NINE TENTHS

Dear Jane,
I hope you
enjoy

Ed xxx.

by Edward Payne

About the author

Edward Payne is an award winning Radio Presenter, Drama School Graduate and Author.
He graduated from drama school in 2009 and began writing his first novel "Mr Impossible". In that time, as a Presenter on Whitechapel AM, he won Silver in the Best Newcomer category of the Hospital Broadcasting Association awards in 2011. In 2012 he won Bronze in the Best Male category.
He currently lives and works in Cheltenham, presenting on Radio Winchcombe and writing.
"Hell Wears A Neckerchief" is his first short story, released in 2015.

To my boys...

The four-legged and the two-legged.

PROLOGUE

There was no tremble in her voice when she spoke. Odette had always admired that in her and had forcefully disciplined herself to maintain a similar balance in her own manner.

Madam twirled a gold pen in her immaculately manicured fingers. "We have reason to believe," she began, in her soft, Scandinavian accent, "that sensitive materials have been brought into the Gloucestershire town of Cheltenham. You know where it is?"

Odette nodded. Of course, she knew. Even if she hadn't, she would have nodded regardless and hot-tailed it straight to Google Maps after the meeting was over.

"Charming place," Madam continued. "I hear it's the perfect juxtaposition of old money and no money."

Odette smiled politely at the cutting remark.

"We don't know who was responsible for bringing it into the town, though a plushly-garmented, female miscreant in a red and white floral dress was seen alighting a train from Birmingham New Street to Cheltenham Spa at around 9 am on Tuesday 15th October, armed with a small, black suitcase. She was noticed by several members of the circle who have alerted us with an understandable level of concern. This woman then proceeded to walk down the Queens Road, onto Lansdown Road, before turning right onto Montpelier Terrace and up Vittoria Walk to get onto the Bath Road. She didn't take a shortcut via the High Street, probably so as not to arouse suspicion."

Odette nodded as she frantically scribbled these details down. She pulled her Armani blazer sleeve up slightly, lest it impinge on the speed of her shorthand.

"She took a left onto Hewlett Road and then a swift right onto Hewlett Place. It was there that she deposited the suitcase." Madam put the pen down, a signal for Odette to pay close attention. She placed her own pen on the pad and leant forward in her seat.

"It is without question that we will need you to go in and investigate," Madam said. "However, I am sure that you are aware it will not be as simple as merely knocking on every door in that street with a writ in your hand."

Odette gave one nod in agreement.

"You will need to talk to our ladies there. Find out why it has arrived and by what force. I am counting on you to assess whether the problem is catastrophic enough for me to intervene."

Odette opened her mouth to speak. "Forgive my questioning Madam," she began, "but do we know what it is?"

Madam lowered her gaze to meet Odette's, her eyes a crystal blue. They were full of wisdom yet weathered at the edges. Like a burning ember in a char-fringed fire. "I'm afraid it is something I've not come across before," she said, with a sternness that both excited and unnerved Odette. "And I've been around a hell of a long time."

It was only when the meeting had ended, and the heavy door had shut behind her, that Odette had put her hand to her head in dismay, Madam's last words still ringing in her ears.

"Find the perpetrator and look after our ladies, Odette. Whatever you do, you must protect the coven."

ONE

Rebecca Dawlish never thought herself to be particularly special. She wasn't cosmopolitan enough to misspell her name, nor did she particularly want to be. All these girls who spelt it Becki or Becci—or, even worse, Bekki—were far too ridiculous for her taste. Becky just liked it to be spelt simply. Otherwise, people might get the wrong idea about her and think her leftfield to any degree.

She grew up in a small, semi-detached house on a quiet residential street in Hendon, North London. Raised by her mother, Beatrice Holmberg Carrington, and father, Derek Carrington, she had one brother, Benjamin, and a family dog called Nelson, after Lord Nelson. A typically British name for a typically British family. It drove Becky slightly mad.

The Carringtons never went on luxurious holidays, nor did they drive around in some flashy four-by-four with tinted windows. They would take their modest Ford Cortina with detachable trailer tent on the ferry to Normandy and hire bikes to take them around the local area. They would sample the local jam and maybe even the cheese but that was enough foreign culture for them.

In the day, while other girls Becky's age would laze around the pool, trying to catch the eye of the European waiter who served them squash without water, she would sit between the calico curtains on her side of the tent and write in her shop-bought journal with the funny French paper. She would scribe stories about simple girls who met well-meaning French boys on tours of museums. Boys who swept them off their feet momentarily and then, after two weeks of secret meetings in dark hallways, would disappear from their lives, never to be seen again. Looking back, they were just thinly-veiled tales of longing for intimacy. Of wishing for a life they might never experience. An all-encompassing romance that was meant to happen, but that may never materialise.

Becky went to Nottingham University in 2006 and studied creative writing. She left in 2009 with a 2:1 degree and a long-term boyfriend named Dominic. Dominic was born in Gloucestershire. They were the same age, though he was slightly taller at 5'11, had an uncontrollable mass of thick, sandy blonde hair and a devastatingly unique chin dimple. Becky first noticed him at the student union where he seemed to be a touch lost amongst the gaggle of boisterous lotharios who cohabited with him in his halls. She was similarly directionless. All the girls around her would whine continuously as they rotated in front of their floor-length mirrors, moaning about how Becky could look so pretty without makeup and stay so slim on a student diet. The real reason was that Becky's parents had taught her to cook, which she would do while the other girls gorged themselves on the fast food that their parents would never have allowed them to devour in such quantities had they still been living at home.

One night at a Halloween party, dressed as a simple black cat, Becky got very drunk on pumpkin shots and Dominic was kind enough to hold her hair back while she vomited in the garden. Luckily, he was dressed as a mummy so there was plenty of available cloth for her to wipe her mouth on when she was finished retching. He walked her home and made sure she was in bed safely. He then returned the next morning to check that she was okay and presented her with some Lucozade and half of a punnet of grapes. Not quite the hangover cure that she was expecting, but Becky thought it was sweet. He invited her out on a date there and then and she just had to say yes. They dated steadily for a few weeks before making it official and showed it off by holding hands in the student union bar. Suddenly her self-penned novels from back in that trailer tent didn't look so implausible after all.

He told Becky that he loved her a few weeks later. She hadn't really known what to say, so she returned the favour. She thought that she would grow to love him if she didn't already feel it. She thought that love would just fall from the sky, but she found herself actively trying to love him more because he was a good man, rather than because she was hit by a bolt from the blue.

On October 20th, 2010, he asked her to marry him and she said yes. They married in the spring at St Mary's Church with a simple reception in the local bowling club. Their first dance was to *Angels* by Robbie Williams. They stayed in London for a few years, living in a modest flat in Golders Green. He got a job as a junior Equine Veterinary Nurse and she worked in an office for a training company. Each night they would cuddle up on the sofa and watch animal programmes before reading in bed for an hour. At least once a week, Dominic would make love to her. Always in the missionary position and never anywhere other than on their double divan. He would caress her breasts and she would think about how simple and happy her life had become.

One morning, Becky was unbelievably sick. So much so that she had to take the day off work, for the first time in the five years she had worked there. Dominic left her in bed and went to work. She looked up her symptoms on the internet.

A quick trip to the chemist and a rather undignified toilet stop in the local shopping centre confirmed her suspicions. She was six weeks pregnant. Dominic was overjoyed—Becky was nervous. Dominic decided that he didn't want to raise a child in London and began looking for work away from the throbbing metropolis. Becky was happy to up-sticks and find work in a similar office, although she would miss everyone. Well almost everyone. She wouldn't miss Beverley, the company secretary, who wouldn't shut up about her polycystic ovaries. She would also miss the sense of adventure that London had, that she had never grabbed hold of. Dominic thought it would be best to move closer to his home since work was so good in nearby Cheltenham for an equestrian professional such as himself. Becky liked the sound of Cheltenham. It was pretty without being expensive and small without being claustrophobic.

They found a darling little house in Winchcombe, a few miles from the town centre. It was a two-bedroom terrace with red roses around the door. The locals who walked their dogs to and from the front gardens of nearby Sudeley Castle waved as the couple unloaded their things from the back of their car. People here liked to smile and wave their sticks in the couple's direction.

Dominic carried Becky over the threshold and sat her on a box in the lounge. He opened a can of lager and she sipped an apple juice. He put his hand on her belly and looked into her eyes.

"My darling Becky," he said. "Isn't it wonderful how everything has worked out? We are going to be so happy here, you and me."

She nodded in agreement and smiled back at him before he carried her on up to bed.

Becky now wondered how she could have been so clueless.

TWO

It began on September 27th, about four days after the last ornament had been unwrapped from its cardboard box home and placed carefully on the oak bookshelf. It was a porcelain woman holding a parasol. Another hideous wedding gift from nobody special, Becky thought. She stood back and admired her handiwork. No, that wasn't right. She should be facing away from the sun, else it wouldn't make any sense for her to be shading herself with the parasol. Becky switched her position. Perfect.

As she walked past the dresser, her eyes fell once again onto an aggressive black mark that festooned the adjacent wall. It had irked her since they had moved in and, although Dom hadn't really noticed it, Becky had meant to get a scrubbing brush to it, but not yet had the chance. It was as if someone had thrown a handful of soot at a blank wall in a pretentious attempt to replicate modern art. Had the walls not been such a brilliant white, Becky might not have been so bothered, but since it was in such an obvious place, it angered her every time she caught sight of it. She would see to it this afternoon.

As Becky walked back into the kitchen she patted her belly. It was still flat, despite the fact it was housing an actual human being. By now, she was twelve weeks gone and ready for a scan. She brushed past the doctor's appointment slip that was blu-tacked to the side of the microwave. As Becky dried the last of the dishes, she cast her gaze out over her new garden, set against such an appealing bucolic backdrop. It was beautiful but unkempt. She would have to go out and sort it. Prune the overhanging leaves and mow the grass. She'd never tended to a garden before but years of watching typically English television programmes had taught her a few basics. It was another thing to add to the already growing "to-do" list. As she dreamily pondered her new shrubbery, Becky noticed something moving in the back bush, near the disintegrating bird table. It looked like a hunched figure. She silently gasped—they had an imposter in their garden! A robbery was being committed, mere days into their new life.

A million panicked thoughts ran through her head. Would they try to break in, steal her things, attack her and her unborn baby? She breathed slowly and regained her composure. Walking slowly to the back door, she picked up the rotting broom handle that leaned against the doorframe.

She wasn't sure what to do with it and inwardly scolded herself for all those years she spent not watching domestic horror films to pick up any tips in the self-defense department. She might just have to act on impulse and throw it like a javelin. Becky tentatively pulled the stiff door from its encasement and leaned out of the arch.

"Hello?" she called in a feeble voice that would never ward off an attacker—she would have to give it more gusto.

"Hello?!"

The figure lurched backwards, a few yards from where Becky stood, the broom handle trembling pathetically in her hand.

"Got it," the figure exclaimed.

Then it turned, wiping its one hand on a dusty old apron and slipping a thick root into its pocket with the other. It was an elderly woman of about 70. Her white hair and curved frame gave her age away. Her face was lined, her fingers bent inwards as though she were holding onto two invisible rugby balls. She was wearing a moss-green top and dark trousers underneath a thick gardening apron. She looked up towards the back door. When she saw Becky brandishing a spear of wood, her face contorted in shock.

"Bloody Nora!" she shrieked in alarm, causing her to fall backwards.

Becky dropped her limp weapon and ran to the woman's aid. She grabbed onto her apron and pulled her forwards until they both collapsed into each other, locked in an awkward embrace. The unsteady woman smelled of peat and rose-scented soap.

"You scared me!" the old woman cried, pulling away rather abruptly. Becky noticed that her accent was a thick Welsh one.

"I'm sorry," Becky croaked, feeling a little put out. This woman really owed Becky an apology for trespassing, not the other way around.

"No bother!" The woman brushed herself down.

"Forgive me," Becky began, apologising again, "but why are you in my garden?"

The old woman laughed. It was a sincere laugh with no trace of malice.

She fished around in her apron and brought out the root. It was an ugly-looking thing. Green and unnaturally hairy.

"For this." She presented it to Becky as though it were something of mounting value. "Malva sylvestris, or High Mallow. A common weed to you, but highly useful to me."

Becky frowned as the woman continued.

"Inexplicably good for indigestion, heartburn, skin inflammations and sore throats. Tastes foul, but then all the best things do." She pushed it back into her pocket before extending her hand. "Do excuse me, child. I'm Gaynor. I live by the church. The humble dwelling with the huge overgrown garden."

Becky shook her hand limply. She wasn't sure what to make of all this. Wasn't this woman committing a crime? She was being mugged in her own back garden.

"I hope you don't mind, I thought the house was still empty. You see, I walk my dog Pluto in that field every day and noticed that there was a stem growing here, poking right out from that gap in the bush there."

Becky followed her crooked finger to a gaping, man-sized hole in the garden hedge. An opening which, sure enough, gave way to a public bridle path. She would ask Dominic to put a fence up. She didn't want the entire neighbourhood coming along and thinking they could help themselves to the rest of her vegetation.

"I don't usually go around prying in other people's privets," she said, tracing Becky's face for forgiveness. Her eyes were a glistening green, strikingly mesmerising.

"My stars," Gaynor said in wonder, leaning closer in. "What a beauty you are."

She reached out and took Becky's chin in her thumb and forefinger, keeping her eyes fixed as she turned Becky's head around slowly.

"Not at all," Becky said through pinched lips, attempting to deflect the flattery. She thawed slightly and smiled. This lady was welcome to the root, now that she was apparently harmless and so very complimentary. She didn't want that disgusting-looking thing eating up all her flowers anyway.

Finally, Gaynor dropped her hand and stuffed it back into her pocket.

"I'm sorry," Becky pleaded—for the third time. "Where are my manners? My name is Becky Dawlish, I've just moved here with my husband Dominic. He's working, but will you join me for some tea? I can just pop the kettle on."

She chastised herself for sounding so formal in her own back garden with someone who had just praised her for her attractiveness.

"Good golly, no!" Gaynor said, rather bluntly. "Much to do, my dear. I need to get this plant home and re-pot it for the winter."

She stuffed her hand back into her pocket and made her way back to her hole.

"But," Gaynor said, turning back, "you should absolutely join *me* for tea. Meet my husband, pat the dog. I insist."

"Oh," Becky exclaimed, not expecting the favour to be returned.

"Tomorrow at three?" she called out. "Or anytime really. As I said, we're just by the church. Can't miss it. Foliage everywhere. I like to call it my botanical garden."

Gaynor started to prize the bushes further apart to get back through, making the hole even bigger.

"Are you a botanist?" Becky shouted after her. She was thinking Gaynor might be able to give her something natural to ease the crippling morning sickness that took hold of her most days.

Gaynor laughed. Becky was beginning to like this woman's unapologetic mirth.

"You might say that," she threw a hand over her shoulder in adieu. "Three o'clock it is then. I've got a great little tea you might like. Will sort that morning sickness out a treat!"

And with that, she was gone.

Becky looked down at the grass with a wry smile. A smile that quickly turned to a puzzled frown as she considered what Gaynor had just said.

I hadn't even mentioned that I was pregnant, she thought to herself.

And as she looked up, the hole in the bush had vanished.

■■

The next day, Becky kissed Dom on the cheek as he headed off to work, armed with his bulging tote bag. He gave her the obligatory pat on the head. Since she had spent most of each morning being violently ill, she was too weak to engage in any more affection than this. And so, they had come to recognise this little daily gesture as being enough manageable intimacy for them both.

"What will you be doing today then, little sparrow?" Dom asked as he stuffed a carefully buttered wedge of toast into his mouth.

"Well," Becky said, sliding a second slice over to him across the gingham tablecloth. "Since our internet is still down, I might go over to the library and send a few CVs out. Maybe I can get some local temp work."

"Good girl," he mumbled, wiping buttery dust from his shirt. His collar gaped open, showing a tuft of curly chest hair. Becky stared at the few crumbs that had made a bid for freedom and speckled his tanned skin.

"And maybe later I could go for a walk, check out the church notice board. Perhaps there's a class I could join. You know, to meet people."

"Boss idea. Listen, I must rush." He pulled his bag up his shoulder. "I'll see you later."

She waved him off with a tight smile. In truth, she didn't really want to spend another day moping about the place, rearranging ornaments and picking lint from the carpet like she had the rest of the week.

Becky didn't know why she didn't tell Dom about her afternoon visitor from yesterday. Maybe because she wasn't quite sure that it had even happened. It had been so strange. One moment she was there, the next she was gone. She wasn't sure whether Dom would believe it. Perhaps the real reason was that she didn't want him to get the wrong idea about some crazy old

17

bat helping herself to their shrubs. He may just get all funny about it and storm round there with a trowel, demanding it back. She didn't want to make an enemy in the town so early on in their tenancy. She could just imagine having to avoid Gaynor's gaze at church fetes, resorting to walking past her stall at the community bake sale with her head jammed firmly into an overhead scarf. Becky had also been quite perturbed about her parting prediction. How could Gaynor have known about the baby without even asking? Perhaps she had been a midwife in her professional life and could spot a swollen tummy at twenty paces. Either way, it had spooked Becky a little and she wasn't sure why.

All the same, she grabbed her sky blue hooded jacket and headed for the front door.

It was unusually warm for a late September afternoon and Becky had no need for the coat after all. It hung over her arm like an overlong piece of cling film, useless and forever trailing. She walked up from their house and onto the main road. It was littered with badly-parked cars, squeezed into the most unlikely of places. The same couple that she had seen on moving day were walking their little dog again. They smiled, throwing a wave over their shoulders. Becky politely smiled back and hurried on up the road. Before she knew it, and without really thinking, she was heading towards the church.

Gaynor hadn't been wrong. Her cottage was a darling little ramshackle of a place with a weathered wall that ran along the right side of the property. It looked, however, as if a Baby Bio bomb had exploded within its four walls, sending twirling branches and ivy off into all directions. It was an uncontrollable perm of a garden that seemed to have a complete mind and life of its own. She couldn't help but stare unashamedly at the cacophony of green cascading down the walls and only imagine what it could possibly look like inside.

"Eyesore, isn't it?" a female voice spoke over Becky's shoulder, causing her to gasp and turn around. A young woman stood there, her face dangerously close for comfort.

Becky scrambled for an answer. She didn't really need one.

"Nice enough old dear but as stubborn as a stuck mule. Won't trim the bushes or rebuild the wall or anything. Just lets the weeds run riot. It's a pity really, such a lovely old building in dire need of an update." Her frosty glare settled upon Becky as her face broke into a moderated grin. "I don't believe we've met, I'm Catherine Clements."

She reached out a perfectly-manicured hand, which Becky accepted and shook.

"Becky," she replied. "We've just moved to the area."

"Oh, so you're the new couple in number four?" she asked, as Becky nodded in reply. "Then that must be your husband I have seen driving up the high street in the blue car? He's very handsome."

Becky grinned bashfully.

"I must admit that Saul and I were quite worried. We thought it might have been one of those beastly homosexual couples, taking over the countryside tree by tree. Saul is my old ball and chain." She pulled a face to indicate that she was joking. She was attractive but extremely well-groomed. A Stepford Wife beauty with an undeniable, synthetic glaze. Her hair was golden blonde, pulled into an almost perfect French roll. She wore a simple, white dress with a cherry-red cardigan.

"So," Catherine continued, "what do you do for work?"

"Well, it's my husband—"

"Ah," she interrupted, "you gave up your job and you moved for him. Very nice. Well, I shall have to keep an eye out for potential employment for you. There's not very much around here for a career gal I'm afraid. I suppose you have children?"

Becky blushed again and brought her hand to her abdomen.

"Oh, you have one on the way," her neighbour gushed. "How peachy!"

Becky felt awkward, giving so much away without, it seemed, really saying anything.

"Well, we live on the Broadway Road. Inglenook Cottage. You should come over for coffee one morning. I'll fill you in on all the local behaviour." Catherine looked Becky up and down in one swift motion. "I'll bake a pie."

Becky inadvertently licked her lips as though she could taste some of Catherine's homemade baking already.

"It's lovely to meet you, Becky," Catherine said as she moved away. "Just knock anytime, I'm in all day."

Becky wondered whether people around here actually *did* anything, besides make hot drinks.

Catherine gave a little wave as she marched off back up the street.

Well, Becky thought, *I've been here a total of five days and already had two social engagement offers. I guess I should be grateful.*

Becky didn't make it to the library. She couldn't face another run-in with a stranger, let alone a group of them, all trying to invite her round for a coffee. In whispers, of course, so as not to upset the librarian. She would go tomorrow. For now, she would just sit and watch the birds fly around outside the kitchen window, while the wind tousled the tops of the trees that lined the fields behind the garden. She had never had these views anywhere in London, so she would savour every second. It was so refreshing not to have to look through a frame of high-rise buildings just to see a patch of sky.

It was around half-past two that she thought of Gaynor. Would she be expecting her arrival? Not overly enthused, but also not wanting to upset anyone in her first week, Becky reluctantly put her reservations aside and set off back up the road towards the church. Before she even approached, Becky was looking all around, lest Catherine jump out of the shrubbery, ready to immobilise her with a home-baked lemon meringue pie. She wasn't around, thank God. She seemed awfully nice, but one of those people who would wear you down gradually until you became so exhausted that you just agreed with everything she said. Becky was continuously falling afoul of this tactic with some of her chattier friends and she surmised that Catherine had spotted this in her quite early on.

With trepidation, Becky crept up to Gaynor's door and tapped lightly with the dainty brass knocker. A good minute passed before she began to wonder if turning back and heading for home might be a better idea. No sooner did she think it than she heard shuffling from within. There was a pause before the door was flung open, startling her. Gaynor stood there in identical clothes to those she wore yesterday, just in different colours. Her hands were clothed in two huge, green, sod-covered gloves.

"Aha!" she boomed so loud that Becky nearly leapt three feet in the air. "Welcome, welcome! Betsy isn't it?"

"Becky," Becky corrected her. She suddenly looked a bit crestfallen.

"Oh, that is a shame," Gaynor said. "I rather like the name Betsy. Has a vaudevillian ring to it, don't you think? Well, come in then, dear. Don't stand on the doorstep like a startled chaffinch!"

She stepped aside to let Becky in, ushering her into the stone-paneled, low-beamed corridor. Various watercolours of country landscapes hung in dusty frames along its length. A line of mud-caked boots and shoes toppled about at the base of the adjacent wall.

"Straight ahead," she directed. It was the verbal equivalent of prodding Becky in the back. She followed orders and moved forwards up the corridor. As she did so, she noticed to her left that there was an open door into a cluttered, dusty, old room. From inside, a radio played soft, classical music. As she peered slightly in, she noticed two feet, adorned with slippers, sticking out from behind the left wall, resting on a small footstool. The walls of this room looked to be painted a bright, warm yellow.

"Oh, that's just Dai. Ignore him—he's having a nap." Gaynor broke her off before pulling the door to.

Becky snapped her head back to mask the fact that she was so obviously snooping.

"Oh, is that your husband?" she bumbled. "If I'm disturbing him, I can come back another—"

"No bother, my dear! He's always napping. It's somewhat of a hobby for him," Gaynor laughed.

As Becky made her way up the hall, she squeezed past an old Welsh dresser that looked as though it were buckling under the weight of the photo frames and dusty porcelain figurines it held. They all rattled as she did so.

At the end of the hall, Becky turned right into the kitchen. It opened into a cosy but completely disorderly room that smelled of honey and baked bread. Dusty cookery books that filled long, wooden shelves exploded with leaves of yellowing paper. Disparate pots and pans hung from countless wooden racks overhead and stickered jam jars of all shapes, sizes and colours lined the worktops and ledges. Somewhat out of place amongst the chintz and china was a grubby, old-fashioned microwave that stood in the corner, its oversized dial collecting thick, greying dust.

"That's it," Gaynor chirruped, manoeuvring her ample bosom past Becky and over to the agar, where a huge, old-fashioned copper pot stood waiting for her.

"Now, tea?" She strode over to the tap where she filled the kettle loudly, not really waiting for an answer.

As she clattered about, a tired old sheepdog trotted in from the outside and made its way over to Becky, wanting to inspect the imposter in its home, but unable to muster up the necessary energy.

"Ah, that's Pluto," Gaynor said, without looking over. "He's harmless, poor old thing. He loves people."

The dog nuzzled his wet snout into Becky's open hand and she gingerly patted him on the head. He began to lick her jeans, which made her frown slightly.

When she had rested the kettle on the hotplate, Gaynor turned around. "Now, sit!"

Both Becky and the dog immediately searched for a decent spot to park themselves. Pulling out a chair from the centre table, Becky perched lightly.

"So," Gaynor said, selecting her own seat and settling down. "What brings you to Winchcombe, my dear?"

Becky's cheeks turned rosy. She didn't really like being the centre of conversation, especially where her new environs were concerned. If she had her way, she wouldn't be here at all, save for the beautiful view, which she couldn't deny might just be the biggest pull factor in the whole operation.

"Well, I'm from North London," Becky began. Straight away, Gaynor scrunched up her face in disgust.

"Ah, it's no wonder then," she said. "Wanted to get away from the stalagmites."

Becky was confused.

"I'm sorry, the—?"

"Stalagmites, my dear. My mother always used to say that London is full of stalagmites and chronicles. Her way of saying stuck-ups and their tall tales."

It was a veiled dig, but Becky wasn't offended. Londoners weren't everyone's cup of tea. Even if she had been offended, she couldn't see Gaynor apologising.

"Well, really we moved here because of—"

"Because of the baby. I see, I see," she nodded as the kettle sprang into life behind her. In a flash, she was up and over to the hob, fussing around and retrieving two cups from a low cupboard.

"Well, yes. I guess so. We didn't think that London would be the best place to bring up a child." Becky sat patiently as Gaynor clattered around with her back to her.

"Sorry," Becky said, feeling confident enough to broach the topic, "but how did you know that I was—"

Gaynor stopped fussing for a moment.

"Women's intuition, my dear" she replied. "I've seen many come and go. You can hide the tummy, but you can't hide the glow."

"Oh," Becky exclaimed, smiling and nodding.

She realised that Gaynor was making her a drink without asking for any of her preferences. Before long a brown mug was placed in front of her with an equally brown liquid sloshing around inside. It smelled odd and looked disgusting.

"I'm sorry, Gaynor—could I trouble you for some milk?" Becky asked, hoping to deposit most of the tea in a nearby dog bowl while her back was turned.

"No need," Gaynor said, plonking herself down, "You don't take milk in Arrowood, just choke it down. Tastes like compost but it'll sort your troubled tum out in no time at all. Now, get it down you. You won't get good stuff like that in London."

Becky stared at the mysterious dark brown broth.

"Now, come on girl," she goaded. "Down in one while it's hot and I'll show you the garden. You won't quite believe your mallow. It is coming on a treat already!"

Becky lifted the cup and swallowed hard. Not wanting to be impolite, she blew a little on top of the steaming mass to stall herself a bit of time. Gaynor watched with open-mouthed delight.

"Bottoms up," Becky said feebly and gulped it down.

At first, the brew had assaulted Becky's taste buds and her oesophagus simultaneously. She thought she might wretch it all back up, but she closed her eyes and breathed slowly. At once, a soothing, comforting swell swept across Becky's body. It was as though someone had poured a little trickle of light into the pit of her insides and now it began to spread and glow inside of her.

"See?" Gaynor chirruped. "Not everyone can take the taste—I'm impressed. You can always trust old Gaynor to see you right, sweet child. I have been curing things that Western medicine couldn't for years and years. If you ever feel queer, you come see me, right?"

Becky nodded. She assumed she meant the word "queer" in the old sense. Unless she had the cure for homosexuality in one of those jars.

"Right, up you get then."

Gaynor led Becky out into the garden via an old, disintegrated back door. She had to fight with a few trailing vines that threatened her access before she even stepped onto the stone outside. As they came to the end of the small path that ran alongside the side of the house, Becky let out a gasp.

What can only be described as an enchanted enclosure of bright colours and weird and wonderful fauna opened out before her. A weeping willow stood to the left of a large swathe of flowers that blazed a trio of yellows, lilacs and reds. From the right wall crept a sea of withies and climbers, each clothed in a separate leafy jacket. They suspended over themselves before twisting to the floor. Various roots and shoots lay potted in disparate terracotta pots, some chipped, some toppling and spilling onto the lush grass beneath. Dragonflies hung, frozen in the air. It was a magnificent sight. A hotchpotch of autumnal hue with aromatic, herbaceous scents that drifted amongst the leaves and into her nostrils. She felt like Aurora in Sleeping Beauty.

"Wow," Becky exclaimed. "This is—"

"Quite a sight, isn't it?" Gaynor said. "It's been my baby for years, child. Never had any others to call my own. And it takes the same amount of tethering, I can tell you. I'm out here most of the time, rain or shine. And Dai, if it's a good day."

As Becky looked around her in wonder, Gaynor had picked up a pair of secateurs and went hobbling over to a pot that was growing a horrible-looking, raggedy stem.

"Here she is, old Maria." Gaynor knelt and began to lightly trim the stalk's withering offshoots.

"Oh, that's my root?" Becky exclaimed. It had almost tripled in size since yesterday. It looked like one of those hideous yams that lined the greengrocer's stalls in Ridley Road Market. But fatter and uglier.

"Well, yes." Gaynor gazed upon it wonderingly.

"It doesn't look very, err ... pretty." Becky didn't really know what she was expecting.

"Oh, you blessed English, stripping Mother Nature of her perfumed underskirts. Never noticing that the best fruit is often the ugliest," she mumbled. "I'll have you know that, when this little nugget is in full bloom, she is one of the most beautiful in the patch. She just has to be cared for."

Had Becky known this earlier, she might have been a bit more hesitant in letting Gaynor snaffle it from her borders.

"So, are you some kind of pharmacist?" Becky asked, confused as to how a place that Gaynor seemed to spend so much time looking after could end up look so unkempt.

"I am, child, I am," she said, getting up and stretching her back out. The secateurs jutted dangerously forward.

"But I don't work for no Boots or Pooperdrug. I work for the waxing moon."

Becky frowned—she'd never heard of this brand.

Gaynor sensed her confusion and stifled a chuckle. "Only when the goddess is in her seeding phase, when Venus is strong with Asmodel and the moon turns in the third quarter might my pharmacy do any bloomin' good," she laughed. "Don't worry, child." Gaynor busied past her. "I am a mad, old woman who has traditional values and speaks in an ancient tongue. I don't make a lot of sense to those who don't know me."

Becky felt like her hands were tied. She smiled feebly.

"Ah, you'll find children of your own age over this garden wall," Gaynor said. "But there are also many who are doubters and free riders, and they know nothing of toil and will. They'll strangle the air that the goddess provides for us to breathe."

She stopped a moment and turned to face Becky with a wry smile. "But you seem pure of heart, child—you mustn't entertain these vultures."

Becky agreed that the old woman was slightly bananas, but she did not offend or frighten her. Rather, her words were of a strange comfort.

"You mean in the town?" Becky asked.

"Oh yes," she said, pointing the handled blade over the wall. "There are people over there who want my garden tamed to make way for their concrete and brick. They wish to crush our ancestors' fortune with their parents spondoolies! But they can't. They cannot wage war with the goddess. They do not understand who they are dealing with."

Gaynor now pointed the tip of the scissors in Becky's direction and closed one eye. It was not a direct threat to her, but she could feel the conviction behind Gaynor's upset.

Bidding her farewell and walking back up the road towards home, Becky noticed a sign outside the house on a patch of grass that she hadn't noticed before. *Winchcombe Homelets Project Committee Meeting. 7:30 pm, Friday 29th November*, the sign read, though the curling vines that had wrapped themselves around the base had made the letters barely legible.

■■■

The next morning, Becky had felt positively glowing. So much so that she and Dom had enjoyed a little grope in bed before he got up to brush his teeth and pop the kettle on. Becky watched his beautiful, pink buttocks escape into the bathroom before turning over to mentally plan her day. She must go to the library and start the inevitable job search—she had put it off long enough. Mainly because she hadn't typed up a CV since the death of the Olivetti word processor.

When Dom had left, Becky used the remaining hot water to make herself a herbal tea. Yesterday's brew at Gaynor's had been her last hot drink and, although it had tasted like dirty bathwater, it had certainly calmed her angry tummy. As she squeezed a dollop of honey into the mug, Becky heard the front door creak open. This made her jump and, before she could even reach her weapon of choice, the rotten, old broom handle, she heard someone cooing for her attention. It seemed that no one had any respect for privacy on this side of the Watford Gap. She pulled her cardigan tight around herself.

"Becky? Are you home?" It was that woman from the other day. Catherine, was it? The immaculately turned-out one.

Becky became instantly aware of how bedraggled her ponytail was.

"Err, yes?" she called back, pulling out another cup.

There was no loitering in the doorway waiting for an invite, Catherine came right in. She looked pristine in a cream dress, wrapped in an azure blue pashmina.

"I just had to tell you the good news." Catherine smoothed her dress down as she cast a quick glance around at Becky's belongings. Becky wished she had more things that matched. Or at least more things that came from Zara Home.

"Oh?" Becky stuck a teabag in Catherine's cup and poured the water. She looked to Becky like a coffee drinker, but certainly not any of the cheap muck that loitered in her kitchen cupboards. In that case, mint tea would have to do—she couldn't turn her nose up at that, surely.

"Well, I just dropped Sienna off at school and, as it turns out, they are looking for a part-time secretary. Isn't that funny?" She didn't meet Becky's eye, she just marched straight over to her wedding picture and snatched it from the shelf.

"Oh." So far, Becky had repeated the same vowel twice in as many sentences. Once again, lost for words in her own home.

"Oh, look at you." Catherine turned the frame over, probably to check what country it was manufactured in. Luckily for Becky, it was John Lewis.

As she put the frame down, something else caught Catherine's eye. It was the angry black mark that streaked the wall by the dresser. Becky suddenly flushed a deep shade of red.

"Sorry," she apologised. "I can't quite seem to get the damned thing out. It's driving me mad."

As Catherine tentatively crept over to examine it, Becky fought to change the subject.

"So," she babbled, "what's new?"

Catherine went to reach out her hand and touch the mark until Becky cleared her throat loudly which made her jump. She shook herself back into the room.

"Well," she continued, abandoning her investigation of the splodge and walking towards the kitchen. "I spoke to the headmistress, Miss Eames, on your behalf. She's an old missile really, but she's having terrible trouble finding an experienced lady in Winchcombe who can make up the hours *and* leave the nanny alone with the washing machine while she's working them. After a bit of cajoling, she agreed to interview you this afternoon. Isn't that just *marvellous*?!"

Becky had to hand it to Catherine. She'd not made so much as a bowel movement yet this morning. Meanwhile, Catherine had got up, preened herself, been to school *and* got Becky an interview. The woman was a machine.

Catherine slid the photo back onto the wrong shelf, which made Becky bristle.

"I hope you don't mind me prying. I used to be a recruitment consultant before motherhood and I could tell the second I looked at you that you had the long fingers of a typist."

Becky smiled and offered her a mug.

"Mint." Catherine examined the mug's contents with a judgemental raise of an eyebrow.

"Oh yes, do you—"

"I do, but only fresh. You never know whose claws have been rifling through this bagged, factory muck." She grinned unapologetically and gave Becky the once-over.

"I could *murder* a biscuit though if you have one knocking around. I'm on the 5:2, but today's a cheat day"

"Oh, yes!" Becky seemed to remember that Dom had snuck a packet of Maryland cookies into the shopping basket on the day they moved in. Maryland was the height of sophistication in their house.

As Becky rummaged, she called over her shoulder, "Catherine, you're so kind to think of me, you really are. I'm ever so grateful."

"Oh, it's nothing, my dear. I know what it's like to be childless and bored, running out the clock until hubby gets home. It'll be 2 pm at St Patrick's School. I'll walk with you if you like?"

Becky nodded, haphazardly arranging a crescent of biscuits on one of her least-chipped side plates. She turned and placed it down on the table.

Catherine looked down, unimpressed by the substandard presentation. Becky chastised herself for not picking up some doilies.

"Oh," Catherine exclaimed through pursed lips. "Shop-bought. Haven't seen *them* in a while."

THREE

Catherine, or "Call-When-She-Wants Cathy" as Becky had now nicknamed her, had stayed all morning. She helped Becky pick out a suitable dress for her interview, not that she really needed help but apparently, the one she had chosen herself was too plain to make any sort of impact. Although, what size of impact did she want to make for managing a bit of filing for three hours a day?

Catherine had also offered to "sculpt" Becky's hair for her, which she found to be a little bizarre. She'd not had someone else tugging on her locks since her mother assaulted it with a Mason Pearson when she was about six. It was a memory Becky wished to forget. Her mother had always done her plaits too tight which gave her an overlong headache that refused to let up.

When Cathy was finished coiffing, Becky thought she looked like a lesser-known member of the Windsor family. In other words, just like

Catherine. Well, the Cindy to her Barbie at least. Catherine had chosen a dress that Becky had bought on a whim and had every intention of throwing out because of its brazen, bright print.

"Stand out, Becky," she had chided. "Be *memorable.*"

Becky couldn't help but feel that she would be memorable for all the wrong reasons. She wanted to impress Miss Eames, not blind her.

After a light lunch, Catherine had practically frog-marched her up to the school and pushed her through the gates. As Becky hobbled up the tarmac in a pair of shoes that had been neglected in her cabinet for so long that she'd had to blow the surface dust off them, she came to the realisation that she was fast becoming this woman's project—another child to mould and scorn while her biological ones were absent.

Becky sat in the holding area for a few minutes, comforted by the background hum of children's voices. She stared at an extremely well-organised timeline of Victorian Britain, framed on sugar paper that hung on the opposite wall. Becky liked schools, though she hadn't actually been in one for quite some time. They were a hive of activity and jocularity. The energy that bounded about the place was instantly palpable and made Becky more confident that she would be happy here amongst the collages and books. School had been an indifferent time for her. She had mostly kept her head down and studied, the complete opposite of her peers, who had larked about incessantly, only to endure endless disciplinary measures at the hands of the authoritarian and archaic teaching staff. Becky had looked on, dumbfounded as the other misbehaving teenagers smoked behind the sports hall and sneaked tampons in other girls' open rucksacks for a laugh. None of that appealed to Becky. She simply wasn't wild enough to fall into any of the wayward groups.

She'd had a best friend, Nancy, who used to let her play with her extensive collection of Sylvanian Families on occasion. Nancy had been quite a promising little actress. She had graduated from primary school and went on to bag herself a spot at the National Youth Theatre. They never spoke again, though Becky did hear on Friends Reunited that Nancy had lost a lot of weight in her teens and developed an inferiority complex after appearing in an advert for margarine.

Suddenly the sliding hatch door opened and an enthusiastic, female face popped out.

"Becky?" she called.

"Er, yes." She clutched her bag tight.

"Yes, Miss Eames will see you now. Third door on the left."

This lady must have been the other part-timer, with the technologically-challenged nanny.

"Thank you." Becky smiled nervously and made her way down the hall.

■■■

"So," said Miss Eames, looking down at Becky's papers. "Mrs Clements tells me you're from London?"

She might as well have said Mars.

"That's right, yes. I worked for six years in the Learning and Skills Support Centre as an administrator before we moved to Winchcombe."

This wasn't going particularly well. Miss Eames was a hard-set woman, easily in her sixties. She towered over Becky from the other side of her desk. As she inhaled, she seemed to suck out a little of Becky's life force. Her face was wide like a toad's and marred with tell-tale lines from years of wearing disdainful grimaces. Her bun perched on her head like a solid block of horsehair, cascading billowing swathes of brownish grey from her crown to her ear. It looked like a knackered Shih Tzu that had climbed its way up, passed out and remained there ever since. Her tie-neck blouse looked a little too small for the bulbous double chin that dangled over the bow and her bosom strained the fabric at her chest, exhibiting the outline of a gigantic, matronly brassiere. She was not particularly impressed with Becky, or anything she had to say. She looked up and down with so many sighs that Becky felt as though she was wasting her time just being there. Miss Eames appeared to be compensating for it by asking Becky endless questions with an ironic tinge of knowingness. She spoke again, her deep croak filling the space.

"And what did you do there?" Miss Eames raised an eyebrow without looking up.

"Well, I was responsible for managing the diaries of workshop facilitators, liaising with external contractors and updating and maintaining the database. I'm very good with Microsoft Word." Becky was grappling for any kind of road into a natural conversation but her interviewer was stopping her at every opportunity.

"And I suppose that you like children and are tolerant of their dispensations?" She turned the CV over and seemed surprised to find the back page empty.

"Oh, yes, very much so. I mean, I hope to have many." Becky thought it best to be vague, just in case her current pregnancy jeopardised her chances of employment.

"Ah yes, of course. Catherine told me you were... blessed." The word fell out of her mouth with little enthusiasm.

Marvellous—Becky's meddling neighbour had struck again.

After what seemed like an age, Miss Eames straightened up.

"Well, I must say that I have never interviewed anyone who has a curriculum vitae shorter than the average greetings card, and who has so little to say for herself on the interview front, other than dropping the word 'Microsoft' countless times. However, you seem competent for the task at hand and you have a trustworthy gait, Mrs Dawlish." She looked up and forced a smile that looked almost painful.

"The hours are from 7 am until 11 am or 12 pm 'til 4 and the salary is £12,000 pro rata. Does this sound manageable?" She raised both eyebrows this time. They crept further up her head as if they were on a suspension wire.

Becky nodded in agreement.

"Capital." She smiled again, looking ever so much like Les Dawson in a smock. "And when can you start?"

"Well, I guess on Monday?" Becky was so convinced that she had blown it that this sudden revelation had taken her by complete surprise.

"Yes, that's fine." Miss Eames straightened up her papers. "I'm just grateful that we managed to fill the position in good time. Miss Wicks left us a little in the lurch you see, and I was starting to think we wouldn't be able to replace her."

Becky sat, waiting for her to finish the sentence. She guessed that Miss Wicks was her predecessor.

"Yes, very queer situation that was. Almost like a vapour," Miss Eames said, to nobody in particular.

That last sentence struck Becky as a little odd, but she wasn't about to push this woman for an explanation. With her enormous frame, you couldn't really push this woman anywhere.

"Excuse me," Miss Eames spluttered, once again fussing about with the meagre leaf of paper in front of her. "Ancient history. So, arrive at nine then. If you go and see Melanie on the front desk, she will furnish you with the appropriate clearance paperwork. She will be training you too so try to make a good impression. I'm sure you'll be up to speed in no time."

She shot Becky a brief, latent grin before it disappeared almost immediately.

"Monday then, I trust you remember your way out?" She used the paperwork to direct Becky to the door. At this, Becky stood up and bowed rather awkwardly. Realising how ridiculous she looked, she hurried quickly to the door and closed it behind her.

What an odd woman. She was truly an inveterate old school headmistress, reminiscent of someone straight out of a Roald Dahl book. Headteachers in London nowadays were practically teenagers. They were a bit backward in coming forward in the country, though it was quite nice to know that some purveyors of rudimentary traditions were still around and hadn't yet succumbed to the new-fangled ways of the twenty-first century. It reminded Becky what she had missed out on growing up in the big city: a draconian education.

True to form, Cathy was around minutes after Becky got home.

"Well?" she demanded as she walked in, brandishing a basket with the obligatory gingham tea towel draped over it. She had completely changed outfits since this morning and was, again, styled to perfection.

"Err, I got it," Becky said. Cathy set the basket down and squealed with glee, clapping her beautifully moisturised hands.

"Oh, I *knew* you would," she sang with magnanimous glee, whipping the towel off and revealing the batch of homemade biscuits within. "They'd never turn *me* down. Not with the position I hold in that school, I practically run the place with my fundraisers. Besides, that Eames woman owes me a few favours."

This kind of spat on Becky's triumph.

∎∎

Becky had baked a pie by the time Dom had come home, though she'd put it in the oven for a little too long and the crust had burnt. She sliced the worst off and served it regardless. Dom said he had enjoyed it and feigned a rather overzealous belly rub to back up the statement, but Becky could tell that the beef had not been drained enough so the whole thing had been an unseasoned, sebaceous failure. While Dom swigged the last of his bottled ale, she told him of the good news.

"Well done, little sparrow," he said and gave her a satisfactory kiss on the top of the head before switching on the television. They cuddled up and watched three Nigellas on the trot. Becky thought, perhaps, he was trying to tell her something.

The next morning, Becky's sickness was back, so much so that she was bent double and had to go back to bed. Dom stuck out his bottom lip as he watched her crawl under the covers and lay, prostrate, waiting for the nausea to subside. It was Friday and it looked to be slightly overcast. There was no real need for her to venture out. She asked Dom to lock her in, just in case Catherine let herself up the stairs to criticise her pyjamas.

Around twelve, she felt well enough to drag some clothes on and lurch downstairs to make tea. As she stared at the empty mug, Becky heard a distant whistle from over the hedge. She noticed a familiar shape through a new, offending gap in her shrubbery—Gaynor. Was Becky seeing things? Had the hedge hole reappeared or had she just imagined that it had completely vanished the other day?

Pushing the cup to one side, Becky walked over to the door and wrestled with the blasted, stiff doorknob before making her way out into the garden.

"Hello, my dear," Gaynor called, when she saw Becky advancing, looking pale and waving awkwardly as if she were aboard a sinking vessel. "Feeling any better?"

"Err, not really," Becky whimpered.

"Ah, you need some more Arrowood," she said. "Come back with me if you like, I'll give you some to take home."

Becky nodded and gave her a weak smile as Gaynor looked down at her attire.

"No rush," Gaynor said, "I'll wait here while you go and get dressed"

"I am dressed," Becky said, looking down at her new grey tracksuit.

"Oh."

■■■

On their walk over, Gaynor had done most of the talking. As she did, she permeated her lecture with a swing of the arm, pointing out landmarks that lay, seemingly imperceptible in the undergrowth.

"And over here," she started, pointing an arthritic finger over to a far-off thicket, "was where the Druids were said to collect for the ritual of oak, from as early as 1250 BC."

Becky was finding it hard to feign interest. She felt so sick that she was ready to drop at any second and crawl the rest of the way in the dewy grass. The bottoms of her tracksuit grew soggier with each step.

"It's a magical place," Gaynor continued. "Full of magical practice. It's no wonder so many mystical things happen here."

"They do?"

"Oh yes, dear, ever so many. Some explainable, some a complete enigma."

It reminded Becky of what Miss Eames had said the day before about poor Miss Wicks, vanishing like a vapour.

"Oh, Gaynor, I forgot to say. I got a job at St Patrick's. It's only part-time, but I think it'll be perfect. You know, for when the baby arrives."

"Oh, my stars," she chirruped. "What wonderful news. You'll be around all those darling little cherubs before you beget your own."

Becky waited until they were nearly at the cottage before broaching the subject.

"I don't suppose you know of a Miss Wicks who worked there?"

Gaynor stopped. Pluto trotted on ahead and through her open gate.

"Oh yes, of course. Ever such a strange business that was. Though it's not out of the realms of possibility. It could happen to any of us." She carried on through the gate. Becky quickened her pace to catch up.

"What exactly *did* happen to her?" Becky was undoubtedly curious but, at the same time, reluctant to find out the answer.

"She was a young girl, can't have been more than your age. White skin, fair hair. Lips of cranberry cream." Gaynor hunted around in her pocket for a key. "Completely vanished off the face of the good, green earth."

Becky clutched her chest in astonishment. "Vanished?"

Gaynor turned and looked Becky square in the face. As she did, her emerald eyes glistened.

"Yes, dear."

Becky's brow furrowed.

"But that sounds unfathomable. She didn't just move away?"

Gaynor let out a sweet chuckle.

"What, and leave a babe in arms and a full house to no one—not even a will? I highly doubt it." She finally located the key and slid it into the lock, pushing the door open.

"It's only me, Dai," Gaynor called down the corridor as the door swung open. A strained response echoed down the hallway.

"Perhaps she was taken?" Becky carried on, shuddering at the thought of a poor, young woman being snatched from the street and bundled into a car.

"I don't think so, my dear," Gaynor said as she ambled up the corridor. "When Goddess Moon decides that it is your time to go then it is your time to go."

She shrugged off her coat and hung it on the first available hook that she came to as she spoke.

"But don't worry, child. Her belongings were given to the less fortunate and the babe was given a good home."

Becky pulled the door behind her and turned quizzically towards her companion. Her fascination was as unmistakable as her aching tummy.

"Well," she said, "why should I be worried?"

"Oh, you don't know?" Gaynor replied. "It was in your house that it happened."

Gaynor pushed the kettle over to the hob as she entered the kitchen and reached up for one of the many jars that sat on the higher ledge. Since she was having trouble getting it, Becky helped her out.

"In my house?" she asked as she grabbed the jar and held it for Gaynor to take.

"Yes," Gaynor replied, rummaging around in the glass container for some of the rugged bark within. "They were pretty quick in getting everything out and hosing it down. Went on the market pretty swiftly after that. That's how we knew that it wasn't just an act of random neglect."

"Sorry, who knew that it wasn't an act of random neglect?"

But Becky was stopped short as, all of a sudden, a loud crash rang out from the other side of the house. This made Gaynor stop fiddling with the jar which she threw on the side.

"Excuse me, dear," Gaynor barked as she rushed out of the kitchen and towards the front corridor.

Becky watched after her, wondering what on earth was happening in the other room for a seventy-something-year-old woman to propel herself to aid with such speed.

Becky strained to hear what was going on but all was quiescent until Gaynor returned. She was rubbing her hands on her trousers.

"Silly puppet," Gaynor remarked as she returned to the kitchen. "Knocked over his tea tray again. Dreadful mess."

She trotted over to the sink to locate a cloth.

"Oh, is there anything I can do?" Becky asked tentatively, not really wanting to impose but not wanting to seem impolite either.

"Would you grab those towels, my dear?" Gaynor pointed to some rags hanging on the agar door handle. "Follow me please?"

Becky escorted Gaynor back down the corridor and watched her disappear in through the last door on the right. Apprehensively, Becky stepped into the room and slowly poked her head around the beam.

The room was small, with a low ceiling and, as she had remembered from the day before, the walls were painted a bright, canary yellow. White shelves were scattered about in no particular order. Upon them, primroses burst out of disparate-sized jars of every flavescent shade.

Prints of sun-drenched cornfields, blazing summer meadows and bountiful, daffodil-lined hedgerows hung on the walls in various clusters. Aureate curtains plumed over dusty, white nets covered the large front window. Whatever sun there was outside on such an overcast day streamed through the perforations in the lace fabric, casting romantic silhouettes on the tawny-coloured carpet.

On the right side of the room, a single bed was made, clothed in fresh, white linen. The pillows were plumped and fluffed where they lay, inviting the head to rest.

To the left lay a tired but comfortable-looking armchair of golden hue. It was a rather ornate piece that one might find in such an old country cottage. The matching footstool lay a couple of paces ahead. An elderly gentleman slouched in the chair.

He was relaxed, almost horizontal. His arms lay at his sides and a vacant, paralysed mask crossed his face. The skin that stretched across his aged cheekbones was so frail, it looked as though it might break. A carefully-brushed sweep of ice-white hair fell onto his forehead. As he saw Becky, his eyes met hers, still blue in their sockets, searching her with a quiet curiosity.

At his feet lay a yellow beaker that had come loose from its lid and expelled tea across the floor. Gaynor knelt on the pile, dabbing at the stain with a cloth.

"This is my husband, Dai," she spoke as she scrubbed. "Say hello, Dai."

The man stayed silent, keeping his eye firmly on the stranger. His mouth didn't move from its perfectly shaped 'O'.

"Fine," Gaynor said. "Be like that." She turned to Becky and spoke in a loud whisper. "He's grumpy now because he won't get another. That's the third one this week!" She gave Becky a wink.

Becky wasn't sure what to do so she worked the cloth between her hands.

"Oh yes, dear, hand that one over." Gaynor reached her hand out to grab the cloth. "This is Becky, love. Just moved into Vineyard Street. You know, the one that was being sold. I told you about it."

She finished what she was doing and hoisted herself up onto one knee before standing. The old man kept watching Becky.

"Take no notice." Gaynor came and stood next to her. "He's just shy. Shy Dai, they used to call him."

"It's nice to meet you," Becky said awkwardly and loudly, as though she was talking to a complete imbecile.

"He's not deaf, love," Gaynor playfully mocked. "He's just had a stroke is all, his hearing is the one thing it didn't take."

Becky immediately blushed.

"So," Gaynor turned towards the walls, "you like the room?"

Becky looked around again and nodded. It was chaotic and jumbled, yes, but rather like Gaynor's garden, the room had an otherworldly beauty about it.

"Yellow, isn't it?" Gaynor asked, running the cloth through her fingers.

Becky nodded again and chuckled.

"Very healing colour," Gaynor continued. "Strengthens the mind and the resolve. When Dai was struck down five years ago, he had to move to the front of the house for his own comfort. He had to relocate to our old living room and it had to be yellow. He gets the most sun in here, see? Our bedroom gets more of the moon. So, I keep the moon, he has the sun."

Dai's eyes moved away from Becky and closed slightly, the rays from the window soaking into his clothes. When his eyes reopened, they were moist with soft tears.

Becky's mouth went dry as she searched for something to say.

"Do you look after him all by yourself?" she managed to croak.

"Of course," she chuckled. "We don't want some stranger coming in here and changing your bed, do we love? Marriage is forever, my dear, not just for hay days and holidays."

She turned to Dai.

"Of course, the goddess helps. But mainly we have each other and we have our garden. And that's all we need, isn't it kiddo?"

The old man closed his eyes again, his mouth still hanging open.

"He looked after me for many years," Gaynor said, gazing down at her husband. "He looked after me and now I look after him."

Becky watched Gaynor as she smiled at Dai. She almost saw a momentary veil of sadness cross Gaynor's face. At once, she suddenly straightened up and balled the wet cloth in both hands.

"So that's our Dai," Gaynor said, making her way back to the door. "Now, let's get back to your tea before it goes cold."

As they left the room, Becky turned back to say goodbye, but Dai looked to be asleep. A slight grin tinged the corners of his mouth.

When Dom returned that evening, Becky ran to meet him at the door with an enveloping embrace. She pushed her face so far into his chest that her tears soaked into his shirt.

"Hey, little sparrow," he said, with an air of surprise. "What's all this?"

"I don't know," she said looking up into his eyes. "I just want you to know that I love you and I will never leave you. Never ever."

She continued to hug him and that night they made love.

FOUR

The next morning, Becky had barely wiped the sleep out of her eyes before she heard Catherine calling through the letterbox.

"Yoo-hoo, sleepy heads! I'm leaving you some breakfast on the doorstep."

Dom looked at his wife with a raised eyebrow. She shrugged and hauled her naked body out from under the sheets. By the time she'd reached the door, Catherine was gone but the obligatory handbasket had been left on the stoop, wrapped in another gingham tea towel. She must have had thousands of these things!

Becky carried it inside and laid it on the table, just as a half-naked Dom came trudging down the stairs for his morning coffee. He put his arm around her and leaned over. She could feel his brittle, golden body hair poking through her pyjama top.

"What have we got here?" he asked as Becky snatched the towel away. The smell of warm muffins hit her as a white card fell out of the fabric. She picked it up. It said, in perfect calligraphy, no less:

B & D, please enjoy the enclosed.

Dinner at ours tonight to congratulate you on your new career venture.

C & S

Knock around 7.

"Just a little something she rustled up this morning at the sound of the cuckoo's fart," Becky said with a sigh.

"Oh dear," Dom said. "A little jealousy in the circle is there?"

She turned to face him.

"I could make muffins!" she spat.

He backed away with his hands up in mock defeat.

"Well, not now obviously. We might as well eat these," Becky moaned.

The muffins were delicious, of course, and since the Arrowood had once again proved its worth, Becky managed to eat two.

After breakfast, they drove into nearby Cheltenham to browse in the shops. Dom wanted a new work shirt and Becky was angling for some of the patchouli perfume that she had read about in Grazia magazine.

Becky marvelled at the beauty of the inner city. Cheltenham definitely played up to its regency heritage. The buildings were tall and made of similar stone. All along the promenade, trees lined the shops and cafes. They sauntered into Cavendish House, a department store that looked as though it would cater to both of their needs. It was huge and ran the entire length of the town square. After walking around the ground floor of the store, they split off to search alone. As she browsed the beauty department, Dom sloped off to choose appropriate work attire for the practice.

Becky ran her hand across the glass shelving as a heavily made-up, middle-aged woman called Karen beamed at her through her thin-rimmed spectacles.

"That is the new Tom Ford." She pointed a crimson talon in the direction of a small, white bottle. "It's unisex, but has a typically fruity scent that reacts differently to both female and male pheromones."

She had clearly recited this verbatim from the Tom Ford training booklet, but Becky humoured her regardless and accepted a quick spritz.

As she went to set the bottle back down, Becky noticed that Karen had suddenly been distracted by a commotion from the opposite counter.

A young girl, no more than nineteen, was being confronted by a female member of staff and an ageing, salt-and-pepper-haired security guard in an ill-fitting, brown uniform.

"She was putting it in her bag, I saw her," the staff member was saying to the guard, frowning as much as her dermatologist would allow.

"Oh, please!" The girl tossed her long, golden hair extensions over the shoulder of her fake fur gilet. "As if you can see *anything* with those false eyelashes of yours. It would be like looking through two black shower curtains."

"Now young lady, is this true?" The guard was holding the girl by the elbow as she attempted to struggle free. By now, the kerfuffle had attracted quite an audience. Mothers started to pull their children into their sides and wide-eyed teenagers watched curiously from behind the relative safety of the greetings cards.

"Of course not!" the girl complained. "I was just reaching into my bag to grab my purse."

"That's rubbish, Harold," the other woman spat. "If you look in her bag, you'll see another bottle in there."

"Miss," the guard said, "I'm afraid that you will have to show me inside of your bag."

The bag in question was a rather fetching vinyl caramel piece.

"You're not looking in my bag," she said, pursing her glossy lips together. "*That* is a breach of my basic human rights."

"Not if you're stealing from my store!" the manager barked.

"Oh, it's *your* store? You own it? Or have you *stolen* it from House of Fraser?"

"Madam," the guard said. 'Your bag."

The girl wrestled free from his grip and clutched both hands to her bag, simultaneously tossing her hair away from her face. She was young but she had that kind of movie-star beauty that transcended her age. Her eyebrows were perfectly sculpted, her hair shone with intense condition and her skin glowed a beautiful, healthy bronze.

She glared at the woman, then back at the security guard. Becky continued to stare, mesmerised as the girl gripped both sides of the bag and wrenched it open. Her fellow shoppers collectively leaned forward to get a good look inside.

The security guard tutted as he reached in and pulled out a large, black box with the word Armani festooned across it. The girl held her resolve and turned back to the woman who folded her arms and nodded smugly.

"There you go," she said, which was good as, "I told you so."

The girl closed her bag back up.

"Well, actually I didn't steal it, I needed it," she scoffed.

"For what?" the other woman challenged.

The girl leaned forward, making sure that each word was well-enunciated.

"Because this whole place stinks like your breath: pig shit," she said, keeping her eye fixed on her nemesis. The shoppers watching let out a unanimous gasp.

"Right. Madam, you'll have to come with me." The security guard handed back the perfume and reaffirmed his grip on the girl's elbow. She didn't fight this time but allowed herself to be frog-marched away from the shop floor, a disgusted look on her face. They advanced toward Becky and, as they approached, the girl gave Becky a warning glare. She dropped her gaze sheepishly as they breezed past.

"I'm sorry about that," said Karen. "It happens quite often. Especially on a Saturday."

Becky nodded and continued pretending to browse.

"Though," Karen said to herself as she went back to staring at her nails, "Armani? At least the girl's got taste."

∎∎

After their shopping, Becky fell asleep on the couch. All the morning's drama had completely wiped her out. Dom had chosen a thick chequered shirt that all the gents in the town centre seemed to be wearing, from the young, muscular farmhands to the ageing, portly bumpkins.

She must have slept for hours because when she awoke, it was five o'clock—she needed to get a move on if they were to be at Catherine's by seven, suitably preened and ready for battle. It would take Becky at least an hour to veto her entire wardrobe, before draping something across herself that wasn't going to meet with Catherine's complete and utter derision.

She chose a simple, black dress and, as she shot herself exasperated looks in the mirror, she sighed. She would be getting big soon. For the next dinner date at Catherine's, she would probably have to wear a burlap sack with tights.

Becky had also tried to straighten her hair so that the natural curl didn't flare up unceremoniously and turn the look of simplistic elegance into 1980's Dynasty bitch. She swept a silvery eyeshadow over her lids and glossed her lips in a nude shade. She went back to the mirror and decided that she looked quite decent. In fact, it seemed she had ever-so-slightly modelled herself on the larcenous girl she had encountered earlier in the department store. Unwittingly or not, she wasn't sure.

Dom looked totally handsome in his new shirt. Although it was meant to be for work, she thought he wore it as a safe bet to fit in. He stood next to her, muscular, tall and gorgeous. Becky was certain that if they couldn't quite keep up with the Joneses, they could at least be on the same race track.

Catherine opened the door and whooped at them as they stood uncomfortably on her porch. The house was amazing, a two-story, gothic property with a Cotswold stone drive and a luscious acre of garden surrounding it. To the left was a conservatory with an accompanying bricked patio, all lit up with dangling white lanterns hanging from a tree overhead. It looked magical in the cool evening air.

"Oh, you two. Come on in!" She beckoned them into the wide hallway. It was brick-floored with various family pictures hung in perfect interstitial symmetry along the length of the magnolia walls. As she looked around, Becky nearly walked straight into an antique end table that was littered with darling little glass pots, each holding separate keys and oddments.

Catherine looked amazing, as always, in a cranberry dress, her hair moulded into the perfect ballerina bun. Her skin was alabaster white, her lips a blazing hue of blush.

"*So* nice to meet you, Dominic," she said, stepping past Becky seductively to kiss him on the cheek. Becky had only ever referred to him as Dom, so she was confused as to why Catherine was calling him Dominic.

"Welcome to our little shack," she joked, punching Becky lightly on the shoulder.

"Oh, Becky. *So* good to see you!" She was being ridiculously nice. In the short time Becky had known her, she had never been quite this pleasant. "Make yourselves at home. Dominic, do let yourself through to the kitchen and grab a beer."

"Right," he said, dancing awkwardly between doors before choosing the right one and tentatively walking in.

Catherine watched him go in before turning to Becky.

"Gosh, he is very handsome," she said. Becky couldn't help but feel a little proud.

"Yes, he is. Very much."

"And you look lovely, darling," she said, looking Becky up and down with a wide grin. "And can I say, I don't blame you."

Becky was confused.

"Sorry Catherine, for what?"

"Your hair," she said, seemingly baffled as to why Becky was confused. "When I was pregnant, I could never be bothered with mine either."

So close.

■■

Dom and Saul had got on well. They were both obviously country boys at heart and, being a property developer, Saul knew this area better than most. He was a good-looking guy, but years of decent wealth and daily grooming from his image-obsessed wife meant that he had the air of an average guy with a thick layer of gloss over the top. He had clearly acquired new dental veneers since the craze had gone global and, though he was clearly losing his hair dramatically on top, what was left of it was well-conditioned. The visible snatches of scalp were also sun-kissed and healthy looking.

They gabbed over home-made canapés while Catherine walked Becky around her meticulously-decorated house. Everything had its place. Even the cat litter tray was set under a Chat Noir gild frame print. At Catherine's instruction, Becky poked her head around the door to what she called the games room. Inside, sat quietly watching cartoons, were two of the most beautiful children she had ever seen: Sienna and Michael. If *The Sound of Music* were to get a 2017 Hollywood reboot, she was looking at two of the Von Trapps.

"They're off to bed soon. I said that you'd be over and they were just *dying* to meet you," Catherine warbled.

"Hi, guys." Becky raised a timid hand in greeting.

"Nice to meet you, Becky," they replied in unison, smiling with impeccable, gap-toothed, good manners.

"Of course, they are both at St Patrick's. Sienna is in year six and Michael is year four, so you'll see them around quite a bit I suppose."

Becky laughed politely as Catherine ushered her out and back to the kitchen.

Catherine's spatchcock chicken, drizzled with homemade lemon and tarragon butter, had been orgasmic. The only thing drizzled over chicken in

Becky's kitchen would most likely have come out of a jar, cooked by Uncle Ben.

Over the raspberry pavlova and a glass of champagne—Becky had sparkling water—the boys were ensconced in a conversation about Land Rovers and so Catherine leaned towards Becky.

"Just between us girls," she slurred, "do you think Saul might be losing his hair?"

Becky instantly flushed as she fought hard not to follow Catherine's wine-soaked gaze. The answer was obvious but she didn't want to seem so brazen in somebody else's house.

"I'm really no expert," Becky mumbled.

"Oh, don't be so diplomatic. He is, isn't he?"

Becky just gritted her teeth and hoped that Catherine would move on.

"Well," Catherine said, pouring the last dregs of liquid from the bottle into her glass, "there is a little clinic in Istanbul that will sort out that little problem for just over three grand. It's only a day operation. In and out. From baldy to Bryan Ferry in one fell swoop. What do you say to that?"

Becky didn't really have an answer. Dom had no problems in that area. Thankfully the only place that he wasn't hirsute was his back. Everywhere else, he was like Chewbacca.

"Of course, it has been terribly difficult for him. It's not right for a man to lose his hair," Catherine sighed and tapped her plate glumly with a dessert fork, "They say it skips a generation on the mother's side, which we thought would act in his favour. Until Saul's mother went and told him that Grandma Clements was the only bald woman in Whitby. Fumes from the munitions factory apparently. She wore a bloody great wig for the majority of her adult life. Since then, Saul's hair has sort of fallen out on its own. One time there was a trail of it from the bed to the bathroom."

Becky stifled the urge to laugh in her face.

"He really wants his old hair back—it's such a bone of contention."

She couldn't help but think that, if this was all Catherine had to worry about, then she really was incredibly lucky indeed.

"And then there's Michael, what will happen there?"

"Catherine, I really don't think there is anything to concern yourself about. Your family are picture-perfect."

Becky wasn't lying.

"Bless you for that," she replied, her shoulders slumped as though a great weight had been lifted off them. "We do try, but it's not easy heading the most faultless nuclear family in the Cotswolds. I wear myself out all the time. You know, sometimes it's a wonder I don't go knocking on that stupid old woman's door to ask for some help."

Becky's ears suddenly pricked up.

"Old woman?"

Catherine looked at her, her eyes heavy.

"Yes, you know, the old woman who lives in that run-down old muck-hole with the *atrocious* garden. Down by the church. The one I showed you. That one! Luckily the Parish Council have got plans to build right on top of that site, so she might not be around for much longer. She can take her hocus pocus elsewhere."

She picked up her glass, sipped it and put it back down.

"Not that she'd help me though," Catherine seemed to mumble to herself. "Let's just say we're not on the best of terms."

Becky thought about how Gaynor had offered her the Arrowood and how it had settled her poorly stomach.

Catherine went on.

"Of course, it's well-known around here, what she is capable of, though she has sworn against it many times."

"I'm not sure what you mean." Becky began to feel nervous. All of her conversations with Gaynor began running through her head.

"Well, I know it's a little backward in this day and age. You know, burning at the stake and flying around on broomsticks and all," Catherine spoke into the air.

Becky knew what she was getting at, but she really needed Catherine to confirm it if she were going to draw her own conclusions.

"And, of course, there are tales that frighten the children senseless. Ones where she turns up on your property unannounced and invites you into her gingerbread house, never to be seen again." Catherine's wine sloshed in her glass as she put it again to her lips.

"Are you saying that she's dangerous?" Becky asked, suddenly feeling hot and cold at the same time. Her dress seemed to get tighter and tighter around her chest.

Catherine gave her an unimpressed look.

"Dangerous? She's a maniac!" she spat. "All that business with Miss Wicks and the cult and such—it makes you shudder."

Becky swallowed hard.

"Cult?"

"Well, no one knows for sure, but apparently this area is notorious for it. Has been since the Dark Ages," Catherine went on. "I'm surprised poor Anne got involved with it at all. I mean people don't just disappear without a trace. She must have got on the wrong side of them or something. I told the police that they should target her with their investigations but apparently without proof, there is nothing they could do. Poor Anne. I never thought she'd go in for all that."

"For what, Catherine?" Becky was pushing her to say it out loud.

"*Witchcraft*, Becky," Catherine said, draining the last of her glass. "I don't want to scare you,

69

particularly in your condition, but I bet you never thought when you moved to this sleepy little town that you'd be living near the local neighbourhood witch. If you ever see her, my God—cross over."

■ ■

When they had returned home later that evening, Dom had dragged himself up to bed. Becky was wide awake, so she made herself some warm milk and sat at the kitchen table, mulling over her conversation with Catherine. She had not let her husband know the finer details of their discussion. It seemed too ridiculous to say out loud: "Oh by the way darling, it appears that I have been fraternising daily with Gloucestershire's answer to Mad Madam Mim."

But, although what Catherine had reported to her about Gaynor's reputation had definitely struck a resonant chord with Becky, she still had to properly assess her belief in the veracity of Catherine's accusations. The fact that this woman allegedly turned up on peoples' property without warning had certainly been true in Becky's case. She had even gone so far as to magic herself a point of entry in the hedge. But was she really dangerous? Could such a seemingly guileless old lady really be a follower of Satan? Granted, Becky's knowledge of witches was limited to campfire ghost stories and films starring Angelica Houston, and neither painted the craft or those who practised it in a very flattering light. She was also familiar with the concept of a white witch. Gloria in *The Wizard of Oz* for instance. But was the idea of someone using any sort of magic for more utilitarian purposes really just an old wives' tale to make the practice more acceptable? Surely the archaic portrait of the wart-nosed old hag with a pointed hat and a broomstick was just a Hollywood take of one of the world's oldest religions, cooked up to scare children on Halloween. If the dark arts were practised so freely across places like Winchcombe, then surely strange and unexplainable things would happen all the time?

Becky cast her mind back to poor Miss Wicks, the part-time school secretary who had disappeared so inexplicably. What had happened in this very house that had caused her to vanish, leaving a baby behind? Had it been magic? Had something evil happened within these walls? Nothing had given Becky cause for concern so far. She hadn't woken up in a cold sweat or felt unfamiliar eyes watching her. She was, in fact, quite comfortable here. Surely if bad things had taken place, Becky's paranoia would be at boiling point.

Perhaps these were all questions that she needed to put to Gaynor when she next saw her—if she ever saw her again. Catherine had warned her away but Becky needed to make up her own mind. She had empirically witnessed the way Gaynor had cared for her ailing husband. She had felt the softness of her hand and been touched by the kindness in her voice. That couldn't just be a smokescreen to veil a more sinister character, could it? There was no way Becky could make up her mind about the situation without further extrapolation. She would go and see Gaynor tomorrow, not to give away what she knew, but to try and get some answers. This jigsaw did not yet fit together.

■ ■

Sunday arrived with its own complications. The toilet had decided to completely flood the downstairs bathroom, sending a river of dark water careening through the doorway and into the kitchen. Dom managed to contain the slurry while Becky stood in a pair of wellingtons, scooping up the excess with an old plastic measuring jug and sloshing it into her one good bucket. They spent the next hour in the queue at the hardware superstore, choosing suitable plastic plumbing apparatus.

By the time the whole business had been sorted, it was far too late for Becky to call in on her neighbour. She was unsure of what Gaynor and Dai did on a Sunday and didn't really want to disturb them. Instead, Dom let her choose a movie for them to watch online. It was no surprise that she picked *The Wizard of Oz*, though it offered nothing new on witches that she wasn't aware of already.

■■

Becky arrived at St Patrick's at half-past eight on Monday morning, following a sea of children into the building. They all eyed her with close curiosity, wondering whether she was a new supply teacher that they had to be wary of or just one of those nasty groomers that their parents had warned them about. Becky half-expected to be strong-armed in by Catherine again, thrusting a lunch box into her chest and placing a dry kiss on her cheek. Thankfully, she was absent.

Mel, Miss Eames' long-suffering PA, who was incredibly thin and had dark circles under her eyes, was the first person to meet Becky. She was extremely pleasant and welcoming from the get-go. Her plain features were framed by an even plainer haircut that hung from her crown like medieval chainmail. She introduced Becky to the rest of the girls in the office: Janice, Tracy and Kay. They were all ex-pupils, now in their forties. They were also all in loving marriages and had pictures of their various, gap-toothed offspring as babies propped up at their desks.

The office was spacious but cosy, with lots of natural light, which illuminated the grand, high ceiling. Various student artwork adorned the walls, from crudely-drawn ladybirds to huge faces with bulging eyes and rosy-red, daubed lips. Multi-coloured storage boxes separated disparate filing and a gigantic, illustrated tree trunk sprouting leaves of staff headshots stretched the length of the back wall. Becky supposed that these must be portraits of the current workforce, though there were quite a few for such a small parish.

"We have about one-hundred and twenty-five students at present," Mel said, once she had furnished Becky with a cup of tea and plonked her on a neighbouring chair. Becky noticed a raggedy bit of tissue sticking out of her cardigan sleeve. She'd not seen one of those in quite some time.

"Your job will be to make sure that student files are all updated on the system. Answer any incoming calls, process tardiness and sickness slips, organise the fun days and fundraising forms, filing security checks, paperwork—that sort of thing." She smiled as she gulped a hefty swig of black coffee. "For instance, this Wednesday we have the Harvest Festival at the church. We are slowly getting bookings in from the parents, so that's probably a good way to get familiar with our students, make a few calls, chase some people. Get to know some of the parents that you'll be communicating regularly with."

"Right," Becky nodded. It was a lot of information that whizzed straight past her at this stage.

"So, we just need Jason, the IT man, to set you up with a login and we can get you onto the database," she sighed, putting her cup down. Her hand slipped into her sleeve and out came the hanky.

"So, Becky," she said, unceremoniously digging around in her nose with the bit of tissue. "How about you? Where do you come from? Where were you before you came here?"

Becky felt all eyes on her.

"Well I come from North London," she said, waiting for the statutory collective gasp from her new office mates.

"Gosh, London!" Mel said. "I bet you find it a bit different around here."

"Well, kind of," Becky blushed. "There are far fewer people for a start."

The ladies giggled sympathetically.

"And are you married?" asked Tracy, a mousy-looking woman with a mass of curly, blond hair.

"Yes, I'm married to Dom and we are expecting."

Cue the rush of congratulations and thanks.

"Oh, I don't blame you not wanting to bring up your child in London," said Kay, the only one of the three with short hair. "My cousin's daughter moved there to go to university. One year in and she's dying her hair grey and sharing a flat with someone from Wigan—it's crazy!"

"I love London," said Tracy, pushing her glasses up her nose as she spoke. "We went there to see Mamma Mia and it was *so* good. And on the way out, we saw Ben Fogle getting into a taxi!"

The ladies shrieked in unison.

"Oh, now I do like Ben Fogle. I would trade my Mark in for him any day!"

"Oh Janice, you are awful!"

Becky smiled. She was either going to love it here, or it was going to send her absolutely barmy.

∎∎

When her shift was done, Becky walked home. It was a nice, crisp afternoon, so she decided to take a little detour past Gaynor's house. There seemed to be little activity going on from her spectator's spot on the pavement, so she thought it best not to bother her. Besides, the morning had gone so well that Becky thought pressing her neighbour for any information that could mar her good mood might not be the best idea. Instead, she swung by the local shop and bought some chicken for dinner.

Later on, Catherine called to catch up on the day's events.

"Yes," Catherine agreed after Becky gave her a quick lowdown of the office, "they are a sweet bunch of girls, I must admit."

"And how was your day?" Becky asked.

"Oh, fine. I'm just putting together a few notes for the Parish Council meeting on Friday. I'm the secretary now since Saul is on the board. We're discussing the plans for the new housing estate that was proposed last summer. Such a good idea!"

Luckily Catherine didn't invite Becky along. She was barely aware of the dimensions of her own airing cupboard, let alone the locations of Winchcombe's avenues and cul de sacs.

"Of course, not everyone is happy with the proposal so we're having to put together a fairly tight pros-and-cons list that has been taking me *forever*. But once it's done, it's done."

Becky had a fairly good idea who would be most upset by the aforementioned proposal.

"So," she began, changing the subject, "will you be coming along to the Harvest Festival?"

"Oh, of course," Catherine exclaimed. "It's one of the pivotal events in the autumn calendar, along with Rachel Power's annual Halloween party. I need to hand out a few flyers for the meeting while I'm there."

Becky wasn't sure whether a children's religious concert was the best place to hold a Parish Council press campaign, but she kept quiet.

"Well, I guess I'll see you there," Becky said, desperately trying to get away.

"Oh yes, I'll introduce you to some of the parents. Only the high-flyers—not the yokels."

Her portentous digs were beginning to make Becky feel uncomfortable.

"And then we *must* do coffee in Cheltenham this weekend. I know a darling little café that does a decaffeinated mocha that is to *die* for. Toodle pip!"

And with that, she rang off.

■■

Once Jason, the undeniably cute IT impresario, had set Becky up on the in-house system, she could start getting on with some work. Mel was an omnipresent aid, thankfully. She blew her nose incessantly and talked non-stop about Michael Bublé, but she was too sweet to be impatient, which was good. Especially when Becky cut and paste the wrong surname three times in an attempt to appear more efficient.

"Just keep typing it Becky, rather than cutting and pasting. Only because we can't really afford mistakes on personal records. Miss Eames still hasn't forgotten the terrible trouble we had when Mr and Mrs Wrankers won the Christmas raffle. That typo went out on all the newsletters—even the vicar's," she sighed dolefully.

Again, everyone that Becky spoke to on the telephone seemed charming enough, though they were all overly interested in finding out her lineage and past employment history. They were quite enamoured with outsiders in this little town.

Miss Eames had breezed through a few times, surreptitiously glancing over her shoulder to check on Becky's progress while pretending to fill her coffee mug.

"How do you get on with the headmistress?" Becky asked Mel once the old girl had sloped back into her office.

"Well, she's a traditionalist," Mel had replied, "so none of the kids or their parents dare square up to her. But she has a good heart. She came to this school after being orphaned. She was separated from her sister who got sent to another city, I think."

Becky imagined Miss Eames squeezing her large breasts into one of the girls' tiny, little hockey shirts and managed to suppress a giggle.

She couldn't see herself ever warming to the woman. She was someone who would only ever live and work on her own terms and, therefore, she would probably only ever do it alone.

Later on, when Mel was on the phone and Kay had popped off to the toilet, Becky walked over to peruse the back wall for faces that she had not yet encountered. Mr Heap and Miss Bowles, the years three and four teachers, she had met briefly when posting some flyers on the staff room notice board. She had also run into a few of the shiny-faced teaching assistant girls on her way back and forth down the classroom corridors. However, when Becky looked a little further down the school office's branch, one picture suddenly leapt out at her. Above the plaque marked 'Miss Wicks' hung a small, passport-sized photograph of a young, plain-looking woman with shoulder-length hair tied back into a French pleat. She was smiling an ineffectual smile that indicated that she didn't really like having her picture taken. Her cheeks were rosy and her skin was glossy as she posed in a woollen, cream cardigan. She looked young and ever-so-slightly sad as she peered out of the photo. An English rose whose bloom had begun to fade—a ghost of someone else.

When Becky turned back after a few seconds, Tracy and Janice's eyes flicked back to their computer screens. Becky didn't have the nerve to ask any questions, so instead she asked whether she could make anyone a cup of tea, before popping out to the staff kitchen. When she returned with three steaming mugs on a Typhoo tea tray, she cast her eyes back to the picture but noticed that it had gone.

FIVE

Wednesday's Harvest Festival suddenly arrived. Becky had only met a few of the children in passing, so having to round them up all in one go was quite a daunting task. She felt like she was doing a particularly sub-par job at the national sheepherding trials.

But then, it wasn't up to her to discipline the kids. That's what the teachers were there for, and they were out in full force. Miss Wilson and Mr Smethwick were leading the event. They were both middle-aged and fiercely authoritarian when it came to barking at loud and obstreperous minors.

Miss Plumb, the reception teacher oversaw the percussion segment, an unruly bunch that contained a few children who were well-meaning but tone-deaf. Peppered amongst them were a few troublemakers who were being made exhibitions of by being forced to tap various misshapen tambourines throughout the whole chorus of We Plough the Fields and Scatter.

Becky had only heard strained versions of the children's musical numbers thus far, mainly since their rehearsals were confined to the assembly hall, which was quite a way down the corridor from the office.

She did, however, stop to listen to a beautiful rendition of There Is a Season by Year 3 when she snuck out to the toilet earlier that morning. Miss Ware, the greying choirmaster and long-standing piano teacher, who was due to retire the following year, had led the group in a delicate rendition of the sixties pop classic, which brought an inner glow to the infant in Becky's belly.

Mel had given Becky the general lowdown. There would be a merging of popular autumnal hymns interspersed with contemporary pop tunes, before the children approached the altar and offloaded whatever muck their parents had loitering in the back of the cupboard, to be sent off to the less fortunate. Looking around at the tins being cradled, Becky was hoping that those in third-world countries would appreciate the endless supply of Bigga marrowfat peas.

The festivities got underway at 2 o'clock, which meant everyone was out by three, satisfied that they had made enough of a religious contribution to be forgiven for Halloween, before reconvening for more God-bothering at Christmas.

Becky was supposed to be on the front door, shadowing Mel and Kay as they guided parents in, armed with one of the leaflet-sized programmes that were printed on various shades of sugar paper, but she had been called into the main church nave to count the heads of year six, who had a tendency to drift from the flock on the walk over.

As the children filed in, Becky noticed a familiar pair of blue eyes singling her out. Sienna Clements had obviously been instructed by her mother to be polite and courteous in Becky's presence and so, having spotted her, a full-lipped, childlike grin spread across Sienna's face. Becky nodded back to the girl as she made for the stage, her hair a cavalcade of perfectly-curled ringlets. It was a welcome break from the sea of faces of initially anonymous children, who eyed her with suspicion, their mouths agog and expressions dead.

"Now class," Miss Ware piped up before the big show, standing at her piano and tapping a chopstick-like baton on a superfluous lectern to her right. "Sienna will lead us in the first verse of We Plough and its everyone in on the chorus."

Becky had to hand it to the teachers. They had single-handedly assembled out of a sea of schoolchildren, a set of three copacetic, House of Commons-style lines of infant bodies.

Sienna stood proudly at the front, like an angel with a perfectly-pressed cardigan on. The epitome of an impeccably well-behaved little girl. Catherine would be sure to laud this over Becky at the post-service Coffee 'n' Mingle.

Another few minutes and the parents would be let in, so Kay stalked over to Becky to give her further instruction. Heaven knows why Kay was looking so stressed—she only had to hold a door open.

As they travelled back past the huge pampas grass and pumpkin installations, Becky was filled with nostalgia from her own Harvest Festivals in London. They were a little more raucous than this one. Guaranteed that some poor girl would end up with an upturned can of baked beans down her blazer, while the rambunctious boys would pray for "Our farter, who art in Devon" and make suspicious flatulence noises when the teachers' backs were turned.

At the porch door, the parents were all hanging around, exchanging polite small talk and picking through the names in the programme, as if they were choosing from a Saturday night takeaway menu. Catherine made a beeline for Becky, sporting a beautifully-cut mocha dress that accentuated every curve of her slender body. Becky suddenly felt incredibly old and totally underdressed.

"Oh, Becky!" she said. "Don't you look the part!"

"Don't you look like a part-time school secretary," was what she really meant.

"Catherine, lovely to see you."

Becky noticed that she was holding a few suspect leaflets in her hand. True to her word, she appeared to be distributing them around to bewildered parents.

"I suppose you've seen Sienna," she gushed. "I believe she's leading the school from the very beginning."

"That's correct," Becky nodded, "she looks adorable"

"I should hope so," Catherine said, smoothing down her dress. "Her hair must be the only crop in St Patrick's that *doesn't* have a natural *curl* and I'll be damned if that Rachel Power's precocious little brat outshines my baby. I've had three sets of curling tongs on it since last night. She nearly had to sleep standing up!"

Becky became briefly distracted as she noticed a glob of spit launch itself from Catherine's mouth, coming into land on her cardigan.

"Well, she truly does look amazing. Incidentally, who is Rachel Power?" Becky asked, slyly patting her cardigan dry.

"She's Erin's mummy and a total social climber. She really puts the desperate into 'desperate housewife'."

Becky laughed, and Catherine smiled. It was nice to see her crown slip a bit when gabbling about the onerous relationships she had with her fellow contemporaries—it made her more human.

"I mean, of course, Erin is always the star in the school play. We were all in awe watching *Oliver* when she debuted her Nancy to the parish, but this year the Clemency will overtake the Power."

Nicely put.

"Well, I must get on," Becky said, gesturing towards the programmes in her hand.

"Oh yes, do. I've still got some of *my* leafleting to do. Honestly." She nodded in the direction of Gaynor's house. The trailing vines were just visible from this side of the churchyard. "How she can maintain that jungle all by herself is beyond me. I mean, she's an old woman. It won't be long before she keels over on her own path and the blasted things will grow over her. Something needs to be done, and fast."

Becky was certain that, regardless of her years, Gaynor could probably outdo both her and Catherine in stamina alone, but she said nothing—she just smiled and walked back to her post.

When the parents had all settled, each attempting to catch the eye of their respective infant and perform a non-committal wave in their direction, Becky perched next to Mel, waiting for the performance to commence. Miss Eames was seated a little further down their line, in an unflattering grey tunic with an ominous-looking smile on her lips, waiting for calm before she could fully relax. She had probably sat through one of these festivals every year since time immemorial.

Miss Ware took a step up to the centre microphone, cleared her throat and dropped her glasses from her nose so that they dangled from a chain around her neck. She was wearing what ladies of a certain age might call a "jazzy" jumper. It was a worn-out, muted pink and had the texture of tinsel.

"Parents, teachers, boys and girls," she said, in a weary voice. She had probably heard these tired old choruses more times than she'd had a proper night's sleep. She stood slightly hunched over as if years of sitting at that damned piano stool had finally taken its toll on her poor old back. "I do hope you enjoy this celebration of Harvest by the pupils of St Patrick's and All Angels. We are going to rejoice with some music you may know and some you may not. But we hope you have fun and do join the children in singing the songs on your hymn sheets. Firstly, please put your hands together for year six, led by Sienna Grace Clements."

There was modest applause as Miss Ware popped her specs back on and took her seat at the piano. The crowd parted as the radiating beauty of Sienna Grace made her way up to the microphone, a stretched grin festooned across her face. The girl was so confident for a ten-year-old—she had the makings of a star already. She tossed her hair over her shoulder and put her lips to the mic.

Miss Ware played a few wonky chords before Sienna opened her mouth to sing. When she did, a beautiful sound simply floated around the room. Becky didn't have the nerve to check behind her, though she could almost guess the expression that Catherine would be pulling, looking around at the other awestruck parents, as smug as smug could be.

Sienna continued, backed only by the piano for another few chords before the chorus was due to begin. All the children in the room collectively inhaled as they prepared to sing.

However, just before they began, Miss Ware's hands slammed down on the keys. The music abruptly stopped with a loud crash, causing the most unpleasant, off-key chord to echo around the arches of the small church. One by one, every head in the congregation looked up towards the piano, including Miss Eames', whose brow furrowed as she leant forward. Becky's eyes shot to Miss Ware, who appeared to be looking, not at the music in front of her, but somewhere over the heads of the audience.

A small group of children continued to sing, but most sat totally silent as they watched their teacher in total amazement. Had she fainted? What was going on? A few staff members began to move towards her.

Just as they did, Miss Ware let out a large gasp and began to quickly rise to her feet, turning to face the audience. Some parents began to whisper amongst themselves, some giggled softly from their seats, but Becky's heart began to race. Something about this was totally bizarre and she had an awful feeling about what was about to happen.

Miss Ware continued to rise up onto her toes, her shoulders pulled back and her neck curved. Everyone in the room heard the snap of vertebrae as her back straightened out. Suddenly the air in the room turned dark and cold.

Once Miss Ware was stood fully erect, she began to convulse in a pernicious manner. Slowly at first, from the fingertips, but then it began to move up her body and into a violent shake. Children began to scream as she opened her lips. Her glasses fell from her nose and began whirling around her chest on their seemingly-unbreakable chain.

"F-F-F-F—" she began to mumble, her face now contorted in a horrendously malevolent mask, her fingers like spikes and her back arched inwards like a cobra.

"My God," shrieked Mel from Becky's right, "she's having a seizure!"

As the piano teacher caromed against her beloved instrument and the parents at the front began to come to their senses and claw their way over to the children, Miss Eames pushed past Becky to get closer to the arresting Miss Ware.

"Brenda!" she shouted. "*Brenda*!"

The whole church began to erupt as Miss Ware's eyes bulged out of her head. She continued to blubber and jackhammer against the piano frame as bodies scrambled to get away from her.

She dropped down to flat feet and began to emit a violent choking sound as she grabbed her throat. An audible gasp of terror rose up from the auditorium.

Suddenly, her cheeks filled and with that, she spat a cool jet of blood which travelled straight from her mouth and onto the opened piano lid. At the sight of this, almighty screams filled the nave as teachers and parents alike fought their way back to the church doors in a cacophony of cries and shrieks.

Miss Eames launched herself toward Miss Ware, but the woman's hand shot out towards her chest, disarming the headmistress.

"G-G-G-G," she rasped at Miss Eames, her face twisted and demonic, a trail of fresh blood trickling down her chin. "G-G-G-*Get it out of me*!"

She let out a sudden, deep-throated snarl before a deafening snap bounced off the church walls. A shot of blinding, white light radiated outwards from the piano, sending Miss Ware careering backwards and dropping like a crumpled heap to the floor. She toppled halfway down the altar stairs and lay, a mass of broken limbs, her eyes stretched open, looking up at her boss.

"My God," Miss Eames said to herself before turning around and booming through the chaos. "Everybody remain calm and evacuate the building! Teachers, parents, please assist the children in getting out safely!"

"*Fuck*," Becky mumbled, totally forgetting that she was in a church. The whole thing had played out like some possession-style horror film. She looked around desperately and realised that she was alone in the pew. Everyone else had catapulted themselves away from the stage, leaving only a few bewildered stragglers, a perplexed Miss Eames and the smashed body that once belonged to Miss Ware.

"Miss Dawlish, I suggest you get outside *now*!" Miss Eames snapped. Becky dizzily felt her way from pew to pew, to get to the back of the church.

Once outside, she slinked past inconsolable children and angst-ridden parents, all making their way back down towards the school in haste. Becky moved towards the north transept to get some space. She suddenly felt completely dazed by the whole event. Pushing herself through, she staggered to a seating ledge, where she collapsed in fatigue. Whatever had just happened, it had not been normal. People don't just freak out in the middle of the Harvest

Festival and start spitting blood in the Lord's house—this was *abhorrent*.

She was sure that an ambulance would be called, but there was no way that woman was alive. Becky had seen the light extinguished from her eyes. What on earth had happened to her? Whatever it was, it was not something that Western medicine could cure. This was the work of some kind of paranormal entity. Becky couldn't just stand by and do nothing—she had to get help.

Her mind suddenly raced back to her conversation with Catherine as she'd garbled soggily at the dinner table.

"Of course, it's well-known around here, what she is capable of, though she has sworn against it many times."

Perhaps there was one person who might be able to come to the rescue. It was risky, but worth doing if something could be salvaged from this terrible situation. Becky shakily got to her feet. Luckily, her destination wasn't far.

■■■

Gaynor looked totally bemused when she opened the door. She certainly wasn't prepared for some crazy woman to be banging against it at half-past-two in the afternoon.

"My goodness child, whatever is it?" she had said calmly.

Becky was out of breath.

"Gaynor, something has happened," she gulped. "The service. Miss Ware, lifted into the air. Blood everywhere. She needs help!"

Gaynor's mood suddenly clouded over. She looked at Becky with a stony seriousness.

"Call 999," she said, "there is nothing that I can do."

With that, she went to close the door. Becky quickly stuck her foot in between the door and the frame.

Gaynor looked down at Becky's foot and back up with a dark solitude in her eyes.

"Oh, come on Gaynor," she whispered. The afternoon's events had unleashed something unbridled within her. "Both you and I know that you can help. You must have a potion or a balm or something. She won't make it if she has to wait for the services. She might die!"

Gaynor still looked unmoved and unimpressed.

"We need help," Becky pleaded.

It was a moment before she spoke.

"Let me get my coat."

■■■

As they pushed into the church through the remaining crowd of disturbed parents, Miss Eames headed them off at the door.

She took one look at Gaynor and then at Becky. She was even more unhappy than usual. Her hair had escaped from its Kirby-grip prison and lay in strands across a forehead that glistened with perspiration.

"What on *earth*?!" she snarled.

"I'm sorry, Miss Eames, but Gaynor thinks she can help." Becky fought for composure.

"I am surprised she can even set foot in here without spontaneously combusting!" Miss Eames spat.

"Oh, pooh, Alice. You know I don't believe in that rubbish, now let me see the casualty." Gaynor pushed past the headmistress and hobbled her way up the aisle.

"We are waiting for the ambulance, we do not need your sort of help. It was imprudent of Becky to ask!" Miss Eames called after her, following her steady journey up the centre of the nave. A few brave people were dotted about, trying to sneak a second look at Miss Ware's twisted body.

"And while you are waiting for those mobile pallbearers, the spirit will be seeping from the bones and making its way into the unknown, scared and alone. Is that it?" Gaynor shouted behind her. "As well as continuously putting the safety of a hundred frightened children in jeopardy, do you really want *that* on your conscience as well?"

Miss Eames did not respond.

Gaynor strode up to the mangled heap that vaguely resembled Miss Ware on the floor and held out a hand. Becky stopped a few paces behind Miss Eames who had stopped behind Gaynor.

Gaynor appeared to be whispering as she stood with her hand out, hovering metres above the body. After a few moments, she turned.

"She's gone," she said, eliciting a few gasps from the few people still loitering in the church. "But with any luck, our lady has led her towards the light."

"She's dead?" Becky said, cursing herself for not contacting Gaynor earlier.

"Yes, child. A part of life will always be death. But it is only one part of a greater journey." Gaynor turned back to the body and knelt down. Both Becky and Miss Eames looked on as Gaynor appeared to sniff the air around her.

She tutted, shook her head, stood back up and turned to face them both.

"Terrible business," she said, "not her time to go."

"Well, obviously not," Miss Eames scoffed.

"Ah, you doubt me, Alice. But then, you never did accept the facts in favour of the propaganda." She began to make her way down towards Becky.

"Come, child, you don't want to see that."

"What happened?" Becky asked, not knowing whether to be shocked or in mourning.

"Poor soul was hexed," she said as if she said that sort of thing every day.

Becky held her hand to her chest.

"It was strong too. Just look." She pointed behind her and Becky's gaze followed the direction of her finger.

A deep, angry, black mark was streaked across the piano. A mark that was all too familiar.

SIX

Wing was at work when she got the call. St Helen's Nursing Home had been so busy that morning. Elsie had refused to eat her porridge, screaming intemperately as Wing attempted to ladle the creamy mush into her open mouth.

"Nurse, nurse!" Elsie had screeched as her arms flailed wildly, sending a globule of slop down Wing's plastic apron. "This one's trying to kill me, just like they did in 1941—she's trying to poison me!"

Wing couldn't be bothered to remind Elsie for the umpteenth time that she was from Bangkok, not Japan, and that the Thai had nothing to do with any sort of invasion in 1941. She was not likely to retain this information. She had dementia and every day for the past 726 days, her memory seemed to have reset itself to factory defaults. Whether Wing was helping her onto the commode or giving her delicate parts a much-needed sponge bath, Elsie would crow that Wing was trying to dispatch her until the sorry task was complete. If it weren't for crippling staff shortages, Wing may have asked another carer to take over from her, but it was no good. She just kept her mettle and carried on scooping the liquid up from the bowl.

"I'm onto you," Elsie had said, milky goo cascading from her open mouth. "I have twenty silver coins under my pillow and you're not getting them."

Wing sighed and put down the bowl. She got up to her feet and walked slowly back to the kitchen, scraping her long, black hair from her moist forehead.

"Is she doing it again?" Alison asked from her position by the sink.

Wing nodded, slightly defeated but smiling nonetheless.

"Silly old coot doesn't know what day of the week it is, love. I wouldn't worry."

To be honest, Wing wasn't worried. For the most part, the patients were harmless, so frail and drugged up that the only thing to normally cross their lips was a watery, toothless smile. It was only Elsie that looked at her with an expression void of any sort of recognition or trust. The fact that Wing had worked at St Helen's for nearly three years counted for absolutely nothing through the eyes of dementia. Elsie had accused her of everything, from Pearl Harbour to the Triads. She had even branded her responsible for the rise of one of Mao's sympathisers. Wing had simply discarded the comments as quickly as she did her disposable gloves.

If only Elsie could be more like Jacqueline. She was Wing's favourite and although you weren't supposed to have favourites in this line of work, Jacqueline was so much more than any of the others. Wing couldn't help but migrate over to her private room when the going got tough.

"Go and grab yourself a coffee," Alison said. "Then I think Jacqueline might need some personal care."

She gave Wing a wink, knowing that this would appease her for all the trouble she'd suffered at the hands of the cantankerous Elsie.

Wing did as she was told and made her way over to the kettle, flipping it on and grabbing for her phone in the pocket of her coat.

There had been a missed call. That was strange. It was nine o'clock in the morning—who could possibly need her at this hour? She didn't have many friends, certainly not any who might contact her so early. Richard and the kids were at work and school respectively.

She looked at the screen. It was Joanna—things must be serious. She looked over her shoulder to check who was about.

Alison was busy with the dishes, slamming each one on the side while singing along to Wham on the radio.

"I just need to make a call," Wing called over. Alison nodded in response.

She grabbed her coat and pushed open the outside door into the crisp, cold, morning air.

"W." Joanna picked up on the first ring. "How are you?"

"I'm fine," Wing said. Although she understood English impeccably, her accent was still strong and made her words sound jumbled, "You okay?"

"Yes, fine. However, something has happened. We need to meet—*all* of us."

"Right. Can't now though, I working."

"Yes, I understand. Though I think we need to meet post-haste, something has come up and we all need to be present."

"Okay."

"Come to me at six this evening."

"Okay."

"Good. And bring some of that tea that you make. Mine has run out. Bye."

Wing sloped back into the kitchen, pulling off her coat. There appeared to be some sort of commotion happening in the day room. Elsie was screaming again.

"Sorry, Wing, could you see to it?" Alison said. "I'm up to my elbows in suds here."

Wing nodded again. Walking past the boiled kettle, she flipped it off and trudged out of the kitchen door. As she approached Elsie, the old bird stopped yelling and gave her a deathly glare.

Wing noticed a big milky pool in the lap of Elsie's brown corduroy skirt.

"Oh, Elsie," Wing sighed. "What happen?"

"Well, what do you think happened?" Elsie snapped as spittle dripped from her gummy sneer. "Your fuckin' poison made me sick!"

∎∎∎

Wing was the first to arrive at Joanna's front door since it was closer to work than home was, and it was more than her life was worth to be late to a meeting. Joanna always said that a good witch was a punctual witch and Wing wasn't about to challenge one of her inviolable rules.

She knocked feebly on the glass and watched as a familiar, wonky silhouette appeared in the frosted pane.

"Oh, hello dear," Joanna cooed as she grabbed Wing by the shoulder and practically manhandled her off the step. Before Wing had a chance to reply, the same hand was forcefully steering her into the lounge and, seemingly, away from the display cabinet that threatened to topple from its position if met with Wing's protruding gut. She proffered a clear bag full of tea leaves which Joanna snatched with an imperceptible grunt of thanks.

Joanna's house was a mish-mash of chintz and ornaments. Yet, to be fair to her, it all matched in colour—gold and claret. Pictures large and small hung from every available inch of wall space, and varying dusty glass and gilt dangled from the ceiling, poised and ready to decapitate any soul who failed to spot it before it caught them.

"How are things at the nursing home?" Joanna called as she whisked past into the kitchen in a blur of cranberry viscose, not bothering to wait for an answer. Wing was far too taciturn for Joanna, who always had something to say. "Is this tea the milk or non-milk stuff?"

"No milk," Wing answered from the lounge, suddenly feeling entirely dispensable. She was still stood in her coat, unable to move, lest she knocked something over, kicking off a domino effect of falling trinkets. She felt like a daft dung beetle who had lost its invitation to the ugly bug ball.

Joanna came back through into the lounge.

"Oh, don't stand on ceremony, W, make yourself at home. Here, give me that." She held out an open palm for Wing to deposit her coat. Wing tried to ignore the incontrovertible grimace that crossed Joanna's face as she transported the wadded turquoise fabric to a hook in the front hall.

Wing looked around for a suitable place to sit. She usually perched on the small red pouffe chair, not ever feeling good enough to warrant sofa space or a whole armchair to herself. Once she had located it, Wing squeezed her dumpy, squat frame onto the cushion and looked despairingly down at how her stomach stuck out over her short legs.

As she let out a bashful sigh, the doorbell rang.

"Ah," Joanna called, breezing from the hook to the door in one sweeping motion that created a draught. "It's Laura! Laura my dear, how are we?"

"Oh, hi Joanna. Yes, I'm good thanks."

Wing could hear the strain in Laura's voice before she even entered the room. It was no secret that the entire circle of ladies found Joanna incredibly hard work. It was her overbearing need to rule and discipline everyone that the women found onerous. She was not only the most experienced witch in the coven, she was also the one who lived most centrally.

Laura entered the room and immediately looked delighted to see Wing.

"Hey, you," she said, striding over and stooping down to give her a tight hug. "How are you?"

"Oh, I fine," Wing said with a guileless giggle that made her feel like a schoolgirl—and an overweight one at that. "You okay?"

"Yeah. Just work, you know."

Wing nodded. She knew. She knew all too well.

In complete contrast to Wing, Laura was young and tall, with tumbling curls of bright, auburn hair. She had pure, white skin and long eyelashes. Beautifully lithe, she always looked casual but extremely well-groomed. Wherever she went, she carried a notepad and pen with her.

"I've left Ben alone tonight. He's a bit annoyed. Still, Grand Designs is on, so I don't think he'll miss me all that much," she said, rolling her eyes.

Wing laughed.

"I know. Richard have to pick up the kids. He won't be happy."

They both sniggered at the misfortunes of their better halves. However, neither partner had cause to complain. It was a solemn vow of each witch that, while they should protect the anonymity of the other members of the coven, they were not allowed to lie to their own spouse about their chosen practice. Since both Laura and Wing had practised magick as soon as they were deemed old enough to read a spell aloud, they had both established an early mutual understanding with their respective husbands that they were witches before they were wives and that the coven would always come first.

Laura settled herself as the doorbell sounded once more.

Joanna led Robina into the room, a flurry of bias-cut fabric and tousled, blonde hair. She sat down next to Laura, frantically running her fingers through her tangled ponytail, apologising profusely for being late, even though she was three minutes early. Robina was one of those slim thirty-somethings who kept themselves unbelievably trim by living on cups of camomile tea and the edge of their own nerves. An inherent worrier, Wing often wondered how Robina ever reined her own consternation in long enough to ever cast a spell at all, let alone one weighty enough to have any sort of clout.

"It's so lovely in here," Robina had sighed as she gazed longingly around at the cramped lounge, with its ageing tapestries and dark oak carvings. She said it every time as if she were discovering the place anew with each visit.

Abbie clomped her way in next, a beautiful but insolent young woman of nineteen who barely threw a "hey" in their direction as she frowned at her mobile phone, tossed her long blonde mane over one shoulder and dropped onto the sofa with an undignified thud.

"Hey, that's my seat," Joanna scolded her on her way back to the kitchen, unmoved by Abbie's insurrection. The girl audibly scoffed and dragged herself over to the next cushion, continuing to text as Robina smoothed out her skirt and wiped a floury fingerprint from her cheek.

"I've been trying to bake my own bread," Robina cooed, "but I think I forgot the yeast or something. I don't know. It didn't rise anyway, so I haven't brought it with me."

Wing was glad. Robina had the kindest heart in the world, but her baking was decidedly sub-par and, though home-cooked focaccia is hard to master at the best of times, she nearly lost a crown to Robina's last attempt at home baking. An old root canal throbbed at the back of her mouth at the thought.

"Tea, Laura? Robina? Abbie?" Joanna called from her position by the kettle.

"Yes please," came the reply from the first two ladies.

"Do you have hemp milk?" Abbie responded, bathed in the blue light of her phone screen.

"No, I've never even heard of that. Hemp milk? Hemp as in mary-juana?"

Abbie stifled a snort.

"No, why would I drink that? It's just cows' in this house I'm afraid." There was a hint of exasperation in Joanna's tone.

"Yuck. Did you know that the human stomach isn't developed enough to process cow's milk? It just lies in your stomach for days like dead custard skin." Abbie pulled a disgusted face that made the other ladies screw up their own in empathy.

"That'll be a no to tea then?" Joanna barked.

"I have some water in my bag," Abbie replied with a petulant scoff.

Robina waited for Joanna to clatter about before she leant forward to the others.

"Does anybody know if Bernice is coming tonight?" she said in a clipped whisper. Laura gave an imperceptible shake of the head.

"It's still under investigation," she said quietly.

The doorbell chimed right on the hour. It made Robina jump out of her skin.

"That'll be Gaynor," Joanna said as she rushed through, mug in hand.

The ladies waited patiently as Joanna exchanged greetings with the last guest. Abbie shut down her mobile and slid it into the pocket of her jeans, before fishing around in her bag for an available lip-gloss.

"Hello all," Gaynor said as she hobbled into the room, Joanna behind her in hot pursuit. "How are we doing then?"

They all nodded and answered in mumbled greetings. That was the thing about Joanna's place, it had the look of a comforting Arabian souk, but with all the atmosphere of a prison visitation room.

"How is Dai?" Joanna asked sympathetically, sneaking around Gaynor's side, still brandishing a china mug.

"Oh, he's still Dai. Good days and bad days."

Joanna was trying to encourage Gaynor to step aside so that she could continue with the tea, but the old woman wouldn't budge.

"But he's under lumelight tonight so he should be alright." She nodded, walking out of Joanna's path and lowering herself into the big wicker chair at the back of the room.

"Lumelight?" asked Robina, her eyes wide with intrigue "Does that really work?"

"It works temporarily," Joanna intercepted before anyone else got the chance. "Of course, it has to be strong, else it fades almost immediately and becomes just a redundant glow."

"Mine keeps sputtering out," Robina complained. This prompted a patronising smirk from Joanna.

"Ah well, you're brand new aren't you, lamb?" Gaynor laughed and rested her hands on her knees. "These old, worn out fingers have had a lot more practice than you. You'll get there"

That was the thing about Gaynor, she was wise and generous, unlike Joanna who was learned but used her wisdom as a weapon.

"I can do lumelight," Abbie piped up, not even looking up from her compact mirror. "It's easy. You just have to concentrate and not piss about."

Laura put a reassuring hand on Robina's knee, as her face fell at this flagrant swipe in her direction.

"Many people's aren't great," Laura said in a conciliatory tone. "They can be intermittent."

Joanna tutted at Abbie's language before changing the subject swiftly.

"Right, tea Gaynor?"

"I'd rather not," Gaynor said. "Could we crack on? I'd rather be home, to be honest. No amount of magick, intermittent or otherwise, compares to the care of a nagging wife."

"Of course," Joanna agreed, stepping into the kitchen to deposit the empty cup and pick up three full ones. She distributed them around the room before taking a seat in the centre of the sofa. "Would you like to start then Gaynor, since you are the one who called this meeting?"

"I suppose." Gaynor took a deep breath and put her palm to her chest. The ladies leaned forward, drawing their attention towards the old woman. Even Abbie glanced up for a nanosecond, pursing her lips as she did.

"Well," she began, "I'm afraid that it has happened again, ladies."

Eyes around the circle widened as Robina gasped and looked desperately around.

"But I thought it was a one-off," she uttered. "Joanna?"

"Just listen." Joanna placated her with a firm hand gesture.

"Well, I don't think it is, love. I think it might be a bit more serious than that." Gaynor stopped to steel herself for a moment. A fraught silence filled the room. "You see. This afternoon—"

She was cut short by the sound of the doorbell ringing through the centre of the circle. The ladies all looked around at each other, wondering who else was due to join them. Since all who were meant to be present were accounted for, there was no obvious answer. Joanna rose to her feet, taking Gaynor by complete surprise. She walked over to the curtain mumbling about Bernice.

Joanna took the curtain by the edge and peered around it inconspicuously.

"Oh." Joanna's face dropped as she stared through the pane. "It's not. Excuse me, ladies."

She marched through the lounge door and closed it behind her.

Everyone in the room sat stock still, gazing in the direction of the door, where a muffled conversation could be heard.

"Do you think we should grab the books?" asked Robina, her eyes expanding with anticipation. Usually, if an uninvited guest called unexpectedly, Joanna would get rid of them. However, in an emergency, she had a large chest full of copies of *Jamaica Inn*. Each person would ultimately select one and open at page fifty, pretending they were having a book group meeting.

Before anyone could react, the door was pushed open. Joanna walked slowly in, her expression one of forced reverence.

"Err, ladies. We have a visitor," she said morosely, stepping aside to let another figure through.

It was a woman, immaculately dressed in a black pantsuit with patent, charcoal, pointed-toe shoes. Her hair was a short crop of sculpted blonde and sitting on the nose of an extremely handsome face was a pair of thick, purple spectacle frames. She must have been in her late fifties, though her skin was taut, and her lips were full. She smiled as she stepped into the space, brandishing an identity card that smiled back from the plastic casing of a black leather wallet. Both faces showed the same set of sparkling, white teeth.

"Good evening, sisters," the lady said. Her accent was clipped, and her voice was soothingly deep. "My name is Odette and I come to you from The Oracle."

Every spine in the room immediately straightened. Abbie smoothed her hair out with the palms of her hands, unwittingly discarding her lip-gloss in the process. Gaynor put her hand to her mouth and Robina slammed her palms to her knees.

A visit from the High Oracle was absolutely unheard of in these parts, indeed this region. This must be serious business and each woman in the room knew it. If the queen herself had entered the room, she would have struggled to have mustered such a reaction.

"My stars," said Gaynor who inched forward in her seat to get a good look at the picture on the ID card.

"Indeed," Odette said, flipping the wallet shut and tossing it into her black Mulberry shoulder bag.

"Now," she went on, "I don't want you to be worried. There is something we need to discuss, if I may intrude on your meeting."

Laura and Robina instantly moved up the sofa to allow Odette to sit.

"Thank you," Odette said as she pulled the bag from her shoulder and went to sit down. Her movements were sleek and, as she sandwiched herself between the two women, she scanned the group person by person.

Joanna, who had spent the last few seconds in a frozen panic, suddenly sprang into life. A million questions fluttered around her mind as she parted her lips. Why was this woman here? What could be happening? Was she going to relieve her of her duties or was there a threat to the safety of the coven?

Had that damned Bernice been granted full acquittal, on her way to make a mockery of their sacred order?

Any one of these wild accusations could fly off her tongue at any moment but she fought to keep her composure under Odette's intense scrutiny. It would never do to lose her cool in front of a member of the High Oracle and risk exhibiting herself as some sort of country bumpkin farceur who couldn't hold her tongue with the necessary decorum. As she fought to find the right words to say without looking as panicked as she felt, she suddenly grabbed them.

"Right, Grand Sceptre," she blurted out, a little over-loud and completely at random, making every head turn in her direction, Odette's included.

"I'm afraid I'm out of maharaja milk, so cows' will have to do."

SEVEN

Bernice looked at the telephone and exhaled loudly. It was never going to ring—staring at it wasn't going to change that.

Why did it bother her so much?

Perhaps the fact that Joanna had finally got her way. Primordial, pedantic, ascetic Joanna. She really was a witch with a capital 'B'. Bernice could accept that Joanna had won the first round, but the war was still up for grabs.

If Bernice had been a man, Joanna would never have treated her with such contempt. But then, if Bernice had been a man then her initiation into the coven would have been pulled completely off the table. There was simply nothing she could do.

The manner in which she had been denuded so bluntly had left the bitterest taste in her mouth.

Joanna had literally emerged from the kitchen and said quite calmly, "Bernice, I cannot possibly allow you to continue to come to meetings until the matter has been logged and investigated by the Admissions Department at the High Oracle. It is simply not a decision I am authorised to make."

Everyone had just sat there, not saying anything or standing up to the nefarious actions of the old hag. She supposed that Joanna's rulings had inculcated such a sense of reason within these ladies for so many years that any change must have seemed implausible. It was only Robina who had fought her corner in the end. Poor, sweet Robina, with her nails bitten to the quick and a big blob of dinner down the front of her blouse. Bernice knew how much nerve it would have taken for Robina to stand up to Joanna, especially given her usual passivity.

"But Joanna, surely the High Oracle don't really need to know. I mean, Bernice fits the criteria, save for one small, technical detail." Robina had looked over at Bernice with a mortified squint.

"No offence."

Bernice nodded in gratitude.

"Robina, that is quite a technicality." Joanna's eyes had burned with a portentous glare that mirrored her dislike of being challenged. "The coven is protected by laws that cannot be contravened. One of which is that its members must have one-hundred percent muliebral solidity. She has to be a woman."

"But, Joanna," Robina had continued, albeit in a whisper rather than a voice. "Bernice ... well, she *is* a woman."

Joanna had sighed condescendingly.

"Bernice," she'd scoffed as if Bernice had not been in the room, "has only been a woman since 2012."

The atmosphere weighed heavy as this statement hung in the air. Nobody had the tools with which to construct a further debate. Only Bernice could argue the toss for herself.

"But Joanna, if you truly understood my condition," she had said slowly, "then you would know that I have actually been a woman all my life."

Joanna had neither the gumption nor the guile to question her at that point.

"I'm sorry," she had said, and politely opened the door for her to walk out through.

And now Bernice was sat by the phone, waiting for someone, anyone to update her on what the next step might be.

■■

Once Odette had finished, the ladies had all remained in a frozen tableau, the information sinking into their brains.

"So," Joanna had said eventually, verbally puffing out her chest, "what you are telling us is that we are under threat?"

Odette set her mug on the coffee table and turned to her interlocutor.

"Not necessarily," she said in an officious manner. "I mean, the locale may be under threat but not the coven directly. That is pre-eminently what I am here to ascertain. It is no secret that there are other denominations in the area that can aid us in fighting this, many who are stronger than us in number. It is of concern to the High Oracle if the coven, and the coven only, is in any sort of danger."

Gaynor unlaced her hands and inched herself forward.

"But Grand Sceptre, with all due respect, the area has been under threat with impractical magick since the Dark Ages. We have always survived the fallout. Why should we need assistance now?" She smiled at Odette who returned it with a generic grin that was framed in dark plum lipstick.

"It's a good question," she said calmly. "This is a kind of magick we have not witnessed before. It seems to take the form of some kind of advanced process that is synonymous with the modern-day lifestyle. To put it bluntly, this is twenty-first century, black witchcraft. We have reason to believe that it will be harder to contain unless we have first-hand evidence of what it can do."

"Well, what is it doing?" Laura spoke up, rolling her pen over and over between her palms. "I mean, what are we being threatened by?"

Odette shifted around to face Laura.

"We believe that what is currently in force in this very community is a spell that allows the victim to not only be bewitched but to also partly combust," she replied. "It places a sort of mark on the possessed soul, disallowing it to pass to the other side. Why, we do not know. But it seems then that this mark, this brand, can be used as some sort of tracking device to bring the corpse back to life."

Odette looked down.

"But as something inherently different from the person that they once were."

A collective gasp echoed through the space.

"So, you're saying," Robina chimed in, after a moment of quiet, "that the magick stays in the soul of the victim so that their body can be used again, like some sort of puppet?"

Odette nodded.

"And this kind of spell has not been used before?" Laura asked with intrigue.

"Never," Joanna answered, sitting up. "It's somewhat advanced. I mean, bewitching has been around since the dawn of time. We all know that one can be bewitched into doing all sorts of things, even taking their own life. However, once the soul is gone, the magick evaporates and becomes spent. It is another level of cruelty to leave something embedded so that the body can be collected like a chattel."

A smile curled at the corner of Abbie's lips.

"Wow," she said, which caused a few raised eyebrows. "I'm sorry, but that *is* pretty cool."

"Cool or not," Odette said, pointedly, "it is highly criminal and militantly treacherous. Akin to a war crime. What we need is to find someone who has witnessed what happens when this magick takes effect. We need to understand how it manifests and trans-mutates within the body. We need to be aware of what the outward signs are so that we can join the dots and find out what we need to refer back to in our history to fight this—this cancer. I will be residing in this community while I make this investigation and would ask you all for your assistance."

It was a moment before Gaynor sat even further forward.

"I wouldn't bother unpacking your overnight bag just yet, Grand Sceptre," she said, "because I believe I can help you find what you're after."

■■

When Becky and Gaynor arrived at the strange house on the corner of the park, a nervous-looking woman with her greying hair in a bun welcomed them at the door, introducing herself as Joanna. She looked inherently sweet but slightly aloof.

Joanna's eyes had searched Becky's face as she stood before her. In her available hand, she clutched a worn copy of *Jamaica Inn*. Becky wore a bemused frown. She didn't know why she had agreed to come to this stranger's house in the middle of the evening, but Gaynor had been adamant that she had needed to speak to someone about the events at the Harvest Festival.

"Oh, you must be Becky, do come in my dear," the woman said as she led Becky in, lightly grabbing her by the elbow. Gaynor followed behind.

The room was stuffy and cluttered, with all sorts of knick-knacks of varying shapes and sizes, accompanied by an abundance of cushions and throws, all in gold and red. Becky didn't really know what she was doing here.

Dom had seemed grateful that this charming septuagenarian who he had not met before was able to talk some sense into Becky. Ever since he had returned from work, she had been scrubbing at the wall, trying to erase some kind of soot mark from the paint. She was agitated— disturbed, even. Dom had never seen his wife like this and didn't seem to know how to handle it.

Just as she had started to elucidate on what was troubling her, the old woman had arrived and advised that she go with her for an hour or two. She seemed pleasant enough, and even though Becky had seemed a tad vacant, he didn't really want to have to deal with it after such a long day in the surgery.

As they entered the room, Becky noticed a silver-haired woman sitting cross-legged on the carpet. She too was ensconced in *Jamaica Inn*, but her copy was brand new. When she saw Joanna, Becky and Gaynor walking in like The Beverley Sisters she looked up and smiled. This anonymous woman had crinkles at the side of her eyes which made her look of an age, Becky would have guessed she was in her seventies. Her aquiline nose gave her an interesting beauty.

Becky smiled back, at ease but still slightly uncomfortable.

"Oh, Becky," the woman said, "come in. We've heard so much about you."

"Have you?" Becky stuttered incredulously as Joanna pushed past her to get into the room. She still felt as though she were in some sort of daze.

"Yes, we have. Gaynor's been so complimentary of your good soul," Joanna spoke as she passed.

"We were just reading Daphne Du Maurier, have you read her?" the silver-haired woman asked, her eyes a twinkling river of blue.

"Err, no. I think I've seen some sort of adaptation on the television"

"Oh yes, much more fun than reading the book I'd imagine!" she laughed.

Becky laughed nervously in awkward agreement.

"Sorry, where are my manners?" The silver-haired lady lifted herself into a squatting position before stretching her legs slowly up to standing. She was remarkably slender and tall, with a yoga-toned body. When she stood upright, her long hair fell nearly to her bottom. She approached and reached out for Becky's hand. "I haven't introduced myself. My name is Temperance."

"Oh," Becky said, slightly bewildered. "What a beautiful name"

As Temperance leant forward, Becky smelled honey and milk.

"Thank you, my dear," she said. "It means virtue, purity. Untainted by troublesome forces. I like to think I am all those things."

"I'm sure you are," Becky said, politely.

Temperance led her to the sofa where she tentatively sat down. Gaynor nestled herself in a wicker chair as Joanna crossed them to enter a separate room.

"Temperance and I go way back," Gaynor interjected. "She is a holistic healer. She uses my garden for some of her ingredients. In turn, she has taught me the valuable powers of the herbs and plants. She's only here for tonight so I thought you might be interested in meeting her."

"I see," Becky said, still slightly apprehensive. Although she trusted Gaynor and had no reason to doubt the motives of the otherwise charming Temperance, she never felt comfortable in the homes of people that she didn't know. She'd never been able to understand how people on Come Dine with Me managed it four nights on the trot.

"I am very interested in what you saw today," Temperance smiled as she resumed her position on the carpet. "Gaynor was just filling me in and I was wondering whether I could help. Some might say that it is one of the more inexplicable elements of my expertise. My understanding is that you witnessed some kind of ... possession?"

Becky looked at the two women one after the other, unable to formulate a response that wouldn't sound as if she was utterly mad. She had been playing the scene over in her head ever since she had left the church and marched straight home. She had wrenched the door of the cupboard under the sink open so hard that it had almost separated from its hinges.

Armed with a scrubbing brush and bleach, she began to ferociously tackle the huge, black mark that decorated her wall. She wanted to eradicate whatever evil had taken hold of Brenda Ware from the hold it had on her house.

"What is this mark?" she said to herself as she scoured. "Why here? Why in this house?"

As she had scrubbed, she thought of Brenda's juddering body, her bulging eyes, her strangled voice. It terrified her so much that she began to sob. To pacify her tears, she scrubbed harder.

Joanna came back into the room and gave Becky a cup of steaming liquid.

"It sounds hideous, what you've been through." Temperance's soothing voice was reassuring and placating, but Becky could feel the upset bubbling up again.

"Why don't you tell us what happened?" Joanna asked as she sat down on the adjacent sofa.

Becky suddenly became aware of the situation she was in, sat in the house of some woman, with another lady that she did not know, holding a cup of some miscellaneous brew. It was all a little strange. But then, hadn't the whole day been sort of strange?

Becky didn't want to be so impertinent as to ask the ladies whether they, like Gaynor, were witches as well, but she had a fair idea. They both seemed so nice, like women you might see at Green Party Conference rallies. They certainly didn't fit the description of your archetypal Wicked Witch of the West.

Becky inhaled the aroma of the liquid in her hands. It was sticky smelling, sweet, like strawberries and lime. It was a heady concoction that sent her straight back to the days of children's parties when her mouth had been tacky with the residue of jelly and ice cream. Her tongue became instantly dry and she longed to quench her thirst. Almost involuntarily, she lifted the cup to her lips and poured a little into her mouth.

The scourge of the day's events was instantly lifted as she gulped down the sweet-tasting, warm fluid. She closed her eyes as it coated her palette, slid down her throat and warmed her chest.

When she opened her eyes, the two women were still smiling back at her. Only Gaynor looked a little put out. Her mouth was crumpled, almost as if she was annoyed by something. Becky watched her eyes flicker between the two other women.

"Now," Temperance said, soothingly and seductively, "why don't you start at the beginning?"

EIGHT

The wind had been cold against Abbie's cheeks as she walked to the bus stop, wrenching her bag further up her shoulder.

Damned witches. Why had they called her out here on such a tempestuous night? She had college work to do and now her head was full of questions. What was happening in this fucked up little town? Did she really care?

It was her mother's idea to entertain this Wiccan bullshit by introducing her to this dreary group with their old-fashioned bollocks. Of course, now that her mother was dead, it was a lot harder to argue with her.

Abbie had thought that being part of such a movement would mean doing cool things like they did in the Harry Potter movies. In reality, it wasn't like that at all. Spells were tedious, boring and written in old-fashioned writing that she didn't give a shit about deciphering. You had to practice reciting them for years before you got anything right, and before you even got to that stage you had to read pages and pages of dull literature that sucked the fun right out of it before you'd even opened your mouth. It was beyond yawn-inducing. Witchcraft was like the martial arts, something you studied how to do for years, knowing full well that you were never going to use it.

Her mother had presented her to Joanna after Abbie had managed to use some innate telekinesis to rob some biscuits from a jar placed on a higher shelf than tippy-toes could reach. This was at the age of eight. Her mother had watched in horror as the jar did a lap of the kitchen before clumsily falling at Abbie's feet. Even then, the treats were covered in shards of porcelain, rendering them inedible. Her mother had dressed her in the most funereal-looking coat she could find, even though Abbie had protested, wanting instead to wear her new snazzy, red jacket. Apparently, anything other than dark and floor-length was not an option when you were going to meet the local neighbourhood kook.

Her mother also looked as though she was going to a wake and, in convoy, they bowed their heads and walked into the town, in the driving rain no less.

Her mother had muttered something to this lady about a great aunt and some sort of gift. Even at such a young age, Abbie had suspected that the gift in question was not the Bratz doll that she had set her sights on. Joanna had welcomed her in, deposited her coat, led her into the front room, which looked exactly the same then as it did now, and asked her to do it again. Without really thinking, Abbie had managed to send a disgusting memorial plate soaring across the room, missing them both by inches. Joanna had smiled, but Abbie had not responded in kind. She was not sure that she wanted to share this talent with anyone else. From now on, she would keep her little secrets locked up tight.

And now it had been so long since Abbie had been allowed to perform anything remotely similar that she had almost forgotten how to do it. From the ages of eight to ten, she was tutored after school in Joanna's study room for hours on end. Endless dusty, old pages in overflowing, leather-bound books. The grey lint would get in her hair and stick to her eyelashes. Joanna would poise over her, the soft, fine hairs on her chin dancing in front of the lamplight, her sinewy fingers poised over a box of matches—ready to light yet another fucking candle. At the end of each session came the stern warning that should Abbie be tempted to "try out" any of these spells on her unsuspecting classmates, then there would be serious repercussions. Of course, Abbie had never wanted to use her craft for herself. Once she knew how boring the theory behind it all was, her curiosity was temporarily quelled.

That she knew she had any sort of power at that age had been a sufficient enough secret.

It was the hell of other people that made her want to capitalise on her talents. When she began attending high school and was denigrated and ridiculed by her peers for having long, golden locks and even longer, delectable legs, she was eager to call upon her supernatural expertise to punish those who had enervated her for so long. Their taunts made her irascible and, in turn, she wanted nothing more than to fight back with a leonine indignation.

But it was not meant to be. A true witch was someone who channelled her power appropriately, who used her gift to gain an inherent sense of self-worth that was far more prodigious than the short-lasting effect of even the most spectacular flash-in-the-pan revenge spell.

Of course, it was all contradictory. As a practising witch, one could use natural resources to concoct a truth serum but couldn't bewitch someone into consuming it. It had to be an act of free will or nothing. Anything that contradicted this rule would have you hauled up in front of the High Oracle as fast as your puddle-skimming coat could take you. Where was the fun in that?

When Abbie had been fifteen, she had rebelled against the system by turning a year eleven girl's hair crimson. This girl was responsible for putting a used sanitary towel inside of Abbie's gym kit. The putrefying blood had seeped into her white gym vest and left a pink stain that both intrigued and disgusted Abbie at the same time. Abbie had bagged the towel and set up her own little experiment at home. The next afternoon, Joanna had appeared out of nowhere as Abbie had alighted the bus and led her forcefully back to the study room. What Joanna had shown her that night terrified her into never performing unauthorised magick again. Yet Abbie still felt that she had missed an opportunity. She should have made the rebellion worth it and burnt that rotten bitch's face off.

Now that she was older, she had to attend endless meetings where they sat and discussed laws and policies, festivals and solstices, all for nothing. She had found herself forced into a preservation group for this anachronistic institution that she had never asked to be part of in the first place.

And there was no escape. Even in death, there was no escape. She was bound to these women for life.

That cold night, when her mother had slipped away from her in a hospital bed, she held her lifeless, white hand in her own and made an avowal. Mainly to protect herself in the afterlife, as she had failed to do so far in her real life. That meant keeping her nose clean—and her spells under wraps.

When Abbie got home, she flung her bag on the floor and clambered onto the bed. Her flatmates were in and giggling over some dumb reality TV show in the lounge. Apparently, a fifty-something Real Housewife had just lost her knickers getting out of a cab, or something. She wasn't interested.

She pulled her iPhone out of her pocket, noticing that she had a text message. It was an unknown number.

"Who's the fairest?" it read.

Abbie didn't answer numbers that she didn't know, but tonight she would make an exception. She was pretty sure it was the arsehole from Moo Moo's who she'd tongued in the alley outside the club. He'd clamped his cold fingers into her skirt and prodded at her clitoris before she wrenched his hand back out. She was surprised that he knew how to text since he hadn't a clue how to finger fuck. What a loser.

She typed two words.

"Fuck you."

And with that, she rolled over onto her side.

∎∎

Robina was stood, desperately wringing her hands in the kitchen. Jessie-Cat stared back at her from the worktop, seemingly affected by her owner's angst.

So many questions were running through Robina's head after the tense meeting at

Joanna's, an event that ranked way above the usual herb and candle girth chit-chat of the meetings that had come before it.

Why had this woman suddenly appeared from the High Oracle out of nowhere? What was this crazy new type of magick that was robbing people of their lives? Who was it targeting? Would she be next?

Robina remembered the advice that her therapist, Sylvie Patrouche, had given her, as she sat in her office, next to the huge vase of lilies that always made her nose twitch.

"When you feel the attack coming, take a couple of deep breaths. In and out … in and out."

Robina had sat there, drawing in a breath that was so painful, it was practically barbed. She wondered whether this was helping at all, indefatigably puffing as though she was blowing up an invisible dinghy.

Sylvie had smiled as she threw a chiffon pashmina over her right shoulder.

"Imagine the panic bouncing off your head like a beach ball."

The analogy was fair enough, but this particular beachball was giving her concussion.

As she bent down under the sink to fish out Jessie's dinner, Robina sucked air in through her lips, held it for a second and then blew into the cupboard, scattering some surface crystals from an open bottle of Shake and Vac. She located a dish of Sheba and rose to her feet.

As she peeled the foil back on the tray, she glanced over at the rack of pathetic-looking muffins that she had baked earlier. They looked like leftover artefacts from an archaeological dig. She couldn't possibly serve them to anyone. Even the diseased pigeons in Cheltenham town centre would wrinkle their beaks up at those.

She upturned the tray into a dish and slid it across the table top. Jessie was a tiny, black assassin, pouncing on the food before the plate had stopped sliding. She held on for balance with her paw.

Robina was tired. Tired, it seemed, of trying to live an ordinary life. Her bakes were barely edible at best, her craftwork was lopsided and, after an unfortunate incident where the thread of her homemade skirt had unravelled while she was chatting to the vicar at the Winchcombe Country Show, it was clear that she was not the best seamstress either.

She even doubted her solidity as a decent witch, seeing as she was never allowed to use magick to assist her in all these domestic activities. But then that would negate the need to live as an ordinary human being. How can you be ordinary when you possess extraordinary powers that set you apart?

Her mother had been a good witch, by all accounts, and Robina had been relentlessly reminded by other witches in the other local covens.

"Oh, Robina," they would say, "what a paragon of the sisterhood your mother was. It's such a shame that she died so young."

Iris died when Robina was just eleven. In retrospect, she had always seemed like a normal mother. There were never any kitchen utensils flying around the house of their own accord, cauldrons bubbling in the garage or broomsticks propped against the stairs. In fact, she and her brother had had a stable childhood, full of homemade strawberry shortcake and clips around the ear for acting up.

It was only on her deathbed that she had told Robina the truth. She hadn't made it sound overly fancy—just said it how it was.

"Robina, you possess powers beyond your understanding. You need to nourish them, respect them, learn from them and carry on the legacy of the sisterhood."

She had looked so frail in her hospital bed. Skin so thin it looked like tissue paper. A red scarf wrapped around her head and dark circles below her eyes. Far from the badminton-playing warhorse of the early eighties. Robina hadn't really wanted to see her mother like this, but she had insisted.

Robina had fought to find the words to say, as she sat there in her itchy dress, under the heat of the hospital lights, her neckline strangling the words inside her throat.

"You may not know it now, but all the magick I embodied was put into you both," she whispered. "The strongest spell I ever cast was for your protection, you and your brother. I never needed to cast another."

And then she slipped away, seemingly because she had syphoned out her subcutaneous energy, drip by drip to her children throughout her short, rather plain existence. So much so that she forgot to leave any for herself.

Robina had felt angry at the time. She still felt angry. When all was said and done, wasn't her mother just a martyr? Why give someone else everything you have to the detriment of the time you get to spend with them? What's the point?

And now her mother's legacy was like a shadow that would follow Robina around, allowing her out into the light, only to step back in front and plunge her into darkness. She was the daughter of Iris the brave—she could never simply be Robina.

Yet her anger was suppressed since she could not refute peoples' kind words and gestures. When Joanna met her at the funeral saying how sorry she was and asking if she would like to allow her to carry on her mother's tradition, Robina became placated with the healing power of forgiveness under the parentage of the Goddess Moon.

But she was clumsy. She often felt as though her mother had foolishly arranged for the heart of a witch to be deposited into the body of a blithering idiot. She had no natural aptitude for botany or alchemy, she was not a particularly adept spellcaster or acolyte. She had just waddled along behind everyone else for twenty-three years, never progressing. If the arrival of Odette spelt a serious threat to her sisters, she wondered whether she would be of any use to the coven at all.

■■

The candle in Joanna's sitting room burned bright, filling the air with an intoxicating incense.

"So, what do we think?" asked Temperance, as Joanna closed the front door and walked tentatively towards the sofa.

"Well," Joanna began, "from what the girl said, it sounds to me as though the bewitching is of the old Titubonic kind. The kind that will never appear through divination or retrospective regression, lume-crystals or Backlat oil trances."

"That's what I thought." Temperance had her chin in her hand and was slowly stroking it in a clockwise motion. "It was the description she gave of the possessed woman's distant gaze, the dearth of depth in her eye and then the ferocious convulsion. I mean, we are talking quite archaic spellbinding here. Not the work of an expert."

"No," agreed Joanna. She ran her finger around the rim of her mug as she cast Temperance a sideways glance. "I'm not sure that the spell was actually formulated. I mean, for the victim to even speak, let alone plead with her audience. That sounds like a break in the anaesthetic."

"Unless she performed it herself." The two women's gaze met, and Temperance saw a flash of herself in Joanna's eye. "Oh, this is ridiculous. Excuse me."

She stretched both of her hands out. Little jolts of blue electricity crackled between her fingers as she swept her palms over her head. As her physiognomy reappeared from under her hands, Odette was, once again, in the room.

"Does this woman have any sort of history with the coven? Any relatives who were past members perhaps?" Odette's brow creased.

"I think I would be aware," Joanna said with a slight scoff as if she hadn't thought of this already.

She was still uncomfortable with Odette performing the mimicry spell so readily in her house. Partly because Joanna did not believe in the use of magick as deception, but mainly because Joanna had not been able to perform the spell with such ease since 1977. She understood, however, that Odette was a High Sceptre, here on orders from The Oracle. It was imperative that her identity was masked to the unmagickal, so that any trace of her could be erased should a police investigation take place.

"I am quite happy to do any research—that is what I am here for," Odette said, missing the enmity completely.

"I have kept the records of this coven since I have been old enough to say the Grand Oath," Joanna said, clutching her mug to her chest. "I have studied every witch who came before me, known every witch who has been since me and taught every witch who will continue on after me, High Sceptre. I assure you, the research has already been done."

Joanna realised that she was beginning to sound shrill, something she hadn't wanted to do in front of her innately impassive houseguest.

Odette sighed and slid her perfectly-manicured hand out across the coffee table.

"Joanna, you must understand that I hold your honour to the charge in extremely high regard. I am here to do my job and when it is done, you will continue on as you have always done." She waited a moment for Joanna to thaw.

As Joanna nodded, Odette lost her smile and set her eyes firmly on her target.

"However, I am not a sentimentalist Joanna. This is business. If any of these matters are a threat to the coven, then we need them eradicated. No question. I am not here to overthrow you or undermine your position within this coven. You are its appointed leader and that is not in dispute. But you are not granted the autonomy to simply teach some random group of disparate women who happen to share an esoteric belief about the ways of our order, like some kind of charlatan. You are governed and managed by an atavistic order older and higher than any one of you ladies, regardless of how long or to what extent your devotion to The Order might be."

She stopped as Joanna looked up, her face a ghostly mirror of amazement.

"This is a gravely serious matter and I am afraid that I cannot and will not hesitate in stepping over you if I have to protect The Order and The Oracle. And, as I am sure you are aware, as a High Sceptre, my final decision is unassailable."

Odette stood up slowly, grabbing her bag as she did.

Joanna resisted the temptation to snap at the air with her open mouth as she fought for the words to come back with. She could feel the temper rising up in her, yet she was powerless to do anything about it. Odette was the boss and that gave her the temerity to lay down the law, even if it was in Joanna's living room. She choked down a bile-like blockage of rage.

As Odette turned to stand over a seated Joanna, looking a little ridiculous with such a severe haircut against Temperance's mother earth attire, she stooped lower to grab her coat from over the arm of the sofa.

"Joanna, I will have no choice but to rescind you from your duties if you compromise my investigation. Please don't make me," Odette said finally. She hesitated before walking over to the door. "I shall see myself out."

If Bernice had been there, Joanna was sure she would have punched the air.

■■■

As Catherine tucked Sienna into bed, she touched the lamp so that it dulled a little in the darkness.

"Goodnight sweetheart," Catherine said, kissing her daughter lightly on the forehead. She didn't really want her bright red lipstick to stain the Egyptian cotton sheets.

Sienna looked up at her with angelic innocence, a porcelain doll face set in a mane of blonde curls.

"Mummy," Sienna said, her blue eyes wide with expectation, "what happened in the church today? Did Miss Ware die?"

Catherine gulped. She didn't want to have to weave a web of untruth—she was such a terrible liar. She could never quite hide the look of disdain on her face when Saul's meddling ox of a mother asked whether her stringy, squelchy beef wellington tasted like the boots that shared its name. She just smiled and shook her head, swallowing hard as she did so. And as for Father Christmas, well, she left the fibbing to Saul on that one and just beamed along like she was in the audience of some pedestrian poetry reading.

'Err, no darling. Miss Ware is fine," she stuttered. "Sometimes, ladies of a certain age ... well, they have episodes like that."

"Like what?" Sienna asked, desperately scrambling up onto her elbows. Catherine just knew that she had made the situation ten times worse.

But she posed a good point. Like what? Like they were having a blood-spitting, levitating, epileptic seizure with a lightning-bolt finale?

"Sienna, don't wrinkle the bedspread darling, it's Jasper Conran. What happened to Miss Ware is what happens when people don't take their medicine," she lied, not really knowing where she was going with this tale. Her mouth dried instantly, and she avoided looking anywhere but at her fidgeting hands.

"Anyway," she continued, feeling entirely fatuous under her eleven-year-old daughter's inquisition, "it's nothing to worry about. It will all be forgotten in the morning."

Catherine smoothed out the sheet and hot-footed it out of the door before any more questions were thrown her way. She would be lucky if either of her children were to sleep tonight, the day's antics having been utterly devastating for everyone involved. Catherine was still uncertain that she hadn't dreamed the whole thing.

By the time they had got home, the children had invented a much more cinematic version between them to regale to their father. A story that involved wings sprouting from Brenda Ware's back and a lizard-like tongue that darted out of her mouth. It had been so utterly bonkers that Catherine had trouble remembering what had actually happened. Now, she wasn't sure if she herself had made up the more unfeasible parts in her own head.

In the end, she had just told Saul that the woman had had a fit at the Harvest Festival and fallen into a basket of pampas grass—hence the wings.

And where had Becky escaped to that day? Catherine had scaled the grounds looking for her, but she had been nowhere to be found. She was possibly, and understandably, concerned for the safety of her baby, and who could blame her? She just wished that she hadn't left her with that tiresome bore, Rachel Power. Rachel had simply scooped her children into her arms, a picture of composure, and whisked them away in their new silver people carrier while casting a condescending smirk in Catherine's direction as she flapped like a troubled goose in the middle of the melee.

She bet Rachel Power had never had to lie to her children. She had probably explained it in a very straightforward and succinct manner.

"Sometimes Erin, things happen that mummy and daddy can't explain. I'm guessing that your ageing piano teacher was encased by the very devil himself, and we all should be very afraid for our own mortal souls. Sweet dreams."

Erin! With her perfect hair and beautiful, long eyelashes. Catherine was sure that perfecting Erin's faultless ringlets didn't take the hours that Sienna's did, with Catherine sweating over a set of hair tongs. Not to mention the following day when Catherine would have to wear wrist length gloves to cover up the horrendous scorch marks she had suffered. She blanched at the thought of the acrid stench of hairspray fusing with the scent of her own singed flesh.

She would do anything to wipe that smug grin off Power's face. To claim back some of the integrity that bitch had purloined when she rocked up here from London with her flawless carrot cake and homemade bunting. Catherine had been the queen of the castle before Power arrived, telling the mothers at the gate that "Polly was about to be knocked clean off her perch". From then on, the enmity between them had been palpable.

And, if there was one place that she could upstage her arch-rival, it would be at the annual Halloween party, held every year at the Power household. The seminal children's party of the season, where the costumes were judged, and the stakes were high. After the fiasco of 2014, where Catherine, much to the amusement of Ms Power, had been in charge of proofreading the marketing materials and, due to a little oversight, had invited everyone to a Halesowen Spectacular, she was adamant that this year the Clements children would take back the crown.

She had already drawn up the blueprints for Sienna's outrageous headless horseman outfit with its detachable papier-mâché skull and exploding cranial cannon of homemade crimson blood. Saul's Audi would drop them at the venue, spilling a red, gushing carpet from its open door on arrival, to the attached MP3 player that would emit bubbling liquid noises on a continuous loop. Thank goodness for her father's rather macabre side-line working as a lighting man for the Hammer Horror film studios in the early seventies. Mixing with the likes of Christopher Lee and Ralph Bates behind the scenes as a youngster had lifted the curtain of fear that other children had with horror. To Catherine, threatening, razor-sharp teeth were nothing put enforced porcelain fangs and pulsating, bloody wounds were simply soaked gauze and corn syrup. These little tricks would stand her in good stead when it came to whipping the shit out of Rachel Power's slim efforts. Her exhibition at this party would make Brenda Ware's freak out look like a performance by Pan's People.

She smiled to herself as she rubbed her hands together in her mind. Rachel Power might have the monopoly on meticulous calligraphy and symmetrical cupcakes, but it was Catherine Clements who had the sick and twisted imagination.

■■

When Becky got home from Joanna's, she was undeniably serene.

Dom had tentatively asked her if she had felt any better, to which she replied that she had been temporarily disturbed by a very real seizure at work. It had frightened her at first since it was new and shocking, but Gaynor had been comforting and reassuring. Gaynor was their neighbour, she told him.

Not wanting to get overly involved in his wife's affairs, Dom said he saw seizures all the time, but mainly equestrian ones, so he didn't really know what else he could contribute.

Becky nodded and, as if in a trance, took herself off to bed.

Dom had been thankful that the whole situation had not escalated out of his control.

As she climbed into bed, Becky licked her lips. The taste of strawberry and lime still coated her tongue.

With a deep exhalation, she pulled the cover up to her chin and closed her eyes. Tomorrow was another day.

She slept well, her dreams were untroubled by jets of blood, or black scorch marks.

In fact, her head was empty.

NINE

Becky slept as if she were dead that night. So much so that she nearly missed her 6 am wake-up call. If Dom hadn't have been getting up anyway, she might have slept through and missed her entire shift.

Her head still housed a warming tingle when Miss Eames called the entire staff into the eight o'clock assembly. She guessed it was from the heady mixture she consumed last night—if only she could remember what had happened after.

There was an air of fraught electricity about the school today. Nobody was able to explain what had occurred, nor were they even keen to broach the topic. The girls in the office talked in stunted, innocuous sentences that hung in the air like abandoned boots on a washing line. Becky couldn't help but feel a little left out of something, although she felt completely included in the awkwardness of mood. From what she could ascertain, since nobody was prepared to tell her, Miss Ware had not clocked into work today. It seems that Gaynor had been right.

When everyone had filed in and taken their seats, a few children were noticeable by their absence. The rest were impeccably well-behaved, which felt rather ominous after the carnage in the churchyard twelve hours previously.

"It seems, children" Miss Eames began in her ineffectual drawl as if she were addressing a room full of drugged up pensioners, "that what happened yesterday was a result of a mixture of things."

Her eyes scanned the room before lazily dawdling back down onto the paper in front of her.

"It appears that Miss Ware did not have a good heart and yesterday, she had forgotten to take her important heart medicine. This resulted in her heart giving her a few jolts to let her know that it needed help." She looked down at the front row, who returned her gaze with slack-jawed curiosity.

"But there was much more to it than that. You see..." She paused, looking up into the air as if she were studying some kind of scripture in the sky. Her dry lips flapped together a few times and the room seemed to sway collectively with each parting. "Miss Ware, I'm afraid, was being punished."

A miniature gasp erupted from the captivated children. Even Becky put a hand to her mouth.

Immediately a hand shot up. A little boy of no more than eight wiggled his fingers in the air.

"Yes, William." Miss Eames addressed him as though he were a military cadet.

"Miss, what was Miss Ware being punished for?" he asked in the impressionable, untarnished way that only a child could.

The harrumph she gave in response was slightly condescending and highly inappropriate.

"Well, my boy, it's very simple," Miss Eames continued with impenetrable calm. Her expression had the same air of impassiveness as a Chinese salamander, chilling out on a rock. "You see, Miss Ware was never one for saying her prayers."

Becky looked up in disbelief. Did she just hear correctly? What was this woman saying? Had she lost her mind?

Miss Eames continued, heaving her bosom up so that it rested on the lectern.

"And when one does not take the time to thank Our Lord for all he has given us—the food that we eat, the earth on which we live, the people we love—well, it makes him upset."

A swarm of chatter started to develop throughout the room.

Inside, Becky was outraged.

A few more hands shot up, which Miss Eames flatly ignored.

"So, you see," she continued, "God was making sure that Miss Ware knew that he had seen her forsaking his church, and so he punished her."

Becky's mouth dropped open as she looked around at her fellow staff. Most stood with their arms folded, hanging on every pious word that came out of this woman's mouth. To lie to little children and make them think that their poor, old piano tutor was a sinner, worthy of the full wrath of a vengeful God, was preposterous and wrong—she was dead, for goodness sake!

Miss Eames carried on.

"Now, you all saw what horror befalls those who do not offer God their thanks and praise. So, I suggest that we think a little harder when we ask Mummy if we can skip church on Sunday, or forget to put our hands together before bedtime."

The colour drained from a hundred faces as the headmistress looked down upon the room through her spectacles. She was careful not to catch the eye of anyone other than the gullible, innocent school children. She waited a moment before breaking into a forced smile that made even Becky's cheeks ache.

"So, let's begin right now with a verse of Lord of the Dance," she said, searching the stand for a hymn book. "I think, in light of what I have I just told you, we will need to sing it extra loud. And since we no longer have piano assistance, could someone from year six help me with the CD player?"

●●

After the assembly, and slightly hot under the collar, Becky marched straight up to Miss Eames' office door and gave it a sharp knock. The more the assembly went on with Miss Eames at the helm, who clearly only attended when she wanted to fill the children's minds with such elaborate, offensive lies, the more riled up Becky had gotten. Most children had been so terrified of what might happen to them if they didn't recite The Lord's Prayer at the tops of their voices, that it was uncomfortable to watch.

"Come in," Miss Eames bellowed from the other side of the door.

Becky pushed the door open and stepped inside. Miss Eames was busy tidying papers on her desk in a vain attempt to appear too busy to get into a debate.

"Ah, Becky," she said, "you've caught me at a bad time I'm afraid, I'm just—"

"I won't take more than a minute of your time," Becky said timidly, the after-effects of her blind rage beginning to wear off.

Miss Eames stopped her fussing and looked up. Her face remained unchanged, a perennial, placid mask that wouldn't have looked out of place on a large, cartoon sea bass.

"Okay, what is it you want to say?" she challenged, with one eyebrow raised.

"Um..." Becky's mouth became dry. She didn't know how best to broach the rather onerous subject of calling her boss of less than a week a dirty, fascist liar, "I just ... I'm just not sure that what you just said—I mean, to the children—I'm not sure it was right."

Miss Eames looked less impressed than usual. If that was at all possible.

"Oh, really?" she said, moving her chair back so that she could lean back and enjoy watching Becky's consternation. "How so?"

"Well..." Becky was beginning to lose her mettle. But then she had to say what she felt was right and to do that would take some spunk.

"For a start, it's terribly frightening." She couldn't look her boss in the eye, so instead, she hovered awkwardly by a bookcase, looking out of the window behind her.

"Well," Miss Eames responded, "heresy *is* terrible."

"But, what happened yesterday had nothing to do with religion. I don't think it's fair to mislead the children like that and it's certainly not fair to make Miss Ware out to be some kind of ... heathen!" Her outburst came from nowhere, but it made Miss Eames sit forward and lace her hands together.

"Interesting," she said steadily. "Very interesting. How someone without a smidgen of experience with children, including not having any of her own, has the insolence and effrontery to question my methods and ethics."

Becky found herself slinking back towards the door like a scolded child might.

"I have been running this school under the watchful eye of my maker for thirty-seven years and I am *fully* aware of the difference between what is beneficial to the children's development and what isn't."

Miss Eames stood up slowly, outstretching her hands on the desk.

"I suppose you would like me to tell them that this ... this hula mockery was the result of witchcraft, would you?"

This comment struck Becky as rather odd since it half-confirmed her own knee-jerk suspicions.

"Well, it may be a practice that is etched way back in Winchcombe's ancient history, but it is certainly not relevant today." Miss Eames cheeks began to redden, and her hair looked set to burst from its cottage loaf-like prison. As she went on, her anger gained momentum.

"That your friend, Gaynor Richards, feels she can just wander on-site and conjure up some sort of *spell* against an evil that somehow managed to barge its way onto hallowed ground in the middle of a sacred festival, is positively ludicrous and immature."

Her eyes grew wide and as she spoke, her cheeks flushed an even darker shade of crimson. On a face that changed as little as Miss Eames' did, it was disturbing to see it vastly alter in hue.

She continued, while the rubber band in which her bun was lassoed seemed to stretch in every which way, as the ball of hair ricocheted back and forth on her head.

"Letting children believe that the *horror* that took over Brenda Ware in front of our very eyes yesterday could be avoided by striving to become a better, more grateful, God-fearing individual is a bad thing, is it? *That*, my dear, can only ever be a positive thing. Much more so than the hokum beliefs of that old woman and her hanging gardens of blasphemy."

She took a moment to steady herself as her bosom continued to rise and fall dramatically. She slowly seated herself back down.

"Now, if you have finished your little lecture, I suggest you get back to your position. I have parents to ward off and governors to pacify. Even the local press wants to get involved—so unless there is something else?"

Becky shook her head. She knew better than to question this woman after the dressing down she had just received. She hung her head.

"That," Miss Eames concluded, "is a very sensible idea, young lady."

And with that, Becky was shown the door.

Wing had spent the morning sweeping, laundering and pureeing foodstuffs.

She seemed to spend half of her life-changing solids into liquids so that she could dribble it into the open mouths of the residents peppered about the bedrooms and communal areas of this place, only to have to clean the same juice up as it came squirting back out, covering their fronts only minutes later. She sighed as she threw another sausage into the blender. In fact, she would have jacked all this in ages ago if it wasn't for Jacqueline.

Her name brought a subtle grin to Wing's face. Jacqueline, with her slender fingers and soft, apricot skin, her gentle smile, blossom lips and perfect, white teeth. Jacqueline made this whole experience seem worthwhile, simply by being so beatific. All the times Wing got splattered with anaemic rice pudding, for all the "chinks" and "nips" that got thrown at her on a daily basis, Jacqueline had simply mopped the misery up, squeezed the overspill into a jar and filled it with a bunch of summer roses.

Wing had been so nervous on her first day and, while tens of pairs of untrusting eyes glared askance at her as she walked through the corridor in an ill-fitting tabard, Jacqueline had spotted her vulnerability and made her way over. Taking Wing's podgy, pink hand in hers, she led her into a private room. She asked Wing questions about her homeland, reached out to touch her long, blue-black hair, twisting it around her index finger and marvelling at its condition. Wing's English was not great at the best of times, but Jacqueline corrected her without ridicule, sounding the words phonetically as Wing watched her crimson tongue do cartwheels within the fleshy cave behind her teeth.

And as the weeks passed and their friendship strengthened, Jacqueline had told her stories of the ninety years she had spent on the planet. She had shown Wing private photographs from her many collections, portraits of her family, all with identical lithe, gangly legs and purple clusters for knees, with perfectly-sculpted hair, held together with bobby pins. And her favourite picture of Jacqueline's dear husband Wilfred, who had died from complications during heart surgery, and who Jacqueline had never quite got over the sudden passing of. He looked handsome as a young man, in a stiff Air Force uniform. The sepia of the photograph brought a solemnity to his eyes. They almost looked as if they had tears in them.

Wing listened to Jacqueline's strained inhalations as she fought to catch enough breath to emit a solemn sigh, tantamount to a loud and long ululation. She could listen to them for hours. The deep trench that Wilfred had left burned its way from Jacqueline's sorrow into Wing's heart and she had no choice but to capitulate.

Wing's own mother had never taken an interest in her daughter, though she had been one of seven. Her mother had never known how to spread what little love she possessed between them all, so instead, she didn't bother trying. She just doled out the contempt that she seemed to harbour in spades.

"You know, Wilfred and I could never have children," Jacqueline had said one day as Wing had perched on the end of her bed. A strand of hair had escaped from Jacqueline's teal-coloured headscarf and danced on the wind of her breath. The shallow creases at the corner of her mouth dropped a little as her smile fell.

"We thought of adoption. We wanted to give another poor child a chance." She looked at Wing with tired eyes. Like pulverised glass, they glinted a dull blue. "Of course, it was a different time then, easy in some ways, but not in others. Wilfred's military connections proved fruitful."

"We were promised a baby from Ubon Ratchathani after the French moved in in 1940. She was a beautiful baby girl whose parents were afraid that she might not survive the attacks in the city. People in that time were desperate, they didn't know what was happening. They had to get their children out."

Jacqueline kept her eyes fixed on the window, imagining the French Army advancing on the small Thai village over the horizon in the distance. Young boys, with barely any hair on their top lip, the taste of blood at the backs of their throats. They were conditioned by fear to uncoil and unleash at the slightest provocation. The perspiration of rage and the eagerness to slaughter anything in sight, men, women and children cowering in fear.

"We were set to receive her in July," she continued, "but she never made it."

Jacqueline's eyes pricked with tears as she brought her hands to her chest.

"She was shot," she cried, a look of horror and despair flashed across her face, as her mouth contorted into a trembling 'O'.

"A group of soldiers broke into their house and shot them, one by one. Our baby, our beautiful daughter—Sarah—was murdered."

As she said this, she reached out to touch Wing's cheek and wipe away some of her own tears. The story was wrenching Wing's heart into two separate halves. The fact that anything could penetrate Jacqueline's imperturbability brought bile into Wing's mouth. A marble of guilt that she could not swallow down. The shame that Wing held for not being there to protect her friend.

And at that moment, Jacqueline had made the connection between Wing and the daughter she could not save. And they held each other's hands with an affirming grip. Looking down at herself, Wing couldn't help but feel, with her dumpy frame and plain looks, clammy skin and nails bitten to the quick, she cut a more disappointing silhouette than Sarah might have, had she lived.

But Wing was just happy to be a cynosure for once in her life. Although she understood her importance to both Richard and the kids in the long term, in the short term, she could never square up to *Top Gear* or the Xbox in either party's affections. She was just the reliable heap in the room. Functional, barely noticeable, but always there. And that's how she had come to feel about herself.

But with Jacqueline, her being had meant something. Wing would tell her stories from her childhood. From when her father would take her to the lantern festival at Chiang Mai. They would walk around the Three Kings Monument, through the temples and houses, decorated elaborately with flowers and coconut leaves. Wing would clap and laugh as the khom were released into the air. A thousand lights sailing over the small town and across the Ping river.

Her father would whisper in her ear.

"See, little spirit. Each light here pays respect to our deity. To release our dark memories from the past and make them into bright, shining wishes for the future."

And she had giggled as she felt his beard scratch against her round, pink face.

Shortly after, her father had died in a tragic boat accident while fishing on the same river and

Wing could no longer stand the lights that sailed above the water, as her father's soul lay shackled below.

Instead, her mother dragged her through the dusty streets of Lampang. Past the whorehouses and massage parlours to the dirty, ramshackle buildings, the doors guarded with angry-looking corrugated shutters, their metal teeth curling up at the base.

Within these buildings were hard-faced women who would shout at her to sit, while her mother disappeared through a beaded curtain, sometimes gone for hours, retreating with rheumy eyes and scars across her skin.

Wing's grandmother, Yai Yai, always said that her daughter was not the same after Noo died. Wing's mother spent a great deal of money on bad medicine in a vain attempt to lift the indignation that grief had bestowed upon her. But, in return, she felt more cursed leaving this dark place than she had when she'd arrived. Her features became hardened, her touch was rough and dry. Her hair became short and severe and her skin sallow. Even her voice changed. Though it was never smooth, it now sounded like a penny being dropped into a drain. The uncomfortable clatter of syllables that assaulted young Wing's ears like copper pots being jangled loudly together.

Wing's brothers had never been taken on these trips. According to Yai Yai, her mother had only wanted her daughter present. It was a rare demonstration of maternal affection that she had never quite bettered.

And no matter how much Yai Yai told her daughter that she should have looked to her ancestry to find that there was good magick within her, it fell on deaf ears. If she reminded Wing's mother that grief was never an affliction, but more a rite of passage, she would be told to "mind your own damned business, old woman" and not to speak again.

"You cannot be rid of something that is meant to live with you," Yai Yai had said to Wing. And misery clung to her mother like a hermit crab to its shell.

Yai Yai always taught Wing that if she prayed to the deity, her family would come to her. She would take Wing into the hills and teach her the sacred calling to the spirits, the elements, the sun and the moon. She would teach her the four signs of worship and the ancient spells of protection, preservation and prediction. Wing's fat little legs would dangle over a rock as she watched the smoke from Yai Yai's lantern form into shapes through the humid breeze. Yai Yai had wiped away Wing's tears of grief for her father, assuring her granddaughter with the prediction that she would be an accomplished sorceress, adept at healing with the power of the mind, through the guidance of the spirits. One of which would always be that of her beloved Noo.

Wing left her mother after an insuperable depression had rendered her almost entirely empty. No longer recognising her children or her home of half a century, her once rancorous features were now a mask of vacant vestige in which pain and torture had ploughed deep striations that no amount of water and soap could wash away. A shell of a body in which a human heartbeat but the soul had long ceded. Her mother went to live with her older sister in the mountains of Chiang Mai, ironically close to the river that had stolen her husband—and her sanity—all those years ago. Ravaged by grief that had torn a chasm of bitterness inside of her that not even the witch doctor could pacify. Wing wasn't even going to try, though with Yai Yai's many teachings in the years before she had died, if Wing had wanted to heal her mother, she could have.

Instead, she travelled to England with little money and not much in the way of prospects. Away from the constant feelings of loneliness and the now-empty rooms that had, for so long, made up her existence.

A year in and she had met Richard while cleaning in an office. He worked in IT and often took the graveyard shift to upload computer systems while the other employees were out enjoying their downtime.

Richard was a lonely man, Wing could see. His demeanour was shrunken, defeated through the threat of continual repudiation, from women to work, to tables at restaurants. He was simple, and their pairing had been easy.

They had dined at a sushi bar on their first date since he had assumed that all East Asian people were Japanese. She had appreciated the sentiment, if not the ignorance. Richard had eaten a piece of wasabi by accident and spilt his green tea all over himself while trying to calm his burning taste buds. His clumsiness had made Wing laugh. At last, she had found someone who was as uncomfortable in the real world as she was.

When they had kissed, his beard had tickled her top lip and their glasses had knocked together clumsily. They were the perfect awkward clowns. Sex had been equally as slapstick. Richard had been so nervous that he had talked his way through his undressing regime. It was a rudimentary commentary as he stripped himself of his garments like the bonus material on the DVD of a bad sex tape.

Wing had lain in bed watching this farcical display, feeling a little embarrassed herself in the mismatched two-piece she had forgotten to change. Her protruding stomach lay like a paint spillage before her. Richard, pink and disproportionate in his snug underwear, had finished his little speech with "and now I shall remove my glasses" after which he promptly plucked his specs off, slipped them into his non-existent top pocket and dropped them on the floor. As he sauntered haphazardly over to the bed, she heard the ominous crunch of plastic and glass and winced at the sound.

The next day, they had spent two hours in the opticians while Richard tried his best to shrug off his utter mortification.

Marriage followed not long after and subsequently, Dara had been born.

Richard managed to get a promotion to the local government offices and Wing had applied for a job at Cleeve Hill Nursing Home.

When Dara was two, Kit came along, and Wing had realised that, without realising, she had built a family all her very own.

And as she rocked her perfect babies to sleep, dewy-eyed with emotion at how much love she could feel for two such small bundles of skin, hair and teeth, Yai Yai's voice rang in her ears.

She knew that it was now time to begin her prayers to the deity.

Night after night, she had prayed to keep her family safe and secure, yet they already were. There didn't seem to be much point in funnelling all her energies into something that she was in control of, with or without the deity's help. And so, she redirected her prayer, instead asking the deity to keep Jacqueline protected from the degenerative disease that was enervating her.

But each time that Jacqueline begged Wing to brush her silver hair, Wing noticed that more handfuls would become entangled in the firm bristles.

And as Jacqueline's skin became more and more contused, her speckled flesh made way for angrier, more irascible bruises. Wing would notice that bloody tissues began to pile up in the wastepaper basket by the bed and Jacqueline's breathing had become more laboured, a sure sign of the strain that mere existence was putting on the poor woman's failing organs.

"Keep her safe, Pra. Give her hope. From her face, Pra. Take the ghost," Wing would whisper as she lit a candle at the makeshift altar she had erected in the laundry room. She would click her tongue three times and set a strand of Jacqueline's hair into the flame, watching it scintillate, making sinuous shapes dance through the sweet smoke.

That same night, Wing would toss and turn in her sheets as the pain was syphoned from Jacqueline's body into hers, giving her cramps, headaches, sore guts and bones. And though the ritual might bring Jacqueline a meagre two days of comfort, where she would sit up in bed and wax lyrical about wanting to venture outside beyond the care home window, the bloody tissues and painted blemishes would always return to seek their revenge.

Today, Jacqueline was supine in her bed as Wing walked over to her tiny body. The curtains were wide, framing the beautiful scene of the town, spreading the length of the valley below the hill like a carpet of tiny lights.

Jacqueline's headscarf had slipped slightly as she slept, revealing a bald patch of skin that her illness had claimed for itself.

Wing crept in and straightened the scarf. She tidied away a few breakfast things before Jacqueline, watching the imperceptible rise and fall of her chest.

"Sleep well, Jacqueline Mae," she whispered and walked softly from the room.

How long Wing had waited to finally call somebody "Mother".

∎∎

Laura was upset.

She looked again at the plastic wand in her hand. It seemed to laugh back up at her.

Not pregnant ... *again.*

She didn't know how much more of this she could take. What the hell was going on in her uterus? Was it like the film Platoon in there? With little cells dressed as the US military, targeting Ben's sperm cells and shooting on sight?

She tossed the test in the bin and pulled her pants up to her knees. It clattered around before landing with a clunk. The final knell of the death bell. The end of fertility as she knew it. Getting off the seat, she pulled her undergarments up further and dragged herself over to the mirror.

How could this be happening? At 37, she wasn't exactly old but then time was marching on and she didn't want to be one of those archaic mothers she had seen in doctors waiting room magazine articles. The ones where the baby is dribbling onto its bib whilst the mother is dribbling into her incontinence pad.

Laura turned her face to different angles to catch the light. Her Botox would need to be redone. She could just see the wrinkles at the sides of her eyes reappearing.

She lifted her hand and pulled the skin on her neck taut. Perhaps she could get that done too if only she could afford it. With all the money she'd spent on bloody pregnancy tests, she could have probably saved up for a face-lift by now.

It was so unfair. Unemployed teenage girls throughout Cheltenham were pushing double-decker prams stuffed to the brim with obnoxious-looking children. They were shooting babies out like some kind of log flume ride and yet Laura, a professional with a great house, a good-looking boyfriend, a competitive sales wage and an ambitiously experimental sex life was still completely barren.

She wrenched the bathroom door open, stepped out into her immaculately scrubbed kitchen and straight over to the fridge. She had been avoiding that glass of wine all evening just in case she was up the stick, but she would damn well have one now.

Ben came in with the Echo, just as she closed the fridge door. She slammed the bottle on the black marble counter-top.

"Well?" he said, folding the paper in his hands.

"It didn't work," she said, haphazardly slopping the wine into a tall-stemmed glass and a little over her Zara skirt.

"You're joking," he said, looking glum.

She curled her hands into fists and spun herself around to face him.

"Yes, Ben, I'm joking. We're not pregnant. Ha! Shall I start on my female genital mutilation gags now, to *really* bring the house down?!"

She was being a bitch—she knew it. She was pissed off and taking it out on him. The feeling that she might be inferior in the womb department weighed heavy on her conscience. She drew the glass to her lips.

She simmered down after a hefty glug. "I'm sorry. I'm just disappointed. I thought it would work this time. I put so much effort into making sure it was to the letter—"

Ben came over to her and put his hand on her spare one resting on the counter.

"I know it's frustrating, baby", he said, which made her automatically prickle. She hated it when he called her that. It reminded her that, until she had one of her own, she would always be the baby of the relationship.

"But we can't give up"

She snapped her hand away from him.

"Who's giving up?" she spat, shooting him an accusatory glare.

"I just meant—"

"Look, Benjamin, if I have to fuck you every night until your dick goes red and detaches from your pelvis, then that is what I will do."

She picked up her glass and stormed into the front room.

Giving up? She was a recruitment sales manager. She never gave up.

■■■

Becky thought it only right to call round at Catherine's after her shift. She wanted to know how she had managed with yesterday's activities, and whether she shared sentiments with the old titan, Miss Eames, but Catherine was not there. Instead, Becky found herself vacillating between wandering over to Gaynor's house and making her way home to sit and stare at the black mark on her wall with a furrowed brow for the next few hours. In the end, and seemingly without consideration, she was knocking timidly on Gaynor's front door.

After hearing a scuffling from the hallway within, Gaynor opened the door to her, wearing a sanguine smile.

"Becky, my dear," she said in a convivial manner, "thrice in two days. To what do I owe this pleasure?"

169

"Forgive my pestering," Becky said self-consciously, "but I think we need to talk."

Gaynor waited a beat before moving to one side to let Becky step in.

■ ■

"You must forgive me," said Gaynor as she pottered from one shelf to the next. "I'm very restive today. It's a turning moon this evening, the best time for making good decisions and warding off bad ones, but I am never, ever prepared."

"Oh, I'm so sorry to intrude when you're busy, Gaynor," Becky blushed. She had been ushered in and a mug of bitter Arrowood plonked down in front of her, as though it had now become routine. Becky couldn't help but feel a little unwelcome as Gaynor hovered between the hob and the sideboard, her back to Becky and mumbling quietly to herself.

Becky gulped a little more liquid down without wincing. She seemed to be getting used to the taste. It was becoming more palatable, like the first time she started drinking coffee without sugar—she would certainly warm to it. It seemed to be giving her an extra jolt of confidence.

"Gaynor?" she said, her quizzical tone stopping the old woman in her tracks.

"Yes, love?"

"I hope you don't mind me being direct." Becky set her cup on the table.

"Oh, stars love us, I welcome it," Gaynor said as she stopped and leant her arms on the counter. "I don't like anything to be squirrelled away. You can't open a locked trove with anything less than the key."

Becky smiled. Experience had taught her to pick the best flesh out of Gaynor's sentences and leave the non-sequitur analogies to one side.

"I'm still totally confused about yesterday," she said, shaking off a cold cape of memory. "I mean, what happened to Miss Ware was crazy. Super-duper crazy! But then to have to explain it all to Joanna and Temperance, who were very nice, but I didn't really know them. And they fed me some drink, which I think made me talk more than I'm used to. It doesn't add up and yet, in some mad way, it makes sense."

Gaynor's eyes darted around as Becky's words tumbled out of her mouth.

She stopped and looked up at Gaynor, who was listening without prejudice.

"I just need to know," Becky said slowly, "am I … am I in some sort of cult here?"

There was a short pause before Gaynor began to laugh. It sounded like soft rain dancing on a tin roof.

"Good heavens! A cult?" She threw her arms up and began to hobble over to the first available chair.

"Well, I suppose it depends on what that word means to you, my dear," Gaynor continued. "I mean, even a book group is a cult."

Becky's mind flashed back to when she entered Joanna's house. The two women both clutched copies of *Jamaica Inn* yet the books had been all but abandoned once Becky had arrived. The memory was gone in an instant.

"I think what you mean to ask is whether you are playing the starring role in some kind of horror movie. The one where Christopher Lee dresses like Crystal Gayle and they all worship a giant, wooden gingerbread man." She reached for a cup, which she filled from the kettle as she let out a little chuckle of mirth.

Becky felt a little bit silly now. It did sound like the plot of The Wicker Man, not that she'd seen it all the way through.

"Well, I don't blame you for being vigilant. The Shire is very different from the big city." Gaynor went on. "There have been pagan rituals and sacrifices going on around here since man walked the earth. And of course, the story-tellers amongst us have always liked to fabricate the facts. The bogeyman under the bed, the beast in the forest, the monster in the closet. All works of fiction. But then—"

Gaynor stopped for dramatic effect as she leaned in.

"I'm afraid that these are just stories."

Becky let out a big sigh that she had been holding in. It was quite comforting to know that there was nothing untoward going on and that she was just, in fact, being dramatic.

"What we see in front of our noses, what we witness, what we become involved in: *that* is what we believe is real life." Gaynor stopped.

"What we *believe* is real life?" Becky echoed.

"Yes," Gaynor nodded, "I mean, science can't explain everything, can it dear?"

She took a sip before adding pensively, "I mean there are some things that defy science— they are a complete enigma. But just because we can't explain it, does that mean that it doesn't exist?"

Becky must have looked as confused as she felt. It made Gaynor rise up off her seat.

"It's like the age-old riddle," she said. "How do we know that a tree falling makes a sound if there is nobody there to hear it?"

Becky took a moment to process this information. She'd heard this quote many times but was finding it challenging to apply it to this situation.

"So, are you saying that what happened to Miss Ware could have happened before?" she asked, with a look of perplexity.

"Oh, many times." Gaynor took another, longer sip of her tea. "I think it frightened *you* because you have never seen something like that before. But there is a first time for everything and we cannot assume that just because it hasn't been presented to us in our lifetime, that it hasn't happened before."

Becky swallowed with a dry throat.

"Have you seen that sort of thing before?" she asked.

"Of course," Gaynor said, holding her cup in both hands. "So have most folk around here I would imagine. It doesn't make them any less scary for parents who are protecting their children, but things of that nature have been going on in these parts since the days of the Rollright Stones"

Becky frowned as she had not heard of this before. She was imagining a setting as sinister as the name suggested.

"The Rollright Stones?"

"Ah, you see. You have so much to learn, my child," sighed Gaynor as she put her cup down. "The legend of the Rollright Stones has been passed down this way from generation to generation."

Gaynor sat back down in her chair and leant her elbows on her knees.

"They are a circle of rocks in Long Compton, not too far from here, in sunny Oxfordshire. Back in the days before brick houses and running water, they say a king was riding with his knights on the moor. He was a vain and proud man, who wore a long cloak of gold and many rings on his fat fingers."

Becky's eyes widened as the story unfurled.

"Suddenly, he came upon old Mother Shipton, a wise fortune teller from one of the neighbouring villages, coming in the opposite direction. Shipton was decrepit and disfigured. She had been exiled by the villagers for frightening their children with her predictions of their future misgivings, so she was not in the best of moods."

Becky pulled her cup slightly away from her lips.

"She stepped in the way of the king's horse and, just before he was about to strike her, she offered to read his fortune in exchange for being spared his hand. He was a fearless man of curiosity, and so he agreed. She looked into the mist on the moor, conjuring images before her. She told the king that when he dismounted, in just seven long strides, he would see the hills of Long Compton through the fog and he would surely be king of all England. He laughed, mocking her with his arrogant mirth, believing that he would surely be able to complete this meagre task. He jumped off his horse and set about making his seven strides toward the town. Mother Shipton's eyes sparkled as he made his way forth from the first and second, to the third stride. However, when he came to the seventh stride, she clawed her fingers together and reached up to the sky. This made the earth in front of the king rise up, blocking his view of the hills ahead. She cursed him for being a greedy man who did not consider the consequences of his actions. For that, she turned him and his men to stone."

Becky was captivated by the electricity that seemed to spark in Gaynor's eyes as she told this story.

"The circle of rocks is still there to this day. On dark nights, the locals say that they come alive and move about the field, trying to get a glimpse of the hills before them."

Gaynor leaned back, at which point the energy in the room shifted back to normal.

"So, you see? Strange things have been happening since the dawn of time. We just need to open our minds to it."

Becky thought for a moment, as the vision of Mother Shipton swam around in her head.

"Miss Eames told the children that Miss Ware's possession was an act of God," she said flatly.

"Pah!" Gaynor walked around the table. "I'm afraid that Alice is a stubborn old ox. A Victorian authoritarian with a mind as tunnelled as the Castleford Caves. She doesn't want to believe in anything that isn't black and white. She is rigid— she always has been. She shouldn't be imparting her popish nonsense on the young and impressionable."

"I agree," Becky pondered, "but then, what do you tell children who witness such a thing?"

"The truth. Children need to know the truth. That if you get yourself involved in black magic, then it's curtains for you. End of story. A vengeful God, I ask you."

Becky chewed on her lip.

"But why would a retiring music teacher dabble in the occult? It doesn't make any sense."

"Ah, you never know what goes on behind closed doors." Gaynor stood up again and went over to the sink. "Folks have been around here for a long time, they have a lot of connections to the netherworld of dark magic. There have been so-called Satanists living in Painswick for centuries. She could have made a bargain with the wrong demon. You don't know what people will do when they are desperate. Voodoo, Jinn, the Shaman—they're all waiting in line for a hopeless, reckless fool."

Becky nodded.

"And what about Miss Wicks? Do you think she made the same bargain?"

"Anne is a mystery I'm afraid," Gaynor said forlornly.

"But those scorch marks on the walls. The one in the church, the one in my house. They are identical. Could they be some kind of calling card?" Becky said.

Gaynor shifted uncomfortably in her seat.

"I have no idea, child. I'm a daft, old woman who grows a few plants and looks after her disabled husband. I am not a fairground soothsayer." She laughed but there was a slight suspicion behind the eye. She realised now that Becky's curiosity might land her in trouble. She would have to discourage her from ploughing any further, getting closer to the sickening truth. That someone from the highest order of witchcraft had been sent to investigate a potentially catastrophic and dangerous threat to the world of practical magic and that Brenda Ware had, most likely, been used as a pawn to experiment with a new craft that could harm anyone in its path.

Becky saw the anxiety cross the old woman's face and took a deep breath.

"Gaynor," she said calmly, "please don't be offended by my next question. But are you ... are you a witch?"

Gaynor smiled.

"My dear," she said with a measured smile, "*witch* is such a horrible word, with such destructive overtones. If you're asking whether I wear a pointed hat and fly around on a broomstick enticing little children into my gingerbread house, then no—I'm not a witch."

Becky felt relieved, but she wasn't sure that she had received the answer she was expecting.

"I am, what you might call, a Wiccan," Gaynor continued, as she ran the tap and rinsed out her cup. "It's a pagan religion that some associate with witches, but not the kind that Hollywood has dreamed up. A Wiccan believes in nature, the earth, the sun, moon and stars. I cast what some might call healing spells. I prefer to call them 'good thoughts'. I grow and use herbs and plants for medicinal purposes, I pray to the goddess Moon and I can predict the weather—a bit, anyway. I'm trying to break into crystals, but the instruction book might as well be written in Flemish for all the sense it makes to these old eyes."

"I always thought..." said Becky cravenly, "I thought witches were kind of ... illegal?"

"Good gracious. The government might be able to stop immigrants coming into the country, but they can't stop me from lighting a few candles and brewing up some Arrowood now, can they?" She turned to face Becky. "Child, I know what you are saying, but my religion is not responsible for what happened to that poor, old lady. It's like asking whether because you are British, you are personally involved with the war in Afghanistan. The two are entirely separate."

She walked back over to the chair and sat herself down.

"It's the Christians who decided that, since we did not believe in their god, then we must worship the devil. But we don't believe in either! We trust in our Goddess Moon and the power that she gives us through the earth and its elements."

"And what about Temperance and Joanna, are they Wiccan too?"

"Oh, mercy, no!" Gaynor touched her chest in mock surprise. "They're just a couple of old acquaintances really."

Gaynor was thinking on her feet her, but she was conscious that she must not unmask her state of unrest.

"They've only since taken an interest in the paranormal for some kooky book they're writing. I thought your story might interest them enough to get their expertise involved somehow. To be honest, I get a bit fed up with their importune goading. They believe anything I tell them if there's some chance of snaring a spectre."

"No," she continued, rising to her feet again. "I'm the only Wiccan in Winchcombe and it's been that way for some time. It upsets some people, but I'm willing to face a few naysayers for the respect of my Goddess. I'm not sure where the nearest fellow Wiccans are. Gloucester's bound to have some lurking somewhere, it's that kind of place. We don't really congregate though. As a religion, we're dying out."

Becky sensed that she had outstayed her welcome. There were a few moments of awkward silence before she got to her feet.

"Well, thank you for being so honest, Gaynor, I really appreciate it. I've got a lot to think about." She nodded as she made her way toward the kitchen door.

The last sentence chilled Gaynor slightly. She wasn't one hundred percent certain that Becky had swallowed her untruths.

"No problem, my dear," she said, a little relief in her voice.

As Becky walked down the hall, she found herself biting her lip again. She turned slightly as she put her hand on the door handle.

"And you think that Miss Ware probably got involved in something she shouldn't have?" Becky reaffirmed.

"Probably," Gaynor answered nonchalantly. "In which case, it would appear that the score has been settled. Goddess Moon can't be responsible for stupidity and curiosity. If you wander off the path she has set out for you, then things are bound to erupt. If, of course, you believe in that sort of thing."

Becky's mind flashed back to Brenda Ware's horror-stricken face, her ashen skin, the burbling words on her lips, the stuttered gibberish that she continued to recite before she fell.

"And you don't think," Becky mused, "that she might have been trying to tell us something? That the perpetrator was trying to give us a message?" she asked assertively.

Gaynor stopped a moment as she seemed to register this information.

"I really couldn't say," she eventually replied. "I mean, who on earth would a message of that kind be for?"

Becky shrugged as she stepped out and waved in adieu. Gaynor slowly closed the door. On either side of the frame, both women frowned.

Becky, because she did not buy Gaynor's story one bit. Gaynor, because she had just been given some food for thought.

TEN

Bernice wandered around her kitchen, looking for her favourite wine glass. Ever since that television producer had departed a few months ago after a meeting, proffering a bottle of Shiraz for her troubles, Bernice had acquired a taste for it and was now partial to an early-evening glass before dinner.

When she located it, hiding behind a large packet of Sugar Puffs on top of the fridge, she gave it a rinse under the tap and set it down, ready to be filled.

That producer lady had been nice, she remembered. She had graciously addressed Bernice by her real name and not tacitly mocked her with smirks and innuendo like that last tabloid journalist. He had incredulously referred to her as female and leafed noisily through his papers as she gave heartfelt answers to his facile questions. She was glad that she had not chosen that particular rag to tell her story or, should she say, tell her story *again*.

In fact, she had rehashed the potted version of her biography more times in the last few weeks than she had changed wigs.

And now, in the age of Caitlyn Jenner and Laverne Cox, if the media wanted a piece of her, why shouldn't she capitalise on it?

She sipped at the glass, letting her full lips touch the rim before she soaked them with wine. She often liked to feel the liquid on her skin. It was the one moment in her otherwise topsy-turvy life, that she ever felt sensual. Like a real woman in an eighties American soap opera, and not the rough builder in a pinafore dress that she felt like most days.

Her mind drifted back to the television producer. How might she present Bernice's journey? Since it was a mid-morning discussion programme, Bernice would probably be made out to be a survivor, a champion. Someone who had overcome adversity and been spat out the other side with a better hairdo and more glamorous footwear.

But then the matter of her son had come up, as it inevitably would. Would the audience side with Bernice or her 11-year-old son, Matthew?

Some people were more sympathetic, saying that it shouldn't matter what gender she was as long as she was as good a parent in stilettos as she was in brogues, but these were mainly the views of do-gooders and television councillors.

Others would call her selfish and impulsive. A quixotic and nefarious attention-seeker who put her own sexual duplicity before her responsibilities when she tired of the confines of the family unit. Then came the insults, the stones, the bricks. The tripping in the park, the taunting at the bus queue. The times where she had never felt more like she was wearing a costume in public by dressing as a woman. Like a clown handing out balloons at a shopping centre.

And then came the guilt that attached itself so indefatigably to her like a child to its mother's leg. Never easing up or releasing its grip. She continuously put herself through every form of self-persecution until it had become an entrenched ritual that happened moment to moment, like breathing in and out.

Every glance in the mirror was done with scorn, every bump in the road was like a disembowelling tremor in her recovery. That in being herself, she was robbing Matthew of his own freedom. The freedom to shrink into the background if he so chose, rather than being thrust into the spotlight every time his father's story was aired.

And then there was Claire. Sweet Claire. Bernice's ex-wife who had stood tall and linked her arm in Bernice's. She had agreed to let the press in, even giving her own contribution, not for her own gain, but because she knew that the reward would support Bernice financially, freeing her of the indignity of having to decide between using the female or male staff toilet.

In the beginning, Claire would try to be so cool and okay with everything, even though her demeanour told a different story. She suddenly grew exhausted overnight and the fug of fatigue refused to leave her side. Her hair became unwashed, her gait hunched. It was as though Bernice had somehow taken Claire's femininity away when she had strived for her own. And though Claire would thumbs-up every magazine article and tell Bernice she looked fantastic, even though her skirts were too short, her makeup too thick and wigs far too young for her face, Bernice could tell that her ex-wife was defeated.

Claire was balancing on the parapet, threatening to topple into the gaping abyss of confusion mixed with grief. The support group had helped Claire understand the art of letting go. She had trouble realising that Bernice's new life was not just her old life painted with pan-stick and swathed in glitter. It was a complete refit. A transformation of global proportions.

But the bullies were unwilling to allow Claire or Matthew to let anything go. The children would goad, and the mothers would whisper, singling them out as lions would a wounded deer. Mocking Claire for her bravery and Matthew for his innocence.

In the end, it was Claire who had suggested that she leave for Bristol and take Matthew with her. Paradoxically, in order for her to face up to things, she had to run away and escape the scourge of the small town before it engulfed her whole.

Bernice's heart became severed in two, but such was her mete for being so honest with herself. The cottage was now an empty shell that echoed with the voices of the lost family that once inhabited them. She would wander from room to room, standing silently in each one. A skyline written on the walls by the furniture that used to stand against them.

In their absence, Bernice had begun to unravel and unhinge, enjoying a bottle here and there, ordering greasy food in and forgetting to clean up after herself. The vacuum cleaner was now the dustiest thing in the house. The air lay thick with a fusty aroma and the carpets teemed with fresh layers of detritus.

Bernice read endless trashy magazines and watched hours of reality television hoping that, in some way, immersing herself in the lives of others might distract her from having to combat her own. She chatted online to other transgender people, who she found inherently boring and continued to completely shun the life that she had given everything up to participate in.

She had no want for intimacy. The only one she wanted was her wife. Her love for Claire had not ceased when the hormones she was taking kicked in. It was entrenched within her.

It had been late one night, as Bernice dozed in the empty room. The light from the adjacent window cast an ethereal glow on the white bedspread she lay clothed in, a voice spoke to her through the dark. It was not one of the usual questions that plagued her, but one that she instantly recognised from thirty-or-so years ago. It pierced through the rest and scissored towards her.

"I told you," it said, "the winds of change would blow. Didn't I tell you?"

Terrified and baffled, Bernice had sat bolt-upright in bed, straining to get a sense of the source of the voice through the limited light. She followed the whisper to a soft, white glow that had appeared in the corner of the room. The light was dull, and yet she could just make out the shape of a blurred figure, hunched over like an elderly woman. Bernice moved slowly onto her elbows and peered closely over to the glow. Was she imagining this? She could be in some kind of drunken trance, the last of the three bottles of red still sloshing about in her stomach.

The figure continued to radiate veins of white light that danced from its body in the darkness, like gossamer.

The voice laughed. It was friendly but cold. There was no depth in the tone of the words that were spoken.

"You have forgotten me, girl," it said with a knowing scoff.

An icy stab of recognition pierced through Bernice's sternum

"My god," she whispered to herself. "Agatha, is that you?"

"Yes, I see you are quick to lose me, child." The voice was dusty and weak. "But I remember you girl—I remember you."

Bernice shivered in the dark. She was sent back in time to a memory of being a young boy, knees pulled up to his chest, crying silent tears into his pyjamas as he willed the voice to go away and stop talking to him when the rest of the house had gone to bed, wondering why it always referred to him as a girl and had chosen him to terrify with its nightly visits.

"You mustn't forget, child," the voice spoke. "Try to remember who you are and what you are. Where you belong and why you are here."

Bernice's old anxiety came back in full force. Her mouth became dry and tiny beads of sweat pricked her forehead. It had been so long since Agatha had visited her. Why here, why now? She had blocked the whole episode out of her thoughts, dismissing them as some kind of delusion brought on by pre-pubescent stress. It was totally unfeasible that Agatha should return when she felt so vulnerable.

"I can sense your fear," the voice said, "but you are not one to feel fear. You are the one to be feared."

The light started to dull and fade as the figure dispersed within the blackness of the wall.

"You will find out soon enough. All will become clear. When you are ready, they shall see things as you see them."

And with that, Agatha was gone, leaving Bernice silently sobbing into her nightdress.

■■

Suddenly, Bernice's phone sprang to life. It gave her such a fright that she nearly spilt her wine all over herself. She fumbled about to find it in her bag before grabbing the leopard-print case and pressing the set to her ear.

"Shit! Hello?" she bellowed into the receiver, dabbing at the excess fluid on her lips with her index finger.

"Good evening. May I speak with Bernice Williams?" said the voice on the end of the line. She sounded officious whoever she was. Not the kind of woman who would currently be wiping freshly-spilt wine off her blouse with a pair of dirty tights like Bernice was.

"This is she," Bernice said as she abandoned the rag and grabbed her glass with her free hand.

"Hello Bernice, my name is Odette. I am a Sceptre from The High Oracle. How are you?"

Bernice went cold.

What the ever-living fuck was someone from The High Oracle doing on the phone to her? Had Joanna really twisted the knife by getting a High

190

Sceptre involved? Surely, Joanna would want to deal the fatal blow herself and not give someone else the glittering opportunity. Bernice wasn't prepared for this sort of interrogation from on high. Least of all when she was half-cut.

"Oh," she exclaimed, "I'm sorry High Sceptre. I mean Your Grace. I mean Priestess Mother—"

"Odette is fine," she said. Her voice was firm but friendly.

"Thanks, Odette."

"I understand you've been experiencing resistance with the Winchcombe order. One of our sisters has put in a complaint against you regarding your gender reassignment," she said. Her tone was insensitive and succinct, just the way Joanna would have wanted it.

Bernice's heart leapt into her throat. Perhaps Joanna was sending Bernice a barbed message— "*stay away or be restrained.*"

Experimenting in her youth, Bernice had put a binding spell on some trappy, little bitch, to render her completely mute for four days and was raked over the coals by her foster mother. God knows what The Order could do to her if they put their mind to it.

"Yes," she agreed.

"Right," the woman replied, pausing as if she were giving a final glance through a file that was in front of her.

It was a moment before she began to speak. With each second, Bernice's heart pumped faster.

"Well, Ms Williams, it is my job to inform you that we are overruling this recrimination. As far as we are concerned, your duty to the coven is not under any dispute and we would like to welcome you back without reproach."

Bernice audibly gasped. Involuntarily, heavy tears began to roll down her cheeks. She tried to reply but the words got lodged in her throat.

The woman continued.

"We expect to see you at the next meeting, Bernice. Joanna will be in contact soon, no doubt, to inform you of when and where this will be."

Bernice nodded, which Odette seemed to sense.

"I'm sure that you remember the sacred oath that your sisters and The Oracle entrust you with. That you are still on strict instructions, under the scrutiny of The Order not to practice magick under any circumstances for your own gain or for any malevolent charges against others. And it is with my power that I accept you into the circle by the will of Goddess Moon. So mote it be."

Bernice just managed to blurt out the sacred response in choked syllables.

"So mote it be."

She clutched the phone so tight that her hand grew numb and her fingers ached.

"Well, thank you very much, Bernice." The woman's coolness began to thaw.

"No, thank you, Odette," Bernice blubbed through thick tears of joy.

"My pleasure," she let out an exasperated sigh, which sounded out of character adjacent to the studious delivery of the oath. "After studying your credentials, it really should never have been brought to my attention."

She carried on.

"Well, good evening then," she said, "and might I remind you, Bernice—this decision is without reproach."

"Yes, Odette."

The phone went dead, but a resonant thought still rang in Bernice's mind.

It seemed that Odette had the measure of Joanna, but she had far more clout and she wanted Bernice to know it.

■■■

The next morning, at school, Becky felt that she should attempt to make peace with Miss Eames. She knew that by inviting Gaynor into the church, she had sent the moral compass of the old battle-axe into a tailspin, so she felt she'd better ameliorate their relationship and at least try and salvage her job if nothing else. Inside her, the baby seemed to somersault in agreement and so Becky rushed to the loo for a nervous emergency pee.

She'd gotten into work super-early, to appear keen.

Yesterday, she hadn't been brave enough to broach the Harvest Festival debacle with the other girls for fear of being shot down in flames and, to their credit, they had remained as tight-lipped about it as she was. Everyone carried on tapping away in fraught silence, the bashing of their keyboards sending rhythmic clicks around the small office. Luckily, Kay broke the tension around mid-morning by asking Mel about Rachel Power's infamous Halloween party which severed the ice, the office once again erupting into a flurry of chatter and jocularity. Becky was relieved. She had felt partly responsible for driving a wedge between herself and her colleagues, even though no one had said as much. She couldn't help assuming that, in questioning Miss Eames' motives, she had subliminally breached the trust of the entire school. It sounded ludicrous, but there had been something about the office ladies' behaviour that morning that seemed a little odd.

"Any idea what you're going to the party as?" Mel had quizzed Becky. She noticed a slight reticence in Mel's voice as if she didn't really want to ask.

"Well," Becky replied timidly, "I haven't been invited so I'm not sure whether I'm allowed to go."

"Oh, everyone from the town is invited, silly," Kay scolded her playfully. "It's the social event of the school calendar. Well, apart from Christmas,

Easter and the May Bank Holiday scarecrow parade. But it's the costumes that everyone attends for. The better your costume, the more likely you are of winning the prize."

"What is it this year?" asked a wide-eyed Tracy, holding onto her coffee cup with both hands.

"Well," mused Mel, "a couple of years ago it was family cashmere."

"Then the weekend in Berlin," chimed in Janice from her seat.

"It gets better each year," said Mel. "It could be an all-expenses trip to Paris? An iMac for the family? It will be something good. Hugh Power is a big wheel in Dulux emulsion paint. He was solely responsible for the surge in popularity of Floribunda Pink in the nineties."

All four cooed in response. Becky must have missed that fad.

∎∎

"Come in," Miss Eames bellowed from the other side of the door.

Becky had pondered appropriate moments to face the music several times that morning. She eventually decided to go and see Miss Eames after lunch, when no doubt the old mare's hunger would be satiated, her mood hopefully lifted. She now found herself turning the office door handle and stepping, rather cravenly, into the stuffy room.

Miss Eames didn't look very impressed with her new visitor since her attitude was practically anathemic. Becky could tell that it was going to be an onerous task to get back on this woman's good side. The distance between one side of her and the other was a prodigious bulwark to cross.

"Ah, Rebecca," she said, her tone flat and nonchalant. "What can I do for you? I'm afraid that I am rather busy. The fire alarm in the hall keeps sounding and not one teacher in this whole, unfortunate school can seem to locate the battery pack."

Becky eased herself into the opposite chair. She had noticed the electrics beeping like the fulminations of some renegade parrot all morning, but it had now somewhat blended into the background noise.

"I wanted to apologise for my behaviour yesterday," Becky said feebly. Miss Eames raised a perfectly-pencilled eyebrow and leant back in her chair slightly. She looked like a toad on a lily pad, watching the fly squirm about before lassoing it with its long, translucent tongue.

"It was imprudent of me to question your instructions, particularly since your primary concern will always be the protection of the children."

Miss Eames remained silent, her large lips sealed firmly across her face like a purse that might never open.

"In retrospect, I'm not sure how I would have handled the situation and I was foolish to challenge you on that." Becky sighed as she felt her face redden. She couldn't help hanging her head like a naughty school girl, cowering under the thraldom of the draconian headmistress.

"I am very sorry, and I hope that this will not affect our professional relationship."

Miss Eames nodded imperceptibly as she processed this information. She studied Becky's face, searching for any hint of insincerity. What seemed like a huge epoch passed between the two women before Miss Eames leant forward to speak.

"Rebecca," she said, the icy tone of her voice beginning to thaw, "I appreciate and understand your compunction. But you must remember that I have been in this position for many years and seen many things. As you said, the children's interests and welfare are at the top of my list of priorities and that will never change. So, thank you for coming to see me today. I accept your apology and you may now return to your post."

Becky was about to ask what Miss Eames really thought had happened to Miss Ware, but she thought it unwise to tempt fate. She didn't want to slip up yet again and undo the good work she had just done. She smiled meekly and got up out of her chair.

"Oh," Miss Eames exclaimed, spurring Becky to look up before she crossed the room. A cloud of contempt had crossed the headmistress' face, which made Becky's own freeze in submission. "I do have one word of advice. I wouldn't mix too closely with the likes of Gaynor Richards if I were you. Her sort of belief system is not one we favour around these parts. Some call it harmless, some call it devil worship. I couldn't possibly comment. But it is not the sort of practice that we would like the vulnerable children of St Patrick's to be exposed to. I hope I am making myself clear."

The look in her beady, black eye was one of warning. Becky thought she should remove herself as quickly as possible from the room. She nodded back at Miss Eames with a look of defeat on her face. Just as she was about to turn and head out of the door, a loud siren filled the air, pulsating through Becky's eardrums and bouncing off the empty corridor walls. She put her hands on her tummy as if, somehow, she could cover the baby's ears.

"Oh, for goodness sake," cried Miss Eames, "this is beyond a damned joke!"

She hoisted her bulk out of her leather-bound chair and stomped around her desk, nearly pushing Becky out of the way and scattering a pile of papers as she did so. She marched to the door and wrenched it open.

"That will be all, thank you, Rebecca. You may return to the office!" she called over her shoulder as she strode down the vibrating hallway.

Becky stood alone in the headmistress' office. Before she left, she took a quick glance around. It was fairly plain, painted in a shiny magnolia, with endless book-lined shelves placed haphazardly on the walls, collecting dust. A hideous, dried piranha fish on a stand was the extent of Miss Eames' personal, decorative touch.

As she stepped forward, she noticed the plume of papers that Miss Eames had dropped in her wake. Becky bent down to scoop them up. As she did, one fell out of her grip and landed, face up on the beige carpet. Becky stooped to retrieve it when she noticed the heading on the sheet.

It was a letter, with 'Toxicology Report' written boldly above Miss Eames' name and the address of the school.

Becky quickly glanced behind her to check whether Miss Eames had walked back into the office, but the room remained empty.

She put the other sheets on the desk and picked the letter up, speedily scanning it before setting it down amongst the others.

As she did, her heart raced in her chest and her eyes widened.

Shoving the letter back between the other papers and straightening them up on the desk, she wrapped her cardigan tightly around herself and exited the room.

It had been a letter from Cheltenham General Hospital and, from what she had read, she had picked up three things about the case of Miss Ware.

One. Miss Ware was dead.

Two. Cause of death was poison from amygdalin, whatever that was.

Three. Miss Ware had had no family and Miss Eames had been her next of kin.

Becky was perplexed and terrified in equal measure. She had guessed that Miss Ware might have been in a bad way after Wednesday's ordeal, but to read that she was dead, right there in black and white, was something of a sledgehammer to the heart.

Dead.

But how? And why?

She cast herself back to Gaynor's theory that Miss Ware had got herself involved in something dark and mysterious. As soon as Becky had mentioned the possibility that the piano teacher's possessed babbling could have been a cryptic message, a light bulb had gone off above Gaynor's head. It was written all over her face.

And what was the significance of the substance in the toxicology report: amygdalin? Becky had never even heard of it, but then, why would she have? She had failed chemistry and had never read so much as the back of a household cleaner bottle in her life.

Becky chewed her lip again as she meandered along the hall towards her own office. She knew that this situation wasn't as cut and dried as

Gaynor had made out. However, it seemed the whole town was simply willing to accept that it had happened and was now ready to move on. Why couldn't she?

Because, coming from London or not, she wasn't willing to accept that this type of thing was normal. If this woman had been possessed by someone who was an expert in the dark arts, then this was murder.

Becky felt as though she had a responsibility to report this to someone. But who? The police? Did they deal with this sort of thing? Would they think her crazy and question her mental stability in being able to take care of a new-born baby? She needed someone to confide in, to seek advice from.

Talking to her immediate colleagues wouldn't be wise. Becky didn't think they could ever be persuaded into jeopardising their little footholds in education administration on the fantastical whim of a stranger. Perhaps Catherine might be a worthy ally. But then, she was not exactly the kind of woman who might open her mind to this sort of thing. Plus, Becky didn't really feel comfortable confiding in her about anything. She was very critical of Becky already and would only become more so if Becky starting accusing people of bewitching and spell-casting.

Gaynor was the only person who might willingly help. She was certainly open-minded enough, but Becky was sure that she was withholding information. Would she be prepared to believe that there was some sort of motive behind this attack? Did she already suspect it? She seemed to defect the notion when Becky had suggested it yesterday.

Dom wasn't an option either. He'd think she was making up little stories to pacify her boredom. Yet another excuse to leave this place and set up home back in London. Besides, he was far too busy at work to be bothering with the ins and outs of a bunch of supernatural mumbo-jumbo. He'd think she'd gone gaga with hormones and ban her from getting involved for the sake of the baby.

Maybe Temperance and Joanna? They were local oddballs looking for a story. Perhaps they would be the easiest to convince that this was a mystery worth investigating further.

As she pushed open the office door, she was met with a gaggle of laughter.

"Oh, Becky, where have you been? You just missed a great suggestion from Mel for the Halloween party," giggled Tracy. "She reckons us five should join forces and go as a group. You can be our fifth Winchcombe Witch!"

An epiphany struck Becky like a bolt of lightning as they all looked at her, open-mouthed, for a response.

She came to her senses instantly.

"That's brilliant!" Becky shrieked, to herself more than to the group.

Mel gave the others a smug grin.

"I told you she'd go for it," she gloated as she reached for a hanky.

■■

Gaynor pulled open the door after a series of frantic knocks took her completely by surprise. An excited-looking Becky was standing on the other side of it, slightly damp but not glum about it.

"Sorry Gaynor, but do you mind if I come in?" she said as she huddled further under the porch out of the rain.

"Why, of course," Gaynor said, a little taken aback. Not that she was complaining, but she hadn't had this regular a visitor in a fair few years. Particularly one who went through such a range of emotions while under her roof. She was beginning to wonder whether Becky was on drugs.

"Thanks," Becky said, pushing past her and marching on into the stone-flanked hallway. The first door was open and so Becky rather uncharacteristically popped her head through.

"Afternoon, Dai!" she chirped to the motionless figure within. Dai groaned in greeting from the comfort of his armchair, which also knocked Gaynor for six. He'd never responded in such a way to someone he knew so little.

Gaynor watched as Becky bounded up the hall and into the kitchen. How had this once sheltered and confused little creature suddenly done such a U-turn and ended up all bright-eyed, gregarious and full of confidence? Gaynor hoped she hadn't mixed up the Arrowood that she had given Becky to take home in a little bag with those unidentifiable mushrooms she had found behind the greenhouse. Gaynor bit her bottom lip in angst.

"Gaynor, I've had an idea," Becky said as she tripped into the kitchen and sat in her usual chair.

Gaynor followed her in, slightly reticent but also intrigued. As Becky spoke, Gaynor surveyed her pupils for any signs of unusual dilation.

"Oh yes?" she said, squinting in Becky's direction.

"I've decided," she said, beaming with zeal, "that I want to practice Wicca."

The room went silent as the exclamation sank into Gaynor's head. The clock ticked on as the room went silent, both women frozen like puppets.

Becky broke the silence.

"Well, you see I've never joined any religion before. I used to go to Sunday school as a child, but I never really believed in it. I have thought about what you said to me last night and I think I should like to learn more."

Gaynor struggled to find the words to respond. She had *never* had someone approach her and ask to *become* a witch. Usually, they were spitting at her in the street or clutching their St Christophers as she walked past. Oh, why had she invited this girl in? Why had she answered her questions and led her to believe that she was just a harmless, old woman with an overgrown garden? Why had she not just left well alone?

Becky went on.

"Because I *do* believe in the earth, in the power of nature. And I want to give thanks to whoever gave us these beautiful things that we so take for granted. So, I would love to be a Wiccan. And I would love you to teach me."

Gaynor took a few steps over to the kitchen side to steady herself. She hadn't wanted all this. Perhaps in her youth, when she loved nothing more than striding in the woods and building circles of light in the now-reclaimed dogging spot on Birdlip Hill, but not now. Her days of being a rebellious necromancer were long over. Now, she just wanted to make a few lotions and look after her husband, not set up her own witch school for the terminally curious.

"Err, I..." she babbled as this train of thought rattled through her head. "I mean ... where has this come from?"

"Well," Becky said, "I think you are right about what you said. People should know the truth, they should be open-minded and willing to see and accept things that they may not fully understand."

Becky propped herself forward in her chair.

"For years I have been a frightened little girl. Too scared to look people in the eye, too suspicious to do anything frivolous. I have always settled for the safe option. I am the most closed-minded person I know."

Becky got up from her seat and walked over to her friend. She took Gaynor's delicate hands in hers. Her skin was soft, with fine folds in her fingers. It made Gaynor smile.

"But since I have moved here and met you, I have realised that I have been ignoring a whole world of possibilities and eventualities. And best of all..."

She looked deep into the old woman's eyes. They were little pools of deep green that glittered with sparks of life. It was as if the skin had grown old around eyes that had never lost their youthful twinkle.

"I believe it all," Becky said. The words were cookie-cutter, but the sentiment was sincere. Gaynor couldn't see how she could deny this desperate, delicate little bird.

Of course, she would never be introduced into the coven since she was not linked to The Order. You had to possess a supernatural power bestowed upon you by an ancestor to become a real witch. But that was not to say that she couldn't practise the religion if that's what she wanted. There were many Wiccans out there who went through the motions without ever being able to cast real magick. And Becky was the perfect candidate for it, a fragile sister who had removed the shackles of ignorance and opened her spirit to the earth.

But Gaynor had never tutored anyone in Wicca before—she wasn't sure if she knew how. This was more Joanna's domain and she had bigger fish to fry with Odette on her case at every corner.

"So," Becky said tentatively, "do you think it's a good idea?"

Gaynor exhaled as she searched around her, seemingly for some excuse to decline that may or may not be lying about the room.

"Well," she said finally, her search proving fruitless, "I suppose it will be a learning curve for both of us."

Becky let out a joyous shriek as she threw her arms around the old woman, embracing her with a tenderness that she had not felt in what seemed like an age. Not since Dai had been on his feet, holding her close to him as they waltzed around their kitchen to the strain of Frank Sinatra. It brought her to tears slightly.

"Oh, that is wonderful," Becky said as she pulled back. Gaynor shielded her face momentarily to hide her dewy eyes. She suddenly felt embarrassed and vulnerable. It reminded her that the tough skin she had built up through years of being shunned by society was only a smoke-screen that hung as a thin veil over a soft soul.

"So," Becky continued, unperturbed by her friend's sudden coyness, "when do you think we begin the lessons?"

"Well," Gaynor said, dabbing her eyes secretly with the sleeve of her over-shirt, swallowing back her tears and straightening herself up, "they always say there is no time like the present, and Goddess Moon waits for no woman."

She moved around the table and to the opposite doorway. It must lead to a room that, so far, Becky had not entered. Gaynor had never imagined letting anyone into that room since Dai had become unwell, but she had a new friend now. Everything had changed.

"So, I guess you better follow me," she said phlegmatically, and slowly opened the door.

ELEVEN

Abbie searched her room for her lip gloss, but no matter how much she overturned everything, she still couldn't find it. That bitch Kayleigh must have nabbed it. She was such a fucking psycho, going into the other girls' bedrooms and taking things that didn't belong to her—it was abhorrent.

Abbie had hunted through inside-out jeans and endless discarded single shoes, but still, it remained elusive. She put one hand into a mass of rubbish and waved it around a bit, hoping to suddenly find something, but it was hopeless.

Grabbing her cigarettes from the side table, she pulled one out of the packet and reached over to lever the window open with her free hand. Once lit, she took a long draw from it and blew the smoke through the gap in the glass.

She shouldn't have been glossing her lips anyway, she should've been getting started on her coursework. Two thousand words on Pinter had to be submitted in a few weeks and she'd barely made a start. How could she, when she had so much going on? It wasn't just Kayleigh who was playing on her mind.

Ever since she'd met Xander, the grunge-loving, pierced and tattooed Adonis, who had a bizarre but compelling fascination with blood and dark, guitar-led murder ballads, the significance of obtaining a degree in theatre studies had all but vanished into thin air.

Xander, with this bleached skin and his dark eyes. The way he looked her in the eye as he slid his finger into her underwear. His crimson-painted lip that jutted out like a juicy slither of raw meat, punctured with a small steel ring. She would bite it when they kissed, imagining it bursting in her mouth, the warm sensation of the fluid within cascading down her own lips and onto her chest. She had to have him, she thought, as she drew in and blew another plume of smoke out through the open crack.

She looked around at the random paraphernalia strewn about her bedroom. It was totally arbitrary. Bags and belts here, scarves and boots there. Crude drawings of lifelike dolls with stitched-up smiles and wide, curious eyes were patched up on the walls, alongside dusty shelves, thick with joss stick ash and the dust from unread books.

This was her life. One chaotic trail of mismatched jumble that was neither use nor ornament. She had no care for her surroundings, no interest in categorising objects in order of her need of them, for getting good grades or acquiring a decent career. The only thing she really had going for her was her slender legs and long, tumbling locks. And then, she supposed, she had her craft.

If her mother had been a good witch, then she certainly hadn't let on and Joanna was under strict instructions not to ever tell Abbie of her family's history within the world of magick. It was the best-kept secret since NATO HQ.

All Abbie ever wanted was to make impulsive decisions in the moment and suffer the consequences if need be. If she wanted an eyeliner she couldn't afford, she pocketed it. If she wanted to stay out drinking rather than studying, she just did it. If she ever sought revenge, she would get it. And if she wanted Xander, she would simply reach out and snatch him.

She leant over to her side drawer and pulled out a small bottle, holding it up to the light to view its contents. It looked just like a clear pill bottle with a glug of translucent liquid inside. She knew she didn't have much left and she wasn't sure that she could get any more. If Gaynor knew she'd taken this bottle, then she hadn't acknowledged it—Abbie wasn't sure she would be so lucky with the next.

She released the lid and poured a small amount of the liquid onto the tip of her index finger, careful not to spill it as she had done before. That night, she cast her memory back. She had panicked when the fluid seeped into the carpet, filling the air with its intoxicating fumes. Unable to rescue any, she gave up trying and took to her bed. All night, her dreams had been dark and frighteningly real. So much so that she had woken up in a pool of her own sweat, tears rolling down her petrified face and twisted in the sheets as if trapped in a spider's web.

She shuddered as she rubbed the dab of oil between her fingers and then into her temples. It quickly absorbed into her skin and, as it did, her eyes rolled back into her head. Her head flopped backwards as her neck became soft. Her jaw hung open and she made a gurgling sound from the back of her throat.

In this trance, her mind's eye raced like a Rolodex, through snapshots of earlier images from her room. Some fragmented, some pitch-black. One from moments ago, others from further back. Dust particles moved back and forth as the sun's light cast shadows across the walls in a counter-clockwise fashion. It was almost as though she was rapidly flicking through a photo album of various shots or watching a silent movie in reverse.

She stopped the reel and focused in on one sole frame. In this blurred tableau, she saw Kayleigh stood by her mirror, holding her lip gloss. As if that weren't enough, the girl was looking around at her dishevelled belongings in disgust, daring to cast aspersions on Abbie's slovenliness when she was the sewer rat, scratching around for a find.

Abbie had all she needed.

Suddenly her head snapped back forward, her eyes relaxed and her jaw rose back up to meet her top lip. She moved her head lightly from side to side as her vision returned to normal. Thoughts jostled against each other in her mind as she regained consciousness. She shouldn't really have used the oil for something so trivial, particularly when she had so little remaining. It should have been saved for a more pressing issue. But then, whatever happened in this town that was important enough to warrant a bit of time-inversion? Fuck all.

Once she felt more stable, she picked her cigarette back up and grabbed her phone that was resting in her pocket.

With her free thumb, she texted Kayleigh.

"My lip gloss had better be back in my room before I turn yours over."

As she pressed send, she began composing another message—to Xander.

"Meet me."

She shoved her phone back into her pocket and stubbed her cigarette out. Throwing the phial back into an open drawer, she stepped over the mess and out of the door.

Joanna scratched her head.

She didn't like this at all, this lack of control. The absence of information was driving her potty.

Who was this woman? And why had The Oracle sent her without contacting Joanna beforehand? She went to college with Constantine, one of the secretaries at HQ—why hadn't she dropped her a line off the record as usual?

She would have to raise this with her when she was next at one of the regional meetings. She was continuously generous to Constantine. Always sliding a jar of chutney or fig biscuits over the sign-in desk and proffering a knowing smile. Well, she needn't bother in future if Constantine was going to neglect to keep her abreast of the matters that concerned her coven. She could bloody whistle. Greedy old busybody, with her tapestry dresses and bad chemotherapy wig.

Joanna scolded herself for being so awful and threw a look up towards the ceiling. Goddess Moon knew she had a temper, and she was sure that she would forgive her for it.

That Odette woman had absolutely no business being here, dealing with a regional matter that, had Joanna been aware of it, she could have sorted sufficiently well by herself.

Joanna knew black magick better than she knew her own family. She had studied and dissected it, she had witnessed many possessions, both real and fake, and had stood watching as acts against the goddess had been carried out right under her own nose. She was lucky that nothing of that nature had ever reared its head in Winchcombe until now, but she was certain that, with her power and knowledge, she could snuff them out competently and without the need for involvement from the higher ranks.

But then, The Order had become so PC nowadays with its new HR policies and health assessments—it was ridiculous. All this tripe got in the way of practising the craft as it was meant to be practised.

In days gone by, a witch could throw anything she wanted into the cauldron if it meant she got a good froth building. But now, everything had to be carefully monitored and modified so as not to affect those with allergies.

Allergies!

What kind of decent witch could be allergic to nettles, dandelion stalks and the bark of a sycamore tree?

But The Order had stood fast, even going so far as to appoint Laura as their HR lackey. She stood there with a pad and pen, seemingly making sure that everything was done by the book under the holy law. Not that this naïve little girl was up to the job. She just fumbled about in endless paperwork, unable to answer any question without giving it a day's thought first, pleasant as she was.

Joanna straightened the objects on her candle table.

What was Odette being sent to do anyway? How could she protect the coven without knowing anything about any of them?

Joanna had tried to figure out Odette's function since her patent black heels had click-clacked into her house—and dug welts in the pile of her carpet. Joanna's strategy in such a state of emergency was always to rule with fear so that she got her own way. She would capitalise on the coven's ignorance to manipulate them into following her lead. It was rudimentary but effective. It was also incredibly easy, she just played the old visionary wisdom card, letting them know that she did, and always would, know more about witchcraft than they did. Exploiting their vulnerability and getting them to hide behind her in the fight against evil was her modus operandi.

Robina and Wing were easy to mould—they were both so damned docile. Laura was slightly more sceptical and Gaynor ... well, Gaynor could go either way. She certainly seemed drawn to Odette, but then the sycophantic old girl always had been a pushover when it came to craft hierarchy.

But the plan was all thrown to the wind now that Joanna was being scrutinised. Odette would see through her plan and thwart it on the spot.

Of course, Joanna herself could have been an Odette if she hadn't been overlooked when she applied to be elected as Grand Sceptre of the West. But just because she didn't have a bit of parchment and a brooch, it didn't mean that she wasn't still capable.

And why hadn't she been allowed to campaign? Because of some ancient allegation about one of her classmates and a leaked prophecy back in her college days. She had been young, foolish and completely at the mercy of several other girls. At least that is what she had told the authorities.

The girl's family had just wanted their fifteen minutes of fame. That quarter of an hour had disgraced Joanna's mother, a renowned prophecy archivist, and put shame upon the family. Hadn't she suffered enough? And now this smooth-talking, preened madam was strolling in here and rubbing Joanna's face in it.

She walked over to the end table and removed a heavy, claret cloth that hung over her lume crystal, a milky dome of light no bigger than a football that swirled with purple and green, the two colours of infinite divinity. It stood before her on an age-old, oaken plinth, the last vestige of her grandmother's estate that had been passed to her in secret before the old woman died.

She would have to be one step ahead of Odette if she were to redeem herself with The Oracle. She could not be disgraced yet again, least of all in front of the sisters she had helped to raise, teach and guide. No stranger could just turn up on her turf and rubbish the name that she had worked so hard to reconstruct—High Sceptre or not.

She looked deep into the globe for signs of activity but nothing immediate presented itself. She closed her eyes and whispered sanctions. The words babbled on her lips, inscribed and woven into her very being. She could recite them on cue, as church-goers did the Lord's Prayer. Unlike Christians, however, her spiritual offerings actually worked. They weren't just a placebo to satisfy those who did not trust themselves at the hands of temptation.

She slowly began to open her eyes and peered once again into her shining sphere of light.

A face appeared, incredibly faintly. A soft, plain face, young, with long, dark hair. It was a face she recognised from the other night. Studying the image intently, Joanna watched curiously as the face slipped from view and into the shifting anomalies of the dome.

It was obvious to Joanna that this person may be the answer to what she was after—but why?

That she would have to figure out for herself.

Now, where had she said that she lived?

Of course, Anne Wicks' old place. Joanna knew it well.

She might have to go over tomorrow for a little visit and make nice with some special tea.

She covered the globe back over and smiled to herself.

■■

Becky looked at the items in front of her as she sat cross-legged on the rug. They were a curious bunch of objects, but it made sense that they were grouped together for religious purposes, as they were all monuments of faith in one way or another.

Gaynor had pulled them out of a large velvet bag and set them out without any sort of explanation. She then hobbled over to an old bookcase, jam-packed with leather-bound volumes of every shape and size.

Her sitting room was another hodgepodge of knick-knacks and jumble, garnished with the occasional plume of dried flowers. It reminded Becky a little of Joanna's living room, but with less cohesive style and more of an unapologetic irregularity. It was astounding to Becky how Gaynor managed to find anything in this unholy mess, but there had been no rummaging so far— she had located everything with ease.

Becky noticed that much of the floor space was taken up with large, ornately-carved, antique, wooden chests, bound with clunky, aggressive-looking locks and covered with a fine layer of surface dust. It was evident that Gaynor did not use this room much, less so to entertain.

Gaynor selected a book and came back over, easing herself into a comfortable chair and quietly flicking through the pages, like a monarch on a throne. It was a few moments before she spoke.

"I think," she began, "that we will begin with the first doctrine of Wicca."

She looked up at Becky, who remained blank.

"It is based on seven laws of magick," Gaynor continued. "One rede—that means a piece of advice—one principle and one truth that should govern everything that you practise or feel in the name of the religion."

She appeared to be reading from the book, and yet she spoke naturally, as though it had been entrenched in her and seeped out of every pore.

"Firstly, the principle," Gaynor continued. "A true Wiccan must be pure of heart."

She looked up again.

"*Totally* pure of heart." She drew the words out, making them sound long, heavy and fraught with conviction. Her old eyes ran deep with severity.

"In other words, you begin from now. First, you let go of your old way of thinking. Only then can you clear the necessary space to make way for this new path."

She rested her hand on the open book.

"But this is a marathon and not a sprint, my dear. Goddess Moon will know whether you are sincere or not, and there is no hiding from her." She shot Becky a stern look. "The truth is the complete and utter worship of the goddess and the god."

This took Becky slightly aback.

Yes, she was aware of the Goddess Moon. She even had a picture of a celestial woman in her mind. White-skinned, with arms outstretched. Like the painting of the Lady of Shalott that someone had given to her on a greetings card many moons ago. She had been so mesmerised by it that she had taped it to her bedroom mirror.

But this was the first Becky had heard of there being a god in this religion. She had supposed this to be an all-female cast.

Gaynor sat forward.

"In the beginning, there was the goddess. Divine, nurturing and all-encompassing." She moistened her lips and inhaled shortly and sharply, as one does when they are telling a tale of great magnitude. "She created Earth and covered it in a blanket of grass. The grass was a sign of eternal existence."

Becky listened intently, her lips parted. As Gaynor spoke, her words encircled her, soothing, enticing and entrancing.

"The goddess grew trees, and these trees would bear fruit as a symbol of everlasting fertility." Gaynor illustrated her words with sweeping hand gestures. "But the goddess still felt alone. The isolation made her cry. She shed great tears of salty water that pooled as vast oceans upon Earth. To abate her loneliness, she impregnated herself with a seed—a representation of life-force."

A scene played out in Becky's head, like the pages of a children's book that she remembered from years ago. Where the sun and the earth joined hands across a wide ocean, and the people on the planet smiled up at the sky with squinty-drawn eyes and full, red lips.

"For ten full moons, the goddess carried the seed in her belly. And after that time, she gave birth to a baby boy." Gaynor's words were full of reverie, and yet they were succinct and direct. In all the time she spoke, she never once looked back down at her book. "The child she birthed gave the goddess so much warmth that she gave him the sun as a symbol of light and placed it high in the sky for all to see and feel."

Gaynor held her arm aloft, with her hand cupped into a bowl-like shape.

"And he grew from a boy into a god," she went on. "Soon, the goddess became fertile again. But in that time the god had become weak. As he faded, so did the sun begin to dull. The hours of daylight shortened and in those hours, the air was bitter and grey. Earth grew cold and the god died."

Becky shook her head with sympathy.

"After another ten moons, the goddess gave birth again. The cycle repeated itself. And so, the seasons were determined. A time for seeding, a time for growing, a time for harvesting and a time for dying. The goddess had created the cycle of life. So mote it be."

Becky looked confused as she watched Gaynor finish and lean back in her chair.

"So, the god is both the father and brother of the goddess' new baby?" she asked incredulously.

"Yes, my dear, you could put it like that. But this is not an example of what we in the modern world see as incest. This is a process of the Divine. The goddess, the god and the seasons of nature, they transcend the human ideals of what is right and what is wrong." Gaynor's words were clipped but languid and as she gazed, her eyes still glistened.

Becky nodded. She wasn't sure she truly understood, but then religion had always been a bit of a puzzle. Christians, Muslims, Catholics— they were all crazy in their own way. I mean, if the Bible was to be believed, Adam was procreating with his own rib. Surely that would be a cause for concern as well.

Gaynor gazed back upon the open page in front of her.

"The concept of magick and performing spells is not for the benefit of personal gain or to harm others. It is to draw energy from the earth and restore it into something physical. Every spell, every wish, every potion must be approved with the blessing of the goddess and the god. Failure to comply with this is seen as a slant on the holy order and will not be accepted or tolerated." Gaynor's face suddenly fell.

"If, however, the principles of our practices are used for any sort of dark purpose, then we cannot accept responsibility for the torment that the perpetrator might suffer at the hands of the goddess."

Becky swallowed with a dry throat.

"When you say dark ... do you mean satanic?"

Gaynor sighed.

"Well, you notice that we do not mention the devil in any of our teachings. He is the Christians' enemy. We do not believe in him. Our religion teaches that anything the goddess condemns is the enemy. Those who use spells to conjure up dark or black magick, for example." Gaynor's brow furrowed. "Many people assume that we, as Wiccans, are responsible for encouraging the practice of evil magick but, since the goddess forbids it, it is the antithesis of what we do."

The room seemed to darken a touch as Gaynor leant back once again.

"And what might the goddess do to those people who practise dark magic?" Becky asked, her eyes wide with curiosity.

"Well," Gaynor answered, "there are many theories as to what happens to the person who gets themselves involved in that which is forbidden. It all depends on who you offer your soul to before you go to such ends. We believe that, in the end, the goddess will punish you for the crimes you have committed against her. But many simply suffer at the hands of the magick they have evoked. A dark spell will come home to roost before the goddess need be worried."

"What might happen to them?" Becky was pushing for an answer, hoping that Gaynor might describe what she had seen in the church.

"My, you are inquisitive." Gaynor steadied herself for a moment. She had ventured a little too far into this topic and would have to now appear aloof just in case Becky suspected anything more. "If people aren't careful, then they could invite a mischievous spirit to latch onto them. Tortured souls who have been banished from the goddess' heavenly after-life, who roam the world forever with unsettled, dark recompense, will always stick to the person who pays them attention."

That wasn't as casual as she had meant to sound. Gaynor stopped, slowly moistening her drying lips with her tongue.

"Or, of course, there is The Chasm," she said sombrely.

"The Chasm?" Becky's eyes were wild with anticipation, yet she still sat, frozen to the spot with intrigue.

Gaynor looked down at her book before answering. She was hesitant to even respond.

"The Chasm," she said, "is an ancient curse. It is only, however, bestowed upon those who practise what is known as Mariana's Magick."

Gaynor waited a moment before continuing.

"Mariana's Magick is the darkest of the dark, a truly perilous kind of craft that is so named after the trench that marks the deepest part of the world's oceans. Anyone misusing this magick can be punished eternally, with infinite damnation that is inherently brutal. The result is your magick backfiring on you four-fold, damaging the outer layer of your soul, like puncturing an embryo. Every movement, every touch, every breath from there on in becomes unadulterated agony. Your life becomes unmanageably terrible—and your death, even more so. Those who use Mariana's Magick are not just banished by the goddess, they begin to banish their soul from themselves."

Becky also began to move her tongue around her mouth for moisture.

Gaynor stopped. She knew that she had said too much and appeared far more knowledgeable on the subject than she had originally wanted to.

And yet, it was something far too close to her heart to just skirt across. She still remembered the faces of the three inflicted, from all that time ago. Grey eyes in sunken sockets, charred bones poking through ripped skin like the torn remains of a refuse sack. A bag of bodies emptied into a pile of ash. The final remnants of the three girls who had tried to burn themselves in the wood, knowing full well that they would never be rid of the torture, even when their bodies were gone.

"So, you see, my child," Gaynor began, her focus shifting back to her guest, "you have to be fully committed to this."

Becky looked back down at her book in exasperation, as Gaynor's lips curled up at the corners

"Right," Gaynor said, breezily, "shall we move on to the seven laws?"

■■■

Nurse Tyler looked down at her watch. Another long shift was ahead of her and it did not fill her with glee.

Three more days of insufferable monotony before she could finally rest for the weekend. She wouldn't have minded, but nothing ever happened in this hospital.

Old folks came in with splintered hips, limbs and joints all hanging on by one sinewy vein. The staff either forged them back together with bits of metal and force-fed them recovery sludge with nonchalant grimaces on their faces, or the sorry unfortunates had the good grace to shuffle off this mortal coil and make everyone happy.

On the hour was yet another round of medicinal distribution. Keeping the ancient lungs breathing for yet one more day, another twenty-four hours of wheezy rasping, punctuated with pathetic little coughs that cut through her concentration like a million tiny knives. Then stacks of paperwork to suffer through once they had nuzzled themselves into the stiff bed linen. Endless hours of making sure a log was taken of every pill popped, every meal given, each shit expelled. God, it was hell.

The only moment of excitement in living memory had been when that schoolteacher was wheeled in a couple of days ago.

Nurse Tyler had very little to do with it all, but she did manage to sneak a look at the body. She had heard the patter of gossip around the staff room about how all the young orderlies would have loved to have been involved in the case.

But Nurse Tyler had taken one look at the cold, white corpse and sent it straight to the morgue to be bagged up and carted off to Birmingham for a proper examination and burial authorisation.

There was not much to report really. She had been old, some minor bruising to the torso, a couple of broken limbs. She could have been jolted about a bit in transit as the dead often were by the time they reached Cheltenham Royal Infirmary. It was not out of the ordinary for a body to acquire some fresh marks, even if the blood no longer pumped. Paramedics could often be quite heavy-handed if they knew that the cadaver was no longer breathing, stiff enough to be tossed onto a stretcher once the rigor mortis had set in.

Some kind of possession, the student nurses had whispered on a tea break. Involved in witchcraft—what a load of nonsense. Nurse Tyler didn't have time for these silly girls and their Now Magazine approach to modern-day nursing. You simply couldn't get involved in idle gossip, there wasn't the manpower or the resources. Just get them sent off to where they need to be and wash your hands of the responsibility.

No doubt the woman would rot in hell if that was the kind of thing she did in her spare time, but that was for a vengeful god to decide, not her, a simple matron.

Just as she was about to drain the last of her coffee and make for her hourly ward round, the phone rang shrilly.

She heaved a world-weary sigh and picked up the receiver.

"Tyler." Her voice was flat and perfunctory.

"Hi, Marge," said the grainy voice on the other end, mired in tension. She recognised the dulcet tones of the senior morgue technician.

"Oh, hello Dennis." She looked down at the grains sloshing around in her mug. They resembled a jagged map of Australia. "What can I do for you?"

"Err, I don't know if you can, to be honest. I'm just sort of doing the rounds here." Dennis was hesitant.

"Try me." She was losing patience, which was ironic, considering her job.

"You know that body that came in the other day? Ware, something. Beatrice? Brenda? Brenda!" His tone lightened as he seemed to locate the correct name on his paperwork.

"Yes, I was just thinking about her actually. Don't think I can help though Dennis. I was only on site to authorise her going to your department. I know virtually nothing about the case. You'll have to talk to Doctor Reynolds or the paramedics, I'm afraid."

She was about to hang up. Usually in this business, if you allowed another member of the team to prattle on, you'd end up signing yourself onto a job that you had no intention of doing. Plus, she had a sneaking suspicion that Dennis was after some info on the possession rumour— information that she was not willing to furnish the old gossip with.

"Yes, I will Marge, I will. It's just ... I have to ask. Did you check the body before you sent it down?"

She suddenly snapped back into the conversation.

"Of course I did, Dennis," she said slowly, making sure she hammered home that her lack of enthusiasm, during this call or otherwise, was not indicative of how seriously she took her position. "Are you questioning my medical competence? I know a deceased body when I see one."

"Yes, I know that Marge," he replied, "and I'm sorry to probe you but—"

"Dennis, I have been a matron for nearly fifteen years, a district nurse for another ten and an auxiliary nurse for god knows how long before that. I think I am able to recognise a dead person, don't you?"

She was beginning to lose her temper. This stupid, jumped-up little Hitler was trying to question her authority and judgement—and she was not about to let him get away with it.

"Yes, yes. I know all that Marge. And I'm not trying to challenge you. I mean, our assistants this end have confirmed it as well. It's just that, she's been lying down here for a couple of days now. I came down with the Birmingham boys to collect her this morning and, well ... she's gone."

Nurse Tyler frowned as she tried to comprehend this information.

"*Gone?*" she said, her mouth agog. "What do you mean she's *gone?*"

"The body," Dennis sputtered down the phone, "it's completely vanished."

There was a moment of silence as Nurse Tyler's mug dropped out of her hand and toppled onto the desk.

"Marge..." the voice on the other end of the line said. "Are you still there?"

TWELVE

Becky was stood at her kitchen sink when someone rapped on the front door. Dom was at work and she was just trying to keep a salad down. She hadn't felt like eating and was a bit tired after a rather long afternoon with Gaynor, the terror of The Chasm still floating around her head.

Becky couldn't quite grasp the idea of something slicing a segment of your soul, leaving you in infinite pain, even when deceased. Could this be what happened to Miss Ware? Was that why she had spat blood across the church steps? Was that an indication that something had severed her from within? It didn't bear thinking about really.

She meandered over to the door and opened it, still lost in thought.

Two police officers were waiting on the step. The female officer—a plain looking redhead with a long coat and a wry smile—was the first to speak. The tall gentleman behind her grinned bleakly. Becky was so surprised that a glob of half-masticated lettuce nearly fell from her open mouth.

"Hello," the woman said, "are you Rebecca Dawlish?"

"Err ... yes. Yes, I am." The baby suddenly did a backflip inside her belly which made her want to run to the toilet.

"I'm Officer Debbie Almes, and this is Officer Michael Wilkinson, Gloucestershire Constabulary. Do you have a moment?" she continued, thrusting a badge out in front of her.

"Sure, come in." Becky felt herself go cold.

She stepped aside to let them through. As she led them to the sofa, she tried to look cool and unintimidated. Unfortunately, she was so tense that she walked behind them like an aluminium robot. What on earth was the police force doing at her door?

"Would you like some tea?" she asked mechanically as if they were all in a play.

"No, thanks—we won't keep you," Officer Almes said, looking around as she rested her leather bag next to her chair. "I like what you have done with the place, it's very cosy. I've always loved this house."

"Oh, thank you," Becky replied with a nervous smile. When had this woman been here before? Maybe to inquire about Miss Wicks and her mysterious disappearance. "We've not been here long."

"I see."

Becky looked over at the other officer, whose eyes were tracing the room with inconspicuous curiosity.

"The reason why we are here," Officer Almes went on matter-of-factly, "is because of the events that took place in the church on Wednesday afternoon. We are doing the rounds, just making sure that all those who were present have corresponding stories."

The officer bent down to remove a pad from her bag and, as she did, her hair fell about her shoulders. She was not unattractive, but brassy. The sort of woman who would get a bit too drunk at the Christmas do.

"Oh, okay," Becky blushed.

"If you wouldn't mind going through the afternoon's events with us and I'll make a few notes. Then, hopefully, you shouldn't see us again for a while." Officer Almes placed her pad on her lap and took a pen from her pocket.

"Yes ... yes, that's fine," Becky agreed and sat between them on the right-hand side of the two-seater, brushing any moisture from the corners of her mouth.

"If you could start at the beginning of the service—what you saw, who was there. I understand that there were quite a few in the congregation and you might not know everyone's names, being new to the area, but try and give us as much information as you can." Her tone was friendly and welcoming.

Becky instantly trusted Officer Almes, but she was dubious about the silent Officer Wilkinson who remained ineffectual and glum. She didn't really want him in her house.

"Well," Becky began, "I suppose it started on the way to the church."

As the story unfolded, Becky could see how implausible the situation had been. She wasn't sure whether she was doctoring her version just so that she didn't sound too crazy. She made excuses for the levitation, claiming that it could have been a simple optical illusion, and skipped over the theory behind the blast and the scorching—it just didn't seem relevant.

"One thing I am interested to know," Officer Almes asked, taking her pen from out of her mouth, having chewed on it as she listened, "would there be any reason why someone would want to—allegedly—poison Miss Ware? Can you think of any possible motive?"

Becky exhaled through her lips.

"As you say, I haven't really been there long enough to know the relationships between the staff and the parents, or any connections Miss Ware had outside of the school. But I can certainly say that she was well-respected, and the children liked her. From what I saw, she never raised her voice or doled out harsh punishment. It's hard to tell after three days, I can only tell you what I witnessed." Becky remained a shade of mortified pink. She felt as though she was sitting there in just her bra and knickers.

A few moments passed as Officer Almes stared at her paper. She looked up and smiled.

"Well, I think that's all," she said, nodding to her male counterpart who had remained on his feet throughout the entire interview. "Thank you so much for seeing us. I hope we didn't disturb you."

Almes stood up and Wilkinson joined her on her way to the door. Becky got up and followed.

"No, not at all," she said as she leant forward to open it, "I hope it was useful."

"Oh yes, of course."

They both stepped through the gangway and onto the pavement before Officer Almes turned back around to face Becky.

"I suppose there is just one more thing," she began tentatively as if she was reluctant for an answer.

"Oh?" Becky leant on the door to stable herself.

"I don't suppose that you have seen Miss Ware since that day, have you?" Her eyes squinted up as she looked at Becky, the knowing confidence from her previous line of questioning suddenly evaporated.

Becky was a little taken aback by this curveball.

"What, you mean, after she was taken away?" she asked.

"Yes. Since Wednesday."

"Well," Becky stumbled, "I mean, nobody has said anything to me officially, but I was thinking that it wasn't going to be good news. I mean, I assumed that I probably wouldn't see her again, if you know what I mean. I mean, she wasn't breathing ..." She trailed off nervously.

Officer Almes' face broke into a polite beam.

"Okay. Thanks again for your time," she said, and they both made their way down Vineyard Street away from the house.

As Becky closed the door, she felt a sudden chill again. What on earth could she have meant, asking whether she had seen the teacher since Wednesday? Had the body gone missing? Or, more bizarrely—was Brenda Ware still alive?

■ ■

Joanna had seen two officers leaving number 4 Vineyard Street and decided that, perhaps, it wasn't the best time to go around and consult with her new neighbour.

Damned police! They were like a navy sock in a white wash, always turning up when they weren't wanted. They were a total waste of time, resources and taxpayers' money as far as she was concerned. They were perfectly aware that it was the responsibility of the coven to clean up any mess of a paranormal nature that occurred in this town. And there hadn't been any of that since the eighties when Ouija boards made something of a comeback. If it fell into the supernatural category, they were to keep their meddling noses out and let the experts drive the investigation. For pity's sake, one of their top brass was part of a circle in nearby Tetbury—she should know that, sometimes, shit happens. Goddess forgive her for swearing.

She pulled her shawl over her head like Meryl Streep in *The French Lieutenant's Woman*, mumbling to herself as she went.

Why, oh why did the police insist on sending out ignorant, clueless megalomaniacs to prod and pry into affairs that her coven should be tending to? They were messing everything up and jeopardising her own investigation.

She would have to have a word with Tamsin at the Constabulary and let it be known that The Oracle was involved in this one, so their people should pull out pronto. Joanna would remind her that The Order had been catching criminals long before some magistrate called Henry Fielding put together a band of vigilantes and named them the Bow Street Runners. Magick had been around for centuries, and yet the law, in mankind's insatiable desire to find the logic in everything, had refused to recognise the use of magic as a weapon. This was simply because they didn't want to lose the respect of the British people and become a national laughing stock. They knew that Joe Public would have to see a paranormal crime to believe it and occurrences were so rare that it wasn't worth opening such a huge can of worms. Keep it simple—keep them ignorant.

Besides, if the police started locking people up under suspicion of being witches, civilization would have to jump back a few centuries and undo all the good work that it had done in promoting the freedom of spiritual choice.

That's why there was a sort of unspoken rule that the police and The Order could both exist to keep their own peace, so long as one didn't tread on the other's patch. Of course, there had been some major incidents where the police had to take charge. That woman who had been spotted levitating over the Thames was a case in point. However, for the most part, dark sorcery and its aftermath usually went by unnoticed on the streets of every day Britain.

And if that was the case, then why couldn't they leave this one alone? At least until they had consulted with The Oracle.

Joanna frowned as she pulled her coat tighter around herself and made her way home.

■■■

Abbie flopped herself down next to Xander on the grass and pulled a cigarette out of her pocket.

She always enjoyed feeling him thrusting away at her in the outdoors, all charged up like a Duracell bunny. They had both been shivering with the cold, which had sent another impulse through her already-quivering body. The saliva that he spread up her neck with his tongue instantly turned to ice in the bitter wind and her fingertips numbed as she scratched the taut skin under his t-shirt.

"That was great." She was out of breath and her thighs ached from being wrapped around him. He held his cigarette in his teeth as he zipped up his fly and abandoned the used condom with his free hand.

"Yeah, it was," he laughed, smoke pulsing out of his mouth in small plumes.

"So, what are you up to tonight?" she rolled over to face him, pulling her knickers up her legs.

"Going to a band in town. Hammer Swing. My mate's their manager."

She laughed condescendingly.

"Their manager? Aren't they, like, sixteen?"

He didn't appreciate her mocking him or his friends. The sparse fur that ran atop both eyelids knitted together.

"No, they're fucking nineteen and they're really good." He spat on the ground, a clear indication of what she could do with her sarcasm.

"Okay, fine." She took a long draw on her cigarette. Any chance of an invite to said gig was probably now shot to shit.

"What are you up to?" he asked, as he began tucking his denim shirt back into his black, skinny jeans. The sleeve on his right arm pulled up to reveal the word "DESTROY" written on him in black ink.

"Coursework—I haven't even started," she exhaled deeply. "It's due in, like, yesterday."

"Rock and roll," he scoffed.

Xander swung his legs around so that she almost got kicked in the face by his battered Converse.

"So, when do you want to meet again? I mean, aside from this essay, I'm not that busy." She was trying hard to sound avoidant, but in that vain attempt, she had managed to do the exact opposite.

"Dunno, I'm pretty busy with the demo— barely have time to wipe my backside."

This must be the demo for his band, Army of Men. The one that had broken up and reformed that many times that their four-track demo tape had been delayed more times than the final *Game of Thrones* novel.

"Sure, well ... just let me know then."

"I did have this idea," he said, turning towards her with his cigarette between his teeth and a lascivious smirk on his lips. A lock of hair from his slicked-back quiff fell onto his face, making him look infinitely sexier.

"Oh yeah, what?" she leant up on her elbows. She almost caught herself batting her eyelids.

"Have you ever, like, fucked on Halloween?" His eyes went dark as he spoke, enjoying the words as they rolled around his mouth.

She bit her lip, then shook her head. Every night was Halloween to a practising witch. The significance was minimal

"It's supposed to be amazing. Outside, in the woods, in the light of the moon. The spirits and the wolves and the night all around us." His white face lit up.

Abbie was nonplussed. Being a genuine witch, Halloween was only a replication of a thousand movies and stories. It had nothing to do with the real magickal world, but she liked the idea of him being so into it. She noticed a small tremor in his crotch.

"I'm up for it," she said, slowly rising to sitting.

"Cool." He looked pleased with himself as he removed the stub from his mouth and threw it into the grass. "You never know—I might even write a song about it."

This offer did not impress her much. She had heard his seminal, self-penned anthem, *Lisa's Left Finger*, and decided then and there that his songwriting skills were less-than-impressive. Anyway, if it was to be anything like this infamous demo, it would be years before she heard it. He rose up to his feet and brushed the flotsam from his jeans.

She got up and followed him back through the field.

■■■

Catherine had had just about enough of this bloody papier-mâché, hanging off her hand like an unwanted, raw poultry skin.

"Hold still, Sienna," she barked, as her daughter twisted and turned through the mass of chicken wire.

"But mummy, it's digging into my arm."

"Well it's going to isn't it—I haven't stuck the felt on yet," she scolded, "and if you keep bloody wriggling, it's going to stick in further."

She pulled yet another shred of newspaper out of the gloopy mess and slapped it onto the wire structure.

In fairness, the project was not really going very well. She had hoped that the chicken wire would bend easily into the shape of a bulky trunk so that no one would suspect that Sienna's head was supposed to be under there. It needed to be twice her size and, with that in mind, it needed a fair amount of padding.

"Can't I just go as Lizzie Borden? The girl from the poem?"

Catherine frowned. She was attempting to turn a young girl into a headless horseman and was getting absolutely no recognition for it.

Where was the skill in running up a drab, Lizzie Borden-style pinafore dress, the likes of which you could probably buy for less than twenty quid? That would never cut the mustard if she were to rub Rachel Power's smug face in the dirt.

"No, Sienna!" she scolded. "It's not special enough. I'm afraid that if we are ever going to win that prize, we need to think outside of the box."

She stood back and admired her handiwork. Ironically, a box was exactly what it looked like.

Well, at least the trunk was in place. The arms were a little bit long, but she could always trim them down before glue-gunning the marigolds stuffed with clay onto the ends.

The head was the best bit. While out shopping early on Saturday, she had found, protruding from a sack of abandoned jumble outside a charity shop, a perfectly acceptable mannequin head. She couldn't believe her luck. Rather than waiting for the shop to open, she had wrestled it from the refuse bag and popped it into her own large shopper. And so as not to seem uncharitable to the disgruntled passers-by, she had then slid a five-pound note through the letterbox and backed away quietly.

And with a bit of white paint, talcum powder and the savage bowl-cut she had given it with a pair of secateurs, the head now made the perfect accompaniment to the giant torso. It would be wedged under the arm once all the paint was dry.

She would then have to fashion the rubber tube drainage system to carry the ketchup-syrup concoction from the neck to the squeezy pump valve in the waistband. It was constructed out of an old garden hose and could squirt thick, gooey blood over whichever poor, unsuspecting partygoer happened to be around whenever the button was pressed. Yes, it was hard work, but it would all be worth it to see the smile wiped off Rachel Power's smug face. How anyone could still grin like a Cheshire cat with all that filler in their cheeks riled Catherine even more.

As she carefully removed the pins from her mouth she smiled inwardly. Yes, her daughter might have to spend the most fun evening of the year in merciless agony, but that was a price that Catherine was willing to pay.

"Darling, please stop squirming—you'll ruin the midriff."

"But I'm hungry, and Daddy said he'd help me with my homework."

"Daddy is busy in the study right now, I doubt he'll have time to help you this evening."

In truth, Saul was spending less time around the dinner table, making the requisite noises of appreciation after gulping down Nigella's peach cobbler, and more and more time in his study. She was beginning to wonder whether it was just *brick* erections that he was developing up there.

Why couldn't he understand how much pressure she was under to keep up with the Joneses? And not just the Joneses but the Powells, the Taylors and Rachel Bloody Power.

"Right, unfasten the back then," Catherine said, striding over to help her daughter out of the wire lung that she had encased her in.

"And place the body *carefully* over there by the radiator to dry. Then can you call your brother, please? Dinner's nearly ready."

As soon as Sienna was released, she hot-footed it into the playroom, shouting to Michael and swinging her arms around to get the feeling back into them.

Catherine didn't have long to complete this mammoth task—the party was only two weeks away, but she was sure that she was up to it. For heaven's sake, she had managed to stitch the bunting for the Diamond Jubilee in less time and with less fuss. Seventy-five little triangles of fabric and all on a Sunday. It was just a bugger that the fabric shop had been closed by the time she'd remembered how to thread a bobbin, so she'd had to sacrifice a perfectly good pair of Cath Kidston curtains to the cause.

Perhaps Becky could give her a hand. It would be the perfect way to get her involved with something more community-based, out of the house and into the party spirit. Plus, she felt as though she needed a friend. She was sure that she was losing her husband to a website of single, Eastern European waitresses and, outside of the school gates, she wasn't really part of the Yummy Mummies group anymore. She spent so much time trying to outdo them that she had forgotten to get to know them.

After what had happened on Wednesday, she felt as though she should really discuss it with Becky, especially since it had probably frightened the poor girl half to death. It had been such a shocking event: Brenda gabbling away like that and then nosediving into the stone floor like United 93. Catherine hadn't stuck around. She had been too busy ferrying her children out of the church and away from the gruesome sight. After the event, she had been expecting Sienna and Michael to be so traumatised by it that they would suffer for weeks to come—nightmares, inquisitive probing, perhaps a bit of sleepwalking or bedwetting—but no. They just switched their iPads back on and carried on as normal.

Her mother had been the first to comment when it came to strange occurrences in the town

"Never trust what goes on behind closed doors," she had said. "Devil worshippers, witches, gipsies, socialists. No amount of strange behaviour shocks me anymore."

Catherine remembered when she was nine, seeing an old man collapse once as he got off the bus. He started to froth at the mouth and convulse against the kerb right there in front of her perfect, pink plimsolls. As he dribbled and fought for the words to scream, he had looked her dead in the eyes. They were bulging and yellow, his face stretched in fear and terror, completely in the know that his time was up.

She had never forgotten that moment when she had literally stared death in the face. Her mother had pulled her away—she didn't want her daughter staring at the unfortunate. When they had walked back that way later, the body had been removed and only a few rubberneckers remained at the site.

"His heart," she had heard a female voice say. "You never know when it's just going to give up on you. One moment you're here, then poof—you're gone."

The possibility that your life could be over so quickly, without so much as a word of warning, made Catherine obsessively fearful of death. She became so consumed with the idea of leaving a legacy in the event of a spontaneous fatality that it had almost governed every decision that she had made.

Her house had to be the best, her muffins the fluffiest, her buttocks the tightest. But was she truly happy in this picture? Was everything perfect?

Yes, her children were beautiful, but Michael hadn't acknowledged her since she'd bought him an Xbox. He had immediately cut himself from her apron strings and run straight into the arms of Master Chief. Sienna was always immaculately turned-out but, like Catherine had been at that age, she could be a precocious little bitch. It wouldn't be too long before she was coming home reeking of cigarette smoke, with ripped tights and some tell-tale marks at the base of her neck.

And Saul. Well, Saul was just Saul. He only made love to her when they were drunk and even then, it was like stubbing a fag out in an ashtray, heaving himself on and off her like he was boarding an inflatable dinghy on a choppy afternoon. He kissed her as he left for the day and again on the way back in, and that was about as close as they got. Two pecks per day after twenty or so years of marriage.

His real passion was in a world that he didn't inhabit, in the Bond films he so often watched and the John Le Carre novels he tore through with more gusto than he ever did at her underwear.

He said "I love you" as though the words were a plaster to be temporarily stuck over an open wound. To pacify her when she begged him to make her feel as though she were of some worth to him. Instead, it made her feel fatuous for even bothering. Her husband always managed to make something so heartfelt sound so bloody evasive.

Maybe it was really someone like Becky who was perfect. Supreme in her banality. She had the husband, who was so gorgeous that he made Catherine giddy. She had the child on the way, who would be blessed with its mother's lack of craving for social supremacy. She was plain without being ugly, quiet without being vacant, shy without being irritating. She had the good grace and humour to be openly manipulated without being scornful or unkind. Maybe that's how Catherine should have played this one.

Perhaps she should get more involved in Becky's life to see whether she couldn't learn a few things from her. To dilute her own magnificence with just a touch of Becky's mundane.

Yes, she would call her and invite her over. She smiled as she patted down her apron, ready to dull a little of her own sheen.

■■

Becky upended the bag onto the table as the myriad of items fell out and began cascading across the surface. She had had to wait for Dom to go to bed before she tackled this lot. Luckily, he was so tired after spending half the night at the surgery, untwisting the temperamental guts of an old mare named Firefly, he barely tasted her al dente cauliflower cheese before sloping off upstairs to lie down.

She unravelled a script from her pocket and smoothed it out before her, selecting the specific items as they met her eyes on the page.

First, she picked up the three candles. One was thick, hard and cold to the touch. It looked like the kind that you might throw through a window if you were ever trapped inside a burning building—it was rock solid. This candle represented the god, so she put it at the top-right corner of the table. Gaynor had told her that she needed to find an appropriate table on which to perform her spells, but the only supportive ledge she had at her disposal was an old tea-tray that her dad used to enjoy doing jigsaw puzzles on—it would have to do.

The next candle, by comparison, was long and thin, like a church candle. This was to represent the goddess and went to the left.

Lastly, the unity candle, which wasn't as tall as the second, nor as thick as the first. This candle would unify the power of both the goddess and the god and so it was placed in in the centre, between them.

Laying out candles felt strangely spiritual. She felt the need to bow her head in prayer as she had when she attended church with her mother all those years ago, her cuddly toy dangling from her hand, brushing the dusty floor tiles.

"Remember," Becky heard Gaynor say in her head, "you must not light these candles. I only lend you these instruments so that you can practise laying the altar out correctly. You cannot start using them until you have learnt more about the religion. This will come in time. First, you must get used to the altar being in your life."

She wasn't sure that Dom would agree with all this. She knew that she would have to tell him sooner or later, but their communication was limited at the moment, with his hours at the surgery getting longer and longer. She would rather keep him in the dark for now, presuming that his little sparrow was more likely to be taking part in sociable knitting than casual witchcraft.

The next ornament was a small, metal oil burner which went in the middle of the table. She hunted around in the bag for a bottle of scented oil, but she wasn't sure that Gaynor had given her any. No matter if not—Becky was sure she had some Body Shop Oceana left over from the nineties when that type of air deodoriser had been fashionable. So fashionable, in fact, that it had stained the cuffs of every cardigan she had ever owned during that era.

She then lifted out a small brass cup. This was to represent the chalice that would hold the potion or liquefied spell. Becky suspected it was a beginner's chalice because it looked like one of her old school trophies, built sturdily enough to withstand any blunders or mistakes.

Last but not least was a felt sheath that housed a small, ornate blade. It was no bigger than a few inches, but the carvings around the steel handle looked age-old and intricate.

Gaynor's voice returned to her. "This is the anthame. I have hundreds, but this was mine when I was being schooled. Its purpose is not to threaten, but to summon the four quadrants of the moon. I ask that you look after it and guard it well. And please don't put it in the dishwasher— it won't last a full cycle."

Gaynor had then written a list of the items that she would need to supply herself.

A container of clean water – Evian will do.

A small dish of salt – Sainsbury's own.

A cauldron.

She had looked at Gaynor in confusion.

"I don't have any that I can lend. Mine has been with me for decades, I can't part with it. A good cauldron should be able to hold a decent fire and a small volume of liquid. A cast iron pot that will not topple over and can be stored easily."

"Will Le Creuset do?"

Gaynor sighed.

"I suppose so"

After a quick rummage in the kitchen, she found the items and rearranged them in front of her.

It looked like the Halloween Special on *Ready, Steady, Cook*.

Becky frowned. Something was missing.

"Don't forget the pentagram," Gaynor's soft voice spoke to her. *"A five-pointed star that points to the five Wiccan elements: earth, fire, air, water,*

254

and spirit. This must go in the centre of your altar."

Having no other paper around, Becky drew the pentagram on the back of the list and placed it in front of the unity candle.

This was her altar.

Becky thought about lighting a candle, just to see what might happen. Whether the winds would suddenly blow, shattering the windows like it did in the movies. But she didn't know what to say or how to begin, so she thought better of it. She also didn't know whether you had to use a ceremonial flint, or whether good old cook's matches would suffice.

Gaynor had mentioned something about opening a circle, but Becky had no intention of opening anything without at least knowing where the exit was.

She drew her hand to her belly as she sat there in the dim light. She suddenly felt very connected to the life inside her. It was as if she was fulfilling some sort of purpose by doing something for herself rather than going along with it because her husband said so. It was empowering.

She knew that she was a country mile away from finding out what kind of magic it had been that took over Brenda Ware, but at least she was embarking on a journey towards understanding it better. This was the beginning of an opportunity, and who knew what this new opportunity would bring? She could end up being a bonafide witch, or a woman bishop of Wicca, whatever they were called. The options were limitless, and the thrill was enticing. She felt connected to the female spirit as she never had before.

She heard movement upstairs as the light clicked on. Becky began collecting everything to the top of the table and searching about for an old sheet to cover it with. Instead, she slid it behind the sofa for the time being. She would tiptoe downstairs early tomorrow and pack it all away before Dom got up.

It felt odd to be keeping things from him, but she smiled a little to herself, discreetly impressed by the nous she had acquired to delve deeper into a world that she was totally unfamiliar with. She would have to tell him in time, but she wasn't ready to share her little secret with her husband just yet.

■■

The next afternoon arrived, and Becky found herself mooching around town after a fairly uneventful morning trapped within the blizzard of chatter that had overtaken the office. The four girls were now planning their witch costumes in infinite detail. It was only cut short when Kay rather tactlessly suggested they get a stuffed cat and tether it to a broom for maximum impact.

Becky had kept out, not really needing to be vocal in the conversation to be a part of it. Their psycho-babble ribboned over her head as she sat, trapped in her own thoughts. She kept chewing the situation over in her mind, weighing up the evidence as she did so. Her own sense of investigative prowess gave her a feeling of *Juliet Bravo*—she sat with her lips pursed and a pencil held to her mouth.

Okay, Brenda Ware was dead. She knew that.

And the cause of death was poison, as stated in the toxicology report.

Yet Gaynor, who was not a witch, but a Wiccan (if Becky believed her) thought that she had been bewitched into taking poison when some sort of dark arts that she had been dabbling in had backfired. That was hearsay.

Apparently, according to Gaynor, this sort of thing happened all the time in Winchcombe. It was like the Midsomer of the sorcery world. Why that was, she had yet to find out.

As fond as she was of Gaynor, she had a feeling that she wasn't really used to having someone as close to her as Becky had been of late, and that closeness had duped Gaynor into letting some sort of cat out of a bag—now it seemed she was frantically backpedalling to try and get the thing back in.

So, what was the motive and who were the suspects?

Well, anyone could be a suspect at this stage. From the toddlers in year two to the hunchbacked caretaker with the moustache like a little, bristled nail brush.

But, at present, the big finger was pointing squarely at one person. One fat, miserable person.

Miss Eames.

Her of stiff, pleated skirt and hideous, tie-neck blouse fame.

She had seen solid evidence that Miss Eames was Miss Ware's next of kin. She had already tried to pacify the children with her crazy theories, which suggested that she was reasonably skilled at inventing elephant-sized cover-ups, and the staff didn't seem to be questioning her either.

And, through the school, she was also directly connected to Miss Wicks, who had disappeared before Becky's time, but who was certainly linked to the mystery somehow.

Perhaps one had led to the other, from Miss Wicks to Miss Ware. Had they practised black magic together? Had they both been bewitched by Miss Eames? Whatever they had become involved in, had it somehow sent them ricocheting into the claws of The Chasm?

Becky's head hurt.

It was so strange how people in this town reacted to something that was so inconceivable. They carried on regardless. As if the broken, despatched body of an uninteresting and unthreatening woman was not worth activating a sweat gland over. It was crazy.

She frowned as she browsed around Cavendish House. She would spend a few minutes in here before catching the bus back, arming herself with a tray of mince that she would, no doubt, turn from an attractive, fleshy pink into a dusty grey merely by introducing it to her kitchen.

She bit her lip as she spun the cap of a perfume bottle around in her hand.

Where should she start with all this? Perhaps it made good sense to go back to the beginning. She put the bottle down and turned to leave, inadvertently hurling herself into the path of another person.

A bag instantly dropped to the floor, sending an array of items scattering away noisily, like a detritus bomb had exploded.

"Oh, god!" the woman cursed. "Oh god, oh god, oh god!"

"Oh, I am so sorry!" Becky babbled. "I wasn't looking where I was going. What a fool I am. Here, let me help."

She bent to the floor, where the woman was on her knees, scrabbling to get the items back into her large shopping bag.

Becky reached for a runaway lip balm and handed it out as one might an olive branch. The woman reached to retrieve it and, as she did, caught Becky's eye.

She was blonde, around the same age as Becky. Plain looking but youthful, with apricot lips and skin like white porcelain. Her hair was slightly messy, and her eyes were tinged with fatigue. Her smile was limp as she took the lip balm back.

"Thank you," the lady said, "it was me really—I never look where I'm going."

She threw the lip balm back in her bag and picked up the last item, a diary with a kitten on the front.

Becky half-laughed.

"That's a cute, little book," she said, "I love cats."

The lady got to her feet and nervously swept a lock of hair from her eyes.

Becky noticed how thin her wrists were, as though they might shatter under the weight of her thin, silver bracelet.

"Oh, you do?" the lady said. Her voice was soft.

"Yes, I hope to get one, but we've just moved so…"

"Oh really, where to?" The lady looked around, as if slightly uncomfortable.

Becky was rarely the confident one in a social situation. She couldn't help but revel in it somewhat.

"Well, not far from here really. In Winchcombe."

The woman's eyes lit up as she heard the words.

"Oh gosh, that's where I live," she said, pushing her hand to her chest.

Becky laughed. She was glad this lady lived near her. She already felt reassured by her presence, as if she had found some sort of kindred spirit by the Tom Ford perfumes.

"I don't suppose you know what time the buses are, do you? I can't seem to get the timetable on my phone," Becky lied. She knew the times—she just wanted an inroad to a conversation or, perhaps, even a lift.

"Oh, there's not one for another thirty minutes. I'll be getting that one back too. I get it every day," the woman blushed, pulling her bag further into her side with a coquettish grin.

"Oh, fantastic. Perhaps we could sit together. You could give me the guided tour," Becky joked, hoping that the woman wouldn't sense her desperation to meet new people who weren't as odd as Gaynor, or as overbearing as Catherine.

The woman laughed, and an awkward silence grew between them.

"Well," Becky said, extending her hand, "I'm Becky."

The woman hesitated slightly before reaching out her own hand in greeting.

"Nice to meet you, Becky," she said. "My name is Robina."

Becky smiled. She liked the name Robina.

They went a little off the beaten track and sat in the window of Boston Tea Party. Becky had always liked the look of it in there. She usually walked past, mouth agog, trying not to stare as hipsters stirred their coffees sulkily, under the watchful eyes of their girlfriends in their funky, oversized specs.

How she had longed for someone to drink with in there but had never had the opportunity. It was far too contemporary a place for Catherine, who would prefer a sweet tea and crumpets in a hotel lounge, and not contemporary enough for Gaynor, whose hot drinks range was far more medicinal than your average Starbucks.

But Becky liked her new friend, she had a good feeling about her. Often it was Becky who felt socially awkward. While other people were speaking to her, she found herself looking through them instead of at them, wondering whether her breath smelt or if her cheeks were noticeably red. She was continuously waiting for the other person to break the conversation, just to tell her she had something on her face, but it never came.

Robina seemed just as clumsy, if not a little more, and it was empowering to find a union that Becky could take control of for once, rather than be controlled in. Robina dithered over the menu and laughed nervously at the end of every sentence.

She was only half-groomed, with wiry, bedraggled strands of hair poking out from the brushed sweep, and threads hanging from a floral skirt that her iron hadn't quite managed to press the creases out of.

Becky wasn't sure whether it was selfish to admit that she didn't see Robina as any type of threat and so she assumed that their friendship would be easy.

When they had ordered their homemade lemonades, Becky had led her over to sit in the window.

"So," Robina said, "when are you due?"

Becky took a long sip of lemonade. It was bitter and sour, not really to her taste, but she imagined that it was healthier than a full-fat caramel latte.

"I've not long had my twelve-week scan, so I'm due for a July baby. In fact, if it's a girl, we may well call her Summer."

That was a lie, but she was feeling relaxed enough to talk garbage.

"That's lovely," Robina sighed, looking out of the window.

"So, what about you? How long have you lived in Winchcombe?" asked Becky, eager to delve a little deeper into Robina's background.

"Oh, I grew up there," she said, mildly astonished that anyone would be interested. "My mother was a fairly proactive resident. On all the committees—she practically made the place what it is today."

Becky raised her eyebrows. Though it was a bold statement, it sounded rehearsed with a slightly disingenuous undertone.

"How interesting, she sounds like an amazing lady. Is she still there?"

"No," Robina said, stirring her drink casually with the accompanying straw, "she died when I was young."

"Oh, I am sorry."

Robina shrugged.

"No amount of town meetings can stave off cancer, I'm afraid." She exhaled again and abandoned the straw.

"No, it's just me and Jessie-Cat now. We have an easy sort of life."

So much of what Robina said was tinged with sadness—Becky's heart ached a little as they spoke. She suddenly felt extremely guilty for having a husband and a child on the way, and not being single with only a cat for company.

Robina wiped a phantom tear from her eye and continued to sip her drink.

"So, do you miss London?" she asked.

Becky shifted uncomfortably in her seat.

"I'm not really sure," she said. "There are parts of it that I miss and parts that I don't. It's a very different way of life here. It's not as crowded, and you don't have to put up with other people and their neuroses. You can get from A to B without feeling like you're wading through treacle. And here, you don't feel entirely anonymous."

Robina looked forlorn as if she would give anything for a day of anonymity. As she began to fidget, something seemed to catch her eye over at the counter. Becky turned to follow her gaze.

Stood at the counter was a girl with long, blonde hair, scratching around in an open bag. Becky recognised her instantly: it was the girl from Cavendish House, the one who had been forcibly removed by the elbow.

The male barista was rolling his eyes as he clutched a takeaway coffee cup in his right hand.

"Miss," the man said with a weary sigh, expelling his last shred of patience, "that will be three pounds fifty ... and we don't do store credit."

"Yes, yes," the girl said, tossing her long locks over her shoulder and digging further into her bag. "I know I packed my purse, it's in here somewhere."

Something about the whole performance made Becky think that the girl was clearly looking for something that she knew wasn't there at all. Becky's mouth hung open as she turned back to Robina.

"Do you know her?" she said.

Robina looked uneasy and set her glass down.

"I've seen her around," Robina said, grabbing her bag with an uncharacteristic sense of haste. "Now, we really must make tracks if we're going to get that bus."

■■■

The next day, Becky sat at her desk, poring over yesterday's events. After they had left the coffee shop, Robina had been noticeably withdrawn and nervous. It was as if seeing that girl had completely spooked her—she had been unable to mask her discomfort, try as she might.

Becky had thought better of inviting her new friend around to see her garden in light of this shift in her behaviour, and instead waved meekly as Robina stepped off the bus a few stops before her, clutching her bag to her chest.

What was it about that girl that evoked such a negative response in everyone? She must be known as some sort of intimidating troublemaker. Becky recognised her type from high school. There had been one absolute horror, Leigh-Anne, who had tormented the entire form for the whole five years. But for a thirty-something woman to be frightened of an eighteen-year-old in this day and age was a bit strange, and Becky just couldn't fathom it.

"Earth to Becky..." Mel's voice permeated her train of thought.

Becky looked down, her face still pensive.

"Sorry," she said, focusing back on her computer and the student records that she had done absolutely bugger all with. "I'm not too far away from the end of these change-of-address forms."

"Never mind that," Mel said, beaming like a Cheshire cat, the ever-present handkerchief dangling from her cardigan sleeve. "We're discussing our Halloween costumes and you're away with the fairies—we were hoping for some input."

"Oh!" Becky gushed, looking around at the other three expectant faces gurning at her.

"What's up with you today? You seem to be in a world of your own." Janice's tone was weighed down with an air of duplicitous prying.

"Oh," Becky stuttered, "Just … err … thinking of baby names."

All four girls cooed in unison, looking at each other in succession.

"So, we're thinking black," Mel said, spinning in her chair, pen and pad at the ready. "I've got a long skirt and cardigans. My whole wardrobe is basically black."

"Slimming..." Becky heard Kay whisper to Tracy from over her desk, which made her smile inwardly. She was starting to think that Kay could be a bit of a handful.

"Well, I think I've got a pointy hat left over from years ago. And I'm sure that balloon place in Cheltenham does plastic witch noses," Tracy chimed in.

"Yes, and those fake, crooked fingers could be a hoot." Mel started sketching things on her pad.

Becky screwed up her face. She didn't fancy spending the whole evening dressed like a crazy, old cat lady with arthritic fingers. It wasn't the kind of first impression she wanted to make to the likes of the infamous Rachel Power.

"You don't look convinced," Mel said, raising her head from the jumbo jotter she was clutching.

"It's not that," Becky protested, "It's just that ... well, I was hoping we could go for something a little more adult."

Kay's mouth turned up at the corner as she dropped her eyes onto her desk.

"Adult?" Tracy asked, leaning forward. "Becky, there will be children there..."

"No!" Becky exclaimed, spinning around. "I don't mean with our doo-dahs hanging out or anything!"

"Heavens," Mel gasped, clutching the pad to her chest.

Becky inwardly cursed her mother for ever having used that terminology to describe any part of the female anatomy.

"I mean, you know, like, sort of ... sexy witches," Becky put forward meekly.

All the girls collectively sat back in their chairs, looking around and pondering the thought.

"We don't need to be the archetypal old hag from the fairy stories, do we? We could be like … Anjelica Houston before she takes the mask off, or the girls from *The Craft*. Or *Charmed*—or *Buffy*!" Becky said, getting rather carried away in her desperation to convince her colleagues that this was a good idea. "I mean, none of us really knows what a modern-day witch looks like, but I highly doubt that they have green skin with warts and wrinkles, like Grotbags or … Pongwiffy."

Janice raised an eyebrow.

"I bet they look, well … sort of like us."

The young girl in the coffee shop searching for her invisible purse suddenly sprang to mind.

"Like, Tracy could have long red hair and dark eye makeup, pointed heels and a broom."

Tracy visualised the look as she chewed on her pencil.

"And Kay could wear fishnets and long, red nails and a black cardigan. And Mel and Janice could be like twins with white skin and tattoos and a black cat."

She wasn't sure how this was going. Nobody seemed to be responding much, just pensively pursing their lips as their eyes roamed around, trying to envisage what this might look like.

Mel was the first to speak.

"Do you know what," she said, "I really like that idea. My legs haven't had an airing since 2007—it's time."

∎∎

Following the success of her earlier suggestion, Becky treated herself to a quick stroll around the playground, checking for any lost property that may have escaped from the children's hands or pockets at playtime. She carried a large box around with her that she could deposit said items in before the lunchtime rush.

As she made her way to the side of the school, she could see a flash of blue in the undergrowth behind the sports hall. This must mean that the door to the sports kit storage room had been left ajar. She tutted to herself. The children knew that they were not allowed in here at break times, not only because it was shrouded in sharp, thorny brambles from which there seemed to be no escape, but also for their own safety, in case the ancient shelves crumbled under their touch and showered them with a deadly avalanche of netballs.

Becky dropped the box and headed over to the rogue door, quietly perplexed as to why any child would want to go in through the back way instead of around the front, thus avoiding the nasty thicket. Unless, of course, they were trying to be inconspicuous.

As she approached the door, she wrapped her sleeve up around her hand, ready to push the thorns aside. She dodged the few stems that threatened to shred her cardigan to pieces before eventually reaching the door. She slowly poked her head inside to see whether there were any children lurking in the storage space. If they were doing anything rebellious, she wanted to catch them red-handed.

The sound of paper crinkling came from beside one of the shelves. The room was small but long. She craned her neck in to see what was going on in the secretive corners of the supposedly empty room.

What she saw surprised her momentarily, and she clasped her hand to her mouth to stop her audibly gasping. It was not the figure of a child who was standing with their back to the door, a little more than halfway down the passage, hiding ineffectually behind one of the hockey puck racks, but the rather generous figure of Miss Eames.

Becky crouched down slightly to get a better look at what was going on. Miss Eames appeared to be holding a rather large gym bag in her left hand and was thrusting her right hand into it as if she was loading it with something.

That was strange. She never came in here. Just to look at her protruding gut, anyone would surmise that the woman had to be allergic to anything remotely connected to exercise. What, then, was she doing in the storage area of the school sports hall?

Miss Eames suddenly stopped what she was doing and took a brief glance over her shoulder towards the open door. Luckily, Becky had now stooped below eye level and so remained in the shadows.

Miss Eames went back to her business, stuffing the bag with what looked like red slips of paper.

As Becky strained to get a closer look, Miss Eames once again peered over her shoulder. As she did, the headmistress leaned slightly over, giving Becky a better view of what she was holding in her hands.

Suddenly, it dawned on Becky that it was not red paper that Miss Eames had been shoving into the bulging gym bag. It was, in fact, crumpled up fifty-pound notes.

Miss Eames halted again, this time for a slightly longer period before turning her head back and carrying on, gaining more speed, plunging her hand in and out of the bag before grabbing another set of fifties from a refuse sack to her left and repeating the operation.

What on earth was she up to?

Becky suddenly heard the first lunchtime bell in the background which made Miss Eames stop altogether. This was an opportune time for Becky to make herself scarce, and so she carefully backed away from the door, still bending down to avoid being seen. As she did so, she felt a thorn stick into her from the side and bit hard down on her lip to keep from yelping out in pain. She stepped out of the doorway, rose to her feet and turned around to escape from the mass of brambles.

Becky turned the corner of the building quickly before colliding with a person head-on.

Sienna Clements was stood directly beside the wall. As Becky rammed into her, she shrieked in surprise.

"Oh *god*, Sienna," she whispered, conscious that she was still very near the open door from which Miss Eames might be emerging any second.

"Miss Dawlish," Sienna said flatly, an accusatory look in her eye, "what are you doing back there?"

"I was ... I was just..." Becky fought for an excuse that just wouldn't come.

Sienna continued to glare, unmoved and waiting for an answer. At only three feet tall, she cast a surprisingly menacing stare.

"I think," Becky said sharply, finding her nerve, "that the question is what are *you* doing back here? You know children aren't supposed to come to this door, least of all when they should be in the lunch hall."

Becky rubbed her side as she spoke—it was still sore from the thorn attack.

Sienna gave an imperceptible shrug, her face fixed like a china doll, her beautiful, blonde hair hung over her shoulders. She really was a little brat.

"Now," Becky said, pulling her own hair out of her eyes and wrapping her cardigan tightly around herself, "I just heard the lunch bell, so off you go."

Becky went to place a hand on Sienna's shoulder, but the little girl jerked free, spun around and sloped nonchalantly away. Becky followed behind, quickening her step as they crossed the playground, leaving Miss Eames to her stuffing.

■■

Becky remained tight-lipped for the rest of her shift. Tracy and Mel continued with their work, stopping intermittently to ponder on what they might wear as a "sexy witch", while Janice and Kay went into the bowels of the school to do some archiving. Unwittingly, Becky had subliminally unlocked a secret compartment in her colleagues' minds. They were each transported to the backs of their wardrobes. To the dusty shelves where jazzier garments used only to snag themselves a husband festered, neglected since their single days and tucked away out of sight forevermore.

A Pandora's box of new and exciting shades of makeup was suddenly introduced into the conversation: blood reds and deadly, nightshade purples instantly replaced their translucent powders and No. 7 eyeshadow palettes. It was as though Becky had awoken four temptresses from underneath their thick, Stepford Wife skins.

Becky's eyes occasionally drifted over to Kay, who was watching her colleagues with contempt, unsure of whether she was inexperienced in this field, or jealous that she hadn't come up with the idea first.

No one noticed that Becky was silent, mulling over the events of the last hour. Remembering the image of Miss Eames frantically loading a gym bag with wads of cash had sent a shiver up her spine. It was totally bizarre behaviour.

Not that this place was averse to a bit of strange conduct. Since she'd moved here, she'd been privy to little else. After her chat with Gaynor, who she hadn't seen in almost a week, the old woman fobbing her off at every given second, she had resigned herself to the fact that kookiness was par for the course in Winchcombe and really, she should just ride the wave and think nothing of it.

She couldn't really blame Gaynor for brushing her off since Becky herself had been ignoring Catherine's advances for just as long. She couldn't be bothered with her at the moment. There were only so many tactless, judgemental swipes that one could sidestep before snapping altogether. Any more and Becky would have to

275

snatch that silly bun hairpiece from off her head and throw it in the bin.

Becky sighed—she had yet to hear from the police regarding her statement and it appeared that, with the upcoming Halloween celebrations looming, the whole school had managed to sweep the Harvest Festival bloodbath clean under the carpet. There was a casual understanding that God worked in mysterious ways and, in response, everyone recited their assembly prayers and sang their hymns even louder to compensate for the seemingly random act of wanton violence. The children seemed more alert and impeccably behaved. Whatever Miss Eames' intentions had been in inventing that ridiculous story, it seemed to have worked in her favour. How ironic that Miss Ware's next of the kin should be the one to erase all trace of her untimely passing in a matter of days.

Suddenly, a thought struck Becky like a sledgehammer—a white-hot surge of panic rose into her chest.

Miss Eames. Next of kin. Money.

A theory began forming in her head.

If Miss Eames was Miss Ware's next of kin, then she stood to inherit all the money in her estate. Not that Becky presumed to know anything of the piano teacher's finances, but surely any money that the old dear had accumulated would now go straight into the hands of her employer. And, from what Becky had noticed about Miss Ware, in her sensible shoes and moth-eaten cardigans, she hadn't been out blowing her ill-gotten millions in Debenhams.

So, if Becky's predictions were true, then it could well have been Miss Eames' inheritance that she was stuffing into that gym bag like a burglar doing over a jewellery store. But why was she hiding it at the school? Why not stash it under the bed at home?

Maybe Miss Eames was disguising it in the deserted, old storage room so as not to arouse suspicion. Keeping it under wraps until she could spend it all on a fancy car or an exotic holiday. Not that Miss Eames looked the type to squander a fortune on either of these things. Her kind of splurge would have been on a new bag of kirby grips and a size eleven pair of Dr Scholl sandals.

Her breathing began to speed up as her heart raced. The more she considered it, the more she convinced herself that it was true.

And, in knowing that she stood to inherit a few grand, could it be that Miss Eames may have had something to do with the possession of Brenda Ware? She had been cautious of Gaynor when they had entered the church and gone to some lengths to smooth over the event at the school. She had, in fact, single-handedly cleared up the whole mess, covering her tracks perfectly—it all made sense.

But what would she do with all that money? She had to have a clear motive for wanting a huge sum of cash.

"Becky?" Mel's voice brought her back into the room.

"Sorry, I was miles away." Becky typed a few phantom letters on her keyboard.

"I said have you got any doctors' appointments booked in?" Mel's neck craned around to speak to her.

Becky thought for a moment.

"Err..."

"I have to put any in for the next two months apparently." Mel scrolled down the open calendar on her desktop.

"Is it due to get busy?" Becky asked while trying to recall her midwife appointment dates.

"No, there's always someone here to cover," Mel said, opening an email. "It's Miss Eames— she's going to be off from next week."

Becky's ears suddenly pricked up.

"Is she really?"

"Yes, a bit of an emergency it would seem. She never takes any time off during term-time, it must be something unavoidable," Mel said, her eyes locked on her screen.

"That's odd," said Tracy, "I've never known her to go away. Unless she's off to Wales to visit her sister"

"Not this time," Mel replied. "It says here that she's going overseas and won't be contactable.

No idea why." She shrugged and turned back to the screen.

Becky's heart continued to pound—the old cow was doing a runner.

She had to act fast.

■■■

Nearing the end of her shift, Becky practically hurled herself out of the door and through the open gate. The girls had watched, open-mouthed, as she'd mumbled something about leaving the gas on and tripped clean over her chair in her haste to get out of the office.

In minutes, she was home, scrambling around in the drawers of her dresser. Where was that damned card with that officer's number on?

She found it, hiding under a box of matches. Becky picked the card up and turned it over in her hand. The baby inside her span along with it, making her feel queasy.

Becky wondered whether she was jumping to conclusions with all this. It had happened so fast that she'd not really had time to process it all rationally. Was Miss Eames truly responsible for this madness? Was she capable of bewitching Brenda Ware into poisoning herself so that she could jump on a flight with all her money? How could so much happen in a week? And how had she managed to get herself so involved?

She rushed over to the sink and heaved a few times, but nothing came up. In truth, she hadn't really eaten much in the last couple of days, so it was understandable.

The best thing, she thought, was just to hand the information over to the police and they could make the decision as to whether it sounded like a plausible theory or not. Becky was not the expert—she was just an innocent bystander in all this. She needed to alert the professionals and let them take it from here. And she had to do it before the woman fled to Mexico or wherever and got away scot-free.

She couldn't let that happen. She had to see that, if there was any truth in her speculation, Miss Eames was brought to justice. Becky had to avenge the murder of poor, old Miss Ware, an innocent piano teacher who was duped and robbed by a callous and unfeeling old harridan.

She took the phone from its holder and dialled the number on the card with shaky fingers.

After a couple of rings, a woman answered.

"Almes," she said. Her voice was cold. In the background, Becky could hear voices and typing.

"Hello," Becky whimpered.

"Hi, can I help?" She was officious—no nonsense. It was quite intimidating. Becky wanted to just hang up and forget about everything, crawl into bed and not come out for a very long time. The stress that accompanied the complexity of this revelation could not be good for the life growing inside her. Therefore, she had to pass it on and relinquish herself of this responsibility.

"Hello, officer," she said, with a more confident tone, "my name is Mrs Dawlish. Becky. We spoke the other day?"

There were a few moments of silence on the other end, presumably while the detective searched her memory.

"Ah yes, Becky. How can I help?" Her voice became softer which made Becky relax.

"Well," she said, slightly hesitantly, "I'm sure it's nothing—just me being overly cautious."

The woman did not respond.

"It's the Brenda Ware case. I know something," Becky said, gripping onto the receiver with both hands.

"Okay, Becky," Almes replied, "would you like me to stop by?"

■■

Officer Almes spent a good hour combing through all the finer details with Becky. As she spoke, Becky kept glancing at her. Her simple haircut, her plain features. Her dull, navy, two-piece suit and matte, black shoes. They were sensible, no frills. As though they had been bought for purpose, not for pleasure. She couldn't imagine Almes ever feeling as though she looked a million dollars. She was a practical woman—there appeared to be no room for luxury in her life.

A couple of times, Becky had been so caught up in imagining Almes' backstory that she had failed to respond to her inquisitor. She envisioned her house, her mind awash with magnolia walls and beige carpets. Functional bits and bobs from IKEA that fulfilled duties but didn't entirely match. She wanted to ask her whether she had a husband, children, a pet. But then, it wasn't down to Becky to be asking the questions and she didn't want to seem impertinent if she started screwing up her face at the answers she was given.

She had explained to Officer Almes everything she knew. The toxicology report, which of course the police had been aware of, the fact that Miss Eames was Miss Ware's next of kin, another thing that Almes knew already.

It was when she reached the subject of money that Officer Almes' eyebrows raised. She was interested in how Miss Eames had seemed in the sports hall, her deportment. Was she slow or quick, self-conscious or brazen? Were the notes placed in the bag or were they crammed in? Did Becky know anything more about where the money could have come from?

"Look, I don't really know anything else. I just thought it was odd. And the fact that she is going away—"

"Going away where?" Almes' interrupted, pen poised over open pad.

"I don't know, somewhere overseas. She never takes time off apparently, but for some reason, she's now taking a holiday. Don't you think that's weird?"

Almes half-shrugged and noted it all down.

Becky no longer wanted this woman in her front room, she just wanted to forget that any of this had happened. It made her vision cloudy and her head hurt. The officer was making her feel nervous, like a frightened child who was telling tales on the class bully. She didn't want to feel like this in her own house. She wanted to run away.

As Officer Almes was leaving, she picked up her plain bag.

"Listen, I think you should keep what you saw to yourself," she said firmly. "Until we've run a few background checks, we can't be sure that the money isn't legitimate. We don't want to throw any accusations around at this stage."

Becky nodded. She had no one to tell anyway—friends weren't exactly banging the door down at the moment.

Almes gave her a strained smile before leaving. Becky heaved a sigh of relief as she closed the door and walked back through her lounge.

She had better get the dinner on. Dom would be home soon. She had to go back to her timid little existence for the evening. She might get some time to study the Wicca book that Gaynor had given her if he was tired from a hard day's work and took straight to his bed. In fact, she found herself hoping for more and more time alone than she did time with her husband.

As she crossed to the kitchen, her eyes drifted to the black mark that was festooned across the wall. It seemed to frown back at her with dark defiance. She then thought back to the faded photograph of Miss Wicks that had been removed from the school wall, moments after she had spotted it.

"What the hell has happened in this town?" she said to herself and put her hand to her head.

■■■■■■■■■■■■■■■■■■■■■■■■■■■■■■■■■■■■■■

Laura closed her laptop and sighed. She could hear the rolling credits of *Breaking Bad* in the next room and was certain that Ben would be popping out for a sly cigarette after it was finished.

She hated that.

While they were trying to conceive, the last thing she wanted was his fag-ash breath all over her. As it stood, the sex wasn't very romantic anyway—more of a feat of endurance. An exercise that was carried out more for practical purposes rather than pleasurable ones, but second-hand cigarette smoke made it even less appealing.

How long had it been? Months of endless thrusting and jack-knifing. The moans of ecstasy had morphed into dutiful grunts, the soft touch and foreplay replaced with bruising grips and hard slaps of skin against skin. The climax was always one of release, a pipe bursting with pressure rather than a champagne cork popping in celebration.

They would lie there, side by side, a thin, gossamer-like film of grimy sweat covering them both. She was gluey inside, tilting her pelvis so that the liquid would spill into her uterus, willing for it to coat her with its thick residue.

It had become her obsession. So much so that she wasn't thinking about Ben unless he was inside her. It seemed that, currently, she only needed him for one thing and one thing only. And if he couldn't give her that, what was he good for?

She just wanted a fucking baby.

At first, Ben had suggested it. He had looked at her all doe-eyed and rested his hand on her belly. His touch had sent electric spasms into her and, somehow, that moment had ignited this infatuation within her heart. There was no going back from this point. She had shifted from go-getting career woman to wannabe mother in an instant. Not getting this baby was the same as not achieving her KPIs in the sales office: non-negotiable.

Her success in life had been based solely on her performance, and that is how she intended to continue. Getting pregnant was nothing more than another goal to be achieved and no one was going to stop her. What she hadn't budgeted for was the fact that it takes two people an equal amount of effort to produce a baby. She wasn't sure that Ben was as pragmatic as her when it came to these things. He needed some serious coaching, and that is exactly what she had set out to do.

And he had been a dutiful student, always there, even when he was tired or grouchy. Never flaccid, although it had taken a few pornographic magazines to butter the toast at times. He wasn't averse to trying out even the most ridiculous of positions to try and get a better angle of shot, so to speak.

But then, sometimes, it's not the student's will that is defunct, but more their wiring. There is something within that person that just cannot do the job, no matter how much promise they show.

Sometimes, Laura, she thought to herself, *you just hang your head and admit that you've been beaten. Take on another hobby—move on.*

But defeat wasn't in her vocabulary. She didn't give in—she didn't just hang up her hat and sigh melancholically. It didn't happen with the Bradshaw account, and it wasn't going to happen here.

She needed a plan B—an alternative pitch. She just couldn't lay her hands down and let the humiliation of failure wash over her. She wouldn't be able to look at her husband again, knowing that he was the reason that she had been trounced. She wouldn't be able to look at herself.

She had to now seek a different path, one that could be relied on. If her husband couldn't supply the goods, then she would need to find someone that could. She wasn't intending to repeatedly tap this source, it had to be a one-shot thing. She had to know instantly that it was going to work. She needed to know that the source was fertile.

If she was going to be impregnated by somebody else, she needed him to have done it before.

The door opened gingerly, and Ben's face appeared through the gap. His expression was one of dutiful acceptance.

Laura looked at him coldly.

"You're off the hook tonight," she said, "I don't feel like it."

The words sounded strange coming out of her mouth.

■■

Catherine reapplied her lip liner and snapped the mirror shut.

"Listen," she said icily to the woman stood opposite her, "I've heard that you are good, and I'm not adverse to paying extra for quality."

The woman wrung a tea towel nervously in her hand. She was clearly buckling under

Catherine's scrutiny, and so she should— Catherine could crush this woman like an insect if she was so inclined.

"I just wanted to know how you got my name," the woman stuttered.

Catherine looked around the kitchen. It was simple but homely. The attractive, low ceiling couldn't detract from the thousands of cat ornaments that lined the shelves, depreciating the property's value in an instant.

"Okay, Rowena," she said, throwing the mirror back in her bag, "I have a lot to do before this blasted party, and baking a cake comes decidedly low down the list. However, I am not prepared to just *turn up* without an offering—I'd never live it down."

The woman nodded, her hands not releasing the rolled-up cloth that they were clutching.

"So, what I need is for someone to help me out—for a *substantial* fee—and keep up the pretence that it was I who baked it."

Catherine smiled an acidic smile.

She didn't want to be here, begging this stranger to enter into some kind of illicit, baking-related tryst with her, just to save face in front of Rachel Power. It was just that the construction of the family's increasingly elaborate costumes was starting to get a little out-of-hand and she needed a bit of extra help if she was going to finish them *and* produce some kind of culinary delight to impress the entire town. She had awoken one morning to find that the arm of Sienna's headless monster costume had gone a bit limp and she wasn't sure why. She had clearly remembered leaving the heating on so that it could set, and further investigation proved that the heating had been turned off. The little bitch had probably sabotaged her efforts so that she didn't have to wear the blasted thing. She'd be smiling on the other side of her face when Catherine made her stand by the radiator for an hour with her arm held aloft, just to make sure her little prank didn't repeat itself while Catherine's back was turned.

"I have it on good authority, from one of the society school *moms*," she continued, "that you are an excellent baker and I would really like you to agree to help me."

She usually hated Americanisation's, but everyone was doing it nowadays.

It had been Grace De Monfort, Christie's mother, who had tipped Catherine off that this woman could be counted on for superstar bakes at a nominal fee. The person opposite her now, however, seemed less than convinced.

"But," she began, "I'm not sure I'm the best—"

"Oh, do cut the false modesty, my dear—it's tiresome," Catherine snapped as she fished around for a twenty in her Kate Spade purse.

She proffered the banknote between two beautifully manicured fingernails.

"Your deposit," she said, slamming it down on the kitchen table and sliding it over to the wide-eyed lady. "Now—will you help me or not?"

Robina sighed and nodded reluctantly.

A devilish grin tinged the corners of Catherine's mouth.

THIRTEEN

Bernice was now wide awake.

She found it ridiculous how she could do nothing all day and yet somehow still be tired.

Ever since the call from Odette, her mind had been reeling. Just what had this woman said to Joanna to make her do a complete one-eighty? Had her tormentor really changed her mind or had she been strong-armed into it? A quick call to Laura had not put her mind at rest. She had sounded positively preoccupied and uninterested in Bernice's plight. That seemed odd, since she had not seen or heard from Laura in a long time, and she had always been her favourite in the coven.

"Can you hear me?" A voice whispering through the darkness broke Bernice's concentration.

She tried to ignore it—she wasn't really in the mood. A few taps crept up the bedroom wall and back down.

There was a moment's silence as the air, once again, grew still.

"I'm lost, can you hear me?" The voice was soft but there was a tinge of urgency in it. This didn't bother Bernice. They were always distressed and rightly so. She looked over at the dresser across the room that shuddered lightly, knocking her bottles of perfume together. This was commonplace as well.

"Hello? I think I'm lost." It was a young woman's voice.

Bernice let out a long sigh. If they knocked her Thierry Mugler off the table, she would get really pissed off.

"Hello?"

This one wasn't going to give up.

"Hello," said Bernice. Her voice sounded like a man's—a pissed off man, at that. When she was angry, she couldn't disguise her masculine temper.

The air was still for a moment.

"Are you over by the wardrobe?" Bernice asked. She knew better than to snap the light on. It would startle her visitor and she didn't want to do that. Many would be frightened away from escape if they were intimidated by communication.

"I ... I think so," came the response. "I'm looking for the trauma ward?"

Bernice felt sorry for the woman—she thought she was still in the hospital.

"Can you help me?" The lady sounded as though she was beginning to sob.

Bernice didn't want to appear harsh, but then she had to detach herself from the emotion of it all, otherwise, she would get too affected. Often, she had to appear stoic and, if there was a particularly harrowing story involved, she would shed a little tear later on, out of earshot.

She sighed.

"I'm sorry to have to tell you this, my dear, but you … you didn't make it."

There was a long silence.

Bernice tried again. Usually, she didn't offer them this much attention after dark, but then she was wide awake, so this one had gotten lucky.

"I'm afraid that you have died."

There were a few short gasps, a sign of utter devastation.

"What you need to do," Bernice said calmly, "is to go back to a place that means something to you and wait. All will become clear in a matter of hours."

In truth, Bernice had no idea what happened to the poor, tortured soul in those long hours after death, since no one had ever come back to tell her. She was just there to guide them along to the next life. How and when that happened was still a complete mystery to her. Of course, some revisited, but they were often the sort that never spoke the truth, in life or in death. They were usually overly gregarious and would return with tall tales of white lights, unicorns and black shadows, apparently urging them to depart from the earth. But Bernice, unconvinced, would always have the same response: "Well, why didn't you go then?"

All she knew for certain is that most souls accepted the invitation and left this earth. If they hung around, they generally weren't worth taking.

A few more cries hung in the air.

"I'm sorry," Bernice said, "but that's the only help I can offer. And I suggest you don't waste time. Whatever means you are given to get out of here, it will only happen once. And if you're not there to board it, then it's gone forever."

There were a few sniffs and snuffles.

"Thank you," the voice whimpered. "I'd better go back to our house—Richard might be there."

Richard ... Richard. She tried to place the name. The only person she could think of was Richard Brooke, the gardener. If that was his wife, then she had been young—it must have been spontaneous.

That was always a gut-wrencher. When there was a fatality completely out of the blue, the voices were often bewildered and lost. This one, however, seemed to be more accepting than some.

After one particularly vocal spirit had refused to accept Bernice's help and remained trapped in her bedroom for over three hours, wailing incessantly, Bernice swore to herself that it was not to happen again. And so, she hardened herself up pretty quickly to chivvy them on in a sterner manner. After all, it wasn't her fault that she was able to speak to the dead.

"Could you tell me," the voice asked through choked tears, "did he make it?"

'Sorry?"

"Richard—did he make it to my bedside?" The voice sounded desperate.

Bernice gulped down the rock that was lodged in her throat. Tears pricked her eyes as she nodded in the dark.

"Of course," she said, her throat pinched, "he would never leave you on your own."

She listened for a moment as a tear trickled silently down her cheek, but the voice was gone.

■ ■

As Becky walked up to the school, a bitter chill whipped around her, forcing her to pull her scarf tighter around her neck. October had been relatively warm thus far, but today there was a definite bite in the air that had been palpable from the moment she had wriggled out from under the duvet.

She had flung open the downstairs curtains to be met with a torrent of autumnal leaves swooshing across the pane.

As she stood, cradling a sweet tea in one hand and caressing her bump with the other, she watched the trees in the distance, bending with the pull of Mother Earth.

The goddess is out in force today, she had thought, suddenly taken aback that she had referred to the goddess instinctively without having trained herself prior. She was obviously absorbing more of Gaynor's teachings than she had thought herself capable of. But then she had been studying quite hard recently, out of the sight of her husband. The various notes she had made were hidden in various nooks and crannies in the house where they wouldn't be discovered, and she had rather ingeniously set up a makeshift altar on an old hostess trolley that her mother had given her, shoved right at the back of the cupboard under the stairs, to be wheeled out only when Dom had gone to bed.

Becky liked this sense of purpose, but she felt bad about hiding it, hoping that it wasn't driving a wedge between them. In truth, however, Becky wasn't sure whether they spoke more or less today than they had ever done. It was only now that she was excluding him from this activity that she realised he didn't seem to have any interest in what she was doing with her time. She felt she knew him more, the less time she spent with him.

She smiled to herself nonetheless. Gaynor would be very pleased with her progress. If only she would answer the door every now and again. She seemed to spend more and more time in solitude. Last time Becky had arrived uninvited, Gaynor had looked tired, almost frail with exhaustion. She had not invited her in but instead said quite politely that it was not a good time. Becky had reached a hand out to her and asked if everything was okay.

"It will be," came the answer, and the door was slowly closed.

But now that she was on her way up to the school, it felt as if something had shifted. Not because she had ratted on Miss Eames. The way Almes had dealt with that had made Becky feel even more stupid for ever questioning the old bag's motivations. No, this sudden rush of optimism—perhaps it was because Becky was starting to feel as though she belonged in this town. It was the idea that, though the idiosyncrasies of folk in this town in this town often defied belief, life was really happening here. It was a good place to be a woman.

Women were strong, they were stoic and proud, devious and shrewd. They created magic and had faith in the female spirit that spearheaded their worship. Becky didn't feel like the little sparrow that Dom so often termed her, as she had followed him around in London. Here, she felt as though she shared a perch with more fearsome, predatory birds. She was beginning to feel a connection to something much deeper.

She rounded the corner and noticed that there was an unusual vehicle parked at the school gates. A crowd of mothers had gathered, whispering to each other and pointing across the playground. She strained slightly to hear what was being said.

She could only make out snippets of sentences and gleaned from this that the car had been there some time and that someone inside the school was a "prime suspect".

Becky stopped in her tracks and backed up a little until she was shrouded by some low-hanging branches a few metres away from the throng.

This was an uncommon sight. Usually, the mothers dropped their little darlings off and rushed straight back to their Tassimo machines and ITV2. She tried to look at the number plate on the white saloon car, but it didn't mean anything to her.

At that moment, the main school doors were flung wide open and three figures stepped through. As they came closer, Becky's heart rose into her throat and her entire body went cold.

In the middle of these three people was Miss Eames, her hair was slightly tousled, and she wore a sombre look on her face—she stared at the ground as she walked. Either side of her were the two officers who had not long been sat in Becky's living room, Almes and Wilkinson. They also looked particularly serious as they strode slightly behind their portlier companion.

What the hell is going on?

Becky felt foolish listening to her internal dialogue—she knew exactly what was going on.

As the three figures approached the car, Becky stood out from behind the fauna to get a good look at the old woman's face. Would her cast-iron nonchalance now be replaced by a remorseful grimace?

As Becky squinted to see, Miss Eames took one last look up before she was made to duck into the back seat. It was then that she caught Becky's eye.

Becky was filled with an uncomfortable panic that bubbled up inside from the pit of her stomach. She didn't know what to do or where to place herself under such an accusatory glare. She knew that, in this instance, she should have felt empowered, yet she still felt like a naughty schoolgirl.

Miss Eames stopped for a moment, as her retinas bore into Becky. She was determined not to drop her gaze. Becky tried to keep her cool, although she had never felt more awkward. The woman's face did not change. It was neither a sympathetic or a warning glare. It was just a glare.

After what seemed like an eternity, Miss Eames' lips parted to speak. The entire crescent of onlookers silenced themselves to hear the words. It was like Moses delivering the ten commandments.

Becky could hear her heart thumping in her eardrums.

"I beg you," Miss Eames said, her voice defeated. "Be careful."

And that was all that she said. It wasn't threatening or tinged with malice but said more with an advisory, concerned tone.

Suddenly, Almes sprang into action.

"Okay, Miss Eames, let's move this along," she said, pushing her hand down on to Miss Eames' head to guide her into the car.

Miss Eames dropped her gaze, stooping and climbing in through the opened door. As Almes slammed it shut, she walked around to the driver's seat, catching Becky's eye on the way.

She nodded ever-so-slightly, and opened her own car door, sliding herself inside. As the car backed out, a few of the mothers parted their way to let it through. The car reversed slowly, accelerated and off it went up the main high street, towards Cheltenham.

A few of the mothers noticed Becky, their stares lingering for slightly too long. She didn't know what to do with herself. Whether she could go to work knowing what she knew. Whether other people had guessed that it was her who had called the police on their beloved—but ultimately crooked—headmistress.

In a moment of nerve, Becky pulled her bag further up her arm and strode on through the crowd. She had absolutely nothing to hide, why should she bear the brunt of somebody else's actions? She would have to stay strong for Brenda Ware's sake. That poor, old woman never even got a chance at vengeance. Becky should feel proud that she had given it back to her.

But as she got to the door, the realisation hit her. Her suspicions were true. It really had been Miss Eames who had orchestrated this nefarious deed, right under everyone's noses and, if that was the case, who knows what else she might have done in her time at the school. They must have all been in danger for a very long time. And, in light of such a revelation, was Miss Wicks just another victim? What had she meant before she got in that car? *Be careful.* Was the perpetrator still at large?

■■■■■■■■■■■■■■■■■■■■■■■■■■■■■■■■■■■■■■■

Marge wiped a few droplets of perspiration from her brow.

"Howard, how can you possibly ask me to do such a thing? Have you any idea—"

She had been on the phone with the consultant for well over an hour now and the conversation was going nowhere. After a few days of searching the hospital, they were no closer to finding the missing body that had been sent over from Winchcombe.

This man was now getting on her nerves and making her unnecessarily edgy. She suddenly felt as though she was on fire.

"I'm just asking you to not mention it in your write-up—say you've filed the paperwork and that is that."

His voice was going through her. He had the kind of clipped cadence that she found infuriating. He sounded like one of those private school-educated yuppies who held a scalpel and wanted some sort of award for doing so.

"Howard, that would be totally impractical. I mean, her family are going to want to lay her to rest. How on earth are we going to get around that?"

Marge stole a quick look at her watch. She was already an hour late and Frank would be very annoyed if she didn't get home for the dog.

"Well, have there been any enquiries?" It was a rhetorical question—he knew there hadn't. They both knew. It had been their focus for the last few days as they had frantically scoured the Cheltenham Infirmary together, all the while trying to keep the blunder a secret from their closest work colleagues.

"It doesn't matter," Marge complained, "the press could get hold of it. We could lose our jobs. It would be another Karen Griffiths all over again."

She shuddered at the thought of the legendary case from 1965, long before her time. It had made national news when the body of a sixteen-year-old girl who was meant to be lying in their morgue had ended up on its way to Ostend in a bag of skipped rubbish. All involved were investigated and the hospital nearly prohibited. She couldn't allow for that kind of cock-up on her watch. It was inconceivable.

"Then what?" said Howard, sounding tired and exasperated.

She sighed.

"I don't know." She wiped her brow again. "I guess we can stall for another couple of days. I'll keep the paperwork open—we'll just have to keep looking."

There was silence on the other end of the phone.

"Now, I must go, I need to walk Branston," she said, not waiting for a goodbye before she hung up the phone.

Dragging her coat on, she exited through the back door and heaved her generous body onto the external fire escape. It was worth checking the rubbish bags just once more. Brenda Ware's body couldn't have simply vanished.

■■■■■■■■■■■■■■■■■■■■■■■■■■■■■■■■■■■■■■■

Wing was deep in thought as she washed up the mugs. What was going on in this town? She had never experienced such strange people.

In her homeland, magick had been revered, celebrated even. But here, they seemed to be ashamed of it. It was like her weight. Back home, being round was a sign that you enjoyed life, that your existence was full of flavour and

303

indulgence. Here, it was something to be apologetic for. She didn't know whether she was more disgusted with herself for not living by the traditions of her forefathers, or whether she was more regretful of letting the great English tradition of eternal flagellation rub off on her so quickly.

She shook her head as she swilled a white cup under the running water. This coven she was in, these women—who were they?

They weren't shamans. They were just amateurs playing with cut-and-paste spells, but never really capitalised on their true powers.

Whoever heard of a witch who sits with her head stuffed in a book all day? She should be out, casting and throwing her energies to the elements.

She had heard that, at the solstice, Joanna would go under the cover of darkness with a blunt blade and recite some old poem under the boughs of a willow tree. In her country, they would cover their bare breasts in paint, beating drums and winding string around each other to bind the circle closer and ward off evil entities. Their worlds couldn't be further apart.

These English women—magick needs fire and earth, not moonlight, tea and scones! They came from different parallels and belief systems. It was stifling for Wing not to be able to do things in her own way.

But then, she was not on familiar soil here— she had to keep a low profile. Accepting that was hard, but Joanna had made it clear on the day that they had met: "We do things a certain way in this order. We do things *my* way."

It was clear that Joanna wanted Wing to know who was boss. If the conversation had taken place in the Thai desert, the wind would have laughed her arrogance away. Joanna's wisdom was no match for the energy of the shamanic circle. She would be regarded as a foolish woman who was imprisoned by her own academia.

One day, Wing might just snap and show Joanna the full extent of her powers.

"Wing, are those mugs nearly ready? Judge Rinder's nearly on so they'll be wanting their tea!"

Jane, the other carer poked her rosy-red face around the door.

"Two minute," Wing replied, nodding and smiling.

Jane stopped as if to say something, then thought better of it. She didn't want to have to bark at Wing since she meant well. Even if she was a little bit slower in action.

Wing smiled to herself. Perhaps she would be able to flex her muscles inside the coven one day. She was so tired of being the nervous, shrinking violet. But then, she had the kids and her husband to think of. How would it look if she started turning this little town on its head with powers blowing in from all four corners? It just wouldn't be practical.

She couldn't help feeling that, with all her Eastern magick expertise, being in this coven was a bit like an Olympic swimmer being in a paddling pool—there was absolutely no contest.

But, true to form, she would never, ever say anything like that out loud.

■■

"And she was just … carted off, there and then?" As the words tumbled out of Catherine's mouth, they became more and more shrill. They were beginning to feel as though they would perforate Becky's eardrum.

"Yes."

"And they gave *no* explanation at all?"

"Not really."

Becky was trying to be as vague as possible. Ever since she had witnessed Miss Eames being frog-marched out of the school and into an unmarked cop car, everyone wanted a piece of her. Particularly the local press, who had been scavenging around every café, every pub, every park bench, seemingly all armed with a threatening-looking Dictaphone, just in case a juicy soundbite materialised out of thin air.

The owners of these eateries had been happy enough since those camped out at the coffee tables in their bay window had bought enough drinks to boost the local economy by a few quid.

Becky had read the headlines in the Echo.

Local Head and the Long Arm of the Law.

They had, in fact, managed to keep up the anatomical analogy for an entire paragraph—a sure-fire sign of intelligent journalism. There was something about paying *lip service* and giving rules and regulations the *cold shoulder*. Becky had only skimmed through to see what angle they were giving the story.

According to the Echo, she was wanted on money laundering offences. I guess that was a safe approach. The whole idea of being a prime murder suspect had not yet been uncovered, but it wouldn't be long. Perhaps Almes had been holding back, only giving the press what they needed to hear.

She had heard from Almes that afternoon. It was a short, clipped telephone call to say that Becky's information had been very useful and that it had sparked further investigation. She also hinted that speaking to the press would be a bad idea and to call if she had any other info.

And now she had to put up with a telephone call from Catherine. In truth, she had expected it to be Almes again, or perhaps even Gaynor, so she had foolishly picked it up. If it had been Gaynor, she would have been overjoyed. She missed her and was falling back on her study somewhat with all this happening. She wanted to know what the ballsy, old Welsh woman would make of all this.

She would throw her hands up in the air and say, "The goddess will always sniff out the serpent."

However, once Becky heard the ever-so-saccharine tones of her other estranged neighbour, Catherine, she realised her mistake and automatically felt sick.

Obviously, Catherine had wanted to pick over the bones of what had really happened at school but had thinly disguised the phone call as one of genuine interest. Unfortunately, Catherine Clements was about as subtle as a breezeblock through a plate glass window and Becky had to work overtime to play along with her friend's pseudo-concern.

"Listen," Catherine said after a mild pause, "I wanted to call earlier but I have been so tied up with these blasted costumes. Sienna's chicken wire is cutting my hands to ribbons—and *Michael*! Well, let's just say that making a papier-mâché of one's face might come easily to the likes of Madame Tussauds, but—"

"It's fine, Catherine, honestly. I've been really busy myself."

There was another pause.

"Really, doing *what*?"

Becky didn't know whether that was a question or a dig at the fact that she had zero hobbies.

Becky thought for a moment.

"Baby stuff," she said as if Catherine had been stupid to ask.

"Oh, well of course."

"Listen, Catherine, hopefully, we can have a proper chat about it when we see each other at the party." She was trying to rush her on.

"Oh." Catherine clearly wasn't used to being shunted mid-flow. Becky had learned, however, that if she didn't busy her along, she would find herself falling into the sinkhole of self-loathing and pity that Catherine so often liked to open.

"Listen, I must dash. Dom has just got home and—"

"Oh Dom, how is he?" Catherine's voice began to pick up again.

"He's well, we're all well. Everything's well. So ... bye!"

Becky placed the phone down as Catherine's solemn farewell came down the receiver. She pondered a moment.

She couldn't go on like this, chewing theories over and over in her head—she'd go barmy. Particularly at work, where Mel, Kay, Janice and Tracy were desperately trying to ignore the fact that the school was currently the subject of a massive fraud scandal. Their tiny brains couldn't conceive it and for most of the last two days, they had just wandered aimlessly about with little purpose or direction. It was like the mother bird that was keeping the unit together had flown for the first time, leaving the baby eaglets to fend for themselves.

Becky chewed her lip. She needed to offload her concerns and there was only one person that she really felt able to talk to right now. She made for the door and grabbed her coat, nearly throwing herself full-pelt into her husband, who was arriving home from work.

"Hey," he exclaimed, putting his arms out, "steady on. Where are you off to?"

"Oh, sorry," she said, brushing past him, not really concentrating on her words. "I'm just popping out. But there are some sausages in the fridge."

She slid out of the door and onto the street, the rain spotting onto her face.

"Hey, hang on!" Dom called after her, but she had already jogged to a few doors down.

"I won't be long!" she called behind her as she pulled her hood further over her head.

As she kept walking, the rain started to turn from dots into a mild downpour. The sky darkened as the droplets became heavy and forceful.

Becky kept striding as she felt the water run down her face, soaking into the cotton of her hood. It was really starting to come down now, but she didn't care. Her thirst for knowledge was too strong for even this heavy shower to quell.

She marched on past the school, not looking to her left. She didn't even want to look at the brick building, casting its shadow on the rainy playing field. She had just about had enough of that place. The whole sorry turn of events had spooked her so much that she never wanted to go back, especially after she had been feeling so optimistic on her way to the school the morning Miss Eames had been taken away.

There were only two words to describe what had been going on in that place: fucked up. And she never used *that* word.

She moved on until she reached the wall with the cracked, white paint, the ivy cascading over the other side like water spilling over from a boiling pan. They looked ever-so-slightly unkempt as if they hadn't been tended to in a while.

It had only been a week since Becky had last walked up to the cottage, yet the declining state of the foliage was instantly noticeable.

She rushed past the wall and down the stone path to the door. A dull, grey light illuminated one of the windows. It wasn't late. Gaynor must be in because of Dai—she couldn't leave his side. Becky recalled the image of the old man's face staring back up at her from the bed, features frozen but eyes still twinkling.

Becky hesitated for a moment, then swallowed and knocked on the door. Again, nobody answered. It had been like this the last two times—Gaynor couldn't ignore her forever.

The rain started to pour down now. It ran off the sleeves of her coat, turning her fingers to shards of ice.

She stood back a little, trying to get a glimpse of what kind of light might be shining behind the curtain, lighting up the room. It certainly didn't look like one of the bulbs from the ancient lamps Gaynor had all over the house. It was somehow ethereal.

Becky's voice was loud from outside of the window, but Gaynor kept her thoughts inward and her mind focused.

The lumelight hung over Dai's chest. It rose and fell with all the strength of a piece of tissue paper.

"Gaynor?" she called. She spoke forcefully to be heard over the rain.

"Gaynor, I just want to know that everything is alright—I'm worried about you."

She was being sweet in her concern, Gaynor knew that, but she just couldn't give her any energy, not when she was so low on it herself. She spent all night casting and most of the day resting. Her complexion was sallow, and her bones ached. Even her lumelight was starting to dull a little.

She tried to block the outside noise from her mind.

"I— I just want to talk," Becky continued.

Gaynor reached and touched her husband's frail arm. His skin was cool and soft but, under her touch, she could feel it fragmenting.

Gaynor didn't have the strength to shed a tear—she was exhausted.

"Gaynor, please?" The voice began to crack. "I think I'm afraid."

That one would certainly hurt Gaynor if she let it, but at that moment, her mind was homing in on that small ball of light, the casting energy that hovered above her husband's heart, keeping it beating steadily. To lose focus would be to lose him, and she couldn't do that.

She let her fingers reach out to the light itself. As she touched it, a thin stem of white speared itself from the centre and onto her fingertip. She felt a little jolt in her breast.

"Goddess," she whispered, "Goddess of Light, light his way. Let him not go. Goddess. Let him not go."

The words hung on her dry lips.

She may be able to sleep soon, she thought. How much longer must this go on?

As she heard Becky's steps retreating down the path, Gaynor let out a long breath and the light in front of her pulsed.

She looked down at Dai—he looked so peaceful.

Soon it would be over, and they would both get some sleep.

313

When Becky returned home, she was soaked to the skin. Dom was waiting for her. He sat on the sofa, turning the sport down on the television.

She wandered in, dazed, the rain splattering onto the carpet as she closed the door and dragged herself onto a chair.

"Hey," Dom called to her, but his voice sounded as though it was shrouded in cotton wool. "Is everything okay?"

She turned to him, but he looked different to her—almost alien. As if she had no idea who he was.

"I think he's gone," she said.

FOURTEEN

It was the week of the party and Becky was feeling sicker than ever. She didn't think that she was going to be able to make it. The continuing stress of the situation at the school had taken its toll on the entire workforce. They had been constantly badgered by the press. One pitiless reporter had even dressed as a mobile librarian to try and infiltrate the school boundaries—it was utter mayhem.

Parents had been amazing in rallying together against such breaches of security, even sending some of the stockier dads to parade the perimeter of the school grounds to scare off any slippery journalists who might be tempted to run the gauntlet, barging in and creating a disturbance.

The kids hadn't even noticed the difference, really. They appeared to be as normal as normal could be. One of the governors had turned up, an absolute shrew of a woman, who had stared at Becky down her long, ski-slope of a nose as she

315

waited in the reception area. She addressed the children in an officious and cold manner, telling them that they may be asked questions about what had happened to their headmistress and that they were to direct these inquisitors to their parents or the school. As far as they were concerned, Miss Eames was helping the police with a few questions about what was going on in the town and that was that. Days later, the furore calmed down. The local rags went back to covering bin thefts and bus stop graffiti and life returned to relative normality. Nobody was particularly concerned. Apart from Becky.

"I just don't understand what has been going on," she had said one Monday afternoon. Becky could tell by the look of desperation on their faces that Mel, Kay, Janice and Tracy didn't want to get into it. It was as if the room was bugged.

"Well," she continued, putting down her coffee cup, "since no one around here is going to say anything about it, I thought I should—"

"How about we go through the details of our costumes again?" Mel interrupted quickly, a quiver in her voice as she spoke.

Becky sighed. She should have known better than to bring it up. The only person that she would have been able to talk about it honestly with was Gaynor if she would ever acknowledge her existence. When she thought of her friend, all alone in that house, a sharp pain began to tug at her heart.

What if Dai really had gone? Gaynor shouldn't be on her own, she should be with a friend. A friend like herself. But then again, she didn't want to push her. Gaynor would come to Becky when she was ready.

She looked around at her colleagues as they chatted nervously, papering over the big, white elephant in the room with vacuous stories of weekend plans and the woes associated with fifteen-denier tights.

Why wouldn't they talk about any of this— why were they pretending it was all normal here in crazy lady valley?

It was almost as if—Becky raised her eyebrows as the thought occurred to her—they were under some kind of *spell*.

■ ■

Joanna stared at the telephone. She felt miserable.

Once, it had been her responsibility to telephone the other ladies and let them know that a meeting circle was due to take place— now, even that had been snatched away from her.

Odette had called her in a very assertive voice, to tell her that she was required to attend the meeting this evening. Required? She had never been required to do anything before this woman arrived. In matters concerning the coven, she was usually the one who did all the requiring.

"I suppose you have a location?" Joanna had asked in a similarly blunt fashion, laced with condescending undertones. "It's just that the meetings usually take place in my home."

"Well…" Odette was refusing to bite back, and there was no trace in her voice that indicated any sort of rank-pulling. The woman was effortlessly cool, to the point of liquid hydrogen. "I was going to organise a room at the Hotel Du Van in town, but if you don't mind, then I'm sure the ladies would be more comfortable in a familiar setting."

Hotel Du Van, eh? Very nice, thought Joanna. But this was a serious circle meeting, not an assembly of the Cheltenham Civic Society.

"Of course, I don't mind," Joanna said, instantly regretting it. If Bernice was back in attendance, and Joanna was pretty sure that she would be, then she would have to grin and bear the whole sorry evening. Particularly since it had been Joanna who had so vehemently cast her out. At the Du Van she would be able to mask her discontent with Bernice more effectively, but in her own home, it would be an uphill struggle.

"Very well, I shall inform the ladies." Odette had rung off without so much as a goodbye. Joanna supposed that the concept of good manners was lost on those who were high up at Oracle HQ nowadays.

She wondered how on earth this woman had got to the position she had. It took years, decades to achieve such an accolade as High Sceptre.

Months and months of study, painstakingly combing through leather-bound volumes of Wiccan history to be able to draw comparisons with modern developments in magick and the practices of centuries past. She would have had to hone her casting skills in numerous controlled environments and measured situations over several years, becoming a proverbial nun to the word of The Order.

Joanna scolded herself for harbouring such resentment—she must try to see this as a positive thing. It meant that The Oracle was concerned about her coven. And if they were concerned, it meant that her little town was still very much on the map.

The Oracle ... Madam.

Joanna could only imagine what she might look like now—the High Priestess. She must be getting on a bit, since they hadn't had a new incumbent since the fifties, not long after the queen's coronation.

But then it was The Oracle's fundamental duty to be elusive, therefore no pictures of the High Priestess were ever printed or circulated. Witches could literally walk past her in the street and never know that they were sharing a path with the woman whose life's work was to protect them from evil, to become responsible for each individual witch's well-being, who kept harmful magick from ever touching them.

She truly was a magnificent woman, but was she really that busy?

Most witches would speculate that, over the decades, all sorts of dark magick plots had been intercepted by those at HQ. The High Sceptres and their cohorts were systematically deployed if any whiff of danger was imminent. The Order was bound to have little plants and spies around the globe, picking up information regarding possible attacks on the community. The details of such stings, however, were never released, so Joanna never knew whether HQ was frequently busy, or the High Priestess was just sitting in her office below Marylebone Station, twiddling her thumbs and waiting for some bad news to come down the wire.

Joanna believed that the High Priestess' biggest achievement was not governing by fear as others had in the past. She steered more towards protecting her covens by not allowing mass hysteria to rise within the sisterhood. She remained dignified and tight-lipped when faced with challenges in security, ensuring that no unnecessary panic was caused by propaganda and gossip. She instead stated that a witch's power lay in her confidence and that paranoia was cancer to her development. Therefore, potential threats from terrorist gangs were never spoken about. Even Odette, if nothing else, had been stoic in the face of these possessions in

Joanna's little town. She hadn't trivialised any of it—instead, she was factual and calm.

Joanna had been to Marylebone Station many times and often looked for the HQ's winged gates at the edge of Balcombe Street. Oracle HQ was, however, not meant to be found. Its exact location was a well-kept mystery to those who did not need to know.

People who worked there were meant to be discrete. However, Joanna knew a couple of slippery employees who fed her titbits of information now and again, keeping her in the loop regarding trivial comings and goings. They all knew that the address could not be disclosed, and so she never had the gall to ask.

She often daydreamed, imagining what it must be like in the HQ. Clean, white, opulent, with crushed velvet, gilded frames of the Wiccan aristocracy lining the walls of the ancient banqueting rooms. Cast-iron statues of Tituba and Hecate at the bottom of a grand staircase. Oh, how witchcraft had come on.

The shabbily-dressed peasant women of the Dark Ages were no longer synonymous with the craft. The branding of the modern-day witch was one of wealth, power and strength. The ancestry line of such pioneers had spread far and wide and, since the sixties, the covens had begun to reap their rewards. Now, witches were in parliament, leading nations, controlling the economy or claiming investment banking commissions. And a good percentage of their wage was subsequently being plumbed back into The Order as a gesture of goodwill. A nod to the struggle of the women who had come before them.

Now the old-fashioned HQ was, undoubtedly, getting a new lick of paint, the silver was being polished, and the carpets cleaned.

The study halls were growing vaster, the equipment was brought up-to-date and education in the art was better evolved and governed.

Witchcraft was now big business and one that the government could not regulate. It was a self-running machine. But its success was not measured by wealth, but more so by membership. The number of covens in smaller locations was indicative of the size and strength of The Order. The wider the net was cast, the more innovative women they could employ. But it had not been pushed into the millennium like so many other things had been—it was still a traditional institution. There was no website or YouTube channel. The Order was as sacred today as it had always been, because the essence of the craft was in the hearts of those who had the magickal gift, and it was mainly the older generation who had the most experience and know-how. That was why Joanna had continued. The main principles of her beliefs in The Order would have been the same as her mother and her grandmother before her. Perhaps maybe her own daughters, if she'd had any.

But it was new-fangled witches like Abigail who would be sure to ruin The Order's traditional values if it was ever left for their generation to manage. Years of hard work, toil and discretion down the pan for the sake of a Facebook page and a reality series.

Joanna would never have allowed her child to be as gauche as Abigail. Peter would probably have been more of a pushover. He had always wanted a daughter. He would say that she would be the most beautiful, little thing that ever lived, as long as she had inherited her eyes from Joanna. The way his own had filled with sadness when she'd told him that the baby inside her had not survived was a memory that would haunt her forever. It was with that same sadness that he closed the door on their relationship, unable to cope with the thought of his partner having to bury a dead child. That he had been any part of it hung around his neck like a noose. He walked out and never came back.

Months later, she had read that he'd drowned in the Severn, losing his footing as he walked across the bridge.

Joanna looked down as a tear fell onto her cardigan. She would have to pull herself together quickly as the ladies would be arriving soon. She shouldn't be reliving old memories from thirty-odd years ago, even if the loneliness was as palpable today as it had ever been.

Maybe Odette arriving here was a good thing. For years, Joanna's regimental government over the coven had provided a distraction from ever having to think about those personal and painful chapters in her life that she had kept shut for all these years.

Joanna smiled.

It seemed that she could think of Odette's arrival positively after all.

■ ■

Wing was the first to appear. Once again, she stood politely on Joanna's doorstep, like a timid, fat, little mouse waiting to come in, adopting that same unassuming grin as she had done for years, which always got on Joanna's nerves.

It was quite a liberating feeling knowing that, now the meetings were out of her hands, Joanna was free to think and judge as she liked.

Odette had arrived around ten minutes early, immaculately dressed in a two-piece trouser suit. Joanna had wanted to wear something sartorially elegant herself, but the only thing that came close was a St Michael from the eighties that she used to wear to dinner parties. It didn't look quite right without some plastic, clip-on earrings and a vinyl handbag swinging on a brash, gold chain from her right shoulder pad.

She instead went for a dark grey pencil skirt that she had banished to the back of the cupboard for being too "peppery" and a simple, white blouse. She had smeared her lips with a dark lipstick and awaited the entrance of her superior, feeling somewhat fancy and a little bit smug.

Odette had given her a familiar nod as she walked in. Her pink skin was smooth and showing no sign of senescence despite her being, by Joanna's guess, in her mid-to-late sixties.

The thing that had annoyed her most was that Odette was a such a pillar of professionalism, while Joanna seemed to be floundering. Before Odette got to Winchcombe, Joanna had been the proud peacock. Now, however, she felt like a churlish school girl, stooping to a new, lower level of envy every time Odette's name was mentioned. She should be acting in a way that befitted her respect to the hierarchy of The Order, not pandering to her own insecurities like one of the little people.

Slowly, the ladies filed into the room and Odette nodded to each one. It was immediately apparent that Odette was not here for tea and pleasantries—she was here for official business. Joanna, standing obediently next to her, instantly felt like one of her staff. They should have gone to the Du Van. She shouldn't have been so pig-headed to host the meeting at her place. It was demoralising.

Laura and Robina arrived within moments of each other, both surprised and delighted in equal measure at Joanna's restraint. *Parasites*, Joanna had thought. Now that someone else was in charge, they were more than willing to brush her off as fast as they could. Did the last few years of her dedicated rule mean *nothing* to them?

Under her passionless smile, Joanna's weary heart emitted a dull ache.

Then Abbie arrived. She looked thinner somehow, paler. As though she had lost an element of her spark. Her hair was still a mass of golden curls, each one alive with vibrancy, but her eyes were somehow empty. She barely smiled as she crossed the threshold and into the house.

Joanna couldn't help feeling that her house was filling with snakes. That they could have the audacity to sit on her furniture and drink her tea when their loyalty was so fickle. She moved past Odette and out of the front door to get some air.

At that moment, she saw someone emerge from the shadows and make their way down her garden path. It was the figure of a tall, but broad being, the outline of whom she had not seen for a fair few months. This person tentatively moved toward her as though they were a fox, eyeing up its prey.

Bernice stepped into the dull glow of her outside lamp.

"Hello, Joanna," she said. Her voice had a gruff female sound with the slightest tinge of an effeminate man. She looked well. Her cheeks were blushed in pink and her eyebrows beautifully shaped. Although her hair looked unnatural against such an undeniably masculine-shaped face, it was a lovely shade of chocolate and in good condition. It can't have been real.

Joanna's heart wrestled with her head. There were so many words she wanted to say to Bernice, but she couldn't grasp any of them. She wanted to tell Bernice that her hands had been tied all those weeks ago when she had shooed her away from her property and, although the meeting tonight was taking place in the same vicinity, Bernice was a guest of the High Sceptres and not of hers. Joanna silently scolded Odette for putting her in this position.

Instead of speaking, Joanna pinched her lips together and bowed her head earnestly. Bernice smiled, it was an idiosyncrasy of Joanna's that she had seen many times. A flimsy plaster of a smile that tried to tape over a thousand indignant thoughts. A condescending sneer that only Joanna could pull off.

Bernice pulled her coat around her and stepped over the doorstep before leaning closer towards her host.

"I guess the fat cats got your tongue," she said icily and swept into the house.

Joanna did her usual tea loop, swallowing down a wave of acidic bile as she passed Bernice.

"Welcome, ladies," Odette had said as they all sat down. Joanna could sense duplicitous smiles flutter on the lips of some of the group which turned her stomach over.

She made a mental register of each attendee, seeing as Odette hadn't bothered to do so. Obviously, High Sceptres didn't trouble themselves with the trivial administration duties that were the slightly demeaning but absolutely necessary responsibility of the head of the coven. The only person noticeable by their absence was Gaynor, so Joanna noted to herself that she would have to follow this up with a telephone call. It was imperative that the meetings had one-hundred-percent attendance. However, Gaynor had never missed one in all their forty-or-so years, so there must have been a good reason why she wasn't there. She supposed it must be Dai.

"Let's start, shall we?" Odette said as the last of the steaming mugs were handed around. Abbie was the only one who did not partake in refreshment, deciding to chew on her hair instead.

"I'm afraid that Gaynor will not be here this evening," Odette continued. The fact that she knew this took Joanna back at first, but then she remembered that Odette had doled out the meeting invites this time around and so would have been privy to this information first.

"I noted some irregular lumelight activity coming from her residence." Odette remained composed as she stood in front of the phalanx. "I'm not at liberty to cast aspersions as to why, but I believe she has a sufficient reason to be absent. So, we have no need to elucidate further."

The words dropped, and the ladies obeyed. Odette laced her hands together and began to pace in a line.

"I'm sure you are aware that one Alice Eames has been placed within the care of the authorities, and that is with good reason." She spoke with such poise and control that Joanna could not help but be in modest awe of her deportment.

"It seems that the WHG Team have been working on the case back at HQ and they found out some distressing facts about Miss Eames. In the end, they had to intervene and contact the police."

Joanna spotted Laura lean into Robina, whose eyes were wide with concern. She was probably informing her who the WHG Team were. They were a team at HQ whose sole aim was to protect witches from the so-called Witch Hunter General, an age-old vigilante society that had existed since the Puritan times of the sixteenth century, primarily to seek out those who practise witchcraft and punish them for their supposed crimes.

It was common knowledge that this was mainly a United States movement and not quite so common here. There had, however, been some cases of recent unexplained arson which could well have been the work of the WHG. It was inevitable that some of their ethics would eventually migrate across the ocean and fall into the hands of bored, jobless, anti-establishment proles with social media accounts and nothing better to do.

Odette paused for a moment to let this information sink in.

"Apparently, HQ have had her on watch for some time but believed her to be a dormant link. Years ago, her father was thought to be part of a sect of foreign witches who settled here in the sixties, with a view to propagating the historic concept of *magic-bending*. Magic-bending is the term used when a witch uses a half-reverse spell to bend the magick back onto the spellcaster. As you know, most spells can be deflected by another incantation, but bending it back is a manmade concept. That is, it is against the laws of the goddess' teachings. So, if a spell was cast by a witch to stun a person, for example, the magic-bender could recite a counterspell that would turn the stun spell on the witch herself. The results, however, would be threefold, hence the practice could be catastrophic in the wrong hands. It is now regarded as highly illegal and extremely dangerous in the United Kingdom. The spells themselves and their countermeasures are kept under lock and key at HQ and are considered to be one of the best-kept secrets in The Order.

Although there had been no proof that Mr Eames was directly involved in this unlawful practice, the WHG caught up with him and bargained his retribution for providing them with the names of the witches.

Mr Eames was then thought to have been present at a WHG meeting in which a plot had been hatched to set fire to a farmhouse on the 18th September 1965, thus murdering these women and putting a stop to the whole magic-bending movement."

Joanna was aghast. Not only was this news to her, she was amazed at Odette's encyclopaedic knowledge. At that moment, she felt a brief modicum of respect for the woman. One that she shook off moments later.

"It appears that this meeting was intercepted by The Oracle. The women were saved and extradited back home.

Yet there was no evidence to implicate Mr Eames in the WHG meeting, so he was spared the charge and given a lesser sentence of exile to the United States, leaving his two daughters behind."

Joanna couldn't believe that this entire story had slipped through her fingers. She had known

Alice Eames for a long time and never suspected this of the woman. She had always thought her parents had lived in a small, unpronounceable Welsh village. She mentally chalked one up for Odette.

"The story doesn't end there, I'm afraid," Odette continued. "It seems that Alice Eames had been in communication with an unknown, independent business in Salt Lake City. The business appears to be untraceable on paper. However, it seems to be linked with someone of interest to the WHG, possibly her father or members of his new family. In other words, she was, for whatever reason, transmitting information to this person through business connections."

There was an uncomfortable silence. It was clear that a sense of impending doom was slowly circulating around the group. For years, The Oracle had provided them with an unwavering sense of protection. It was a hard pill to swallow to think that this defence may be compromised, that their sacred order was currently under the threat of a terrorist attack, brought about by someone who had lived under their noses for decades.

Abbie was the only one who failed to look remotely perturbed. She carried on stroking her middle cuticle with the tip of her thumb. She had since spat out her hair and was now chewing on an invisible piece of gum.

"So," Abbie said, obtusely, "what does this mean for us?"

Odette looked her challenger dead in the face, her eyes emitting a slight sparkle.

"Well," she said slowly, rolling the word around in her mouth. "First of all, I guess it means that we need to be slightly more vigilant and discrete in our day-to-day practices. These are vulnerable times for us and we should be hyper-aware of that fact. There are people out there who wish to harm our order, some closer to us than we think, and we must be careful."

Abbie did not buckle under her examination. In fact, she looked more visibly bored than ever.

"But isn't that what The Oracle does? Isn't the High Priestess there to make sure we're safe?" Abbie said, raising an eyebrow.

Joanna was boiling under the skin—she couldn't believe the insolence of this girl. Say what you wanted about Odette, but she was one of the High Sceptres and must be treated with the necessary respect when holding a circle meeting.

Odette sighed.

"Look, Abigail—"

"It's Abbie," she spat.

Joanna suddenly clenched her fists and furrowed her brow.

"Abigail, show some respect!" she barked— her voice was harsh and abrasive.

Abbie flinched.

"Joanna, it's fine, thank you," Odette said serenely, holding out her hand.

Joanna climbed back into her cage as Odette regained her composure.

"Abbie. The Oracle works tirelessly at ensuring that your safety is maintained in the grand scheme of things. What I am saying is that it is up to you to guard your own personal security."

She looked around at the other ladies, who were all slightly unnerved by this exchange.

"Now, while we can't rule out the possibility that an outside influence unconnected with the WHG may be responsible for these random attacks on the school staff, I would say that, judging by the proximity of said possessions and what we know about Miss Eames, I'm fairly certain that we have a suitable explanation for what has been going on in this town—the death of Miss Ware and the disappearance of Miss Wicks. It is no coincidence that both women are connected to the school."

Bernice sat forward.

"Apologies, High Sceptre," she said slowly, bowing her head, "but I'm not sure I understand."

Joanna gave an exasperated sigh. There was no way, after Bernice's long absence, that they'd have time to update her on all the goings on now.

"Hello, Bernice—please do tell me what I can fill you in on," Odette said softly.

"Well," Bernice's voice was similarly calm, "I know that I have been away for some weeks now."

She cast a cold glance in Joanna's direction.

"However, I have spoken to the girls at length about the situation regarding Miss Ware and what happened at the school festival. There is just one thing that doesn't add up."

Bernice looked around her at the expectant faces. Joanna was the only one who looked completely unimpressed.

"I mean," Bernice went on, "are you saying that Alice Eames is somehow responsible for the *death* of Brenda Ware?"

Odette stopped as if checking herself to see whether she'd missed out any significant information.

"Yes," she agreed, "the possession and subsequent passing of Brenda Ware."

Bernice was silent for a moment before shaking her head.

"But that's quite impossible. I know I haven't been present for many of the discussions about the possession and the fine details of how it all came about. But there's one thing I do know, that I can say with absolute certainty."

Odette smiled as she leant slightly forward.

"And what is that Bernice?" she asked.

"Well," Bernice continued as she looked around, slightly more nervous than before.

"Brenda Ware isn't dead."

"What do you mean she's not dead?" Joanna spat. "Of course she's dead—she got carried away on a stretcher for goodness' sake!"

Bernice was delighting that Joanna's crown was not only slipping in front of Odette but that she was about to miss it as it crashed onto the floor.

"Joanna," Bernice said slowly, "you know that one of my enlighters is being able to speak to those who have passed on."

Joanna stopped, her face resting on a final tableau of frustration and contempt.

"Well, everyone comes through my room. Everyone." Bernice looked around the room at her audience, hanging on her every word. "I had three just last night—passed from the hospital right into my bedroom. I can categorically tell you that Brenda Ware, who incidentally used to teach my son piano, has not visited me at all."

Robina, who had sat wringing her hands in despair for most of the meeting suddenly spoke up, as if awoken from a terrifying dream.

"But isn't this what you were saying, Grand Sceptre?" Robina looked up at Odette.

"Please call me Odette," came her reply.

"Odette," the word was choking Robina as it came out, it was thin and strained—it sounded out of place.

"That this magic, this *new* magic, it burns something into the ... bewitched," she continued, her eyes wide and darting around as if possessed herself. "That the magic could attach itself to the unfortunate person and this would enable the spellcaster to use that channel and control the body after death?"

Odette smiled serenely.

"I did say that," she said softly, "and you have done well to remember"

Robina half-smiled into a full blush. She was not used to being commended so highly—she almost didn't know what to do with such praise.

"I think what we have discovered here ladies is that, perhaps, our suspicions about such magick have been correct. Whatever this ... this poison is, the poisoner—possibly Miss Eames—is using it to control those whom she has poisoned."

Laura was the next to speak.

"But why?" she asked incredulously. "What possible purpose could anyone have for wanting to puppeteer a dead piano teacher? I mean, is the WHG looking to put together some sort of piano-playing, zombie army?"

There was a murmur of mirth around the group.

"That sounds like an awesome movie," Abbie remarked under her breath.

"Excuse me," a small voice spoke up from the corner.

The ladies all turned in the direction of the sound.

Wing was sitting timidly on Joanna's pouffe with her hand held aloft.

It was so unusual for the painfully bashful Wing to ever come forward with a verbal contribution that the other ladies barely remembered what her voice sounded like.

Odette stepped towards her.

"Wing, please," she said soothingly, "you don't need to ask our permission to speak. It is an equal floor here."

"Oh," she slowly retracted her hand and giggled shyly. "Sorry."

Robina and Laura smiled in response.

"It just remind me of a story from home," Wing said, blushing so much that she was practically camouflaged against Joanna's claret furnishings.

There was a pause before Odette nodded to signify that she should continue.

"My village," Wing began timidly.

She paused for a moment as if waiting for approval before continuing.

"In mountains of Thailand, we had legend. Wun Yiang Pan—this man, he very rich land and animal owner in the village. He was very bad man who beat his wife and children, and made people work in field for not much money. Under him, many starved and had to eat hay and straw to fill up their stomach. This kill many peasant people, but he would not stop."

She looked up at the faces in front of her. They were all leaning forward, listening in earnest. Even Joanna looked interested and enthused from her position at the back of the room. Wing was not used to this sort of attention, which made her shrink back slightly.

"One winter was very bad—many people and animal die in frost, their limb frozen to the ground as they sleep on floor of hut. The winter was so cold that many of Wun Yiang livestock perish and he could not sell for meat. His crops fail to grow, and his land became barren.

Most of the villagers believed that Wun Yiang responsible for his own misfortune and banished him up into mountains as a broken and penniless peasant who brought bad luck to village. After a few days in mountain, he meet a shaman. He beg the shaman for the power of forgiveness so he could be let back down the mountain to his home. But the shaman was too wise. He wanted to give Wun Yiang a test to see whether he was a good-spirited man who ever deserve his pardon. The shaman tell him, 'If you go back down into the village and work hard for it, your fortune will return in ten years—if you accept a more attractive offer from me, your fortune will return in ten days.'

The shaman offer was to cast an ancient spell that would bring back all of Wun Yiang animal and worker to life to work for him once again. If Wun Yiang take this offer, then he will see his fortune return much quicker than if he work for it himself. Wun Yiang, being greedy and having learnt no lesson from the struggle put upon him, he choose to have magic from Shaman so that all his old workers come back and help him rebuild empire. He knew that way meant he could sit back as he always did and watch his money roll back in.

So, the shaman did as he was told and cast a spell. The shaman then send Wun Yiang back down the mountain to his field.

As promised, when he enter the village, all his old staff were working hard in the field, and as he expect, his animal were back too, roaming the land as if nothing had happened. They work away in silence. But it was not to be."

She looked around and swallowed hard. The pressure of holding court was new to Wing and her discomfort was burning her chubby, pink cheeks.

"You see, they may have been given second chance at life, but they weren't the same. Their body had return but the soul had gone. And behind their eyes, there was nothing. They were not human, but something else. As days wore on and Wun Yiang try to get his house back in order, he notice that the worker began to look at him with a devil's hunger on their face. As he passed them in the field, they licked their lip and they stop and stare at him without looking down. On the tenth day, the field were growing crop again and it look like Wun Yiang was to be in charge of much land. But the workers were no longer silent and obedient.

"One night, they gather around his hut and wait for him to come out. On his doorstep, they pounce on him, tearing at his flesh with their hands and devouring him bit by bit."

Suddenly Joanna stepped forward.

"Oh, for goodness' sake Wing," she said, flustered and aggrieved at having to listen to such a macabre story in her own living room.

Wing flinched a little but kept her resolve.

"Well," Wing said, "it clear that he who use spell to awaken the dead is either a shaman or a Wun Yiang."

"Meaning?" Joanna asked impatiently.

"They have great power," Wing replied, "or they do not know what they are doing."

FIFTEEN

Abbie looked at herself long and hard in the mirror. This was it—this was the night that she was going to allow Xander to shag her in the Cleeve Hill undergrowth.

She must be insane. Giving a handjob in the park, yes, but full-blown sex on top of a mountain? That was just barking mad. Not only was it frigging cold, but it backed onto a golf course. She could only imagine the horror of frantically pulling up her knickers as some old fart in plaid trousers coughed politely before asking if he could "play through".

Oh, pull yourself together, she scolded herself.

She wondered whether there was something in The Order handbook that said she wasn't allowed to do such a thing on Halloween. Maybe it awoke the dead or something. It's not like she could ask any of the other ladies for advice—that would *not* be very well received. She doubted any of them had ever tried anything this daring anyway. The most scandalous thing that Joanna had probably ever done was wearing a brown skirt with black shoes.

Why couldn't Xander suggest doing it in a bed like normal people? Why did they always have to venture into the great outdoors for him to get aroused? Most guys would worry about getting all shrivelled up in the cold and usurp the rough ground for a warm feather bed. Luckily, Xander didn't suffer that trouble, he was always erect. Her tongue brushed against her lips as she thought of his perfect, pink penis.

Perhaps she could get excited about this after all.

She gave her reflection a little, lascivious smirk as she scrambled around in her bag for that all-important lip-gloss.

As she applied, she made a mental note to swing by the shop for some emergency condoms. The last thing she wanted was to get pregnant this evening. Conceiving Rosemary's Baby at this early stage of her life was not part of her plan. She didn't have the time or the inclination for a mishap on that sort of scale.

■■■■■■■■■■■■■■■■■■■■■■■■■■■■■■■■■■■■■■■

A few roads over, Becky was in a similar state of exhilaration. She was just pulling some old, black tights out of the drawer. The ones she had ordered online had arrived with a great, big ladder in them, and she really didn't have time to run into town for another pair—bloody eBay.

The dress that she'd bought had looked a little less slutty in the shop, but now it was on, it rode up a little higher than it had in the changing room. It also accentuated her bust while showing off her little bump—a triumph, she thought. She secretly wished all maternity clothes could pull off such a manoeuvre.

She had spent ages painting her nails a deep purple. They were glinting in the light as she inspected them. The matching lipstick she had chosen also made her look decidedly vampy. All in all, she was quite proud of this look. She felt sexier than she had in a long time, mainly because this was the first time that she hadn't rallied for her husband's validation. She had done it all on her own.

Dom had not been interested in attending the party, after a week of her asking him. He'd had to deliver a foal in the night and was on constant call for the thoroughbred mother, who they had almost lost during the delivery. Instead, he had vegged out on the couch with a sandwich and a copy of the *Racing Post*. As it was, Becky was quite looking forward to a bit of a girly night without him. It was just what she needed to shed the gloom of the recent town dramas.

She could have one heavily-diluted glass of Pinot and maybe even do *The Time Warp*, bump permitting. It would do her good to meet a few more people in the area and expand her horizons a bit. Gaynor and Catherine aside, she really could do with having a few more friends. She wondered whether that pleasant-but-nervous woman, Robina, would be there. She had enjoyed their previous coffee date but never followed it up with a call. It would be nice to see her and arrange another.

As her mind wandered, she clipped some drop earrings onto her lobes and let her long hair tumble over her shoulders.

As she took one final look in the mirror, she smiled. If she weren't already married, she reckoned she could pull tonight.

Grabbing her witch's hat from the bed, she flicked the light off and made her way downstairs.

■■

Robina stared at the fallen mess in front of her. She had iced it far too quickly and now the orange goop was sliding down the sides of the sad-looking cake. It was meant to be a bright orange colour, although it looked decidedly brown for a pumpkin. *Too much muscovado sugar*, she supposed. But then it was hard to measure it out properly when her hands were shaking so much. The buttercream filling that was loaded into the middle wasn't so much a tempting treat as it was a pustulous boil, begging to be burst. The enticingly delicious-looking pumpkin cake that she had found on Pinterest actually resembled a punctured basketball with a face that grimaced back at her in unadulterated pity.

She wiped a forlorn tear away with her finger and streaked a perfect white line in flour across her cheek. She had no time to do anything about it now—she would have to just hand it over and hope for the best. She could always give Catherine her money back if she wasn't happy with it, and Robina was almost certain that she wouldn't be. It wouldn't do to just not turn up. That was the problem with this town—nowhere to hide. Catherine Clements was intimidating enough as it was without adding wrath into the mix. If she were to show up with nothing at all, that would make Catherine think she was a thief *and* a liar. Robina shuddered at the thought. She was in a checkmate situation and she didn't really know how she had gotten there, or why Catherine had ever considered her for this task in the first place.

It suddenly crossed Robina's mind that Catherine could be doing all this solely for the pleasure of making a fool out of her and her hopeless baking skills in front of an audience. But then, while she knew that Catherine had the tendency to be a bit of a bully, she wasn't a total heartless bitch.

Oh gosh, she really was nervous now. She thought of how pathetic she must look, crying in her kitchen, dressed as a cat in front of her own cat, with even the cake gurning sympathetically at her.

Mother would never have done this, Robina thought to herself. She would have had the good grace to bow out and not even commit to such a charge. But Robina couldn't. Even with a healthy dose of pike weed in her coffee, a herb known for its confidence-boosting properties, she just couldn't say no.

She straightened herself up and brushed herself down, leaving yet more white dust about her person. She would not allow herself to cry tonight, not on Halloween, the holy night of her ancestors. She would have to keep her mettle in the face of adversity, just like her mother would have done.

She would have taken her daughter's chin in her smooth grip and said:

"Robina, you don't let anybody grind you down, my dear because you are the light of the world in the meekest of girls."

That sentiment would resonate more with Robina had she truly believed it. Sylvie, her therapist, would have said that the reason she didn't take this advice was twofold: one, that she didn't trust her mother's sincerity, and two, that she didn't value her mother's truth.

Robina wasn't about to dissect her relationship with her mother at this moment. She had to get this oozing monstrosity plated up and out the door.

She looked up at the ceiling as she reached for the spongey, brown mess.

"Goddess, give me strength," she said aloud. "So mote it be."

■ ■

Laura watched Ben from the other couch. He was lazing about again, all that dead sperm just sinking within him. The watery, milky grave of a thousand potential children. She knew that it was unfair to be disgusted by him, but she couldn't help it—he couldn't give her what she wanted.

She shifted about in her seat as the news came to an end.

"So, what time is this party then?" he asked, not looking up. His tone was sweet but ineffectual. It made her feel infuriated.

"I'll leave in about twenty minutes or so," she said, looking at a non-existent watch.

He craned his neck slightly to look at her.

"Are you not dressing up?"

She looked down at herself. She was wearing a long, slinky, black dress and had painted her nails silver. She thought she looked passable for a Halloween party.

"I am dressed up," she replied, slightly whinier than she had intended. He nodded, not really wanting to get into an altercation, which was a wise move.

He must have noticed the change within her these last few days as her fuse got shorter and shorter. It was as if she had drawn a battle line and was just begging him to cross over it and bear the brunt of her wrath. But good-natured, well-mannered, would-do-anything-for-her Ben would not accept that challenge and it drove her even more bellicose.

Unfortunately, it was the poor new intern in the office that'd had to face the full force of her anger. The pretty, but mind-numbingly dumb twenty-something who flounced about the office. The one who struggled with long adjectives and made frequent "oopsies" at the photocopier, costing her department tens of pounds in recycled A4 paper.

That poor girl was the one who had to endure Laura's constant frustrated exhalations and the snappy instructions, the door-slamming and the eye-rolling. Luckily, the girl was not self-aware enough to cotton on to this blatant act of continuous corporate bullying.

Laura chastised herself for being able to get away with this breach of professional conduct and, even more, for enjoying it.

"So, who's going?" he asked, not wanting to push her on any other points, and instead keep the conversation fairly neutral.

"Just some of the girls," she lied, "but we won't really be drinking, as you know."

Of course, he knew. Halloween was strictly off limits when it came to alcohol. For any member of the circle, it was far too risky.

The story of the girl who got far too drunk at a party in Hove in the seventies and started setting off spells like fireworks, frightening guests so much that they dove into the sea to escape her was still a favourite morality tale of Joanna's. Luckily, this was the age of LSD, so many of the partygoers had chalked it up to a bad trip. That must have made The Oracle's job, dealing with the fallout far easier, not that it was ever publicised.

She looked down at her invisible watch again. It must have been a nervous tick because he wasn't even looking at her.

"You know what?" she said, suddenly sounding alert and assertive. "I think I might swing by Robina's and pick her up."

She rose to her feet and pulled her dress down slightly.

He squirmed a little to get a better look at her. His eyes were filled with affection and a slight tinge of something else. Perhaps it was desperation.

"Have a wonderful time," he said.

She attempted a smile, but it looked more like a piteous smirk.

"It's more duty than anything," she said, "I doubt I'll be back late."

She walked to the door and turned to face him again.

"Love you," she said, wishing she sounded as though she meant it.

■■■■■■■■■■■■■■■■■■■■■■■■■■■■■■■■■■■■■■■

Mel had turned up at Becky's door, looking the part. Her purple wig matched her false eyelashes and the coloured, crushed velvet sections of her short, laced-up skirt. She giggled as Becky led her down the front path.

"I had a couple of glasses before I came out," Mel said. "I feel a bit tipsy!"

Becky rolled her eyes jokingly and punched her playfully on the arm.

"I'm going to have to keep an eye on you, aren't I?" she mocked, as a slightly unsteady Mel followed her out of the gate.

■■■■■■■■■■■■■■■■■■■■■■■■■■■■■■■■■■■■■■■

From behind the leaves, something watched as two women walked away from the street, one more in control of her footing than the other. It continued to stare as they crossed over the road and turned right at the corner, out of view. When it knew that it was alone, it stepped out from hiding and darted into the shadow of the opposite row of trees.

It pressed itself low to the ground, so much so that every time it gave a deep breath, it felt its breast touch the cold gravel beneath. The stones dug into its palms and the wind chilled the skin on its back. Inching forward, it ran its dry tongue over its cracked lips.

With trepidation, it began to follow its prey.

■■

Rachel Power's house was a sight to behold. First off, it was massive. A huge, L-shaped, two-storey new-build just off a slip-road outside Winchcombe. As they walked along the hedgerows, the house suddenly appeared before them.

Becky let out an audible gasp as she took it all in. The house was lit up like an enormous Christmas tree.

Orange lanterns hung from the conservatory, right across the length of the guttering—it looked like Disneyland. A battery-operated miniature henchman at the front gate lifted his plastic head off his shoulders while simultaneously welcoming them in. Mel stifled a little scream—Wilko's had obviously gone all-out with the fancy decorations this year.

Every inch of grass seemed to be covered with kids running amok in various, spooky attire. From werewolves to witches, vampires to mummies, they chased each other around the garden, dangerously high on sugary treats.

A wrought-iron fence poked up and out of the hedgerow, circling the house, strewn with orange and black balloons and streamers. A pond that stretched the width of the lawn glistened in the moonlight, a solitary stone ballerina perched in the middle of it wearing, for the occasion, a *Scream* mask.

"Wow," Becky said out loud.

"Oh, I know" Mel agreed, slightly sobered-up after their little walk through the town. "You wait 'til you see the inside. It's like a bloody palace."

She wasn't wrong.

A stone-flanked hallway ran throughout the bottom floor, the walls festooned with a million expensive-looking portraits, presumably patriarchs of the Power dynasty. Fresh flowers in autumnal colours stood in glass vases on every available shelf space and, as a centrepiece, a multi-tiered table-stand held sweets and chocolates of every conceivable kind, flavour and size.

A few people were dotted around, some that Becky recognised from the school gates and some who were total strangers, dressed in varying comedy-horror attire. It was great to see that people had made a real effort. There was an Elvis, an Amy Winehouse, circa 2011—slightly in poor taste, Becky thought— two pirates and innumerable becloaked figures, each with some kind of hideous facial disfigurement hiding underneath their black hoods. They all clutched orange cups filled with a reddish liquid as they chatted.

The Monster Mash played out of a Bose sound system, and Becky had to duck to get past the long stretch of fake web that snaked its way across the ceiling, dangling little plastic spiders from every dark oak beam.

Mel led the way into the kitchen, a vast, country-cottage affair with a middle hob that housed a massive cauldron, bubbling over with the aforementioned liquid. Cookbooks were arranged in order of size. Quirky jars full of dried herbs, bulbs of garlic and the like were spread about the room. A huge tray that held every Carluccio's bottle known to man was on display next to a huge, square, porcelain sink.

This was clearly the hub of the party activity. Mothers dressed in drab, black outfits with questionably dry Morticia Addams-esque wigs were stood around, smiling, yet at the same time surreptitiously sizing each other up. Dads held beer bottles as they discussed the latest Apple gadget and nonchalantly stroked the heads of their offspring who ran in to complain about the behaviour of the others' offspring.

Becky craned her neck to see what else was going on further in. Set amongst the thirty-or-so parents and their various sprogs dashing about the place, three perfectly pampered dogs sat in a line in the confines of a circular pen, decked out with more soft toys than your average orphanage day room. A beautiful, long-haired Cocker Spaniel perched next to a white

Chihuahua and a brown Dachshund. The all had their tongues lolling out of their mouths, unfazed by the noisy bustle of the party and panting in perfect unison.

The decorations carried on down as far as the eye could see. Plastic pumpkins bursting with sweets were uniformly placed in rows along the length of both opposing walls and dry ice cascaded from large, cauldron-shaped bowls.

Suddenly, a burst of laughter grabbed Becky's attention. It came from the group standing opposite her. A large collection of well-turned-out ladies seemed to be swarming around one individual. Becky could only see the backs of these ladies, but she could see that they were all about six stone, with gorgeously-conditioned locks in every shade of the Vidal Sassoon brochure. A real gaggle of Stepford Wives, quaffing pinot grigio and gasping with delight at innocuous anecdotes, just like the characters Becky had seen in those reality shows that she immediately turned off whenever they came on the television.

As the wall of lithe bodies parted momentarily, Becky managed to snatch a glance at the person holding court in the centre.

A tall, fantastically thin brunette stood in the middle of the throng. Her breasts were sickeningly pert and clothed in a sexy, figure-hugging white cheerleader's outfit, splattered with fake blood. Her full lips glistened with the same blood red, and her long, dark curls fell over her shoulders, twinkling with a similar sheen.

She had a flawless, taught complexion that made her look at least ten years younger than she had any right to. As she laughed, her long eyelashes tipped back to reveal glowing, blue eyes that fizzled in the light. She looked simply beautiful. Like Madonna in the *League of Their Own* years, oozing sex appeal but maintaining an air of integrity and class. A beautifully glazed pin-up.

This, Becky thought to herself, must be the ever-elusive Rachel Power in all her glory. Becky had only managed to get a strained glimpse of her through the tinted glass of her Jaguar XJ before now, but she was certain it was the same girl.

In the flesh, she was every bit as awesome as her house was. Becky could now see why it chapped Catherine Clements' backside so much. Who wouldn't want to be this woman? Not Becky, obviously. She knew that she would never be in that league and, somehow, she was at peace with that. However, someone as competitive as "Call-Me Cathy" would surely find it a constant source of misery and frustration. It suddenly all clicked into place.

"Isn't she gorgeous?" Mel said into Becky's ear as she continued to stare, the faintest smell of white wine on her breath.

Becky half-nodded in response, as the wall of bodies closed back in on Rachel Power.

"Hmm," Becky agreed.

"*Bitch*," was Mel's one-word affirmation.

∎∎∎∎∎∎∎∎∎∎∎∎∎∎∎∎∎∎∎∎∎∎∎∎∎∎∎∎∎∎∎∎∎∎∎∎∎∎∎

Abbie stepped off the bus and shot an accusatory glance at the driver, who she had noticed adjusting his mirror earlier to get a closer look at her thigh. There were only the two of them on the late bus on Halloween night and she guessed he might have thought he could get away with a bit of black magic of his own. Had he been younger she may have been flattered, but he was old, balding and had the look of a dirty, old pervert whose mugshot might be seen on the news.

She pulled her floor-length cardigan out of a puddle as she climbed off the steps, turning only to see the driver scrunching his face up in mock ecstasy. As the door closed, she smiled at him as she coolly extended her middle finger.

The bus pulled away and she suddenly realised the ridiculousness of her situation. She was on top of Cleeve Hill, equidistant between home and town. it was cold and desolate, she had barely any mobile signal and she was running out of battery.

Bloody brilliant.

Xander had told her to meet him up on the bench at the top of the hill. She could access this, thankfully, by walking up the steep, stone path that ran alongside a row of cottages. The idiotic, archaic Cotswold bus timetable meant that she was twenty minutes early, so at least she had a bit of time to make her way up there in the limited light, carefully, so as not to fall arse-over-tit onto the treacherous, jagged pebbles.

Rummaging around in her bag for the bottle of Dutch courage she had brought with her, she stepped away from the road, narrowly avoiding a speeding juggernaut that came hurtling down the road at top speed, nearly sending her careering into a nearby thorn bush.

"Arsehole!" she shrieked after it, as the car's taillights disappeared down the hill and away from view.

Pulling her large bag further up the shoulder of her black coat, she began to make her journey to the pathway, stopping to check in all directions for any sign of her not-so-punctual lover. There were none.

She mumbled a few expletives to herself as she made her way up the path. Luckily, the lights from the cottages would illuminate part of the way, but the rest would have to be done either by feel or by switching on her smartphone's torchlight feature, thus using up what little battery she had left.

She opted for the latter.

■■■

Laura sat in the car, drumming her fingers on the dash. This was not her at all, conducting illicit affairs with strangers on familiar, residential streets. Thankfully, there was no end of country hills or historical ruins in Winchcombe—perfect places for a couple who were not meant to be together to go about their sordid business under a veil of shadow.

She hadn't been expecting to find this guy so easily—it just sort of happened.

On Thursday, she did something that she never, ever did. She popped into the Soho Bar in Montpelier after work for a glass of fizz. It just seemed the perfect way to unwind after a fairly tense day. She had spent the entire day at her desk, totally unable to concentrate as she contemplated her biological hourglass, gushing sand at a rate of knots and her not being able to do a single thing about it. It sent her half-mad with anxiety.

When a client had caught her out on a decimal point that she had misread in a fairly large corporate contract, she admitted defeat, picking up her bag and storming out of the office, leaving Lara—the imbecilic intern—with no instructions or tasks for the rest of the day.

It was after a couple of sips of the cool, soothing liquid, that she nearly decided to push the glass away and march back into the office with a fresh sense of audacity. But as she looked around, she noticed a handsome, sandy-haired guy was coming to sit next to her at the bar. He looked similarly crestfallen and before long, they had begun talking. Firstly, about work, though she wasn't really listening—she was too eager to fill in her next sentence. Her mother's voice rang in her ears:

"Laura, you must learn to listen. How are you going to answer somebody if you don't know what they've said?"

No wonder she ended up as a sales manager. In this career path, you only really had to listen to half a problem before you steamrolled in with the solution.

As this guy talked, she noticed how attractive he was. He wasn't self-deprecating like Ben, whose every word seemed to drip with apology for being such a let-down.

Eventually, they got onto their respective partners. This guy was married but felt as if his wife was drifting further and further away. He wanted to be respected again, listened to—loved.

She lied and told him she was single. It was more appealing that way, making herself look young, stupid, impulsive. If he thought she had nobody to lie to, then he only need feel half the guilt than if she was also married.

As she spoke, she noticed that his eyes travelled across her breasts, along her thighs and into her lap. He imperceptibly licked his lips as he mentally undressed her. Though all he drank was lemonade, he appeared to be intoxicated on the mere possibility of something happening.

In the end, they had swapped numbers. He'd pulled out one of his cards to hand her as she drained the last drops of her wine.

She wouldn't have accepted it ordinarily. The idea of ever meeting up again was far too ridiculous to comprehend. She could never do that to Ben, no matter how she was feeling about her current plight.

But it was as he opened his wallet to select one of his green and white embossed cards that something caught her eye. There, amongst the five-pound notes and store cards, lay something that made her insides turn over. It was a small ultrasound photograph. The grainy picture of a forming foetus.

This, of course, changed everything.

She had slipped the card into her breast pocket.

■■

The party was getting into full swing by the time Catherine had arrived. She was wedged into Saul's Audi between a bottle of English sparkling wine (or "the new Prosecco" as Mary Portas had called it) and the giant chicken wire, papier-mâché torso of a headless horseman that was currently encasing her little girl. The little pump sprayed strawberry-flavoured milkshake syrup out of the neck via some cleverly-assembled tubing that she had found in B&Q. The charity shop head was jutted under Sienna's arm and, after a few minor enhancements, it looked almost as if she was carrying a giant, foam television set. In the chest, she had cut a peephole, out of which Sienna's own head poked through. Catherine had abandoned the idea of stitching an adjoining pony onto the trunk, mainly because of time constraints. And so Sienna was, in fact, a headless man—sans horse.

Once assembled, it looked a little *Blue Peter*-ish, but then, no one could possibly mark her down for not being innovative. She was sure that an ambitious, homemade creation would trump anything that Rachel Power would've had specially sent down from Angels in London. In the end, Michael had had to go dressed as a mummy. She had attempted the papier-mâché mask so many times that she was over it. Sienna's costume had taken up the majority of her time anyway and, at the end of its construction, all she could really afford was a few rolls of bandage out of her first aid box. So, she sent Michael up to his bedroom to his own sartorial devices with a roll of Scotch tape.

He had looked quite pleased. It was Sienna who had whined and moaned, pleading to go as a mummy as well and not as this stupid, giant, painful piece of junk that didn't look scary at all.

Catherine had grabbed her by the scruff of her tarred and feathered neck and told her, through gritted teeth, that if she didn't wear it, then her iPad was going on a one-way trip to the orphans in Antigua. Or wherever it was that orphans were situated. Sienna soon shut her sullen mouth and pulled on the humongous, foam-filled headpiece in silence. Catherine stepped out of the car and turned to help her daughter off of the back seat, careful not to scratch the paintwork. Of the costume, obviously—she didn't give a shit about Saul's silver Chelsea tractor. Michael hopped out of the front seat and immediately ran over to where a group of young kids were playing with some outdoor sparklers.

"Careful you don't set yourself on fire, dear!" she called after him, wishing that she had fireproofed those bandages before he had escaped, or at the very least sprayed suede shoe protector on it or something.

"I'm going in," Catherine said to Saul. "I've got to see a woman about a cake. You park up and I'll see you in there."

He nodded as she slammed the door shut, helping Sienna tackle the grass slope that led up to the garden.

"Come on darling," she said as she placed a cold hand on her back. "Only a couple of hours, you can walk away with the crown and all this will be over. Now, where is that silly blonde?"

■■■

Robina slid the tin onto the kitchen side next to the other tins, careful not to be caught. The arrangement was to deposit it there secretly, labelled with the name of her conspirator and then blend into the party and act as if nothing had happened. She was then to leave as quickly as she had come in. The first part had gone well, but she was not sure whether she had the guts to reveal this monstrosity in public. The right thing to do would be to keep it with her and explain to Catherine that there had been a terrible mistake, that they should just abandon their plan and she could have her fifty quid back.

As Robina turned, she noticed a familiar face poking out from under a rather large witch's hat.

"Oh, my goodness—Robina!"

It was the girl from Cavendish House, Becky. She looked very beautiful in her outfit. Now Robina was in a quandary. She hadn't wanted to bump into anyone, lest she got all nervous and let the cake out of the bag, but she couldn't well say nothing and run. She had enjoyed Becky's company last time they were together.

"How are you?" Becky continued with a sincere look of joy on her face.

Robina could feel herself blushing scarlet. She started to splutter as Becky looked down at her attire.

"Oh, you're dressed as a cat. You could sit on my broom!"

Robina let out a strained, nervous laugh.

364

"I was just off to the drinks table, fancy joining me?" Becky was persistent.

"Well, actually I was about to—"

"Oh, come on." Becky grabbed her by the arm, a little tighter than was comfortable. "I'm here with a load of works people who have dumped me to mingle with their friends, and I don't really know anyone. I need the company before I start to look desperately lonely."

Robina didn't argue any further. True to form, she allowed herself to be directed.

■■

As Laura climbed over the seat, she surprised herself at how efficiently she was approaching this—like a businesswoman closing a deal. It was transactional, with very little emotion. She had called him, proffered the service and he had accepted. It was the way she closed all of her deals—quickly, and without ever having to explain herself.

He had said that his place was free tonight, but she didn't fancy that—it was too risky. She didn't want to live with the fact that she had been the other woman. The one whose very scent had to be fumigated out once she had left the building. It didn't really do much for her self-esteem.

She had offered an alternative: her car was roomy, with the added advantage of being able to hide it in the shadows of a nondescript country lane as they set about doing the deed.

She drove to his and as he got into the passenger seat. Without saying a word, they had begun tearing at each other's clothes. His arms were muscular, and they pulled her tight towards him as his mouth made its way from one side of her neck to the other.

He grasped her breasts in his rough hands and worked his fingers around the cup of her bra. She wasn't so sure about doing it on the street outside of his house, but there didn't seem to be anyone around and, before she knew it, she had removed her top, careful not to tear anything for fear of being asked about it later.

She could feel his erect penis pushing up through the seat of his trousers. It was a good size, no doubt full of precious, full-bodied semen. She could almost feel it permeating his chinos.

He was like a starving animal, pouncing upon a freshly gutted carcass. His hands groped at her, hungrily, manically. They found their way in between her legs and, as he pulled back from her, looking her in the eye, he slid two fingers inside her. She groaned with pleasure as she threw her head back. She knew that this was all a prelude to the main event and, if this was going to work, she would need to get there quickly.

Breathlessly, his lips came close to her ear as he panted. His sweat-sodden fringe brushed the side of her cheek, leaving a cold streak of film across her face.

"I don't have any condoms," he growled, his breath laboured and hot against her face, "but I really fucking want you"

"It's okay," she replied, mimicking his desire. "I'm on prescription—it's fine."

She didn't want to dwell on it too much since she was lying through her teeth. After what seemed like an age, he plunged his lips back onto her neck, moving his fingers in and out of her like a piston.

As he worked his way down her neck with his tongue, she fumbled in his trousers with one hand, while simultaneously pushing her knickers aside. She managed to wrestle open his flies and release his rock-hard cock from his fly.

Holding it in her hand, it was practically pulsating, threatening to explode all by itself. But just as everything had begun to rocket by in an ecstatic blur, she stopped rigid.

He immediately looked up, his eyes searching hers with a nervous concern.

He stopped, and his penis seemed to cease vibrating in her hand.

"I just wanted to check whether—"

She swallowed hard, amazed that her sensible, compassionate side was deciding to kick in now she was without underwear and had an incredibly ravenous man clamped to her breast.

"Whether you really want to do this?" She found the words, but they sounded dry and desperate.

He looked around as if she had been addressing someone else.

What seemed like hours passed after this awkward exchange before he gave a little nod of the head, her nerves building up all the while. As he craned his neck to get a better bite on her left nipple, she opened her legs and let him in.

■■

"For fuck's sake!" Abbie cursed to herself as her phone battery died and the torchlight extinguished. She was now officially in the middle of nowhere, with no way of contacting anyone for immediate rescue. *Perfect.*

The wind bit around her ankles and, though it wasn't super cold, it whipped her hair and pulled the strap of her bag off her shoulder. This was ridiculous—she didn't know if he was here, or if he was even intending to show up.

The comforting glow from the windows of the cottages had ceased a while back and now she was scaling what looked to be a never-ending field, leading up to the solitary tree and bench at the top of the hill. Supposedly, Xander knew a perfect spot up there, but she was rather hoping that he might have arrived early and escorted her up there like a proper fucking gentleman would've.

She was beginning to feel afraid, not least because she had Odette's talk of witch hunters reverberating around her mind. Silly, jumped-up old cow, scaremongering in the hope that she might retreat back into her room for all eternity. She needed to take everything that woman said with a pinch of salt. Joanna was exactly the same. If she had her way, Abbie would be at home now letting her leg hair grow and reading Germaine Greer. Philistines.

As she wandered blindly in the pitch darkness, she suddenly heard something rustling a little way ahead of her. She froze on the spot. As she did, she felt her heartbeat in her ears. Whatever it was, she couldn't make it out.

"Hello?" she called, her voice sounding weak and pathetic across the vast expanse in front of her.

There was no echo and there came no reply. The wind seemed to cease for a second. She crept forwards, towards the source of the noise.

"Is anybody there?" she called out again, her nerves making her voice sound pinched and thin.

The rustling continued for a moment and then stopped.

"Listen," she said, stumbling as she began to inch back towards the security of an adjoining hedgerow. "I've got my phone here and I can call for help if I need to."

Her dad had often told her that was the best way to sound confident when facing a potential attacker. Not that he knew. Whenever her dad came out with something inspirational, it had usually come straight from the pages of the *Daily Mail*.

She made the impulsive decision that a shag wasn't worth putting herself in danger for after all. But just as she was about to make a run for it, she gasped in shock as something darted out of the shadows and shot towards her.

■■

Gaynor sat at the bedside, slowly smoothing the covers down on the empty bed. The room that had once been so vibrant with colour could literally have been painted black for all she cared now. No amount of varying shade of yellow could cover the dark place that this room had become. She felt so stupid for ever thinking that a lick of paint could alter the situation. And then she felt silly for feeling stupid. Stupidity was the scourge of the young—she should know better.

The saddest thing was that he had passed in his sleep. There was no death rattle, no struggle, no rage against the dying of the light. It was as if he had given up. He simply let go and went peacefully. It was the goddess' will, which she was loathed to argue with, but she wished that he had called out to her, let her help.

In the old days, running across the beach at Bracelet Bay, they had wrestled each other into the sand, not one of them letting the other triumph. It was always a battle to the end with the pair of them. When they argued, which they seldom did, it would be explosive and last for days. Only when one yielded would the whole sorry business be forgotten, and they could, at last, get back to normal.

And now the goddess had taken him for her own. He was on to better things, their life together a mere dot on the long journey that lay ahead. Oh, she hoped he would remember her.

She rose to her feet, and her old knees creaked as she did so. As she steadied herself on the back of the chair, she noticed the tray that lay to the side of the bed. His beaker. The one she would fill with lukewarm tea and slide across to him at regular intervals throughout the day. There it stood, proudly. As though it was immensely honoured to have provided such a thankless service for all these years and would now be allowed to retire, dismissed of its duties.

A solitary tear rolled down her soft cheek as she made her way over to the open doorway.

Perhaps she would go away for a few days. Somewhere on the coast, where she could see the stars.

"Goodnight, heulwen," she whispered and turned out the light.

■■■

"You're a fucking *idiot*!"

Abbie pushed Xander hard in the ribs. She was not joking—she was trembling.

"Oh, come on," he whined, "it was a laugh!"

She looked at his hang-dog expression, illuminated by his mobile phone screen. He looked young and inexperienced and, in an instant, she felt the lust trickle out of her like a leaky tap.

"I was scared," she smoothed her clothes down, her heart beginning to resume its normal pace.

"Don't be scared baby, I'm here."

She hated it when he called her "baby". It sounded so insincere. As though he'd picked it out of a film or a book. It was void of emotion or meaning, and it made her cringe.

"Yeah, you're here. But you're jumping out at me through the bushes like a rapist—that's not very attractive." She was beginning to get riled. There was a spite in her tone that suggested as much.

"Well, I guess I'll have to sort that out then." He came closer to her, his sallow, cold skin pressing against hers, his lip-ring brushing her neck. She felt decidedly unaroused as his wandering hands approached her midriff and he buried his mouth in her shoulder.

Nimbly, his fingers moved down to her crotch as he softly bit the side of her neck.

"Look," she said, just wanting him off her now. She was pissed off, it was dark, and the moment had truly passed. "I don't think I really want this anymore—"

"Oh, yes you do," he said, his fingers becoming firmer as they buried under her dress, frantically searching for a route into her underwear.

"No!" She was starting to writhe under his grip, twisting slightly to manoeuvre herself away. "I don't think I—"

"Don't be frigid," he moaned as the bites on her neck began to get harder and more painful.

"I'm not fucking *frigid*!" she barked, finally turning enough to wrestle herself away from his body.

As she looked up, she noticed a shadow cross his face. His once tired eyes were suddenly filled with rage. He raised his hand and struck her clean across the jaw. The blow was so spontaneous that it knocked the breath out of her. She staggered back, startled and clutching her cheek.

"Yes, you *fucking* are!" he spat at her, advancing forward. His voice was hard and gruff. "You make out you're a dirty slut but in reality, you're a frigid, little skank."

She couldn't read the expression on his face—it was one she didn't recognise. This was not Xander, the guy who hummed Nirvana tunes and held roll-ups between his yellowing teeth. This was someone else, someone far more sinister. Although it was dark, she could see the outline of his hand moving down towards his fly. Next came the sound of frantic rummaging as he fought with the zip. Terrified, she stumbled as she clambered back down the muddy slope.

"Well, there's only one way to sort that out," he snarled. "Tonight you'll have to face your fears. Tonight, I'm going to make you a soiled, little skank!"

Her eyes widened with fear as she whispered "no" a few times to herself.

Finally, he managed to unzip his trousers and pushed a hand in. He held his other hand out towards her neck as he lunged himself forward and extended his fingers into a claw shape.

Her breath grew heavy and she became extremely light-headed. As if something was taking over the panic that was rising up in her. Suddenly, her head snapped backwards, her eyes rolled back, and everything went black. From deep within her mind, two words resonated.

"*Inverius sanctum,*" the voice said. It repeated the incantation.

She whispered it out loud.

She heard five single cracks, each one in turn, and then an endless, blood-curdling scream. She opened her eyes in time to see the phone drop to the ground, shining its light upwards towards Xander who fell to his knees. He was clutching his outstretched left hand with his right, his flaccid penis dangling through his open fly.

"What have you done, you bitch?" he screamed at her. "You've broken my fingers. You fucking bitch!"

She suddenly lost her nerve. She hadn't meant to do that, to release a spell—but she couldn't help herself. What was going to happen to her now? She couldn't think.

Xander wriggled around on the floor in pain, burying his hand into his stomach, lurching and retching.

"You're dead, you're *fucking* dead!" he shouted, which sent a white-hot hysteria up from the base of her spine. Before she could stop herself, she grabbed hold of her bag and ran, away from the light of the mobile phone behind her and into the darkness of the open fields. Her hair stung her face as it whipped in the wind, while tears cascaded down her cheeks.

She had really done it now. There would be no penance for casting a spell in front of a civilian— the ultimate taboo. She would be hauled up in front of The Oracle for this. She didn't even know what such a punishment would entail. Exile? Prison? What did they do with witches who used their power for bad? Last she read, they were burnt at the stake.

She ran until the screams had faded into the distance. She stopped at a nearby tree, her breath raw in her throat and burning inside her chest. Panting and gulping at the air, half-sobbing, half-retching, she fell to her knees into the grass.

She could see the lights of the houses below her, some three fields away. She pulled her knees up towards her chest and began to rock gently, forwards and backwards. It became clear that, in wanting to fuck Xander outside tonight, she had ended up fucking herself.

■■

The thing was crouched in the bushes, metres away from a huge house, lit up with endless, dangling lanterns. Children played on the front yard in bizarre costumes, running around in flashes of orange, white and black. The retina-searing lights from the hundreds of bulbs that illuminated the front of the house made its bloodshot eyes ache. It slinked underneath the low-hanging branches and rested onto its back limbs. Moistening its lips with saliva, it watched the house for any signs of action. Any one of the people out front would have made a satisfying meal, but its instruction was to feast on a particular piece of meat, and it would know it when it saw it. All it knew was that the target was near.

■■

As Laura climbed off of him, she immediately felt a rush of guilt hit her like a steam train. She felt sticky between her legs—warm and moist.

He had exploded inside of her, as though months of sexual anguish had been building up in his testicles and she had just allowed him to release it. He had gripped her arm as he convulsed into climax. She really hoped that he hadn't left a bruise that she would have to explain to Ben later.

He lay underneath her, deflated, closing his eyes for a moment or two as his penis slowly shrank. His shirt was open, now missing a button, ripped from its home as she had passionately torn at it.

His eyes opened slowly.

"That was—"

She put her hand over his mouth. She didn't want to hear all that bullshit about how good she was. Trying to appease her adultery by giving the experience any worth couldn't have been less appropriate. She was now officially a cheat. Everything she hated about promiscuous, sly women, she had become. She told herself that it was for the greater good. It had a purpose. It wasn't simply an exercise in vanity, addiction or perversity. It was a necessary step towards saving her marriage.

She locked her knees together, hoping that his fertile sperm would start swimming inside of her, rather than spill out over her car seat and be wasted in the process.

"I have to go," she said coldly. She didn't want to upset him, but then she didn't want to mislead him either.

He came to and opened his eyes wide. The words hung in the air for a moment before he nodded and looked around for his things. She knew this was out of awkward nerves and rejection. Everything he had brought with him was still on him. He began to dress, pulling his jeans up and fastening however many buttons were still left on his shirt. He did this without looking at her as if the transaction had been necessary for him too. Nothing more, nothing less.

She couldn't help but feel a little used, regardless.

"I—" he went to say.

She shook her head and looked away.

He slowly opened the door and climbed out. Before he closed it behind him, he turned back and crouched down to look at her.

"I really needed that," he said, in a pathetic voice. As though somehow, she should feel proud that she had provided him with a convenient amenity. What he had done for her would be thought of as honourable, had he been aware of what he was donating. What she had given him was nothing more than what a common slut might have given him in the car park of a local nightclub. Another divide between the sexes.

She nodded as he slammed the door.

"*Me too,*" she thought, as she fastened her seatbelt.

∎∎∎

Becky and Robina were standing next to the punch bowl as Catherine made her way into the kitchen. Robina immediately slammed her cup down in alarm. Becky noticed this panic and glanced up to see what it was that had irked her so. Once Catherine had spotted the two women, she made a beeline for them.

She did look radiant, although not really dressed up for Halloween, but more outfitted for an upmarket cocktail party. Again, she made Becky feel not so much a million dollars as an old, creased five-pound note.

"Oh, hello stranger!" Catherine's syrupy voice came drifting over the music. Becky half-rolled her eyes, almost forgetting Robina's discomfort.

"Catherine!" Becky said, nearly choking on a slurp of her Vimto. "How are you?"

"Oh, you know," she beamed, "living life to the full as always."

What a response.

"How has life been treating you? I thought you'd fallen off the face of the earth!" Her tone changed from sweet to acerbic.

"Well, I've been busy." Becky's voice began to tremble. She was such a terrible liar.

"Oh, of course," Catherine said, "I forgot how demanding part-time jobs can be."

What was more offensive than the comment itself, was the fact that Catherine would say it without even registering how offensive it was.

There was an awkward pause as Catherine's focus drifted over to a reddening Robina, who appeared to be attempting to fit her head into her punch glass.

"Oh," Becky said, glad of the shift of attention. "Do you two know each other?"

There was a slight pause as Robina's eyes continued to bulge out of her head and Catherine regarded her with an acidic smile. After what seemed like an excessive stretch of time, Catherine spoke.

"I don't think so, no."

Becky was doubtful. From the way Robina was acting, they had definitely met somewhere before, and she was clearly hoping that they would never meet again. Becky understood and so refused to dwell on it. Somewhat awkwardly, she introduced the two and they faked their way through pleasantries.

As if on cue, the gorgeous lady who Becky had been fawning over earlier swept by with her entourage in tow. Rachel Power stopped momentarily by their group as she spotted Catherine to her left.

"Oh," she said, halting suddenly as the line of women behind her almost concertinaed into each other. "Catherine! I didn't know whether you were coming or not. I almost gave up waiting."

Catherine instantly went into turbo saccharine mode. Her smile widened, and her eyes looked as if they were about to jump out on stalks.

"Oh, *Rachel*!" she bleated, turning to face her nemesis, almost cartoonish in her capriciousness. "As *if* I'd miss it for the *world*!" she carried on, as the two exchanged air kisses befitting of the *Real Housewives*.

They both cackled in perfect unison like two hammy actors in a bad English farce.

"Well, I saw Sienna wobbling about in that *monster* of an outfit and I thought, 'that can only be the work of Catherine Clements—now where is she hiding?'"

Catherine's skin prickled slightly at that, and Becky thought she saw a slight twitch in Catherine's right eye. Rachel was also studying Catherine's face with fervour—her eyes seemed to glisten as she noticed her enemy's armour denting.

"Well," Catherine said, "I did make *the entire costume* myself!"

Her gaze cascaded slowly down Rachel's outfit in silent judgement. Now it was Rachel's turn to purse her ruby red lips.

"Well, in that case," Rachel said, following a moment of painful silence, "follow us into the garden my dear—we're about to start judging the cakes and the costumes. And I'm sure we'll all be wanting a good look at this *marvellous* culinary creation that you, err ... *made yourself.*"

One of Rachel's associates held up Robina's tin and smiled.

Catherine clamped her lips together and gave a little nod. Becky's eyes were fixed firmly on Robina, who visibly blanched and shifted uncomfortably.

"I'll be *right* there," Catherine replied. She half-waved as the group breezed on by, Rachel grinning like a Cheshire cat at the front of the line.

"Cow," Catherine spat as soon as they were out of earshot. "I suppose we had better go outside."

She seemed to say this directly to Robina, as she fished around in her bag for a mirror. After checking her teeth and slightly adjusting her cleavage in the compact, Catherine threw it back into her handbag.

"Are you coming?" she said, breezily.

"Sure," Becky agreed, quickly glancing at Robina for reassurance. "Sounds ... good?"

There was a momentary meeting of eyes between Robina and Catherine before they made to move.

"It had *better* be," growled Catherine to no one in particular, as the trio headed towards the patio doors.

Abbie waited for a few more minutes. She tried to think of ways that she might reverse the spell, but she just couldn't concentrate. The hysteria in her head was clouding her ability to formulate the words. But then, if she wasn't sure how she cast the spell in the first place, how could she possibly reverse it?

She couldn't just say the words backwards, like some of the other spells, just in case she got it all wrong and broke some other body part in the process. Or could she? That slimy bastard deserved everything he got. She should have cracked every available bone in his disgusting body.

She would have to go back, there was no doubt about that. She would have to face him, call an ambulance—something. She'd have to threaten or bargain with him to keep him quiet. Surely, they both had something to lose if this ever got out—he'd tried to rape her for shit's sake, what she did was self-fucking-defence! But who would see it like that? Young lad advances on a girl who, in retaliation, manages to crush every bone in his hand. She didn't sound much of a victim when she put it like that.

She got to her feet, running her hands down her dress, which was wet and sticky with mud.

Slowly, she started to advance down the hill, back in the direction she had come. He was softly sobbing as she approached him. He had managed to move downhill slightly, towards the shelter of a bush. Even in the dark, she could make out his hunched figure crouching down, clutching his hand.

"You came back then? Didn't leave me for dead?" he snarled at her. She was shaking but managed to keep her composure.

"You're not dead, just a few broken bones, that's all," she said, with a similarly frosty attitude.

"A few? What the fuck have you done to me?" he whimpered. This sudden helpless act was beginning to make the rage rise up within her.

"I haven't done anything you didn't deserve," she said, stooping to meet his face. "You would have done much worse to me. You tried to fucking rape me, you arsehole."

He was silent for a moment.

"I wouldn't have done it," he said, in a thin whisper.

"Like fuck, you wouldn't have," she growled.

"Now, I'll go and get help, but we need to keep our stories straight here. Either this happened in self-defence and we both go down for it, or it was a happy accident and you forget the whole thing." Her voice was steady, but her heart was beating fast.

He didn't reply—she could hear him breathing through the darkness.

"Or I can leave you here to make your decision if you'd rather," she said rising to standing. "But it'll be a cold, long night out on this hill."

She waited a moment before making to retreat back towards the main road.

"Okay," he pleaded. "It was an accident. I'll say I fell, just help me."

She let him wait a moment.

"Please?" His voice was strained. She puffed the air out of her cheeks.

"Okay," she started, "I'll grab your phone."

"On the ground over there."

She walked over to where the phone's screen was still illuminated. Abbie bent down, picked it up and brought it over, shining the dulled light onto his face. His eyes were puffy as he looked at her with a sense of bewilderment. He was like a little boy. A lost little boy. Her heart skipped in her chest and her eyes filled with pity.

"Okay, let's get you up then and—"

She went to pull him up, but something made her stop. In the meagre phone light, she noticed a figure, lying a few metres behind where Xander was sat.

"What?" he said, glancing over his shoulder into the nothingness.

"What's that?" she asked incredulously, moving the phone's screen from his face and over his shoulder. From this distance and by this light, it looked as though someone was face

385

down, covered over with a few leaves and branches.

"How do you put the torch on?" she asked him.

"For fuck's sake! You need my password," he said. "Then you can switch the app on. Look—I'm in pain here!"

"*Wait* a second," she barked. "Give me your password."

"I'm not giving you my fucking password," he scoffed.

"Just do it!" she snapped, urgently.

"Okay, okay—5825."

She keyed it into the phone.

"It's got a flashlight icon on it," he said. "Just do it quickly."

After a bit of desperate searching, she found the icon and pressed it. Immediately, a bright beam of light shone out of the phone's flashbulb.

She inched forward to get a better view as she held the light out in front of her.

"Holy shit" she exclaimed, nearly dropping the phone.

"What?" he demanded.

She swallowed a moment as she tried to comprehend just what she was looking at, stretched out, supine in the long grass. There was no question in her mind.

"There's a fucking dead body here."

■ ■

Once congregated in the garden, Becky, Robina and Catherine found a spot near a large table that had been decorated with various horror-themed paraphernalia and big, gothic candlesticks. Countless tins and dishes adorned the table, one of which was Catherine's orange one with the fanned lid that Rachel had taken from her friend and was now holding in her hand. Robina was beginning to look increasingly more worried by the second. Becky couldn't be certain, but it definitely looked like her and Catherine were in some kind of cahoots over what was in that tin and Becky was intrigued. If Robina's pained expression was anything to go by, something catastrophic was about to happen. Like staring at a car crash, however, Becky couldn't help but watch.

As people began to gather and call their children to stop playing and join the group alongside their parents, Rachel Power stood centre stage, grinning from ear to ear.

"Right," Rachel began, managing to sound charming and authoritarian all at the same time. "If I can have your attention please everyone?"

A hush began to descend on the sea of expectant faces.

"Firstly, welcome to the *tenth* annual Power's Halloween Ball," she said, with all the necessary confidence of a seasoned public speaker. "I hope you are all having a *fantastic* time. Thank you to all of you, but mostly to my old ball 'n' chain,

Hugh, for putting up with me, Erin and Mungo for being such darlings while mummy has been going coco-loco and, of course, our long-suffering housemaid Rosita for decorating the place so *wonderfully* terrifying!"

There was a ripple of applause and a few shouts of appreciation as Rachel scanned the party, winking and waving at anyone she recognised.

Becky noticed that the Puerto Rican lady at the side of the table was trying—and failing—to hide the fact that she looked tired and, ultimately, pretty pissed off, despite the recognition.

"Soon we will be asking your *fabulous* little treasures to step forward to the front for the costume judging, but *first*, we will have the annual Halloween cake-a-thon!" she beamed. "Let's not forget that all the money we raise from the sales of tonight's cakes and treats will be going straight to the Dear Hearts of Gloucestershire charity for children's heart disease, of which I am a patron, so please—*dig deep*!"

Catherine was surveying the crowd and muttering something to herself. She had an unhinged look in her eye as she scanned the row behind her. She locked eyes with someone and started to mouth furiously at them.

Becky followed her gaze. She was actually scorning her husband, Saul, who was cradling a beer a few yards away. He began to reluctantly make his way over as Rachel Power continued gushing.

"So, without further ado, let's have a look at the first one, which I *believe* is from Catherine Clements!" Rachel tapped the lid of the tin in her hand.

Becky swung her focus between Robina and Catherine—one of them looked unashamedly smug while the other looked as though she were about to be sick.

There was another small round of applause for Catherine and she turned to give the audience a knowing grin.

With fervour, Rachel grasped the lid of the tin and tore it off, just as Catherine moved her head back around.

Peering in, Rachel's facial expression was one of mock disbelief.

"Oh ... *dear*," she said, a grimace plastered across her face. The people around her began to look into the tin and employ the same look of shock.

Catherine's face fell so hard, it nearly hit the floor.

"I think your standards might be slipping, dear!" Rachel said with glee, putting her hand in and holding up the contents for everyone to see. It was an orangey-brown, oozing mess of a cake, both flat and ugly. It had the vague resemblance of a pumpkin, but one that had been left out since last year—and been run over a fair few times by Rachel's Jaguar.

A Mexican wave-like smirk made its way around the garden as Catherine's face turned progressively more crimson. Her mouth dropped open and she began to grasp around her neck at an invisible noose.

"Not so much Baked Alaska as Baked *Disast-a*! Better luck next year," Rachel teased. "I just hope the dogs are still hungry."

At this, people couldn't contain their mirth, and a sudden burst of laughter erupted from the partygoers.

Becky felt a pang of sympathy and embarrassment for Catherine who clearly wanted the ground to swallow her up. Her mouth opened and closed like a robotic fish and her eyes darted about the place like she was possessed.

Rachel carried on laughing, hers being the loudest and the most pronounced. She slid the cake back onto the table and wiped her hand, in mock disgust, on the skirt of her outfit.

Catherine turned to Robina and gave her an icy glare before reaching out to Becky.

"I've got to get out of here," she choked, her voice tight and thin. "Now. I've got to get out of here now. Please."

Becky froze in surprise for a moment. She was not used to seeing Catherine like this, vulnerable and afraid. It was upsetting and frightening, and

Becky needed a moment to process it. She nodded and handed Robina her drink.

Becky put her arm awkwardly around Catherine's shoulders and led her through the crowd of onlookers, in the direction of the pond. The laughing began to die down as people saw Catherine's reaction and they moved out of the way to let them both pass. Each face they met on their journey away from the throng had the same expression of exasperated pity. Catherine kept her head down and her eyes on the floor.

As soon as they reached the outskirts of the pond, away from the rest, Catherine gulped back a few sobs.

"She knew," she whispered to Becky.

A few people wanted to come over and console Catherine, but Becky kept them away with a slight shake of the head. Even Saul had the good grace to stand well back.

When she was sure that it was safe, Catherine buried her head in Becky's shoulder and wept as Becky held her loosely.

■■■■■■■■■■■■■■■■■■■■■■■■■■■■■■■■■■■■■■■

Abbie ran the light around the edge of the body, careful not to move anything. She had to check whether it was breathing and, therefore, still alive. She scanned the phone over the figure slowly so that she could examine the state that the body was in.

The clothes were ripped and mud-stained. A long skirt had been torn and shredded at the bottom to reveal stubbly, white legs that were peppered with cuts and bruises. The shoes were women's flats that were heavily damaged and discoloured. A sheer blouse was now thick with dirt and the hair, that had probably been in a plait before, was now tangled and filthy, splaying across the shoulders and onto the ground.

The body lay with both arms outstretched as if it had fallen there. The skin was greyish-white, with splatters of dirt and decay.

She ran the light down the arms and along the fingers. The left hand was scuffed and scabbed, the nails broken and green with grass stains. The right hand was a little more unusual, which made Abbie turn a shade of grey herself. Through the entire index finger, a long masonry nail protruded, almost as if it had been hammered through with force. It didn't look as though it had been pierced accidentally—this was definitely the work of an assailant.

As she ran the light back up to the face, she gasped in shock.

"What the fuck is it?" Xander called from a few yards away. "This is creeping me out—we've got to go."

"Oh *shit!*" Abbie said to herself as she studied the face more intensely. The facial muscles had fallen but it was unmistakable. The long nose, the thin but perfectly sculpted lips, the arched brows. It all made sense.

"*What*?" Xander called impatiently.

"This body," she said, to herself more than to him, "this is the body of Anne Wicks."

Just as she stepped back from the body to get a better view of her face, to make absolutely sure that she had, in fact, found the corpse of the mystery woman who had disappeared all those months ago, she stopped.

There was a momentary pause. And then its eyes snapped open.

■■■■■■■■■■■■■■■■■■■■■■■■■■■■■■■■■■■■■■

"I'm *sorry*, Catherine," Rachel Power said, swooping over to the couple as they stood alone on the quieter outskirts of the garden. "I was only teasing!"

Catherine lifted her head from her friend's shoulder and spun around so quickly that Becky thought she might send them both tumbling. Catherine's lipstick was smeared, and her mascara had slightly run. She looked a little like Boy George, sweltering to death in a sauna.

"Don't give me that, *Power*!" she swiped, spitting venom at her interrogator, "You *gave* me the name of that woman. You set me up!"

■■■■■■■■■■■■■■■■■■■■■■■■■■■■■■■■■■■■■■

The thing watched from its position behind the pond. It licked its lips again as it watched the scene play out. It needed its prey to separate before it could make its move—it slunk back into the undergrowth and lay low.

■■

Rachel laughed as Becky began to feel incredibly uncomfortable.

"Oh, don't be ridiculous. I don't know what you're talking about," Rachel responded, cool and calm. Her countenance remained unchanged.

"You knew!" Catherine blubbered. "You knew that I wouldn't have time to make a cake. I told Grace De Montford! You knew that if I was to do everything myself it would compromise my title as the best baker in Winchcombe. You couldn't stand it, so you set me up!"

Rachel raised a perfectly-arched eyebrow and put her hand on her hip.

"I think," she said, "that what we have here is an admission of fraud."

Becky watched, dumbfounded, as Catherine calmly put herself back together and held her head up. Even though her makeup was smeared, and her hair was all tousled at the front, Catherine's front made her look even more beautiful.

"No," she spat, "what we have here is an admission that you are a fucking *bitch*."

Rachel didn't quite know what to do with this word. She had been called it before, but not since those little sluts in high school had her in a headlock. She taught them a lesson in the end, and she would do the same here.

She laughed mockingly at Catherine, who stood firm. Rachel walked a few steps away, before looking over her shoulder and opening her mouth to speak.

"A bitch I may be," she said slowly, savouring every syllable, "but the only *fucking* I know about is that Grace De Montford is fucking your husband behind your back."

The air stood fraught for a moment as the comment sunk in. Becky saw Catherine's expression turn from one of defiance into one of twisted, contorted rage. Catherine's stance suddenly became feline. She hunched back on her heels, ready to pounce as she lifted her arms up and bent her fingers into claws.

At that moment, Catherine was on the edge of absolute mania and Becky steeled herself to jump in and pull her back.

But before Catherine could strike her arch-enemy, something else tore between them. A flash of white shot across the lawn, galloping at great speed on four nimble limbs—something inhuman and feral. It sped past the two women and leapt through the air, towards its prey.

Before anyone could react, the beast hit its mark and locked its jaws onto her neck. There was no time for anyone to even scream out—the thing had sunk its teeth into Rachel Power's neck. Its head flicked backwards sharply, ripping the entire throat right out and covering the lawn with a fine spray of crimson blood.

Catherine's and Becky's mouths fell wide open as the beast landed on its four limbs, the body of its victim dropping like a rag doll to the floor.

The beast turned its head, a chunk of pink, masticated flesh dangling from its bare teeth.

As it did so, it locked eyes with Becky. She realised, at that moment, that what she had come face-to-face with was not an animal. It was human, and it was familiar—she was staring into the bloodshot eyes of Brenda Ware.

Catherine was the first to scream. She flung herself as far out of the beast's reach as she could and began to scramble across the garden towards the pond.

Becky kept her eyes locked with Brenda as she moved closer, like a rabid, bloodthirsty animal. Becky's heart started to beat rapidly as other party members began to flee and children ran into the arms of their terrified parents.

As Becky's heart raced, she felt as though she was lapsing into some kind of seizure. Her body went hot, and her chest began to rise and fall. As if taken over, her eyes rolled back and her whole head collapsed forwards. Her mind went completely blank as all the muscles in her body relaxed at once.

A voice began to form in her head. It was familiar, but not instantly recognisable. She followed the words.

"Palo Mortis Release Embegum."

The words continued. They were slow, they were deep. They were female.

She felt her lips mould around the chant and, as if encouraged by an unknown force, she spoke the words aloud.

At that moment Becky was blasted back into consciousness, still staring into Brenda's eyes. Her gaze dropped, and her face morphed into a twisted visage of agony. Spontaneously, Brenda's frame began to buckle, and she spat the greying flesh from her mouth as she cried out in pain. Her whole body began to contort as she arched her back and slumped to her knees. There was a loud cracking sound, like a firework exploding, as a black lightning bolt broke free from Brenda's chest and shot up into the air. With that, the body slumped back to the ground.

It all happened so quickly that Becky could hardly believe it. Suddenly, the party was in absolute chaos. People began running into the house in fear, their screams echoing around the garden.

Becky felt extremely exhausted and flopped into the grass. Through the fog of her exhaustion, she heard someone calling her name, but she could feel herself slipping into unconsciousness. She immediately put her hands on her belly. Through the sea of moving bodies, a figure approached her, repeating her name over and over.

Becky felt arms around her, pulling her close.

"It's okay," the voice kept saying. "You'll be alright."

It wasn't the same voice that she had heard in her head just moments before, but it was just as familiar.

"My baby," she said, her vision clouding over.

"You'll be fine," the voice said. Even in her bewildered state, the voice came to her.

"Gaynor?" she called out, her eyes closing, the world closing in around her.

"I'm here," Gaynor said, tightening her embrace.

And just like that, everything went black.

SIXTEEN

Becky's vision went from blurry to hazy, as the shape of a face began to materialise in front of her—it was a face that she knew. The person was speaking, not to her, but about her.

"I don't know how she could have known, I really don't. She's never mentioned anything of the sort since we met."

The voice was urgent, almost defensive.

"Oh shit," Becky said. She wasn't in the correct frame of mine to say anything politer. "What happened—where am I?"

Becky looked around as her vision began to clear. She noticed that her surroundings were a hue of red and gold that she remembered from somewhere. As she went to sit up, she noticed other faces inching their way into view.

"Oh, Becky ... Becky, my love it's me, it's Gaynor. You're safe, don't worry about that. You mustn't move though, my dear—you took quite a tumble." She laughed, but it was depthless. Becky moved her hand to her stomach in a frantic manner.

"The baby is fine, everything's fine." Gaynor's voice was clipped and desperate. It didn't fill Becky with much confidence.

"Why am I here?" Becky asked, slowly coming around. "Why am I ... why am I not in the hospital?"

"You don't need the hospital, love, we've, err ... already checked you over," Gaynor said, still sounding a little unsure.

"*We?*"

Suddenly, another woman stepped into the frame. Someone that Becky had not met before. She was officious looking and pristinely well-groomed. She was the kind of high-powered executive type that Becky was used to seeing in London, but not so much gracing the quiet streets of Winchcombe.

"Hi Becky, how are you feeling? My name is Odette. It's a pleasure to meet you." Her voice was soft yet direct, but Becky was panicked.

"Yes, you too I'm sure, but what the hell is going on here? I shouldn't be here, I should be at home or at the hospital or something. I don't know you and I don't know this house!" Her voice started to rise.

"Now Becky, you need to stay calm," Odette said, almost as if she was scolding her. The gall of this woman was almost too much to bear. Becky clambered up onto her elbows and looked at the four faces that stared back at her: Gaynor, this Odette, Robina—looking extremely upset—and some other woman, the woman whose house this was. Julia? Judith, was it? No, Joanna!

Her side began to scream out in pain and Becky let out an audible cry.

"Please Becky, stay as you are," Gaynor pleaded.

When she regained her composure, Becky slouched back onto her shoulders.

"Gaynor," she said breathlessly, "will you please explain to me what happened, why I am here and not in a medical facility and why are these women around me telling me what to do?"

Her patience was now at breaking point.

Gaynor bit her lip as she looked over at Odette, whose eyes were alive with interest. She nodded back at Gaynor.

"I'm waiting," Becky said forcefully.

"Well love, you remember, you took a fall?" she said tentatively. "You took a fall right after you were confronted by that ... that thing."

Becky frowned slightly as the words sank in. Yes, she did remember. She had come face to face with Brenda Ware, only it wasn't her. It was something else, something more menacing—less human. Tears involuntarily trickled from her eyes as the magnitude of what she had faced now dawned on her.

"Well," Gaynor went on, "you did something, Becky. You recited something, an incantation of some sort—and you killed it. Whatever was holding on to that woman, you released it. You saved her soul."

Becky's frown deepened.

"What do you mean?" she said in a dry, emotional voice.

"I'm afraid I haven't been entirely honest with you," Gaynor said, her voice trembling. "When you asked me if I had powers and I said no..."

Becky looked around at the women. Their faces were stern, apart from Robina who looked unusually impassive.

"We had to bring you to this house because it is one of the only safe places that we could bring you," Gaynor said. "You see, the Arrowood I have been feeding you isn't just to cure sickness. It provides an unbreakable shield around your baby. It's protection. And I know that your baby is fine because ... well, because I have protected her."

Becky went to speak, but she wasn't sure she knew what to say.

"I have what some may call a *gift*," Gaynor continued, looking up and into Becky's eyes. "We call them enlighters. They are unique to each of us. Mine is to heal. I have healed you ... and your daughter."

Becky's was still in total confusion. This must be a wind-up.

"I'm not expecting you to understand straight away, but you must understand this," Gaynor told her, her face suddenly serious. "You have an enlighter too. You used it tonight. You must be one of us."

"So, you're…" Becky said, the words bubbling from her lips as her eyes grew wide. "You're witches?"

Each face, in turn, thawed a little. Gaynor looked around at the others, who looked back at her empathetically.

"Well, I guess you could say—"

"But why should I believe you?" she whispered.

At this point, Odette stepped forward and smiled. She put her hand on the crown of her head as if she were about to pull a wig off, but instead, ever-so-steadily, she brought her palms down across her forehead and over her face. As she did so, the face of Temperance emerged.

"My *God*," Becky gasped in disbelief. She then felt moved to laugh.

"You are real-life witches," she cried incredulously.

"I suppose you could say we are," Odette took over, "and I think, Becky, that you might be one too."

Two thoughts suddenly struck Becky as she lay there on Joanna's sofa, staring up at these four disparate women while still dressed in a witch's Halloween costume. She could well be a real one—and she was having a little girl.

Catherine was manically cleaning her hands, trying to wipe make-believe blood off of them, even though she had scrubbed them for at least fifteen minutes until they were red-raw. Her hair had come loose and was hanging like the branches of a willow tree. Sienna's discarded costume rested, lopsided, against the wall. She had ripped it from her as they all clambered into the back of her car.

Saul had gone to join them.

"I don't damn well think so," her swift response had been. Everything had happened so fast. Hugh running to scoop up what was left of his mangled wife, children screaming—or had it been the mothers screaming? Fathers running. Car's starting, total and utter devastation and chaos.

It was the second time that Brenda Ware had wreaked havoc on an event. In truth, it was the second time she had died at one too.

The police had been called and Catherine had had to make a statement.

"I don't know, officer. She leapt out of the bushes and just ... just *dived* at her. I mean, she was like a ... like an animal! Hunched on all fours like some kind of predatory cat! I mean, it was like something off of a David Attenborough programme."

Saul had gone to put his arm around her, but Catherine had removed it with a stiff, upward shoulder shrug.

"And did she say anything?"

"No, she just ... *growled*?"

Catherine could barely believe she was saying these words, nor that she was in a police station, holding a Styrofoam cup of tea and sitting opposite a female officer who had a moustache and all the grace of Big Daddy Crabtree. The whole situation was completely ridiculous.

And what happened to Becky? She had said something and set off some kind of explosion that threw Catherine back, knocking the wind right out of her. When she had come to, Becky was being carried off by that old hag from the town and that idiotic cake woman. But rather than go through the front entrance, they went around the pond and disappeared out the back. Catherine hadn't known that there even *was* an exit back there.

But she hadn't had time to investigate as people came up to her, checking whether she was alright, wanting to know what had happened. As shaken as Catherine was, she had quite enjoyed basking in a little of the spotlight. She also couldn't resist taking another look at Rachel Power, maimed and deposited on the grass. Even in death, she looked achingly beautiful. Her porcelain skin, splattered with blood and her eyes open, the sparkle

405

extinguished. Catherine only wished she hadn't thrown up at the site of her half-devoured throat.

And in her heart of hearts, even though Catherine resented that old woman and her garden, that stood in the way of council developments, she felt, deep down, that she should keep their exit a secret.

And as Catherine's children made their way over to her, nonchalant through disbelief, she held them close.

"Can we go home now mummy?" Michael had asked, his pupils dilated with concern.

"Of course, sweetie," Catherine said, smoothing his hair down with her hand.

"But your father can walk."

■■■

"Palo Mortis Release Embegum. I mean, that is quite advanced magic. Semantically, it is the formation of two principles which, in effect, shouldn't work." Odette was speaking to the room, but more so thinking out loud. "Palo comes from the ancient Wiccan word for a dark spirit, but its origins would be water-based. It certainly wouldn't be appropriate for this particular possession."

Becky was now fully awake and sitting up on Joanna's sofa, drinking from a china mug filled with spiced tea. The earlier revelations were still rattling around in her head.

"And Embegum, well, that's a fusion of two factions," Odette went on. "Begum is another term for dilution, but then Em means to reverse. So, in essence, it's saying to evaporate the dark spirit from the waters of Mortis. Mortis coming from the French word for death."

She looked at Becky as if Becky should have a clue what she was on about.

"I mean it makes sense, but it is a super-round-about way of saying it. It's almost poetic—like a Shakespearean approach to a direct spell. I'll have to research it. It's not something I have ever come across before. It might even explain your ancestry, Rebecca."

Becky half-shrugged, half-shook her head. All she remembered was that there was a voice inside her head that told her to say it, and she just said it.

Gaynor was the next to speak.

"And your mother never mentioned any sort of coven or circle in conversation? An aunt or a grandmother?"

Becky shook her head again.

"Well ... no," she said. "My mother is not a very open person I'm afraid. I couldn't see her getting involved in anything supernatural."

I mean, for goodness sake, Beatrice Carrington collected Royal Worcester crockery, she was hardly likely to be the Elvira of Southgate. And she hated anything remotely scary—she could barely sit through *Doctor Who* without having to

407

get up and make a cup of tea. But then, perhaps that was a sign.

"And would I have your permission to run your name through our database?" Odette asked, scribbling a few notes down onto an open pad.

"Yes, of course," Becky said finally. "It will be interesting for me to see how I fit into all this. If I do, of course. I mean, this could all be some massive kind of fluke."

"I don't think so," Odette said. "You didn't just say these words—you cast the spell. You need to have some kind of magical authority to do that. Otherwise, women the length and breadth of the country would be casting willy-nilly. You, my dear, have an inherited gift. An enlighter."

Becky would need a little more convincing.

"I need to get back to my husband," she said. "He'll be worried."

Odette stopped for a moment, chewing the end of her pen.

"Of course," she said, after what seemed like an hour of pensive mulling over. She was still trying to work the language equation out in her head.

"But I think it is only right that we hold another meeting with all the others. They should be informed of what has happened this evening. Joanna?" She threw a look in Joanna's direction.

Joanna, who had barely said anything for the entirety of the meeting, gave a small, meek nod. She was utterly worn out.

"I'm telling you, her eyes were open," Abbie told the bolshy paramedic, in between frantic puffs of her cigarette.

"Well, people often die with their eyes open," the man said condescendingly, as he slammed the back of the ambulance door.

"No, they opened. In front of me. She wasn't dead!"

"Look, I'm sorry to have to tell you this love, but the body was decaying. It had been there for some time. If you're that worried, you should really be talking to the police."

He nodded in the direction of the stern-looking policewoman who was directing a police cordon.

Abbie rolled her eyes and stormed over to the figure. She was a hard-looking woman with a rosy-red face and a touch of clear mascara. She was shorter than Abbie, but what she lacked for in size, she made up for in assertiveness.

"Hey," Abbie said.

"Yes, Madam?" the woman eyed her up suspiciously. "I need this area cleared please, so I'd be grateful if you were on your way."

"I'm the one who made the call," Abbie interjected. "I ... that is to say, *we* ... found her."

"We?" The woman still seemed unimpressed.

"Yes. My friend and I. He was taken away by an ambulance about ten minutes ago. He ... fell."

"I see," the policewoman answered. "Well, I think that you'd better be escorted to the police station so that one of my colleagues can take a statement then."

"But she's not dead," Abbie said. "I think you're all making a mistake."

"It was my understanding," the policewoman began, leaning forward as if to make her point abundantly clear, "that the body had been missing for some time and was fairly decomposed at the time of discovery."

"That's as maybe," Abbie pleaded, "but she isn't dead. I think she may be dangerous. That is, I think she might harm someone."

Abbie thought that this is what Joanna would do in such a quandary. After she noticed the body, Abbie used the phone in her hand to call 999. Miss Wicks hadn't moved, but Abbie distinctly saw her eyes open and close. And with the recent events as discussed in their circle meetings—which, for the most part, she'd flatly ignored—Abbie was pretty sure that the police should alert The Oracle if anything suspicious was reported.

"Listen, I would really appreciate it if you went down to the station and answered a few questions," the policewoman nodded. "I can't have anybody in this area at the present time until our investigation is complete."

The woman extended an arm towards one of her fellow officers. Abbie reluctantly nodded and made her way over. The grass crunched under her feet and her bag strap was beginning to make her shoulder sore.

"Err … I was at the scene," she said to the kind-looking man. "I think I need to talk to someone about what I found."

"Right, Madam," he said, feeling around in his high-visibility jacket for something. He brought out a set of keys. "Do you want to do it here or at the station?"

"At the station," she said. "I need to go into town."

He nodded and escorted her over to the car.

The reality of what she had discovered began to sink in. The body of Miss Wicks, the ashen skin, the torn clothes and broken heels of her smart shoes, the nail that had been driven through her finger. What the hell had happened here?

Suddenly, she panicked.

"Sorry, Sir," she said, making the policeman stop in his tracks and look back at her with a concerned expression. "Before I get in … I think I'm going to be sick."

∎∎

"So, what happens now?" Becky asked Gaynor, as the old woman threw one of Joanna's shawls over Becky's shoulders.

It was a few minutes since they had left Joanna's and now they were walking home.

411

"Well," Gaynor said, looking down as they linked arms, "I suppose we wait to hear what The Oracle has to say."

"Right," Becky stopped. "The Oracle being...?"

"Oh, The Oracle is the highest of the High Priestesses," Gaynor said quietly as she hobbled alongside her friend. "She is the high power of The Order and the one that governs the entire operation. She is omnipresent, yet entirely elusive. We don't know who she is or where she is. All we know is that she looks after us. Her and the goddess, of course."

"And is she..." Becky was tentative—she didn't want to ask anything stupid but then after this evening's antics, she was sure that no eventuality could be impossible. "Is she, like ... an angel?"

Gaynor laughed—it was condescending but genuine.

"No, my child. She is a woman, made of flesh and bone like you and me. But she holds the authority to use magick wherever and whenever it is needed, unlike us puritan witches who can only use spells in a controlled and regulated environment. The Oracle is like the Prime Minister of our world. And like a Prime Minister, she makes all of the big decisions. She is responsible for our protection and conservation, yet we will probably never meet her. And the current Oracle has been reigning for as long as our monarch. They often work together to allow both worlds to exist in harmony."

"Amazing," Becky said breathlessly. She couldn't believe that in the space of one night, she had been catapulted into this covert world. A world of mystery and wonder, one that runs parallel with the world she knew and yet was governed by a whole other elite. She had so much to learn about the things beyond her imagination.

"And who can I tell about all this?" Becky asked after a few moments of silence. She realised that this new society must operate solely behind closed doors if she had not been aware of it until tonight. And if she started going on about possibly being a witch to anyone in London, her friends and family would think that living in the country had driven her barking mad.

"Well, since you have now been introduced to The Order, I suppose you will have to have the initiation and official welcome into the circle. After that, it is one of the rules that you will have to inform your husband." Gaynor looked up. "But in most cases, it is customary for the magickal person in your family to be present when you tell him. It softens the blow somewhat."

Gaynor smiled reassuringly.

"But I don't know who that is." Becky was still mentally trying to work out who on earth in her family could be a witch without her knowing. "I mean, I never really knew my grandmother. She was from Ukraine, I think, and lived there all her life. As far as I know, her and my mother never had the best relationship. Perhaps that is why. Maybe it's her?"

"Oh, I am sure Odette will find out for you, child," Gaynor assured her. "She is a High Sceptre, so this will probably be top of her agenda. I imagine that an emergency meeting will be called tomorrow, by which point you will meet the other ladies and we will go from there."

"I see." Becky's eyes sparkled with intrigue.

They neared the end of Gaynor's road before unlinking arms.

"Well, this is me," Gaynor said as she smiled in adieu and made to turn towards her house.

"Gaynor," Becky called out—the old woman turned back around. "Thank you for coming for me tonight."

Gaynor's eyes creased at the corners as she gazed at her friend with a loving affection.

"There is absolutely no way I would have left you," she said. "I am your protector."

There was a moment of comfortable quiet between the two women. Becky had never felt more connected to another female than she did now.

"And," Becky said, the words almost catching in her throat as tears pricked her eyes suddenly, "I really am so sorry about—"

"I know," Gaynor said before she could finish. "I know."

■■■

When Becky got in, Dom was in the shower. His clothes were strewn about the bedroom. She could hear the soft downpour of water as the smell of coconut drifted with steam out through the open door.

She fell backwards onto the bed and lay there for a while. She tried to process the night's events but was far too tired to go through them frame by frame in any kind of attempt to make sense of it all now.

The shower stopped and after a few minutes, a shiny, water-streaked Dom emerged, wrapped in a towel. He looked different, happy almost. She felt as though she had missed his smile, as though it was an echo from happier times. In a few short days, she had really sensed their disconnection. They were acting like flatmates having to share a bed, rather than husband and wife. She didn't know whether it was her fault or his, she just knew that she felt different about him somehow. As if she had found something else in her life that was more important than him—she had found a bond with her people.

"Hey," he said, towelling his hair with his free hand. "I didn't hear you come in."

She let out a breathy laugh.

"I was being stealthy."

He snorted.

"Good time?"

She pursed her lips together and looked up at him. His baby girl was growing inside of her. A perfect, little, magical, baby girl.

"I had a bloody fantastic time," she said and got up to get undressed.

■■■

Wing walked slowly down the hallway, pushing the temperamental trolley. Often, as was her luck at the moment, it would veer off to one side, rattling the cups and sending a shower of milk careering up the wall.

She had come to realise that, the slower she went, the likelihood of avoiding this mishap would increase.

Elsie was sat in her usual place, transfixed on old reruns of *Columbo* on the television and tutting as anyone in a tabard walked past. The new Polish girl, Kristina, had got an earful earlier this morning, as Wing had sneaked out to make a phone call.

"Bloody Ruskies," Elsie had moaned in her spiteful, Gloucester drawl. "Coming over here and taking our jobs."

Matron had reprimanded her in the end.

"Elsie," she had said in a stern voice, thrusting her bosom out to exert her authority. "If Kristina hadn't filled the vacancy then we would have no one to help you onto the toilet. So, I think that is quite enough."

"*I don't see,*" Elise has responded in long, drawn-out words to emphasise her point, "*why* our boys fought in the war if all they were going to do is come over here anyway. It's a bloody disgrace."

"Well," Matron said firmly, "I would hardly call helping you on and off the commode a sterling victory, would you?"

She marched off, stealing a wink at Wing as she went.

Wing had smiled. In truth, it was not that she disliked Elsie—she didn't really dislike anyone. She was just afraid of her. Her vicious bleatings made Wing feel as though English imperialism was still alive and well. And if that was the case, she might be forced to leave the country, and she didn't want to do that. She loved this strange, little island.

Another person who made her feel similarly uncomfortable was Joanna, though she had been much more approachable while Odette had been around. Joanna had telephoned earlier to let Wing know that an emergency meeting was to be called this evening and had sounded almost pleased to speak to her.

There was obviously some advance with this odd possession magic thing which seemed to be threatening the town since they were now meeting every week. It didn't particularly scare Wing—she had seen far worse. She had sat and watched as a small, Thai woman with a hardened

417

face and only one eyeball had cut her own palm and bled into a bowl on the table. Wing had gripped her mother's hand as she watched the eyeball roll around in its gooey socket. The woman had spoken in a voice that came from the depths of her throat. Of course, she had cost a pretty price. No charlatan would ever self-mutilate without asking for a three-figure sum in return.

Wing's mother, however, had believed in the woman's authenticity as a medium and twisted her hand free from her daughter's clutch.

When it was evident that this woman knew nothing of her dead husband and, instead, demanded more money to make better communication, Wing's mother had scolded her daughter for being there at all and ruining the woman's concentration. She then stormed off, leaving Wing to struggle to catch up with her as busy people rushed between them, kicking dust into her face.

As she entered the small care home lounge, armed with a teapot and a plate of soft biscuits, she noticed activity by Jacqueline's room.

Mr Eyre, the consultant was here again. That was never a good sign.

Yesterday, Jacqueline had pulled Wing close as she was smoothing her bed covers. It had startled Wing, as she had thought that Jacqueline was asleep.

"I know," Jacqueline had said weakly, her voice a whisper, her breath soft. "I know that it is soon my time."

Wings heart had broken right there on the floor.

"The pain," Jacqueline continued, "it feels like a separate organ inside of me. It's not going to go away."

She had released her grip on Wing's arm and settled back into her bed. Her eyes had remained closed.

"But, my darling, I am not sad," the dying woman had said, a slight crack in her voice. "My family waits for me in heaven. My Wilfred, my Sarah."

Wing's teeth came down over her lip as she blinked back tears. She had continued to run her hand along Jacqueline's bed covers as she silently wept tears of her own.

And now the consultant was discussing something with Matron, who nodded along sombrely.

Wing would have to cast a different kind of spell tonight.

∎∎

It had been a long night for Abbie. After being asked the same questions over and over again at the police station, stopping only to get a cup of coffee and borrow a cigarette off of a semi-attractive silver fox in uniform, she had only just crawled in at half-five.

Her flatmates were all asleep, but that didn't stop her making a clattering sound as she searched around her bedroom for the small pot of oil she used to rewind the night's events. That was one thing Joanna couldn't stop her from doing. Provided it didn't mess with anyone's well-being, Abbie could use her divination enlighter to her heart's content. The oil helped her to scan both backwards and forwards, depending on what information she was seeking. Thoughts rushed through her head like a series of camera shots.

When she eventually located it, tangled up with an old thong in her top drawer, she dabbed a little onto each temple and let her head flick back on her neck.

Her eyes fell open and rolled back as images from the evening scrolled through her mind.

There she sat at the police station, absentmindedly tracing the rim of her coffee cup with her index finger as the officers eyed her with cautious disbelief.

"She wasn't dead?" the attractive one asked. "You know that is a pretty sensational claim?"

She remembered him instantly falling out of her favour.

The images flew back through to her awkward ride in the police car with the other officer. The one whose ears stuck out of the side of his head like the handles of the World Cup. He tried to make small talk as they juddered along Cleeve Hill. She hadn't felt much like talking—she had just wanted to get away from the scene.

Next, she saw Xander being lifted onto a stretcher, wincing in pain as the paramedic crew bandaged his hands. She was acting in an overly assiduous manner, but he was struggling to keep up the charade, saying that he had fallen with his hands outstretched as he had playfully chased her in the dark.

And then back to her and Xander, on their own, kneeling before the spent corpse. Wondering what they should do, calling out to see if there might be a response and, clear as day, the eyes of Miss Wicks opening in front of her.

She was right.

Bringing herself out of the trance, she massaged her temples slightly as her eyes readjusted. This was serious. There was every chance that this corpse could be bewitched by the same force that was threatening the coven.

She had decided to try and get some sleep before she contacted Joanna in the morning, but the sleep wouldn't come. She had just laid in bed for three hours, staring up at the ceiling as the light came in through the gap in the curtains.

And now, at nine o'clock, she found herself logging on to Facebook and going straight to the search browser to try and find some more details on what type of magick can be used to bewitch people into coming back from the dead.

What to type though?

Odette had made it clear that this kind of magick had never been used before, so there wasn't going to be anything online.

Perhaps she should contact Ebony, she might know. They always had little chats about using magick, but nothing this heavy. They had never broached anything more serious than good sex spells and anti-blemish potions.

In truth, she didn't really know if Ebony was who she said she was, and that's why Abbie kept herself moderately discrete when chatting to her. It was a big no-no to reveal anything about the coven online. But compared to witchcraft, the internet was a brand-new invention and hadn't been given proper regulation by the archaic, old farts who dominated the higher echelons of The Order so, in effect, she could write what she liked. Abbie should really be responsible enough to be suitably secretive, since Ebony could be anyone really—even a member of that group of witch hunters, acting as a honey trap for those who played fast and loose with their personal security.

It was probably not a good idea to talk about this on Facebook.

But then, she could find out whether anyone else had mentioned it in a post, that wasn't giving anything away. As she went to type, a message pinged onto her mobile screen. It was from Joanna, and it was terse and direct.

"We need to talk."

Four little words that carried so much weight. Focusing on the body she had found, Abbie had almost completely forgotten about casting a spell on Xander and ruining his hands. And if she had unlawfully used magick in front of an unmagickal person, she was bound to be in big trouble with Joanna.

How was she going to get out of this one? Whatever the plan, she would have to get it over with pretty soon before it escalated any higher.

"I'm on my way," she wrote and pressed send.

■■■■■■■■■■■■■■■■■■■■■■■■■■■■■■■■■■■■■■■

Laura tapped away on her computer, but she couldn't quite hone in on the screen in front of her.

The intern, Lara, had been sashaying around outside her office for over ten minutes now and it was beginning to wear out her last nerve. The fact that their names sounded similar and some of her international clients were getting the two women mixed up was also exasperating for Laura.

She was just so young. So young and so very, very stupid.

She had made friends with other interns from the other departments, and they had taken to collecting around the kettle and talking facile drivel about housemates, boyfriends and staying out all night, doing shots.

Laura didn't know whether she found this irritating because she didn't like the girl, or irritating because she was jealous of their carefree, unpressured existence.

She didn't have many girlfriends anymore now that she was married—certainly not a whole group of them. A gaggle of fun girls of her age who would enjoy themselves in Fever nightclub, dancing to eighties Madonna.

She had the coven, but it wasn't quite the same. She couldn't really see Joanna sinking three Jägerbombs and dragging her on the floor to do the *Cha-Cha Slide*.

She had picked up, via snippets of conversation, that Lara had just bought her first house with her boyfriend. This was the guy who was always on the sick and refused to eat anything but chicken.

There had been a card going around to wish her well. Laura didn't really want to sign it, feeling hypocritical for writing a puerile, depthless message of congratulations, considering she spent most of the day slagging her off to the podgy, thirty-somethings in Credit Control.

She had instead given a non-committal signature and thrown a fifty pence piece inside of the bulging collection jiffy-bag.

The phone next to her began to ring, which brought her back into the room.

She let out an audible sigh and picked it up.

"Hello, Laura speaking?"

"Hi, Laura Speaking."

"Hi, Donald, how are you?"

It was the sleazy guy from GE Aviation, returning her sales call. She had wanted to offload a new engineering temp onto him, since the previous one had breached his contract and buggered off on a midnight flit to Ibiza to become a tour rep, leaving them in the lurch and her on the brink of losing a contract with a huge, commissionable client.

She hated these calls. She always felt responsible for placing an irresponsible candidate. Even if their CV was water-tight and they had great references, they always found some way or another to completely fuck her over.

After an awkward conversation, where she flirted shamelessly—and he lapped it up—she put the receiver down. Another satisfied customer.

Chewing on her pen lid, she reached into her bag and fumbled around inside.

Perhaps now would be the best time, as she was finding herself disenchanted and grumpy. The result might perk her up a bit.

She pulled out the oblong box and stared at the picture on the front of it.

How much more would she spend on these damn things before she got pregnant?

It was time to find out.

■■■■■■■■■■■■■■■■■■■■■■■■■■■■■■■■■■■■■■■

When Abbie reached the door, she wasn't expecting such a tired-looking Joanna, but the woman looked absolutely spent. And even though Abbie thought of her as a cranky old bitch most of the time, she couldn't help seeing Joanna as some sort of mother figure. Therefore, her well-being was something of a concern to Abbie.

Since she was almost certain that Joanna was going to tear her a new asshole, Abbie only offered a thin smile as she stepped inside.

The room smelled comforting, like burnt toast and the sweet smell of incense—or, at the very least, a Glade plug-in.

"Would you like a drink?" Joanna said in a passive tone, as she breezed past Abbie and on into the kitchen.

"Too early for a gin?" Abbie quipped and was met with an unimpressed silence. "Just water then."

She heard the tap go and a chink of glass before Joanna returned and passed a glass of water over.

Abbie stood awkwardly, never really wanting to sit unless she was invited. Usually one of the other ladies was here to distract Joanna from her austere expectation of Abbie's good manners. She was that type of host.

"Please Abbie, do have a seat." Joanna motioned for her to sit once she had handed over the glass.

Out of sheer nerves, Abbie inelegantly plonked herself down onto one of Joanna's dusty sofas and took a sip of water.

While Joanna fought to compose herself, Abbie was misconstruing her discomfort for white-hot rage.

Both women squirmed under each other's inspection. After what seemed like an age, they both opened their mouths and spoke at the same time.

"Look, I didn't mean—" Abbie started.

"I'm concerned about you—" Joanna interrupted.

"...to cast that spell..." Abbie continued, trailing off awkwardly as she realised her mistake before she could rein in her tongue.

But Joanna knew better than to be caught off-guard and risk missing the opportunity to allow someone to hang themselves with their own rope. Instead of correcting herself, she remained silent and tightened her lips.

Abbie, being slightly thrown, then screwed up her brow before continuing on.

"I mean, I was in trouble—real trouble. It just came out of nowhere. I didn't even know I was doing it. I think if you were in a similar situation as I was then you would have done the same."

Joanna began to process this information and, as she did so, her lips clamped closer together.

First of all, there is no way in abject hell that Joanna would ever make the same decisions as this deluded, little girl. And second, if what she was hearing was what she suspected she was hearing, then could this abominable child actually be admitting to casting a spell? No doubt without being under the protection of a regulated safe-house roof, and in front of someone who was not in The Order?

Did she not understand the implications of such a practise?

Not only was she threatening to blow the anonymity of the circle *wide* open, but she was also committing possibly *the* worst breach of security the coven had seen since the early seventies, on her watch, under her tutelage—and with a High Sceptre watching on and rubbing her devious little palms together.

Joanna had to move her head slightly sideways to check that steam wasn't coming out of her ears.

The fact that Abbie had the gall to sit there, bold as brass, and admit this in her own home was less brazen than if she had taken a house brick out and batted Joanna across the head with it.

Joanna wanted to speak, but her mouth, it seemed, was bolted shut.

"It's just that," Abbie went on, unable to look Joanna in the face, "I'm not sure that I was even able to cast the spell. It's not one that I ever remember learning. I mean, to put such a destructive curse on someone like that. It's ... it's just not my style!"

"Curse?" Joanna said, her temperature starting to rise.

"Well, yeah," Abbie said, leaning back, her jaw hanging open with a passive look on her face.

"Do you mean to tell me," Joanna began, slowly rising onto her feet, "that you placed a *curse* on somebody?"

"I—" Abbie was beginning to think that perhaps Joanna wasn't aware of this at all.

"What kind of *curse*?" Joanna spat, sending a few flecks of spittle across the coffee table.

"It was an atonic one. I think." Abbie was beginning to shrink away from her own confession, abashed that she had let this slip for absolutely no reason. The revelation was tightening a noose around her own neck.

"And what *happened* to this person?" Joanna was now towering over Abbie, who was hoping that the sofa cushions would become a huge set of lips that would swallow her whole and spit her out somewhere else entirely.

"Well," Abbie said in a small voice, "I think it ... kind of broke his fingers."

Joanna was now apoplectic with rage at this and brought a balled-up hand to her lips as she let out a small shriek.

"What—" Her voice was contained but pregnant with fury. "*What* do you think you are doing practising that kind of magick in public?"

"I—"

"*Please let me finish!*" Joanna growled, beginning to pace around her side of the coffee table.

"You, Abigail are the most foolhardy, irresponsible, inconsiderate and obstinate little *child* I have ever had the misfortune to tutor. Your lack of respect, your nonchalance, your complete negligence of regard to the sanctity of The Order is absolutely abhorrent and this ... this act of unabashed rebellion just makes me want to wash my hands of you."

Joanna stopped on the spot, her face turning ever redder.

"I mean," she continued, her voice reaching fever pitch like a singing kettle, "you have not only performed magick in front of a non-magickal, which is going to set tongues wagging and fingers pointing, but you have *cursed* someone with a spell that is not only destructive to the person involved, but also to the very fabric of the sanction that I am trying to uphold."

As she spoke, she could barely bring herself to look at Abbie who sat, looking at the floor like the insolent little brat she was. She had always presumed that Abbie thought herself above The Order, never being committed, always answering back. Strolling in an hour late, blowing on freshly-filled acrylic nails as in-depth, serious topics were being discussed. Joanna had wanted to say something for a while, and now she had broken that wall, she didn't feel she would ever stop shouting.

All the frustration Joanna had with the coven, with Odette, with this ruinous magick that was tainting her beloved town and her social standing within it was literally unwinding her. She was stood in a metaphorical china shop, ready to swing her bat of vexation and bring the whole lot crashing to the floor.

"I cannot *believe* what you have done! Do you never learn from your mistakes? Did I not ignite any kind of fear within you, showing you those pictures of what happens when a macabre spell is cast?"

The images flew through her head of the old, leather-bound book she kept locked up underneath the upstairs bed. Grainy photographs of women hideously aged, their hair sprouting as wisps above their ears. The picture of the unfortunate American woman who had managed to streak a set of angry-looking, puss-filled boils across the top of her head, taking clumps of hair away in the process. The bile-inducing close up of the unfortunate who had begun to grow whiskers on her puffed-out cheeks, clear, glue-like excretions dribbling from her eyes and ratty teeth protruding from under her greying top lip. An age-old catalogue of foolish witches who had tried to use their powers for evil purposes and been hideously disfigured in the process.

"For my sins, I have tried to keep this coven together while everything has begun to fall apart around us, and you are *intent* on making this difficult for me."

"It wasn't to do with you—"

"Oh really?" Joanna spat. "Because I'm going to be the one who is hauled up in front of The Oracle. I'm the one who is going to have to beg and plead with them not to banish you for weeks while the painful process of rehabilitation is bestowed upon you. Have you thought about that?"

In truth, Abbie hadn't thought about that. For some reason, she had thought that the buck would stop with Joanna.

"And I will be the one who will have to pick up the *bloody* pieces when you idiotically do it all again."

"But I won't—"

"Oh, come on Abbie, you can't help yourself! You think I don't notice you rolling your eyes at me? Scoffing when I make important announcements, looking at me like I am past it, unimportant, old and irrelevant. Who do you think you are?"

"I don't, it's honestly not about you."

"Do you think that I am that bloody stupid?" Joanna rolled on as Abbie stood up, steamrolling her point across. "I mean, unthinking, vacuous, little airheads like you are always thinking about yourselves—I don't know why I'm surprised."

At this, Abbie puffed her chest out to square up to her interrogator.

"It was *not* about you," she said slowly, through clenched teeth. "If I hadn't done something, I would have been in serious trouble."

"In more trouble than we're *both* in now?" Joanna sang at her, inching slightly forward.

"Yes!" Abbie shot back. "I could have—"

Tears began to prick her eyes as she began to sob. The hideous images of Xander imposing himself upon her. The fear of not knowing what he would do to her, how she might endure it. And how she would live with herself after he had had his five minutes of fun.

"I could have been raped," Abbie said, through an onslaught of tears.

Joanna waited a beat before leaning in and baring her teeth.

"Well, maybe that would have taught you a lesson," she snarled.

With that, out of nowhere, Abbie swung back her hand and struck Joanna clean across the face. It wasn't necessarily a hard slap, but it was enough to throw her backwards.

Abbie went through a second of shock, before inhaling loudly and bringing her hand back to her side. Her crying instantly stopped.

"You heartless *bitch*," she said coldly. She looked at Joanna. Her old face was frozen in horrified disbelief.

Abbie picked up her bag, wiped her cheeks with the back of her hand and made her way out of the room.

All Joanna could do was clutch her stinging face in bewilderment as Abbie slammed the door behind her.

■ ■

Becky got up early in the morning and travelled with Dom to A&E. She had told him that she had felt some discomfort in the night and really thought that she should go and get checked out.

He was a little put out, considering he was due in surgery early, but he called ahead to cancel a few appointments.

As they sat in the waiting room, watching elderly couples hobble in and out, flicking through an aged copy of *Bella* magazine that had a few pages ripped out and all the crosswords filled in, she placed her hand on her tummy.

She hoped that, somehow, her daughter could read her thoughts as she imagined cradling a beautiful, baby girl in her arms, almost bursting with pride and love. It was only when he coughed audibly that Becky remembered that Dom was even there. She was going to have to plan it just right so that he didn't suspect anything about her knowing the sex of their child before he did.

After half an hour, Becky was ushered into a private room.

The nurse was tall and attractive. She had blonde hair and perfect, white teeth. If she were in *Casualty*, she would definitely have been in the main cast, Becky thought to herself.

"Right," she said, after introducing herself as Nurse Clarke. "What can I do for you today then?"

Becky was slightly nervous at having to fake some symptoms, but it was necessary if she was going to get some sort of medical confirmation that her fall hadn't damaged her baby. She had already had to cleverly disguise a purpling bruise on her forehead with a generous blob of concealer and a new side-parting.

"Err ... I'm just feeling a little bit queasy today. Out of sorts, you know?"

"Right." The nurse's voice was sweet but not condescending. "You're sure it's not just morning sickness or general nausea?"

Becky gave a little shake of her head.

The nurse's eyes shifted from Dom who, as of yet, had said nothing and looked all sullen, and then back to Becky. An awkward silence filled the room.

Nurse Clarke was quick to speak.

"Okay. Hop up on the chair then, we'll have a quick look."

Becky tentatively sat on the cold, blue chair and swung her legs around.

"If you could pull up your top for me?" the nurse asked politely, as she pulled on some surgical gloves.

As she carried out the scan, Becky eyed her face with a cautious frown.

"Everything looks absolutely fine, Mrs Dawlish. Heartbeat is regular, everything taking shape nicely." A smile broke out on Nurse Clarke's face.

"In fact, if you would like to know," she said excitedly, "I can tell you the sex of the baby right now."

Becky pursed her lips together and looked over at her husband, her eyes widened with anticipation.

Dom, however, looked practically cold.

Both Nurse Clarke and Becky looked at him as he straightened his tie and puffed out his cheeks.

"I don't want to know," he said.

■■

The journey back into Winchcombe was frosty, to say the least.

"Look, I'm sorry, but I just don't think it's important at this stage," Dom said as he drove, the radio turned down and the windows up.

"Well, I would have quite liked to have known," Becky answered in a small voice. She was not used to disagreeing with her husband. Or anyone for that matter—she wasn't one hundred percent sure that she knew how to do it.

He harrumphed, which angered her. Why was she forever kowtowing to him? She had wanted to know the baby's sex for her own reasons— why did he have to have the deciding word? Come to think of it, when was she ever going to be part of the decision-making process in this relationship?

She had married him when he asked, she had upped sticks and moved so that he could be closer to home and carry out his work, even though she, a competent administrator, was now slumming it in a backwater school with a bunch of lunatics. He had always chosen their holidays, the times they ate. Hell, they were even cruising along in a car that he had wanted and that she had ended up going along with because he rarely let her drive. How ridiculous was this?

An ember suddenly ignited inside of her and grew hotter and more vibrant the longer the silence lasted.

Suddenly, he accidentally hit a speed bump, jolting her in her seat.

"Argh!" she shrieked in frustration, turning to him with a face like thunder. "Not only do you not want to know what sex our child is, you want to kill it before it's even born—watch the bloody road!"

His mouth opened, stunned, as he briefly glanced towards his wife.

"You know," she continued, "I'm the one carrying this person around with me, the least you can show is a bit of gratitude."

He fought to answer back, but he wasn't used to seeing such a fire in Becky's eyes. It knocked him completely sideways.

"You're never home, and when you are home you're too knackered to do anything. I spend all my time on my own, my hormones are running wild—" she trailed off.

"Hey," he said, his stern look thawing. "I'm sorry, I didn't know you felt this way."

He was speaking softly, but it did little to quell her exasperation.

"Well, of course, you didn't—you never ask!" She was beginning to redden. She looked out of the passenger window, unable to face him.

"What—" he spluttered. "What's brought this on?"

She gave a hostile shrug. She was sure he would put it down to hormones, but she knew it was something different. Deep within her was a seed—something magical. She harboured a power that had lain dormant for ages and neither he, nor anyone else, could take that away. And that seed would be then passed onto her daughter and her daughter after that. The endless legacy of strong, powerful women would continue, and there was nothing he could do about it.

As he pulled into the drive, she unclipped her seatbelt and opened the door. She knew that he only had time to drop her home before driving back to work for afternoon surgery.

As she stepped out of the car she reached her head back to face him.

"I'm having a girl," she said pointedly.

"What—" Dom stuttered after her, trying to crane forward but getting restrained by his seatbelt. "But ... how do you know?"

She poked her head back through the doorway and gave him a stony glare.

"I just *know*," she said, slamming the door.

■■

"So, what happens now then?" Becky asked Gaynor, as she sipped her Arrowood.

Gaynor had a filthy tabard on, fresh from tending to her mess of a garden. Since Dai had been in a critical condition, she'd had to give herself a break from her horticultural hobbies. Now it was obvious how out of control the vines could get if neglected for even the shortest amount of time. They seemed more twisted about than ever.

"Well," she said, diving her hand into her pocket for the secateurs, "I guess it will be for The Oracle to decide."

"Right," Becky mused, holding her cup in both hands while leaning up against Gaynor's back door, watching her friend wrestle with an angry-looking climbing plant.

"At least one good thing has come out of this." Gaynor stopped momentarily and wiped her brow.

"Oh?" Becky asked.

"At least that Clements woman has put a halt to her ridiculous Parish Council meetings and their plans to bulldoze through my oasis. I got a letter about it this morning." She pointed the secateurs to the top of the wall. "She knew she'd have a fight on her hands anyway, but all this hoo-hah has put her petty bellyaching about my garden into perspective."

"Still," Gaynor continued, getting back to the task in hand, "I can't be giving them any more ammunition. As soon as this blows over, she'll be back on my tail I'm sure."

Becky watched the old woman rigorously pulling at the green vine. It curled away from her as if it was aware of what she was trying to do. It was like they were having an argument. Becky looked down at Pluto, who was casually snoozing at her feet, enjoying a spot of autumn sunshine.

"You see, The Oracle will have it all in hand. No doubt, that Odette woman will have raised the alarm. They'll send a few police officers out to throw any public suspicion westward and then back to business," Gaynor said, changing the topic.

"But I saw that thing tear a chunk out of Rachel Power's throat. I mean, how are the police going to explain that to the interrogating public?" Becky was confused.

"Oh, the goddess will think of something," Gaynor said, looking up at the sky. "I mean, they've managed to keep our world a secret pretty effectively up until now. I'm sure they've got this one covered."

Becky could tell that Gaynor didn't really want to get into it, and she didn't blame her—she sounded like she had been through enough.

"Now," Gaynor said, slipping her tools back into her pocket and brushing her hands down her front, "come and see the tree that I am going to plant for Dai. It's an absolute cracker."

She took one of Becky's hands in her own and pulled her down the path alongside the back of the house. Pluto sensed their departure and went to plod along behind them.

The three moved around to the side of the house, where another, smaller patch of grass was covered with similarly chaotic flora and fauna. Becky had not been to this part of the garden before. It was a solemn, more private space, disorderly but strangely sombre at the same time. The leaves on the trees were crisp and brown and some of the more vibrant flowers had their heads bowed to the floor.

Her breath caught in her throat and she suddenly felt the urge to cry.

"Beautiful, isn't it?" Gaynor asked. "This was his favourite spot."

"It's almost as if—" Becky started, almost in a whisper so as not to disturb the peace. "It's almost as if the garden is mourning"

Gaynor let out a little laugh.

"Why, of course," she said, "plants are living, breathing things. You talk to them, they respond in their own language. You suffer a loss, they suffer right along with you."

It was the most beautiful notion that Becky had ever come across, yet it made perfect sense. These were not just plants that surrounded Gaynor, they were living things that experienced life alongside her and mirrored both her sorrow and her joy. Tears crept down Becky's cheeks.

As they walked further into the space, she noticed a small shrub that was situated away from the rest, still in its plastic pot. Its leaves almost glowed a hue of vivacious yellow.

"That's beautiful," Becky said, squeezing Gaynor's hand for support.

"Robinia pseudoacacia," Gaynor replied. "It's going right here, in the middle, soaking up the sun. Keeping us company. Myself and my plants, that is."

She turned to Becky, her eyes moist.

"I'd love it if we planted it together," she said.

"I'd like that," Becky agreed.

Bernice looked at herself in the mirror.

She was looking better than ever. Her hormones were kicking in and not drinking every night was making her appear slender and energised.

She was even beginning to get more notice online. Men would actually contact her now. It was a far cry from weeks ago where she would constantly check her dormant internet dating account like one might sit by the phone, waiting for it to ring.

Now men would message her, saying she looked pretty. She had never been told she looked pretty before. Freaky, yes. Ridiculous, absolutely. But pretty? No.

Of course, she still got hounded by the weird guys who wanted to know whether she still had everything "downstairs". The ones who clearly liked to flirt with both possibilities, to satiate their perverted curiosities. But she was not a vessel or an unusual museum exhibit, to be studied while scratching one's chin and shaking one's head, bemused as to how such a thing could exist. She was a woman. A woman who had been cruelly burdened with hard features, rough skin and innumerate follicles that sprouted dark, thick hair in places where she shouldn't have it.

She had been afflicted with these huge feet, that feminine shoes would never fit, a bristly chin, a receding hairline and two droopy domes of fat where shapely breast tissue should be.

She had been given this and this is what she had had to work with.

She wasn't sexy. She didn't saunter or pout like voluptuous, feminine creatures did. She didn't look great in a fitted dress or a slinky, little trouser suit. Inside of anything tight-fitting, she just looked like a blob of mashed potato wrapped up in cling film.

And the hormones, though they shaped her slightly and curbed some of the unsightly hair from reaching most of her visible parts, they also turned her into a strange, non-binary soup. As though two species had crossbred, and this was the result—some parts of one, some parts of another.

Some days, she wished she could just bottle what was inside of her and simply pour herself into another vessel. She wanted to select a ready-made, female body, and leave her current, messed-up chassis out in a skip for the bin men to take.

It was as though, no matter how hard she tried, she just couldn't make this body match her mind and, just like with a new car, she should be able to take this battered one back and get a model that suited her better.

But it was what it was.

Once upon a time, she had been ready to die, thinking that somehow removing herself from the problem would simply make it stop. But then, where would that leave her son? Her wife? The other trans people who may depend on her to give them strength and inspiration?

And what would she be running from anyway? Other peoples' judgement? Those lucky bastards out there who were fortunate enough to have been born with ten fingers, ten toes and the genitalia they were always meant to have? Who take themselves for granted every single day, kill their brains with recreational drugs, beat their partners, prey on little children and laugh at the unfortunate for being less blessed than they are?

Was she escaping from the possibility that she might die at their hands instead of her own?

She wouldn't let that happen.

Joanna could never get her head around Bernice. She could never see beyond the man's hands and the chiselled features. She saw a bloke pretending to be something that he was not. Bernice saw it in her eyes from the moment the two had met.

You are not welcome here.

She had coated Bernice in a film of discontent that Joanna had no intention of ever rubbing off.

But then Joanna's word was never going to trump Odette's, and Odette had seen who Bernice was from the beginning—the true woman inside. The huntress. The warrior. The witch.

And for as long as Bernice could bear it, she would continue to attend those meetings, if only to prove to Joanna that her kind must be forced to embrace change if this world was ever going to evolve. To understand that things might not be to Joanna's liking, but she did not control them as she thought she did. That life was not so black and white, and that people shouldn't be categorised into two pens—ladies and gentlemen, boys and girls.

Her mobile started to ring so she swept it up off the bed.

"Bernice Williams?" she said, flicking her hair from her shoulders.

"Oh, hi Odette. Yes. Yes. Tonight? I'll be there. Of course—thank you."

She took one last look in the mirror and switched the phone off.

It was time for her to stand tall for herself.

She was ready to take Joanna down.

SEVENTEEN

Marge had the radio on in her shoebox of an office.

The strains of Kate Bush singing *Wuthering Heights* was permeated only by the sounds of frail, old women moaning in their sleep like zombies.

She sighed as she turned the pen over between her fingers. Another day, another mound of time-consuming paperwork.

"Thank you very much, UK Government, for making my job so bureaucratic that I hardly ever get onto the wards anymore."

The NHS was so doomed that it almost made her laugh. Old people who had served their country now festered on these hellish wards, being forced to eat slop and exist amongst the putrid smell of urine and disinfectant, while Johnny-Come-Lately gets shipped off to a private ward, just to have a knot tied in his sperm tube. It was sickening.

She licked her thumb and turned the page. In truth, she quite enjoyed this shift. She was more or less alone all night, so she could get a few things done, drink endless cups of tea and, best of all, tune in to the late-night music show for insomniacs and nod her head along to all the hits she remembered from her youth.

Ah yes, youth. When she wasn't so thick-set with the hardened features she had acquired through years of frowning at incompetent staff and unruly patients. When she wore her hair long and her trousers flared. When she smoked pot and hung around town without her parents knowing. When the Bay City Rollers were every young girl's fantasy and you could watch *Top of the Pops* without feeling guilty about what might be going on behind the scenes when the cameras stopped rolling.

Those days.

Suddenly, the internal phone started to ring. It was unusual for anyone to call at such a late hour—most staff had practically run out of the place when the bell had tolled five.

She knew almost immediately who it would be. She had specifically told him to keep her up-to-date with whatever was going on down in the morgue, even if it was nothing. After a couple of rings, she answered in a flat whisper.

"Tyler."

"Ah, Matron," the treacly voice on the other end exclaimed, "I trust you are well?"

He had a unique way of making her feel special and repulsed all at the same time. Although he exuded a certain charm down the telephone, in truth, he was rather a slimy individual, with a comb-over and ill-fitting trousers.

"Good evening, Dennis," she said, sounding rather like a game show host introducing a contestant. "Any news for me?"

There was a dubious silence on the end of the phone, almost as if he were preparing to lie to her. When she thought about it though, he could be just holding the line to check on the corpses.

"Nope," he confirmed. "Nothing to report I'm afraid"

She sighed. She didn't really know what she was expecting, but then any news might have been better than no news.

"So, they're both still there then?" she reaffirmed.

"Yep," he replied. "Two dead women. Both ashen. Both cold."

"Right." She threw her pen onto her desk in defeat.

"Would you like me to keep these regular checks?" he asked tentatively, obviously itching for her to set him free.

"Oh yes, I think so," Marge said as if the thought had just occurred to her.

A moment passed between them.

"And … the restraints?" he said in a small voice as if he were talking to a mad woman. "Do you want me to keep them strapped down?"

She bit her lip as she considered what the consequences might be.

"Yes, Dennis," she said, "I do."

She replaced the handset and picked her pen back up.

"Does she still want him to keep them restrained" indeed!

I mean, they may be dead, but after the last time, Marge wasn't taking any chances.

■■■■■■■■■■■■■■■■■■■■■■■■■■■■■■■■■■■■■■

Wing had spent the whole day lurking outside of Jacqueline's door, reciting silent whispers to the deity under her breath. Various staff had been going in and out—professional staff, far more senior than her. She had more-or-less been banished to the day room.

At one point, she saw an elderly man she didn't recognise exit the room, hanging his head. He looked handsome for an older gentleman. He wore a tweed jacket and carried a Panama hat in his hand.

Wing watched as Allison had offered him a seat and a cup of tea in one of the guest mugs.

When Wing thought it was safe, she swallowed her reservations and went to sit next to him, taking a jay cloth with her for courage.

"Hello," she said in a mouse-like voice, "are you okay?"

She was aware that she sounded like some kind of East Asian robot.

He was lost in thought, turning the hat around and around in his hand.

She tentatively looked at him and then back at her hands no less than five times. After what seemed like an age, he noticed her.

"Hmm?" he muttered as if he hadn't heard her. "No, not really."

She nodded, her mouth like a line across her face.

There was an uncomfortable silence between them. As if they were in some kind of play.

"You family?" she said eventually, as impassively as her accent would allow.

Again, a few moments passed before he answered, the hat still rotating between his slender fingers. His eyes were tired under his thick, bushy eyebrows. His skin was pocked with the red blood vessels that either severe cold weather or excess drink brought with them.

"Yes," he said, his lips parting underneath his mousy moustache, revealing yellowing, stubby teeth. "Brother."

"Yes," Wing agreed.

The two of them sat like the original odd couple: the middle-aged English gentleman and the portly Thai care worker, united on the uncomfortable Draylon seats that were the staple of every British care home interior in existence.

"Is it bad?" she said, the language barrier getting in the way of saying something more sensitive. They just didn't have as many sympathetic words in Thailand. It was straight to the point and then move on.

He nodded.

"I'm afraid so, I think—" He stopped himself as he choked back a tear. "I'm sorry, is there anywhere I can smoke around here?"

He put his hand to his nose and wiped it slightly.

"Err, outside," she said, pointing to the direction of the reception area.

"Thank you," he said, getting up onto his feet and rushing past her, as he clutched his hat in a balled fist.

At that moment Allison returned with a cup of tea.

"Oh, has he left?" she said. There was a tinge of being inconvenienced in her voice, which annoyed Wing slightly.

"Cigarette," Wing answered, a little defiant in her tone.

"Well, I'll just leave it here," Allison said, sliding it onto a nearby table.

As Alison stood up, she smoothed down her dress and clasped her hands together as if she were about to say something that might make her uncomfortable.

"Wing," she said in a small, concerned voice.

Wing looked up, surprised that Allison had called her by her name. She usually gave polite orders without ever feeling the need to address her.

"Yes?" she asked apprehensively.

"I'm really sorry," she said, reaching her hand out to pat Wing affectionately on the shoulder. "It really is very sad."

Wing swallowed again, but this time it was as if the motion had dislodged her heart and sent it slowly sliding down inside of her.

"Yes," was all Wing said, before looking down at the cloth that she had crushed in her hand.

■■

"So, what we appear to be dealing with is magic-bending. But we expected that already," Odette reported back, not in the same composed, measured way that the ladies had now gotten used to, but in a sort of frantic, excitable manner.

Joanna, who seemed utterly spent, drawn and tired was unperturbed, letting Odette's change in dictatorship wash over her.

Odette had drawn up some sort of chart and placed it on Joanna's coffee table. It had two circles that overlapped each other pencilled in the centre and lots of words branching outwards. Now, in her perfect patent shoes, Odette was walking around it, tapping a pencil on her lip as she went.

"It seems," she continued, "that this particular spell is a splinting together of two spell spheres."

Becky looked around at the sea of confused faces. They had been sat at Joanna's for more than thirty minutes now. She had barely been given an opportunity to introduce herself to everyone before she was ushered in by Odette and bombarded with information, most of which she hadn't the faintest clue about.

She had managed to give Robina a quick hug, and direct modest nods towards Odette and Joanna, seeing as they were clearly in charge.

She had smiled at the larger Asian lady, Wing, who gave her an abashed grin in response before looking down at her hands. There was also the attractive, tall, thin woman with long, brown curls who looked incredibly professional but winked back to suggest she probably wasn't.

Apparently, a girl called Abbie wouldn't be able to make it this evening, according to Odette, but that was fairly swiftly glossed over.

There was one other woman in the room. She had seemed very keen to speak to Becky but hadn't gotten the chance since Odette had immediately started to speak. This was somewhat of a relief since Becky was not really sure what to make of this woman. She looked odd. As if her fitted, red, wrap-around dress didn't really suit her, or her hair wasn't quite right or something. She almost looked handsome under her makeup, which Becky thought looked strangely excessive. This woman's eyes had followed her around the room.

Becky had smiled nervously back at her before trying to return her focus to the chart that Odette was now pondering silently over, marking a pause in her lecture. It was as if Odette was trying to work something out on the spot and wasn't about to welcome interruptions.

"So, in terms of spheres then," Odette said, after this momentary hesitation, "we have this one which has to do with the rising. That's a fairly standard spell base, I think you'll all agree."

She looked up over her glasses—the ladies felt compelled to nod in unison.

"Well, of course, the rising of the sun, the moon. The rising of the god up to the sky when he passes, et cetera. When we cast, we understand that the flame rises upwards and therefore a spell ascends, unless it is meant to be directed into the ground—yadda, yadda, yadda." She moved her hand around in the air as she said this. "But it is *this* sphere—this is the interesting one."

Odette leant over the page and pointed her pencil at the second circle that had been drawn, overlapping the first.

"See, where we would use the rising part, we would often cross it, or fertilise it, if you will, with a volume sphere to quicken the pace of something. It could also be an emotional sphere that crosses a rising fear—the progression of happiness, for example. Even in the dark arts, one might couple the rising sphere with a threat or curse. Even death. It grows, it climbs. But *this*—"

She once again tapped the circle with her pencil.

"This is the sphere of grounding." She stopped a moment to let the information sink in. "In essence, the two counteract. So, the spell rises but then is pulled back to the ground. It becomes *bent.*"

Joanna moved her mouth to speak but thought better of it and shrunk back into her corner.

"So, when we look at the hex placed on this woman, Brenda Ware, we see that, in effect, they are asking her to rise up from the dead and yet remain grounded—that makes sense under the laws of bending a spell."

Odette put her pencil in her mouth again, almost muttering to herself.

"But there is almost a fertilised cell within that command that, first of all, links the infrastructure of the spell together, and then puts some kind of stopper between the rising and the grounded. Almost like the recipient is held in magickal limbo. This cell is the reason that the victims are not dying."

She looked around at the ladies who, again, looked completely baffled.

Odette's head nodded from side to side as she waited for some input.

Gaynor spoke up.

"So, High Sceptre," she asked from her usual seat nearest the door, "if we were to reverse-engineer Becky's spell, could we not figure out the complexity from there?"

"Ah yes, thank you, Gaynor," Odette said, moving back around the table in a whirl of black.

"See, what Becky's spell tells us—"

She halted again to acknowledge Becky with a small purse of the lips. This made Becky blush.

"What it tells us is that the spell used to intercept this possession is based on the waters of Mortis which, in the great Wiccan book, is a stretch of water that ran along the Västergarn Region in Gotland. So, it is Scandinavian in origin, which is really quite interesting."

"Interesting?" Robina asked tentatively, covertly setting her mug down on a spare inch of carpet, in the absence of a coffee table.

"Well," Odette nodded, "the principles that magic-bending is based on originated from Västergarn. Interception spells and their remedies, which are illegal here, used to be fairly common practise there. But we're talking about extremely classified magic here. You would almost have to have been present at that time to be able to recite anything close to that kind of spell unless you had access to it in the HQ vaults."

"So," Robina asked with yet more apprehension in her voice, "how would Becky be able to recite this spell—I mean, if the information is so secret?"

Odette eyed Becky with intense interest, moving her finger up and down her cheek as she nodded. Just as Becky began to feel slightly uncomfortable, Odette shifted her focus.

"I don't know. But it means that, effectively, I am going to have to go back to The Oracle and check this out with her. I do think, however, that this is an act of terrorism and we need to be very careful out there from now on. Be vigilant, keep your wits about you." Odette looked deadly serious.

"Forgive me, High Sceptre," Laura spoke up. Becky noticed a flash of a red bra under her crisp white shirt. "But why us? Why has this threat come to our town? Why here, of all places?"

Everyone looked up at Odette, who gave a small shake of the head.

"Well," Odette said, "this place has been a hive of Wiccan practices for many years. Cheltenham itself is an ancient town and Winchcombe alone stands on two ley lines. It could have something to do with that."

Laura looked up at the ceiling as she mused over this information.

"It could also, of course," Odette pondered, "be a complete mystery."

■■■

The meeting drew to a close after it appeared that the ladies' hands were tied. There was nothing that anyone could do except wait for further instruction from Odette. And since she was almost as confused as they were, it may be some time before anything happened at all.

Joanna cleared the last of the coffee mugs and walked into the kitchen. Odette could see the ladies out seeing as she had more or less commandeered Joanna's house for herself. Arrogant woman.

She turned to grab a cloth when she noticed somebody behind her. She looked over her shoulder and gasped softly.

Bernice was stood in her galley kitchen—all six feet of her, towering over Joanna like some sort of barbarian.

Joanna took a large gulp of breath and stuck her chest out. Bernice cradled a mug that she slid onto the side, a timid smile on her face. It made Joanna cringe.

Behind her, Bernice had pulled the door to, a signal that Joanna was going to have to talk to her, even though she had little to say.

"So," Bernice began, with an exasperated sigh. The gall of it, coming into her house and cornering her after everything that had happened between them.

"I just wanted to check, Joanna, that you are okay," she carried on.

Joanna gritted her teeth and, after a few moments, reached to retrieve the empty mug that Bernice had deposited. She would have to scrub this one extra hard.

Bernice didn't wait for a response.

"You see, we haven't really had the chance to speak since..."

She pursed her lips.

"Well, since you threw me out of your house. I was thinking that, perhaps, you might have something that you wanted to say to me."

Joanna's eyes narrowed as she gripped the porcelain in her hand, so tightly it may well have shattered into a million pieces.

Bernice's eyes flicked up to meet her nemesis'.

"How dare she," Joanna thought. *"How dare she stand there with her fakery, unabashed and brazen, in my house, and browbeat me into an apology."*

What was she thinking saying "she"? Bernice was a he! William Burns was his name and now here *he* was, stood in her kitchen, with imitation breasts poking out of a flashy dress, garish makeup and a ridiculous hairstyle, trying oh-so-desperately to get everyone to play along in his little, sexually-motivated charade. Well, she wasn't having it. This fruitcake of a man was only allowed in this house at all because Joanna had been stalemated into it. He belonged indoors, where husbands who liked to dress up in their wives' dresses belonged. Away from society, away from vulnerable and impressionable little children and, more to the point, away from her.

"Joanna," Bernice said provocatively, "I'm just concerned about you. You're so quiet. It's almost as if you've lost your fire."

Joanna placed the cup down for fear of launching it.

"Don't tell me," she replied in a thin, passionless voice, "that you are concerned about me."

Bernice hung back on one hip, defiantly.

"You don't know the first thing about me, so don't saunter in here with your bogus interest in my well-being. You're just waiting. *Waiting* for me to stumble, like the vulture you are," she spat.

"Oh, come now," Bernice said, her voice changing from soothing and sweet to thick and heavy with vengeful delight. "That's hardly neighbourly. I am just voicing my anxiety as a sister, a fellow kind and loving sister."

"Sister?" Joanna emitted an acid cackle. "You're no more my sister than you are my friend. And you are *certainly* not one of those."

"Why are you so closed-minded?" Bernice said, turning the smugness off like a tap. "You've never accepted me—you've hardly ever been able to look me in the face."

"Well, what does that tell you?" Joanna growled, so enraged that she was close to tears.

Bernice exhaled, flicking her hair over one shoulder like she'd seen Hollywood actresses do in movies. The problem with Joanna was that she had mistaken Bernice's vulnerability for weakness. Bernice had sacrificed everything in her old life to become the person she knew she was supposed to be, and it had taken more than just scanning through Cosmopolitan and picking out a hairstyle. It had taken guts, bravery and strength.

In a way, they were similar. They were both incredibly robust and steely women, with passion, intelligence and integrity. But Bernice had needed to work that extra bit harder to push her voice forward and it had taught her never to give up when the battle lines were drawn.

"You can't say I haven't tried," Bernice sighed. "After all, now that I'm officially back in The Order—"

"If it were up to me, you would *never* have been let back in," Joanna said, her face turning red.

"Well," Bernice was quick to point out, "that's just it—it's not up to you. Nothing is anymore. The Order has finally seen the Joanna-shaped hole in their parachute and they have obviously sent someone down to stitch it up and get rid of the rot."

Bernice looked down at her nails. Now she had jumped over the first hurdle with Joanna, she was going to enjoy every second of rubbing her nose in it. It was more than enough to compensate for the humiliation that Joanna had put her through. Joanna had not banked on Bernice coming back fighting. She had not banked on her coming back at all.

"You might think otherwise," Bernice continued, "but they've obviously found out about you. What you did, who you are..."

Joanna's eyes narrowed.

"What on *earth* do you mean?"

"I think you know exactly what I mean," Bernice said, with a smile. "It seems that, with Odette in position, your post is quite redundant. I mean, you haven't solved the spell—you can't even retain Abbie anymore. Doesn't look good for the future, does it? I think The Oracle may have seen the iceberg coming."

Joanna's face fell. Bernice had incised her weak spot—and with such expert precision.

"Of course, with you relieved of your duties, there might be an opening." Bernice's tone was now indulgently suggestive. "Perhaps for someone who *does* represent the future."

Joanna didn't respond, her mouth began to hang open as she listened. She was too dumbfounded to speak.

Was this creature right? Could The Oracle be replacing her? Had she found out about Joanna's past? How could Bernice have possibly known about that? Who had she been speaking to?

"Well, all this silence is riveting," Bernice said, "but I think I'll leave you to it."

Bernice turned on her heels and began to walk out of the kitchen, catching a glance back over her shoulder.

"I'll see myself out," she said with a grin.

■■■

The walk home for Wing was not a pleasant one. Not only had the meeting finished late, as always, but not one person had offered to give her a lift. Not that she had wanted one—she was too lost in her own thoughts, her own anxieties.

Laura usually stepped in to ask Wing if she wanted to share the journey home, but this evening she had also seemed distracted by her own thoughts.

Wing pulled her coat around her, as the October chill crept closer to her skin. Even concealed under this hefty flesh insulation, she still felt frozen and weak.

What was she going to do when Jacqueline finally left this earth?

She scolded herself for being selfish. Life, for her, would continue on. She would carry on spooning pureed vegetables into Elsie's mouth while she spat it back at her, blended with a fresh mix of racial slurs.

They would wash all trace of Jacqueline from the bed linen, her cards and photographs would be given to her brother or slotted into a manila folder and thrust into an archive box to collect dust, like so many other memories. Everything else would go into the bin.

The stage would be swept, and another show would be brought in. And there would be no tolerance for grief or pity. It was a job, and this was very much a part of said job. No room for sentiment, no room for tears. People die, you live. You were lucky this time—you could be next.

She had stopped praying to the Deity now. She thought it more appropriate for Jacqueline to go to her family, as was her wish. To Wilfred and Sarah. She saw no further point in wasting words on something far less powerful than the scourge of a terminal illness. What was the use of magick if it didn't stop pain, if it couldn't mend a heart, if it wouldn't halt death? And yet she had chastised her mother for thinking it ever could have. Magick couldn't obliterate hope like cancer does—there was simply no contest.

She suddenly felt a searing-hot wave of guilt, despair and emptiness all at the same time. How naive she had been to doubt her mother, when all the woman had wanted was for her dead passion, the feeling of companionship and love, to return to her. Now Wing knew so much more about magick. It was not strong enough to compete with any of these things. It was more like a plaster that held the inevitable together when the very pitfalls of life just ripped them apart.

She got home, hung her coat up and stood in the hallway for a moment, concentrating. Listening to the house as it slept. No doubt, the children would be shattered—it was after eleven. Richard might be reading in bed, pyjamas buttoned up to the neck and smelling of athlete's foot powder. A car passed by the window, its lights casting a beam through the frosted glass of her front door.

Then, stillness.

She suddenly felt her phone vibrate in her pocket.

That was strange—it was a ridiculous time for someone to be phoning. She looked at the screen as she pulled it out. It was a number she didn't recognise. She answered it.

"Hello?" she whispered, so as not to disturb anyone upstairs.

There was an audible sniff on the other line.

"Hello," it was a man's voice, clearly distressed. "It's Morgan. We met at the home. Jacqueline's home."

Wing's chest fell slightly.

"Oh," she said, exhaling deeply. "Hello, Morgan."

"I got your number from the lady at the home, she said you and Jacqueline were good friends," he went on, stopping now and again to sniffle. "I hope you don't mind me calling."

"No," Wing said, putting one hand out to the wall to steady herself, "it fine, I just got in."

"Okay," he said, his voice suddenly tense. "She spoke about you. She always talked about your kindness, your good heart. I just called to thank you."

Wing smiled and nodded. He seemed to sense this and continued.

"And I thought I should let you know," he said, "that Jacqueline slipped away about an hour ago."

She had the urge to be sick, but she held onto it. The nausea that came with disbelief and pain all at once felt like a lumbering dragon, opening its jaws, ready to engulf her in flames.

"I'm so sorry," he said, "but I thought you should know."

"Thank you," she whispered and hung up the phone.

She held it in her hand a moment before letting it drop to the floor. All that time she had been sat there listening to those women wittering on about spheres and spells and nonsense, her precious Jacqueline's final moments had been frittering away.

She felt the dragon travel further up towards her head from her stomach, its nostrils pouring out plumes of acrid smoke. She started to shake and clench her teeth.

She couldn't hold it back anymore. Her eyes flashed with fiery orange sparks and her fingers shot out from her palms like spikes.

The dragon reached her, its mouth open, screaming out a burning hot jet of fire. Her arms flew out as her mouth hung open. Her limbs stiffened, and her mind clouded over with lightning bolts of electric red.

A guttural growl emanated from her open mouth. A silent scream of rage and agony, twisted and entwined, burst forth from the pit of her stomach.

At that moment, the glass window in the front door blew completely out, sending shards of crystal cascading across the carpet.

Wing dropped to her knees and wept.

■■■■■■■■■■■■■■■■■■■■■■■■■■■■■■■■■■■■■

Laura rushed to the toilet as a sudden wave of nausea passed through her. She made it, jamming her head into the bowl just as she began to empty her stomach.

After she had retched a few times, she wrapped her arm around the cistern and pulled her head up, wiping a sweaty strand of hair from her forehead.

She should have been ecstatic, but it was hard to feign excitement when she had just vomited everywhere. She felt like shit on a very real stick.

She knew she was pregnant—the test had told her as much. She should have been filled with unbridled joy and yet all she really felt was a never-ending pang of guilt. Guilt associated with the fact that she could be holding another man's baby. How could she have been so stupid as to sleep with someone else? Why did she have to make this so difficult for herself?

Her mother's voice rang in her head once again.

"You're impulsive Laura. You never think of the process, you just go straight for the result."

Luckily, she and Ben had still been going at it most nights, so she would have no problem in convincing him that it was his. It still could be— she just didn't know.

Since she had found out, the sex between her and her husband had been more romantic and less formulaic. She found herself indulging in foreplay, enjoying the build-up rather than feeling obliged to inelegantly clamber on top of him and lock down on his member.

They had begun to take their time, to kiss each other on the neck. She knew that he liked it when she did this. He had caressed her, traced her body with his finger and covered her eyes as he nibbled on her breast. It had been fun, sexy. As if the transaction had been completed and now they could both relax.

But he didn't know yet that she was even pregnant.

She had decided not to tell him until she knew how she felt about the whole thing. Luckily, he was usually eating breakfast by the time she woke up and so, for the past two mornings, she had managed to disguise the fact that she had been throwing her guts up in the top-floor bathroom as he happily munched on Weetabix downstairs.

She sighed and let out a rather unbecoming burp, praying for relief from another onslaught of vomit.

Suddenly there was a quiet tap on the door. It took her by complete surprise.

Ben's voice came from the other side of the door.

"Are you okay in there babe?"

Shit.

She pulled her robe tight around her and went to climb up onto her feet, but she still felt dizzy. She didn't really want to be sick again—it was too much effort.

"Yes," she grunted in reply.

There was a moment of silence.

"I heard you running across the bedroom like you were going to heave or something."

She rolled her eyes. How foolish to think she could keep getting away with this when her own body was giving the game away.

"Yes, I—"

She sighed as wiped her mouth with the back of her hand.

"I think you'd better come in."

She saw the handle twist as the door opened. Laura looked up through tired eyes. Her husband looked handsome, framed by the sunshine from the hall window. He always looked cute in his work clothes. A smart Ted Baker suit and tie perfectly matched his short brown hair and tailored beard.

She must have looked a bedraggled mess, sat on the floor, her legs spread, practically hugging the u-bend.

"What's up?" he asked a look of concern on his face, his beard speckled with cereal crumbs.

She winced slightly at him.

"I think I might go in late today," she said with a heavy sigh.

He cocked his head to one side in sympathy.

"Daddy..." she added, with a weak smile.

■■■

Whoever was behind this possession couldn't have timed it better. With it now being October half-term, the school would be empty for a week, so Becky had more time to process all that had happened to her over the last few days.

It had all been such a whirlwind, becoming the new blood around the witches' table, that she had almost forgotten the abject horror of the night of the Power's Halloween party.

A vivid memory kept playing over and over in her head. The flash of grey, cold skin diving over her shoulder and latching itself onto smiling Rachel's neck. Even more horrific had been the sound, the toe-curling crunch of teeth against flesh. The vomit-inducing ripping sound as skin and meat was literally torn from the body and then the gushing spray of crimson-red blood. Every time the thought came back to her, Becky had to steady herself against the side for fear of toppling over. It was the very thing she was reliving with Gaynor. After she had pecked Dom on the cheek and sent him off to work, Becky had slipped her coat on and made her way out of the house.

"Gosh, my dear," Gaynor had said, "you're beginning to grow out, aren't you?"

Becky looked down proudly at her swollen belly and put her hand on the bump. She had grown, and yet she hadn't noticed. Her morning sickness hadn't been so bad recently and, since Gaynor had revealed the protection she had placed around her little girl, her concern had been somewhat quelled. Becky had now, in fact, taken to singing to her belly of a morning, as she stood cradling a mug of tea. There had been slight inner twinges throughout her repertoire, which suggested that the baby didn't think much of out-of-key Celine Dion.

"Not long now," Becky said, and though she felt a wave of excitement for what was to come, she felt an air of sadness too that Dom didn't appear to feel quite the same way. In truth, it was as though they were drifting apart. Their kisses weren't full of the meaning that they once had been, they were just perfunctory. Or maybe they always had been, but she had never noticed before.

Gaynor registered a sigh.

"The best miracles come to those who wait," she said, slowly clearing things from the kitchen table as Becky lowered herself into a chair.

"So," Becky said, changing the topic swiftly, "the other night was a bit strange wasn't it? I mean, Odette didn't really know what it was all about, did she?"

Gaynor scoffed.

"Magick is a tricky business," she said, pootling about the kitchen with no real purpose, while Pluto lay sleeping in his bed. "I mean, I've been practising for a fair few years now, but the High Sceptres...! Even the younger ones' volume of knowledge surpasses mine by a country mile. They have brains like encyclopaedias. Always referring to ancient spells from bygone eras and such. I just can't keep up."

Becky narrowed her eyes.

"Did you never want to go for it? To be a High Sceptre, I mean?" she asked quizzically. Their conversations had not been so contrived recently since Becky had been outed as a magickal person. However, she still trod carefully when asking too many probing questions.

"Pfft—no!" Gaynor cackled. "I was a tearaway, dear! I never wanted to sit and study for those exams. I mean, the train from Carmarthen to London in those days would have cost my mother a pretty penny. She wasn't going to squander it on me when she had other mouths to feed."

Gaynor sighed.

"No, Dai and I were too busy gallivanting across the meadows to be tempted by endless book-worming and spell-casting. I couldn't be bothered. It was only in my older years that I took up botany. That's when we decided to move here and build the paradise."

She nodded in the direction of the back garden.

Becky had so much to ask, but she didn't want to interrogate Gaynor and seem like an inexperienced little girl.

"Most of what Odette was saying went straight over my head. Spell spheres and Rivers in Vasterbargarian, or whatever it was called. I don't even know where that is!" Becky smirked.

"Well you're brand new, you'll have all this to come when you begin your proper study. If, of course, that's what you want to do. They can't force you."

"I thought you were going to teach me. If you do, then I'll do it."

Gaynor smiled and turned her back to Becky as she wiped the sideboard.

"To be honest," she said over her shoulder, "it went a little over my head too. It sounded all a bit gobbledegook to me. I mean, the connection to magic-bending seemed obvious, but she isn't going to let us in on too much. Keeping her cards close to her chest. Even through our decades of service, it seems we still can't be trusted with too much sensitive information. Still, she is a High Sceptre, so she must be respected, and her opinion honoured."

"I just don't know where that spell came from, or how I even knew what to say." Becky screwed up her face which made Gaynor chuckle.

"You must be the chosen one," she said, throwing a hand up.

Becky thought for a moment.

"I mean, it's all very well trying to decipher my spell, but that seems to be taking too much time. If Odette wanted to take quick, affirmative action, wouldn't it be more useful to explore a pattern in the victims that were targeted? There must be a reason why those three women were chosen."

Gaynor stopped a moment as if she too was thinking.

"What do you mean?" she eventually asked.

"Well, there were two teachers who went missing," Becky said. "Miss Wicks and Miss Ware. Both opposite ends of the age bracket so no connection there."

"Yes?" Gaynor turned around.

"We know that the spell was used to possess. But why these women? Why were they chosen to be hexed? And Rachel Power? What is the connection there?"

"But wait now," Gaynor said, running the tea towel through her hands, "we don't know for a fact that Miss Wicks was possessed—she's never been found. The two could be totally unrelated."

"Hmmm," Becky mumbled, scratching her chin. "I'm not so sure. I think if we put these things together if we spelt the facts out right here on this table, something would link up. I mean, did Miss Wicks have any money to speak of?"

"Not that I know of," Gaynor replied.

"Because Miss Eames and her squandering could have meant that it was money she was after. If she is, indeed, a suspect in all this."

Becky tapped her temple with her finger while Gaynor raised her eyebrows.

"You knew about that?" she asked.

"Oh yes," Becky responded with a smile, "I was the one who saw her."

Gaynor nodded as Becky stuck out her bottom lip in thought. She was loving this fresh, exciting approach to the dilemma.

"I mean," Becky said, with a sparkle in her eye, "I reckon that if we put our heads together, we could solve this thing before Odette does."

■■

Abbie was sitting on her bed. She had only really stopped intermittently crying in the last hour or so, and she was exhausted. There would come a moment where she would feel alright,

476

but then a wave of panic would grip her slightly and that would set her off again. There was something about her row with Joanna that was still haunting her.

It wasn't the fact that she had hit Joanna, though that was shocking enough all by itself. It wasn't even the fact that they had quarrelled at all. She was more devastated that Joanna had rebuffed her without a second thought. Even to go so far as to say that she deserved to be abused for misusing magick. I mean, what was all *that* shit about?

Okay, their relationship had never been plain sailing, but Joanna had been her mentor for so long that she was used to standing with her head down and accepting Joanna's verbal beatings with good grace and a knowing smirk. However, in this instance, she had been pushed so far that she had actually answered Joanna back.

Perhaps it was because Abbie saw Joanna as a mother figure, and this is how daughters argued with their mothers. She would never learn this kind of thing from her biological mother, who she simply did not get on with. There was no maternal love in their relationship. Her own mother could barely lift a phone receiver to call her estranged daughter, let alone dole out any sort of discipline.

Joanna and Abbie's relationship was more like Stockholm Syndrome. She was trapped under Joanna's tutelage and authority, and yet she felt an indescribable awe for the woman and her wisdom. And through all the criticism and scorn, of which there was plenty, Abbie had never felt that Joanna didn't care about her, or that she did not want Abbie to be the best that she could be.

Now, however, that was all gone. She had performed unauthorised magick. That was enough to get you exiled on its own but striking the coven leader—fuck knows what the repercussions of that would be.

She still couldn't forgive Joanna, no matter what she may have thought about her in the past. It was now clear that Joanna didn't give two shits about her. No one who did could ever say such a dangerous and offensive thing, especially when she didn't know the facts. It was almost as if she would rather side with that rapist Xander if it meant that Abbie was taught a valuable lesson about the respectful use of magick.

But then, Abbie thought, if Joanna was now out of the picture, then surely she no further incentive to live by her rules. Perhaps now she could go renegade. She could finally start experimenting with her gift and putting endless years of painstaking study to good use.

She wondered if there was a special coven for those who had been banished from their own. A sort of *Bad Girls Club* for rebel witches.

Perhaps she could contact Ebony, to see if she knew if there was any such society. They might even be able to start up their own to rival that old bitch, Joanna, and kick her nose right out of joint once and for all.

She could poach the others, who were surely as pissed off with Joanna's dictatorship as she was. But not that fat, Chinese woman, she would be a waste of time—she never spoke!

She wiped her nose with the back of her hand and pulled her laptop lid up.

Looking at the screen in front of her, she scrolled through her messages to select the thread from Ebony.

She began to type.

"Hey babes, got something to ask you. It's about revenge..."

She knew that would get Ebony's attention.

Sure enough, seconds later she received a reply.

"Sounds interesting—how can I help?"

■■■■■■■■■■■■■■■■■■■■■■■■■■■■■■■■■■■■■■

"So," Becky asked, "what is it we know already?"

At this point, Gaynor had pulled up a chair, initially hesitant about trying to do some sort of unauthorised detective work behind the back of one of the Grand High Sceptre's of the United Kingdom, of which there were only about thirteen. Becky's enthusiasm, however, was making her warm to the idea.

Becky had found a pen and was now writing on the back of an old envelope.

"What do we know about Anne Wicks?" Becky momentarily rattled the pen in between her teeth. "Was she part of The Order?"

"Well, no. Not that I know of..."

Gaynor paused for a moment before correcting herself.

"I mean, no—she wasn't. She was just a girl from Plymouth who had settled here with a baby. No man to speak of. Much like yourself, dear."

Becky frowned.

"I'm married."

"No, I mean like yourself in that she came from outside and settled here, went to work at the school. Kept herself to herself." Gaynor sighed. "I would see her walking about. Never stopped by for a cup of tea or anything, much as I invited. I think she was shy. Not very chatty, you know, unlike yourself."

Gaynor gave Becky a cheeky, little smile, which Becky returned.

"And she didn't have any connection to the occult or anything?" Becky's line of questioning was direct, but she was enjoying this new-found confidence. It gave her a sense of importance and power that she rarely felt in her daily life.

"Well, it's not the business of a regional coven to check those kinds of things," Gaynor said. "We don't keep tabs on people unless we think they may be a threat. And we haven't had a threat here for decades. If there were to be such a person entering the town, The Oracle would be sure to know about it and Odette would have told us."

"Right," Becky said, "well there must be some sort of link between her and the possession of Miss Ware."

Becky thought of the mark that was still emblazoned on her wall, under layers of the superfluous paint she had applied to it, and its similarity to the mark on the church piano.

"But I'm sure the only link these two women would be the perpetrator." Gaynor looked at Becky with frustrated eyes. She was too old to play detective.

"Not necessarily. And you're definitely sure that it wasn't Miss Eames?" Becky asked.

"I'm not sure that she would be able to do anything from a police cell, dear. I mean for a spell that catastrophic, you would need an altar or a voodoo sacrifice. I mean, she'll have nothing in there, sat all alone."

"Then could she potentially have someone working for her on the outside?"

"Very possibly," Gaynor said, "but if there was to be anyone, Odette would know. She would have targeted them and put a stop to it."

"But she hasn't," Becky sighed, "she's too busy working out the spell, not following the crime."

Both Gaynor and Becky looked in separate directions, temporarily lost in their own thoughts.

"And there are no people with the necessary enlighters to help catch the criminal," Becky asked, clutching at straws.

Suddenly, Gaynor had a thought that hit her so hard, she gasped and reached out to Becky's hand.

"*Abbie,*" she said in a low whisper.

"Abbie?"

"Yes, she wasn't there last night. I completely forgot. Abbie wasn't at the meeting."

"And Abbie is...?"

"A precocious little madam who resents the coven and everyone in it for taking away her childhood," Gaynor said, rolling her eyes. "But there *must* be a reason why she wasn't at Joanna's. There is no way she would be allowed to miss it. Oh, I can't believe I didn't say anything at the time. I was too caught up in Odette's ramblings."

"And you think she might know something?" Becky's eyes widened with anticipation.

"Well," Gaynor said, "we can but ask."

Gaynor jumped up from her chair and made her way over to a kitchen drawer under the sink.

"Now, where did I put my little black spell book?"

■■■

Abbie saw her phone ring, but she paid it no mind. It was an unknown landline. Who used landlines nowadays? Whoever the archaic moron was, she didn't want to speak to them.

It then dawned on her that it might the hospital, trying to get hold of her. Or worse still, the police.

Maybe Xander had, in fact, ratted her out, even though they had made a pact that he wouldn't. She wondered what the little ditch rat would be up to now? Probably playing the little-boy-lost routine with the nurses, sticking his bottom lip out and pretending he was in agonising pain. Yeah, well—he deserved it.

She scratched the side of her head in thought. She was thinking that she might have to go and see him at the hospital to reaffirm their little deal, to make sure he was sticking to it and somehow, correlate the events of that night into some semblance of order, just so she could get her head around what it was that they had both seen. She was trying not to think too much about what had happened, lest she panic and turn into some kind of unhinged ball of anxiety.

She had to keep her head at the moment. Weird shit was going on everywhere and it was not the time to lose her mettle.

She shook the thought off and went back to typing her message on Facebook.

"Gone rogue—split from the "sisterhood" and want to start trying out some shit. Any ideas where I can go for some advice?"

From what she had gleaned from earlier conversations with Ebony, this girl had done much the same thing. She was always moaning about her coven, saying that she was eager to move forward, to not be hamstrung by all the rules and regulations. Of course, Abbie still didn't know whether Ebony was one hundred percent legit, so she wasn't giving too much of herself away. If anything, Ebony had given more of herself away from what she had written in previous posts.

The reply took longer than she thought it would. Either Ebony was trying hard to make something up on the fly, or she was equally as cautious as to why Abbie was asking this.

The reply came.

"Who are you?"

Abbie frowned. It was unusually vague as if someone else had intercepted their conversation. Who was it? Joanna? Oracle HQ?

"You know who I am."

She only went by her initials in the profile she used for her chats with Ebony, along with an ambiguous photo of her smiling through a thick wedge of blonde hair, so she was suitably unrecognisable.

"No, what is your name? Your name and your coven?"

Abbie started to get hot. Ebony had never been this direct with her before. It was unnerving. She couldn't help feeling, however, that she was on the cusp of getting some highly classified stuff here. She debated whether she should just take the plunge and answer Ebony sincerely.

Well, she'd risked everything else. Performing unregulated magic, breaking her lover's fingers, slapping her elder. What more could she do wrong?

"Abbie Welch. Winchcombe."

Her finger hovered over the send button. Then, in a split-second of impulse, she pressed it.

What seemed like painful hours passed. It was, in fact, about three minutes.

And then the worst thing happened— suddenly, Ebony logged off.

Abbie's heart skipped a beat. What the actual *fuck*?. Why had Ebony just peaced out? Could it be possible that she was really part of the Witch Hunter Generals, posing online as a young witch to entice others to reveal their whereabouts? How could she be so stupid as to reveal her real name to someone online—was she totally fucking crazy? Perhaps Joanna was right, maybe she should be taught a lesson.

Her heart beat through her chest and her breath came out in short bursts. What if someone was coming right now to get her? What would they do to her? The memory of the images that Joanna had conjured up when they had been learning about the goings-on of the WHG from those dusty, old books of hers suddenly filled Abbie with panic.

This was too intense. She had to get out of here, it was too risky.

She searched around for her bag and threw a lighter and a half-smoked packet of cigarettes into it.

As she climbed off the bed, not knowing where to go or who to contact for help, her computer blinked at her again, making her stop in her tracks.

The message box flashed back up onto the screen.

Ebony was back online.

A sentence popped up onto the monitor.

"Charlotte. Glasgow Central Coven."

Abbie's heart stopped racing a touch. She flopped back down on her bed, her bag crumpling to the floor.

The message continued.

"So, you want out of the coven then? Let's get you hooked up."

■ ■

"Do you think she might be ignoring you?" Becky asked, inadvertently biting her index fingernail.

"Hmmm," Gaynor mused, "I can't be sure. I'm not sure how many seventy-something-year-olds she gets phone calls from of an evening."

Gaynor stood pondering for a moment, before seemingly having another thought and springing into action.

"Ha," she said, making for the lounge door, "these youngsters really should know not to try and fool an old witch."

She stopped in the doorway and motioned to her companion.

"Well, come on then," Gaynor barked, "sitting there won't buy the baby a new bonnet will it?"

Becky jumped off her chair and followed along.

Once they had entered the lounge, Becky noticed that the room had been largely untouched, save for a few items having been moved here and there. That said, the energy felt somewhat different as if some casting had been going on since she was last in here.

Gaynor was already on her knees, wrestling with the lock on one of her chests. The throw had been pulled off of it and lay like a dead body on the carpet.

Once she had released the lid, Gaynor reached in and brought out an object. It looked like a bubble, but it was the size of a dinner plate and was so opaque that you could almost see right through it.

It was one of the most beautiful things Becky had ever seen. She gazed at it in wonder.

"What is *that*?" Becky after asked after a few moments of open-mouthed awe.

"This, my dear, is a limelight," Gaynor said, not struggling at all under the weight of such a large ornament. Becky supposed that it must be as light as a feather.

"It's a very basic and very old magickal instrument," she said. "It can be used as protection, as a shield or, in this case, as a peephole—you just have to know what energy to fill it with."

Becky looked confused.

"Don't worry about it," Gaynor reassured her, "once we begin your training, you'll be able to handle this thing like you handle a remote control. It's just about knowing what to do."

That didn't fill Becky with much confidence. She cast her mind back to the last time she had tried to manage the Sky remote and erased all of Dom's pre-recorded episodes of *Countryfile*. That was a tense day.

And as Gaynor continued to look Becky in the eye, she broke into a grin and flicked her wrist. As she did so, the ball went sailing into the air.

Becky's natural reflex was to rush to catch it. She felt herself lunging forward, but the ball stopped mid-leap and she landed, rather pathetically, onto her wrists. Gaynor let out a little chuckle.

"I love doing that to spook the newbies," she said. "Now, hold my hand."

Becky, her ego bruised a little, bashfully got herself into a kneeling position and reached her hand out to take Gaynor's. She was still a little shaken by the thought of the sphere crashing to the floor and shattering. Instead, it remained suspended in mid-air, like a window in an invisible wall.

"Now, close your eyes," Gaynor instructed.

Becky furrowed her brow and tightened her lips. She had no idea what was about to come and, even though she trusted Gaynor implicitly, she was not sure if she trusted the ball dangling above her head as much.

Gaynor squeezed Becky's hand in her own.

"Come on now," she said, "there's nothing to be afraid of."

Holding her gaze with the glimmering dome, Becky slowly closed her eyes. Gaynor's hand felt soft under her own trembling digits.

The next thing she heard was Gaynor whispering softly.

"Tanto versberum. Colossus," Gaynor said, repeating herself a few times.

A strange sound followed, like water rippling on the surface of a calm lake.

And with that, Becky opened one eye.

■■

"So, who are these people?" Abbie asked the girl, whose face had now appeared on her computer screen via Skype.

Ebony—or rather Charlotte, her true name— was, in fact, a Scottish girl of Dominican descent and was around Abbie's age. She was beautiful, with jet-black hair and perfect white teeth. She smiled as she spoke, and her eyes seemed to shine as she did, quite far removed from the picture Abbie had concocted of her in her mind.

Charlotte had been uninterested in pleasantries and had, instead, ploughed right in. She had asked Abbie a few questions concerning her magickal study, just to check that she was who she said she was. She then demonstrated her empathy with Abbie's situation. She too had become disenchanted with her coven and had heard of this covert group from a girl she had befriended in the circle. The group was named 'The New Realm'.

"Well," Charlotte had said, "they are as their name suggests. But I can't give too much away over the computer for obvious reasons. Once you join the network, it will become clear. And don't be worried about online security—it will send copies of your profile back and forth across a range of territories so that, in effect, you become untraceable."

"Sounds cool. So, this is all outside of The Order then?" Abbie pulled a lock of her hair into her mouth, as she was prone to doing when she was engrossed in an online chat.

"They are not affiliated with The Order at all. Think of them as a separate, more liberal front. The core principles are the same, but the ancient, bureaucratic constraints no longer apply.

They're like the second generation of our kind. The world has moved on, so why not the craft?" Charlotte's expression grew stern. It was clearly something she believed in.

"But," Abbie continued, "how do you get in? It doesn't sound like they'll just welcome anyone."

"Oh," Charlotte held out a hand to the screen, "I'll recommend you. It's fine."

"I see," Abbie replied, suddenly extremely satisfied with the decision she had made to breach her anonymity with Charlotte. She had no idea that the rising stars of The Order were splitting away and forming their own alliance. But then it made sense. The whole world had changed so much, with the advance of technology and online communications in the last twenty years—it only made sense that the sisterhood should too. And if even age-old institutions like the British monarchy was now sending tweets from the palace, why should the craft still be lurking in the shadows?

Abbie was overjoyed that someone had had the nous to start the whole ball rolling with it. At last, she didn't feel quite so alone in finding the ways of The Order stuffy, outdated and totally out-of-touch with the modern age.

Abbie looked concerned.

"But if they're a secret society," she said tentatively, "how come you can just recommend me? I mean, you don't really know me that well."

"The thing is," Charlotte said, sensing Abbie's trepidation, "even though The New Realm is pretty choosy about who gets access, I think there is something on the website that every witch should see, especially those from your part of the world."

Abbie pressed her lips together.

"What is it?"

"I can't say too much on here. Just follow the link that takes you to 'threats'. You'll know where to go from there."

Abbie nodded in acknowledgement.

"Well, I've got to go, but I wouldn't hesitate too long. The recommendation will only last for forty-eight hours before your application is rejected and blacklisted. I'll message you when I've made the claim," Charlotte said.

Abbie smiled.

"Okay, cool," she said, "I'll look out for it."

Before she went, Charlotte looked directly into the screen.

"Oh, just one more thing," she said.

Abbie listened intently.

"Be careful not to advertise this. If The Order feels it has unauthorised competition, it will shut us down and have us exiled. It's so important to keep this thing alive. The New Realm offers an alternative to those of us who want change. It keeps us abreast of the things we need to know, the things that The Oracle thinks we need to be protected from. So, we need to keep ourselves hidden, for now."

Abbie nodded again.

Charlotte signed off and Abbie immediately went to her Google browser, poised and ready for Charlotte's message to come up. She didn't intend to sail close to the wind with this one. A fire had been ignited within her and she was eager to see what innovation these girls had come up with. It was about time Joanna was sideswiped by those who were more than capable of filling her pompous, ugly shoes.

She drummed her fingers on the base of her laptop.

What could Charlotte have meant when she said *especially those from your part of the world?* That had been a bit bizarre.

All of a sudden, the doorbell rang upstairs.

For shit's sake, she thought, cursing her flatmates. *Don't they ever remember their keys?*

Confused, and a little weary, she closed her laptop and got up from her bed.

She opened the bedroom door and sprang up the small staircase to the front door.

She was just about to wrench it open, when a cold thought struck her and so, she looped the chain on first—it might be Xander, all bandaged up and ready for round two.

Tentatively, she opened the door and pulled it slightly ajar.

When she saw who it was, her face fell. She closed the door, unlatched the chain and opened it again, swinging it out to meet her guest.

Abbie stood with one hand on her hip and a frown across her brow.

"Hi," she said in an unimpressed tone, "what the hell are *you* doing here?"

Gaynor smiled.

"I don't believe in hell, my dear, and neither should you." One of her eyebrows was arched. "Now, are you going to let us in? It's very rude to keep two visitors standing on the stoop like this."

Abbie still didn't return her grin.

"I haven't had time to tidy up." Abbie chewed on an imaginary piece of gum.

"Well, we're not here for an inspection, so I think you'll be alright." Gaynor looked down at herself and up at Abbie.

Abbie sighed, hoping her nonchalance might have put Gaynor off. Joanna had obviously sent the old woman over here to try and talk to her or something, and Abbie hadn't the time nor the inclination to hear it right now.

That said, she stepped to the side and let her pass. However, someone else was with her. Some brown-haired woman who she hadn't met before, though she did look familiar, walked into her home. She looked shy at first, but when she saw Abbie, her eyes widened.

"Who's she?" Abbie asked

494

"*She,*" Gaynor said, "is a fellow witch. Now, is there anyone home that we should know about?"

"No," Abbie said, closing the door behind the two women.

The three stood about awkwardly. No one spoke.

"And am I to navigate my own way around your house or shall we hold this meeting in the hall?" Gaynor piped up after a while, punctuating the awkwardness.

"Fine," Abbie huffed, squeezing her way past and leading the way into the cramped lounge.

A dusty, old sofa lay covered in various clothing items like it was shedding a skin. Empty cigarette packets lay open on a small table that was marked with streaks of foundation and a thick layer of dust. The air was heavy and smelt of wet towels.

Abbie plonked herself down on the sofa into an undignified slouch.

Gaynor and Becky stepped over the detritus to find a suitable seat on a couple of dining room chairs.

"Well, if she's a fellow witch, how come I've never seen her before?" Abbie asked insolently.

"Well," Gaynor said, smoothing her trousers out over her legs, "if you came to meetings like a decent witch then you *would* have met her before. Now if you don't mind, we didn't come here to cop a load of your attitude."

Abbie exhaled deeply and pulled herself up out of the bowels of the sofa.

"Well, why did you come here then?" she said. "Did Joanna send you over to have a pop at me?"

Gaynor looked confused.

"My dear girl, what are you going on about?"

The other woman's eyes darted about nervously, but she stayed quiet.

Abbie shuffled her feet uncomfortably.

"So, you don't know anything about what happened?" she asked, feeling foolish to assume that Gaynor was out for blood rather than being concerned for her well-being.

"I don't know a thing," Gaynor said. "All I know is that you didn't make it to a meeting and I wanted to know why. Neither Joanna nor Odette know I am here or have put me up to anything of any kind. I work on my own authority, you must know that by now."

Becky stared at Gaynor, impressed by her change in attitude. In front of this girl, she held authority, and it was a pleasure to witness. It was now slotting into place, who this girl was. Robina had known her all along, but Becky now understood why she had denied it.

"Okay," Abbie shifted her focus over to the Becky, who sat politely with her hands in her lap. "So why is this lady here?"

Gaynor looked at Becky and let out a small breath.

"She—" Gaynor started. "*Becky* ... was there when Brenda Ware tore the throat out of that woman at the Halloween party."

Abbie's eyes grew as large as saucers at this. She wrenched herself forward in her seat as Becky smiled awkwardly.

"*What?!*" Abbie spluttered. "How—I mean ... *what?!*"

"It seems that we both have stories to tell," Gaynor chuckled, sitting slightly back in her hard chair.

"Now," she said, "who wants to start?"

EIGHTEEN

"So, Miss Ware, possessed and bewitched, crashed the Power's party and tore the mother's throat out?" Abbie recounted back to them, horrified and delighted in equal measure.

"That's the gist of it, yes," Gaynor nodded. She was parched and could have done with a cup of tea, but she didn't fancy drinking anything out of a mug in this flat.

"Did you *see* it?" Abbie was letting her fascination with the macabre get the better of her.

"I did," Becky intercepted. It was the first time she had spoken since she had arrived. "It wasn't pretty."

She didn't want to elaborate further. She didn't feel particularly welcome in this girl's house and, after recognising her as the light-fingered troublemaker from Cavendish House in the lumelight's glow, she knew what kind of untrustworthy type she was dealing with.

"Well," Gaynor said, resting her hands on her knees, "that's my contribution. Are you going to tell me what happened with Joanna?"

Abbie grimaced and fell back into the sofa.

"We've fallen out. I never want to speak to her again," she said, playing with a make-believe hair on her fingernail.

"Why?" Gaynor asked, with a slight exasperation.

"Something happened to *me* that night." Abbie refused to look either woman in the face. "Something I did, something she said. It was stupid really."

Gaynor exhaled. She didn't have time to deal with Abbie's usual obstinance. She hated having to be so direct with her, but it was the only way she would ever get results.

"I went to meet this guy up on Cleeve Hill," Abbie began. "It all ended badly and so I..."

Abbie stopped mid-sentence, her cheeks turning pink.

"You hexed him." Gaynor finished the sentence for her. There was no trace of judgement on Gaynor's face.

"Yeah," Abbie said, suddenly embarrassed. Gaynor's lack of reaction cooled her somewhat.

"And you fell out over it?" Gaynor continued.

"We didn't just fall out. That horrible cow said that I had it coming. She said if I was going to start performing magick in front of non-magickal people, then I deserved ... for bad things to

499

happen to me." Abbie was now completely red-faced, all her frustrations now pouring out of her.

"Well, she shouldn't have said that," Gaynor sighed, "but she probably said it out of anger."

"Look, if you're going to defend her—"

"I'm not saying it to defend her Abigail, I'm saying it to assure you. Assure you that your actions most certainly did *not* warrant that kind of treatment." Gaynor's tone became firm.

"Listen," Gaynor went on, "do you think, in all my years as a practising witch, I never hexed anyone for being a total and utter bastard?"

This word made both Abbie and Becky turn towards her.

"Of course, I have! I have met some *vile* people in my time and when you know that, as a youngster, you have all this unusual power at your fingertips, there's nothing more tempting than ruffling a few feathers. Just a little."

She gave Abbie a wink.

"And you never got barked at for it?" Abbie asked.

"My mistress was a lot less strict than Joanna," Gaynor replied. "Joanna likes to feed you the worst possible scenario. She's old-school. Government by fear—I used to see it all the time in her generation. The sixties witches all believed that they should provide a solid mast in a sea of free love and experimental drug-taking. Joanna's lot didn't know what they were missing out on, being so bloody frigid."

This made Abbie snort.

"But whatever she does for you, my dear, she does it to protect you. She doesn't mean to bite. I'd be a bit more forgiving."

"I slapped her," Abbie replied, the memory bringing tears to her.

"Well," Gaynor shrugged, "sometimes people need to be put back in their box."

Abbie pinched her lips together in appreciation.

"Thanks," she muttered.

Gaynor leant over and put a comforting hand on Abbie's knee.

"I suppose we'd better go." Gaynor rose to her feet and nodded to Becky who also stood.

"Oh, okay," Abbie said, standing up herself. "Crazy about Miss Ware though. I mean, we all thought she was dead and it turns out she's hiding in the bushes somewhere, ready to take someone out. That is *mad.*"

"I suppose," Gaynor said, as she began to make her way out.

"In a way, it's a bit like the Miss Wicks thing, isn't it?" Abbie mused as she went to lead the ladies to the door.

"Hardly," returned Gaynor. "I mean, at least Miss Ware turned up, we still don't know where Anne Wicks is, poor lamb."

This made Abbie turn around, excitedly.

"Oh my God. Of course—you don't know do you?" Abbie slapped herself on the forehead with her palm.

Gaynor and Becky stopped in their tracks, a bemused look on both of their faces.

"Know what love?" Gaynor asked, hesitantly.

"Miss Wicks!" Abbie exclaimed. "I *found* her."

■■■■■■■■■■■■■■■■■■■■■■■■■■■■■■■■■■■■■■■

An American woman's voice came down the telephone.

"So, Mrs Clements? How can I help?"

Catherine couldn't believe she was doing this. She was finally succumbing to the last bastion of bad parenting—phoning the child psychologist.

She had been through so much in the last twenty-four hours and if there was one thing her mother had always taught her, it was to prioritise the children's needs before anything else.

"My dear, if you don't act fast you may end up with a drug addict on your hands. Or worse still, a gay. Get the creases ironed out post-haste."

Catherine shuddered at the mere thought of taking any parenting advice from a woman never once seen without a gin and tonic in her hand, but she was running low on ideas.

Memories of Rachel Power's fateful party still rang in her mind. The twitching corpse, covered in the blood that streamed out of the torn neck like an unstoppable fountain. Still managing to pout, even in death. The screaming of parents and the blur of darting bodies. How she had managed to scoop her own children up in the melee was anyone's guess, but she had, and they had run as fast as they could to the car.

But her children had been positively calm ever since. Maybe it was them repressing the recollection of what had happened. It can't have been easy for them to witness that kind of commotion at, what should have been, a nice, family occasion.

Perhaps it was the stress of their father not being invited back home that had turned them insular. Either way, they maintained an air of cool acceptance that was both strange and unsettling.

While Catherine panicked whenever she considered the shame that would come with being a single parent at the school gate, the children were quietly watching television together or helping to load the dishwasher. She wished she could act so reserved in these times of crisis.

It was only when the woman cleared her throat on the other end of the phone that Catherine remembered that she was in the middle of a call.

"Oh, I'm sorry," she said in a sleepy voice, "I was just phoning to see whether Doctor Fabril had an appointment this week."

"Okay," the lady said. A faint tapping sound indicated that she was perusing through reams and reams of patient details. I mean, honestly, how many people in the Gloucestershire area could afford private counselling sessions?

Not that Catherine would be paying for it, of course. She'd send the bill straight to Saul. It would come out of his 'you-brought-this-on-yourself' budget. As would the huge bottle of Bombay Sapphire that she had driven especially to Waitrose to purchase.

The woman cleared her throat again.

"The earliest we have is three weeks on Friday," she said as if that was good enough.

In that time, Saul could have successfully manipulated her through fear, getting himself out of the Travelodge he was currently licking his wounds in and back into the marital bed.

Catherine clutched the receiver. Perhaps it was she who needed the shrink, not the children—she felt as if she were going mad.

"Oh, that's too late," Catherine said, sounding like June Whitfield.

"There's nothing sooner, I'm afraid." The delight this woman evidently found in disappointing people was palpable in her voice.

"Fine," Catherine snapped and hung up the phone.

Putting it back down on the table, she listened to the strains of Disney's *Moana* rattling along in the background.

She had to speak to someone.

Her first thought was Becky, but she wasn't sure that Becky was the best choice. She needed to offload onto someone who barely knew her, someone who could just listen and not offer up any sort of opinion. Someone who was so far removed from her situation that they would not judge her or roll their eyes when she looked away.

She opened the Kath Kidston address book that lay on the table and searched for another number.

▪▪▪

"What do you mean you *found* her?" Gaynor had immediately sat back down. "She's been missing for months. I mean what, when, how?"

Abbie was fairly impassive.

"Yeah, I mean everything happened on Saturday. I was in a field up on Cleeve and I found the body," she said.

"Oh, my." Gaynor put her hand to her chest. "Was she..."

Both Abbie and Becky knew what she was getting at.

"Well, this is the thing," Abbie said excitably. "They took her away and covered her over, but I swear... I *swear* that her eyes opened."

"What do you mean? She was dead with her eyes open? That's quite common, isn't it?"

Gaynor was both shocked and intrigued at the same time.

"No," Abbie said, "They weren't open, they opened. Like, she suddenly came to life. I remember it scared me. That's why I ran to call the ambulance. I thought they might be able to save her."

"Well, was she clothed? Bruised? Decomposed?" Gaynor was desperate with her line of questioning, which made Abbie cautious.

"Her clothes were ripped. She was lying on her stomach. She was dirty, you know, like she'd been there for a while." She searched her mind for an image of the body.

"I just remember thinking that she was dead. Almost knowing she was." The magnitude of what Abbie saw that night was beginning to come back to her. "I tried to warn the ambulance guy, but he wouldn't have it. He said she was definitely gone, but I saw her bloody eyes open. I saw it!"

Gaynor took a deep breath, looked at Becky and nodded.

"I think there could only be one person who would be able to answer for certain," Gaynor said. "I mean, I could look in the lumelight and see whether it gives me any frames inside the morgue. I don't think we can be overly cautious on this."

"What?" Abbie said, "You think she could be bewitched?"

"Almost certainly," Gaynor said. "The mark that the dark magick left at the possession site of Brenda Ware was identical to the one at the last known sighting of Anne Wicks. Those two things link the victims. I think we can safely say that there is a strong possibility that Miss Wicks is being used as a host by the person who bewitched her, poor lamb. Knowing what that magick is capable of, we can't take any chances."

"What do you think we should do?" Becky said.

"Bernice," Gaynor replied. "She is the only woman in the circle, indeed in the UK, who is able to speak to the dead. Only she will know whether the soul of Anne Wicks has passed over to the other side."

"But wouldn't she have mentioned it if she had?" Becky asked.

"Before we thought Anne was missing, not necessarily dead. Now we have her body, we can find out whether she was killed, or whether she is still alive at that hospital, ready for use as and when the perpetrator needs her." Gaynor's mood was now so serious that it piqued further concern between the other two ladies.

"Do you think we should go to Bernice's right away?" Becky said, her heart beating rapidly.

"Absolutely," Gaynor said as she started to get to her feet.

"Well," Abbie said, also rising, "I think I should come too. I mean, I was the last person to see the body."

"Fine," said Gaynor, "but I want you to think, *really* think, whether there was anything else you noticed. Any slight bit of info that might be of interest to the circle."

Abbie nodded, and the three women made their way out of the room.

∎∎∎

Robina was nervous. She hadn't really banked on getting an out-of-the-blue phone call from the woman who she made an absolute fool of, albeit unwittingly. She still had trouble figuring it all out. Robina had only really ever made contact with the deceased party when they attended a cookery class together. Well, Robina attended, and Rachel had practically hosted the damn thing.

Everybody else's soufflé had puffed up like beautiful pastry clouds, whereas Robina's had remained a sticky, yellow skin at the bottom of the dish.

Rachel's was positively towering over all the others, and the six other women had cooed over it. The master chef had just stood there, nodding and running an Emma Bridgwater tea towel through her hands. Robina recalled her mesmerising beauty, her lips stained with a deep crimson gloss, her hair perfectly conditioned.

It was only when Robina had arrived home and began to scrape the horrible, cheesy mess into the bin, that she had stolen a look in the mirror and noticed a trickling milk stain running down the length of her blouse. It looked like she had been lactating and had obviously been there ever since she added the milk to the ingredients, very early on in the class. They had probably all been laughing at it behind her back.

Robina should have seen this coming a mile off. Why would anyone recommend her to do anything, let alone cook? And why on earth would they pay her to do it? But when Catherine had appeared at her door that day, she hadn't the nerve to send her away. She had been persistent and intimidating, and Robina would rather have said yes and watched her go, than refuse and be continuously pestered.

Well, there was little she could do about it now. That Rachel woman had obviously engineered the situation to make both herself and Catherine look extremely stupid.

But, that said, no one deserved what had happened to her. Robina had seen the whole thing. Brenda Ware, naked and ferocious, pouncing upon an unsuspecting Rachel. If that is what karma did to you, then Robina intended to live a very blameless life indeed.

She shuddered.

And now Catherine was coming over, seemingly to return her cake tin but, Robina suspected, more so to try and discuss what happened at the party.

Once again, Robina had felt too pressured to say no when Catherine had invited herself round for a cup of tea.

In truth, Catherine had sounded a bit forlorn, not nearly as assertive as in their previous encounters. It was as if she had been crying an awful lot. Perhaps that's what made Robina buckle. No one deserves to be alone when they are that distraught. Robina knew that from personal experience, though hers was much more steeped in anxiety than it was in upset.

And, at her lowest ebb, why would Catherine call the crazy lady who couldn't bake her way out of a paper bag? Surely, she had a myriad of mummy friends who would be on-hand at the end of the phone, with a sympathetic ear and a gin and tonic.

No, something clearly wasn't right at the Clements household.

The doorbell rang, which made Jessie-Cat—and consequently, Robina—jump.

She took a few deep breaths and went into the hall. Closing her eyes, she braced herself.

As she pulled her front door open, a very different woman stood on her doorstep. Rather than the beautifully turned-out glamour-puss that she was used to seeing sashaying around Winchcombe with a mega-watt smile slapped onto her face, the Catherine of today cut a much more sombre figure.

Her usual cascading golden curls were now scraped up into an uneven ponytail. Where her eyes normally shimmered with a vibrant blend of colour, her lids were darkened and her eyes sunken. Her bronzed skin was now pale, and she hunched forward, dressed in a modest, grey tracksuit.

Robina thought she actually looked more striking dressed down than she did all dolled up.

Catherine's eyes grew moist as she registered Robina's sympathetic head tilt and she could feel her throat begin to tighten.

"I'm sorry," Catherine choked, forcing back the urge to break down but failing miserably. She held her empty hands out for Robina to see.

"I forgot your *fucking* cake tin!"

■■

It had taken Wing some time to pluck up the courage to make the call. She knew it wasn't going to be easy, but she had to do it, and now was the best time.

Richard had come down the stairs in the night to see her in floods of tears, sweeping up shards of glass from the carpet.

Rather than press her for answers, the sweet, composed man that he was, he instead made his way out of the back door to the garage to get a stronger broom and a shoe box to deposit the glass safely.

Together, they silently proceeded to tape cardboard panels over the front door and to form a cordon of chairs so that the children didn't hurt themselves when they came down in the morning.

He then took her hand and led her upstairs where they undressed and got into bed. She didn't put on her frumpy, old nightgown that hid all of her wobbly bits, but instead lay naked, facing her husband.

"She died," Wing said, after what seemed like hours of blissful quiet between them. She didn't cry—she felt that she had passed that point.

"I'm sorry," he whispered, knowing exactly who she was referring to.

"Thank you," she replied.

In the morning, she heard him telling the children that the glass pane had simply fallen out of the door and that they had been meaning to get a new door for months.

"It's been on the news," he had said. "Glass shattering all over the country. Mummy's lucky not to have been hurt. I have a good mind to phone the company."

Although it was a lie, his anger was very real. And though the words might not have been the correct ones, his emotion was from the heart, and she loved him for that.

She adored her family so much, which is why, as she had laid there in the dark, she decided that she needed to go.

She held her breath as she keyed in the numbers on the handset.

The dial tone seemed to go on forever before it clicked, and Joanna's voice came on the end of the line.

"Wing," said Joanna. There was a pause before she spoke again.

"I'm guessing this isn't going to be good news."

■■■■■■■■■■■■■■■■■■■■■■■■■■■■■■■■■■■■■■■

Laura swung her car around the corner, nearly clipping the woman coming in the opposite direction. She tooted her horn, which made Laura mouth a very prominent *"fuck you"* through the glass.

She was not thinking straight. But then, how could she?

She had been throwing up all morning, some as a result of being pregnant, and some trying to rid her body of the awful remorseful, dread she had swirling around inside her. Keeping this deep, dark secret from Ben, who had been walking on the clouds ever since she told him about the baby, was literally making her ill.

Her husband was swanning about with pride, where he used to hang his head in shame, lured into a false sense of security, newly convinced that he was fertile and virile and that he had always possessed what it took to make babies— she had just needed some patience.

He had ordered a bottle of expensive wine and then remembered that she couldn't drink, so he pathetically squirrelled a glass away when he thought she wasn't looking, celebrating his mini victory. One that was, in fact, all smoke and mirrors.

How could she be so heartless? How could she deceive the person that she loved, for her own ends? She had never felt so completely and utterly rotten.

And, as if karma had been waiting for her in the wings, Roger had sauntered into her office today to talk about recent redundancies in the recruitment field.

"Some of the sales managers' jobs might be at risk. You will probably have to reapply for your post," he had gloated, in that ridiculous fake Essex accent of his, that had materialised out of nowhere after he'd been promoted to head of department—he was from Somerset, for goodness' sake!

It appeared as though the years of working her way up through the nasty temp desk roles, winning the trust and credibility of the stakeholders, putting up with the "woman in a jacket" comments and drunken gropes at the Christmas party counted for fuck all. She had worked like hell to get to this point, and now it was clear that it wasn't going to be acknowledged by this company at all.

"Of course, you should be okay," Roger had said, cool and irritating. "It's just lucky you're not planning to travel the world for six months or anything—we couldn't promise that you'd have a job to come back to."

Then he laughed that pathetic, nervous, corporate laugh that men do when they have nothing else to say of any worth. She might not be off travelling the world, but she would certainly be getting to know her uterus a bit better. She was fucked.

How would she cope financially if she were to drop the pregnancy bomb on them now? Roger would have a field day. She would be first on the chopping block when the interview stage came around. No one wants to hang onto someone they can't rely on. If you weren't sat at your desk, you were off meeting clients. Being fat, immobile and running to the toilet every five minutes did not suit the job description.

So, not only was she expecting Ben to love a child that wasn't his, she was also expecting him to foot the bill for everything while she, with child, swollen and ill, tried desperately to look for suitable work. It would never happen.

Why did she ever think this would have been a good idea?

She would have cried but the tears wouldn't come. She was angry. So much, in fact, that she had left the office under the guise of sickness and driven home. She needed to sit quietly, get her thoughts together and make out some kind of plan. This is what she was good at, what her entire livelihood was centred around. If she couldn't apply her professional strategy to her home life a bit more, then she was seriously missing a wasted opportunity.

As she parked her car in the drive and turned the key in the ignition, she sat slumped over the wheel for a few moments, enjoying the sweet wafts she kept getting from the Little Trees car freshener that bobbed away under the rear-view mirror.

She sighed. This wasn't going to be easy, but she had to make a hard and fast decision that was going to suit everyone. And it was going to take courage.

■■

Bernice opened the door with trepidation. She was irked. She had just finished a rather lengthy conversation with a potential date online.

Never once had this guy broached the topic of her being a trans woman and yet, in her opinion, it was always sat there like an elephant in the room, even if it wasn't an issue.

It was a trans website for goodness' sake. Of course, people were going to know. But then, they weren't the ones who had a problem with it—she was.

She had just finished a glass of red when the doorbell rang and, as she glanced in the mirror at herself in the hall, she suddenly realised how flushed she was.

It wasn't that the exchange with the man had been particularly flirty or heavy, it was more the possibility that this guy might be visualising her with no knickers on. The only people who had been there were the doctor and her ex-wife. Not even Bernice could look in the doctor's mirror that he had held up to her open legs after the last bandage had been removed. She couldn't help thinking that a gruesome incision would be staring back at her like something from a David Cronenberg film, and it had made her feel depressed.

She winced at the thought. The regretful disturbance that came from thinking that she had voluntarily removed a part of herself and thrown it away was too much to bear. And although she had never felt right with that redundant piece of flesh dangling between her legs, at least it had produced her son—at least it had been hers to remove.

As she opened the door, she wiped the edges of her mouth with the tips of her fingers to remove any tell-tale signs that she had been drinking on a school night, though that was no different to any other night these days.

Three faces stared back at her. Gaynor was first, Becky second and Abbie last. They looked like an amateur production of *The Witches of Eastwick* stood there, looking all morose.

"Oh," Bernice said, not in the least bit welcoming. She had wanted to be guest-free tonight. She wanted to have finished the bottle and continued on with her conversation, let the chat get steamy, turn the lights off and let her imagination run wild in the dark—but alas, no.

This guy was sure to go off her, and they'd only just met.

Only the other night, after she had spent some time at the altar she had newly constructed in the dining room, she had taken her laptop upstairs to see if her new friend had logged on. They chatted for a bit, but she had had to put a stop to their conversation, stating that there had been someone at the door.

In truth, she had noticed that a white light was manifesting at the end of the bed. It was not the same as the other spirits, who appeared as voices in the darkness, mostly frightened, often upset. She knew exactly who this was and was moderately surprised that this was her first visitation since the last one a few weeks ago.

Bernice had closed the laptop and sat forward.

"Agatha?" she said softly, "Agatha, are you there?"

The light had pulsated intermittently before a familiar voice reached out to her.

"My darling girl," it had said, "you always knew what you were."

Bernice felt involuntary tears fall down her cheeks.

"Why, Agatha—why are you here?" she cried. "Why are you coming back?"

The light faded slightly before the old woman spoke again.

"They won't forget you," she said. "You will make them see when you are ready. The fire might scorch, but you will put it out. You had to go through the pain in order to save our souls."

And the light had vanished.

She didn't go back to the laptop after that. She had lain in bed, confused, alone and drugged with fatigue.

And now she stood in her hallway, considering whether she could afford another night of ignoring his advances and, potentially, letting the chance of intimacy slip through her fingers, just when she was beginning to get her confidence back.

"Hi, Bernice," Gaynor said flatly, "I wonder if we might come in?"

■■

"Sorry about the mess," Bernice said, clearing a few magazines from the sofa so that the ladies could sit down. The half-empty bottle of wine smirked at her from the coffee table.

"We won't stop long," Gaynor said.

"No," replied Abbie, looking around in disgust. Not that she had much to be critical of—this place was a palace compared to her front room.

Bernice shrugged. She hadn't really had time to tidy up but then, what did she need to tidy up for?

The ladies sat down one by one, as Bernice seated herself opposite on the single armchair that had fast become her sanctuary.

"How can I help?" she said, flipping her laptop lid down and ignoring the message that had flashed up in the interim.

Gaynor took in a deep breath and got straight to business, telling Bernice the events that had led up to this moment. The finding of Miss Wicks, how she had been discovered supposedly dead, even though Abbie had fervently denied it.

"I mean," Abbie chimed in, frowning at the memory of the corpse lying in the grass, "what was really strange is that her hands were dirty like she had been crawling in the earth or something. Her nails had dirt underneath them. Thick, horrible dirt."

She suddenly let out a little gasp as the thought struck her.

"Oh, shit yeah—there was a nail!" Abbie blurted out suddenly.

"Nail?" Gaynor hunched around to face her on the sofa. Becky remained silent.

"Yeah, a nail. Like a builder's nail. It had been hammered through her index finger. Like, as if someone had driven it through her skin. I could see the pointy bit sticking out of her fingertip," she said to nobody in particular. "I remember thinking it was fucking gross."

Gaynor and Becky looked at each other. Becky furrowed her brow.

"Do you think that has any significance?" Becky asked Gaynor, but Gaynor just shrugged her shoulders.

"What we really need to know, Bernice, is—"

"She's not dead," Bernice said quickly. As much as she wanted to help these women with their quest, she wasn't really interested. She needed to remove herself from this madness—Joanna, the coven—and get on with living a normal life. Dating, getting romantically involved with others and being a normal woman. The dead showing up in her bedroom unannounced was always going to be a fly in the ointment she was never going to be free of. But having to deal with this drama and the narrow-mindedness of folk that came with it was getting to be a pain in the tit.

"Definitely?" Gaynor asked.

"Definitely," Bernice nodded in confirmation. "I would have known. There haven't been many deaths since Halloween, and she certainly wasn't one of them. I suppose that can only be a good thing."

Gaynor and Becky both nodded in unison. She wasn't dead. At least it had been confirmed. Now

521

they could put a plan together. They knew where she was, and they could alert Odette, who would be able to subdue her.

"Yes," Abbie cried cheerfully, "I fucking knew it. I *knew* I saw her eyes open. Telling me she wasn't dead. I know what I saw!"

Gaynor looked back at Bernice with a heavy smile.

"Well, I'm very glad for your victory, Abbie, but—"

Gaynor's voice began to tremble.

"Anne Wicks is far more dangerous alive than she would be dead."

■■

Laura had thought of little else since she was delivered the news that her livelihood might be snatched away from her, and now she was sitting outside his house, across the road in the very car that she had fucked him in.

She turned the ignition off and drummed her fingers on the dashboard.

Could she really go through with this? What if his wife answered the door?

Well, she had never met the woman, so she could make up some bullshit story about knocking at the wrong door. She would be all apologetic and say that she had meant to knock at number 15, not 5. She quickly scanned the area to see whether there even was a number 15. Would she be able to lie to another woman's face? Oh hell, she was a recruitment consultant, of course she could lie. She had made a living out of it.

But what would she say when she got him alone?

She noticed movement in the window, there was definitely someone in. Unless they had a cleaner. She looked up at the top windows. The place was tiny—it didn't warrant a cleaner really. Unless his wife was a slovenly, lazy bitch. A pregnant, slovenly, lazy bitch.

What had happened to her? She used to be such a nice girl. The Oracle specifically recruited her for her polite and discrete disposition. She didn't possess any magickal powers that would, ordinarily, get her into the coven without a pass. It had always been a bone of contention with Joanna, letting non-magickal people in as a last resort, to make sure that policies were upheld, and paperwork was completed. The scourge of new thinking and more inclusive ideals. Apparently, those who possessed magickal powers were too easily distracted to undertake such mundane administrative tasks and, therefore, those non-magickals who passed the stringent vetting process, replete with a complicated series of tests, were authorised to attend meetings and carry these duties out. Joanna thought it ludicrous and abhorrent and had always kept Laura at arm's length. But The Oracle had primed Laura for this type of reaction and so, she had always accepted Joanna's rebuttals with good humour and grace. Laura had simply smiled, without judgement, turned up with a pad and pencil and set about the job in hand. But her constant frustration with the recent chain of events had upped the pressure on her work, in the office and in the coven. It had become personal. And that, coupled now with her insatiable hunger to become a mother, had turned her into a cynical and somewhat devious woman. Worse still, it was a suit that seemed to fit her well.

Of course, she shouldn't really be angry at his wife—she had had nothing to do with all this. She was just a dried-up prude who couldn't give him what he wanted. Otherwise, he wouldn't have come knocking at her door, would he?

But then, wouldn't Laura become the same in a few months when the baby began to sap her energy? He would move on to propagating his seed with some other poor, fertile young specimen, while she was left feeling fat, unattractive and totally alone. Ben was sure to find out she had deceived him. He wouldn't want anything to do with her. She'd be a jobless pram-face with a council flat and debt up to her chewed, saggy nipples.

She shook her head. That wasn't going to happen. She was going to sort it and she'd come out fighting—she had to. For the sake of the tiny body growing inside her, the one that she was going to inspire by being a strong, confident, no-nonsense woman.

And after she had sorted this item on the agenda, she would go to the board of directors at work and threaten them with discrimination, harassment and victimisation of a pregnant woman. She would ask them to look at their competency policy and see whether they were allowed to just throw someone out for being with child. The idea of the press hearing all about it, or perhaps one of their competitors, was the least she could throw at them. She would ask for a rise as compensation for them being so incompetent and prejudiced. She would win on all levels, and Ben would be none the wiser.

Perhaps she didn't need this guy's financial support, maybe she would be okay. But then what if everything went kaput? She couldn't take that chance. She needed a backup plan as insurance that she would not fail.

She unbuckled her seatbelt and opened the car door.

■■

As Gaynor, Abbie and Becky walked back, they mused over what the possible consequences would be.

"She's probably in the mortuary," Gaynor said, "but it's too late to get in there now. I wouldn't even know how."

"I mean, what do we do?" Abbie said. "Just turn up and say, 'we think you've got a live woman on ice'? They'll think we're taking the piss."

"But we can't take the same chance that we took with Brenda Ware. If Miss Wicks is hexed, she could be out there, already sizing up her next victim. Someone could be in real danger," Becky said nervously.

"But who is next in the line of victims?" Abbie questioned. "I mean, we don't even know who we are supposed to be protecting."

"What about Odette?" Becky said. "Perhaps she might have a better idea than us."

Gaynor turned around.

"I'd leave her out of this for the time being," she said. It took the others slightly aback.

Gaynor looked down.

"The Oracle doesn't know our little town like we do. She might send a load more seniors over here and we'll just have to kowtow to them. I don't know if I'm ready for all that just yet."

"I'm surprised she hasn't done it already to be fair. I mean, it's pretty serious shit that has gone down here in the last few weeks," Abbie mused.

"Yes," agreed Gaynor, frowning slightly at the expletive, "perhaps The Order think Odette has got a good enough handle on it."

"But she hasn't really. I mean, Becky seems to be the only one who knows the spell that can stop all this. She's the strongest out of all of us.

But then, Odette will be super-pissed if we withhold information if she's anything like Joanna," Abbie said. "She'd tear us a new one."

"Trust me," Gaynor said, a sparkle shimmering in her eyes, "with Becky as our secret weapon, we could crack this on our own and show those London types what a little parochial coven is capable of."

Abbie cooed at this. "You're a bit of a sort for an old girl, aren't you? I love it!"

Becky smirked at Abbie's blatant lack of filter.

"Well," Gaynor said, "when you get to my age, you grab every bit of excitement that you've got coming to you."

She gave Becky a little wink. Becky smiled. She loved this woman.

"So, is there a link between the victims then?" Abbie said, pulling her coat tighter around her. She'd seen a film like this once and was quite enjoying the drama of it all.

"We were trying to work this out earlier," Becky chipped in.

"Well," Gaynor thought aloud, "there's Brenda Ware."

"Right," Becky said, "and Rachel Power."

"And Miss Wicks," Abbie concluded.

"And the only connection between these three seems to be the school," Becky said. "We've established that they weren't witches themselves or somehow connected to the occult."

"Yes," Gaynor agreed, "and as far as we know, they weren't involved with the Witch Hunter General, but two of them worked under Alice Eames. So, she could have had them hexed pretty easily. But while Eames may be connected to the WHG, she's not a witch. She would have needed a witch's help for that part—and the WHG is against witchcraft."

"So, do you think she was just after their money?" Abbie said.

"Well, we're not sure about that," Gaynor said in a diplomatic way, "but we do know that she was investing funds into a company funded by the Witch Hunter General cult. Brenda Ware's funds by the sound of it. The Oracle must have instructed the police to take her away while they ruled her out—or not, as the case may be. But we can't prove she had anything to do with the possession."

"It's can't just be a coincidence that those two zombies worked for her can it?" Abbie asked. "She's always been dodgy in my view. No wonder she's never had a bloke."

Gaynor paused in thought again.

"But then, what's she got against Rachel Power?" she asked. "If money was her motivation, then how did she propose to get her hands on the Power family's funds without bearing any relation to them? There must be some other reason that she chose to do all this, and in such a measured and considered way. And magic-bending must fit into it all too, somehow."

Abbie thought back to the website details that she had been given by Charlotte. Perhaps there was more information on there. She could've told the others about The New Realm, but she didn't really want to share yet. If this ever blew wide open, Abbie wanted a bit of recognition for being so intuitive as to take a massive risk. She was working on Gaynor's theory: keep your cards close to your chest and a few little titbits for yourself.

"Well," Abbie said, stopping at a junction in the road, "I'm bouncing this way. So, what happens now?"

"I say we get together again at my house tomorrow," Gaynor said. "Arrive early, I'll put a pot of tea on and we'll try again to make sense of all this—lay the puzzle out and slot the pieces back together. I might try and speak to someone at the mortuary. Somehow or another we need to be assured that Miss Wicks is somewhere out of harm's way. That way, we will know that nobody else is in danger until another victim is selected."

Abbie nodded.

"Other than that, ladies, if we have any other thoughts we must let each other know," Gaynor finished. "So mote it be."

Abbie rolled her eyes but repeated the phrase. They both looked at Becky who blushed and recited it too, even though she had no idea what it meant. After all, she was still new to all this.

The three women looked around at each other. A strong, electric tension was held between them that was palpable in the air. It was as if they were about to uncover something bigger than could ever have imagined. And yet, at the same time, they were each eager to get home and find the missing jigsaw piece for themselves.

■■

As soon as he saw her on the doorstep, his face fell.

"What the *hell* are you doing here?" he said.

"Well, that's not much of a welcome," Laura said contemptibly. "Is your wife at home?"

"No, she's not, but she'll be back any minute so—"

"Listen, what I have to say won't take long," she said moving closer to the door.

He said nothing, but kept the door open slightly, looking at her with an obvious disgust written all over his face.

"Look, I can either come in," she said with a turn of the head, "or we can do it out here in the street. Your call."

His mouth tightened as he thought for a second. Against his better judgement, he opened the door fully and she stepped in.

Laura looked around at their front room. It was basic. Functional. Full of little, mismatched trinkets and untouched books on stacked shelves. She could just imagine what his wife must be like—dull, pale and passionless. A proper little vacuous nothing.

He closed the door behind her and she heard it click. She didn't move any further into the room. She didn't want to feel like the scarlet woman any more than she already did.

He stepped in front of her with a sullen look on his face.

"What's all this about?" he said, putting his hands on his hips, trying to look casual but coming across as camp. She almost felt compelled to laugh.

"I'll keep it brief," she said. There was obviously no love lost between them. Whatever had happened in that car had coated them both in bitterness and disdain. Days ago, she had thrust him inside of her—now, she could barely stand to look at him.

"I'm pregnant."

The world seemed to stop for just a minute as the information sank in. His mouth formed into a perfect circle as his eyes darted around her body.

"I don't want you to be involved," she said, in a measured way. "I don't plan on letting my husband know, but I need your assurance that you will help me financially if this doesn't work out."

She hoped to hell that she was coming off as cool as she thought she was. It was just like dealing with a corporate contract. Arrange for a client to receive an incentive and you might just get something nice in your Christmas bonus.

He started to breathe rapidly, his chest rising and falling under his crisp, white shirt.

After what seemed like an eternity, he spoke.

"How do you know it's mine?" he said, his voice panic-stricken and dry.

"Of course it's yours," she said spitefully. "Ben and I haven't had sex in ages."

She knew it was a lie, but she wasn't going to let him know that the chance was probably fifty-fifty. It made her go numb. She hadn't meant to say his name out loud in this house—it made him sound cheap.

"Well," he said, "I want a test."

"You want a *what*?" she spat.

"A test, a paternity test," he nodded manically. "I'm not committing anything to you until I know it's mine."

"Why would it be anyone else's?"

He leant forward and growled through clenched teeth, "You told me you were on the pill."

"I didn't—"

"Oh, yes you did," he cut her off, angrily. "That is *exactly* what you said. You're nothing but a hustler. I know about your sort. Honey-trapping guys and then blackmailing them for money. Well, I'm not buying it. I want proof, or you're on your own."

Laura began to backtrack. His face was so full of rage that it actually shocked her. She hadn't prepared herself for this eventuality. Judging by how placid he'd been in the pub, she half-expected him to just roll over and accept his fate. But here she stood in front of a maniac, his expression contorted into a malevolent grimace. She decided to go.

She turned to leave. She wished she'd never come here. It was an utter disaster. She wondered how long before the deceit and guilt would finally catch up with her. She was beginning to get a taste of it now—a hard lump in her throat that she couldn't swallow down. The memory of Ben's face at the news. His honourable intentions were surrounded by lies and betrayal. How could she do this to the man she had been with since she was seventeen? She hated herself.

She reached out to take the front door handle when she heard the key in the lock and the handle under her hand begin to turn.

She looked at him for some kind of answer, but his face was frozen in horror.

Then the door swung open.

∎∎∎∎∎∎∎∎∎∎∎∎∎∎∎∎∎∎∎∎∎∎∎∎∎∎∎∎∎∎∎∎∎∎∎∎∎∎

Abbie threw her coat on the floor and sat back down on the bed. She was excited, exhilarated, more than she had been in months, and she was including her dalliances with Xander in that. She opened her laptop lid and keyed in her password.

Facebook was already open, and a little notification above her messages indicated that she had new mail. With anticipation, she clicked on the icon and read the message. It was from Charlotte and it contained nothing but a lengthy hyperlink and a password.

This must be it.

She thought for a moment about whether opening this Pandora's box really was the most sensible way forward. Surely, she could be opening herself up to all kinds of online evildoers. Some might offer the answers she sought, while others could put her in extreme danger. It was a risk.

And yes, she liked a bit of risk in her life. She had never been averse to the odd bit of shoplifting when money was tight or batting her eyelashes at generous baristas when she lacked the right change for a coffee, but this was a whole different kettle of fish.

But then, she would never play a part in solving this mystery without taking a few chances. Xander, the spells, giving herself away to "Ebony" when she had no idea of the consequences, rebelling against Joanna. All those gambles had got her to this point. She couldn't very well stop now. She was a young woman in the twenty-first century, they put themselves on the line all the time and worried about the repercussions later. If she was going to gain any sort of power, she had to make herself vulnerable.

So, she clicked.

■■■

Becky just stood, her key still in the door.

"Oh," she exclaimed to her husband. "You took me by surprise, I didn't know that you had a guest coming over."

The two just stared back at her, surprisingly startled by the fact that she had let herself into her own home. She was sure that she recognised this woman from the circle. Was she allowed to acknowledge her? I mean, she had yet to tell Dom about her visits to Joanna's. But then, if this woman was part of her secret life, what the hell was she doing in her house? Becky's heart froze.

"Oh, hi!" the woman said. "It's Becky, isn't it? I'm Laura, remember. We ... err ... we met in that shop, remember?"

Becky smiled a half-smile. This was weird. Why did Dom look so guilty?

She might not know this Laura very well, but she knew her husband, and he looked as though he wanted the ground to swallow him up.

Becky suddenly noticed that she was still standing in her own doorway, clinging onto the key. She pulled it out of the door and let her arm drop to her side.

"Sorry," Becky said, her tone measured. "Laura, why are you in my house?"

A grim reality seeped into Becky's bones like infectious bacteria. She could feel her cheeks redden as she focused on her husband. His eyes were full of sorrow—they were almost pleading for forgiveness.

It reminded her of the time in London, when he had promised her that he'd locked their parents back door when they popped around to water their garden one August. But he hadn't, and her parents got broken into. The shame that he had transferred to her when she had to confess that they hadn't been so particular when checking the house was secure was both mortifying and heart-breaking. She had come back distraught and he had looked at her like he was looking at her now. He was full of remorse and self-pity.

Laura also looked at Dom.

"I'm just here—" she began.

"I'm not asking you," Becky said through clenched teeth. "I am asking my husband."

Dom swallowed hard.

"Look," he said, putting his hand to his chin and rubbing it slowly, "it's not what you think."

His face said differently. Becky felt so utterly stupid. There was no explanation for why that attractive woman was in their living room, with her breasts and her hair. Therefore, it could only mean one thing.

"You *arsehole*," Becky said and turned around.

She slammed the door behind her, making her way back onto the street, not wanting either of them to see her cry. She could hear him calling her from the doorstep, but Becky didn't want to hear his explanations. She just wanted to get away from there.

She felt embarrassed, mortified that she had ever come home. She wished she had left it a few hours longer and let them do their business so that she could carry on in blissful ignorance. She didn't want to be burdened with this sordid imagery. She just wanted everything to be back to normal like it was thirty seconds ago. But now, everything had changed.

Becky looked down at herself, wondered why she was still standing there, outside her own house, riddled with shame.

She could hear footsteps behind her, and so she ran as fast as she could, out into the night, as Dom called her name behind her.

■■■

Bernice sat, holding the glass of red wine as if she was clutching the Holy Grail. She licked her lips as she read the latest message that had appeared on her computer screen.

"Well, I must say that I am always partial to a glass of Chateauneuf Du Pape. Usually with friends, sometimes alone. But more so with a companion and two wine glasses."

This guy was so old-school. Bernice found it funny, yet endearing. The fact that someone could be so *Casablanca* when it came to online dating. He must be new to this game. Talk of a good red wine and smoking a fine cigar by the fire was not your standard opening gambit on this site. Usually, they wanted to know the colour of her knickers and whether she could accommodate if the talk got any steamier.

She found this guy refreshing and, over the last few days that they had chatted, she had learnt that he could actually be as funny as he was endearing. He had also gotten quite flirty and so she had added another layer of lipstick in the hope that it would make her typed messages sound sexier.

"So, what is your village like then?" she typed, trying to get a better idea of his home life and, possibly, his wealth. She knew very little about the world outside of Cheltenham really. But he assured her that he only lived a few miles out—not far in a cab.

As if she should be thinking like this, plotting the journey to some stranger's house in the middle of nowhere. But then, she could never invite him to her place. She imagined the dead coming howling in the middle of the night, as the two were in the throes of passion, would put quite the dampener on proceedings.

A message returned.

"Very little, I'm afraid. A church, some houses. And the hill, of course. Our hill has the most fantastic views in the county. God's own country. Breathtaking."

He was a countryman. She liked that. And, although his pictures had been small and grainy, he certainly looked like he had all his own hair and teeth. She could just imagine taking breakfast in his conservatory whilst staring out at the rolling hills. If he had a conservatory, of course.

"You should come."

"Oh no," she thought, as she pulled herself to her feet unsteadily. She made her way over to the kitchen side where another bottle lay in wait. She carried it back to her spot on the sofa.

He had already messaged again.

"Sorry, was that a bit forward? I'm not very used to this."

She blushed for him, it was sweet that he didn't really know what he was doing. It made her want him all the more.

"No, Oliver," she typed.

"Yes, I'd love to come over if you'd have me. Are you free at all next week?"

She pressed send, thinking that perhaps now it was she who had become too forward. What would he think when she arrived at the door, full of Dutch courage and bawdy jokes. Her masculine frame spilling out of a cocktail dress never made her feel particularly sexy, so why would it light his fire? But then, she had lost a bit of weight with the hormones and such. Why not let him decide what he fancies a bit of?

There were also very few illusions on this website. It was for open-minded people looking for relationships with trans individuals and, since she always put her cards out on the table before she launched into the film noir stuff, he was unlikely to be surprised when they met in person.

He took ages to respond. She stared so hard at the message box, willing it to illuminate that she felt she might cry.

Then it happened.

"How about tonight?"

She licked her lips and unscrewed the bottle top.

■■

Becky sat in Gaynor's kitchen. She was cold and wet by the time she had reached Gaynor's door, to be welcomed in with a comforting hug from her neighbour.

"Listen, love, you don't have to talk about it if you don't want to. The goddess makes gruelling work for idle tongues." She leant forward and put a reassuring hand on Becky's shoulder. "I just want to know that you are okay."

Becky, who had been sat, staring at a pepper pot on Gaynor's table for the last few minutes, shook off her momentary daydream.

"I think—" she started. "I think I'm fine."

Becky had been shell-shocked by what she had seen in her front room, unable to believe that her husband, her hero and protector, was capable of such an atrocity. Perhaps it wasn't what she thought it was. It could have been something entirely innocent. But she recognised the unfamiliar anguish and torment on Dom's face.

He never showed guilt unless it was absolutely necessary and, if it had just been nothing, then what did he have to feel guilty about?

She wondered how he could do that to her. How could he even think about conducting a torrid affair with someone he barely knew, while his wife stood, pregnant in the doorway? Surely, he would have known that she was due to come back at some point, the reckless idiot.

She looked at Gaynor who stood by her agar, busying about awkwardly. Did she know? Had she had looked in her lumelight and seen everything? But then, why would she spy on them unless she suspected something was going on? Becky couldn't start thinking like this, getting all paranoid about it. It made her temples throb with an uneasy tension.

"Can I make you some tea?" Gaynor asked, breaking the silence.

Becky wiped her nose with her hand and nodded.

"I've got a headache," she said flatly.

"Ah," Gaynor said, as if finding a use for herself after all, "you're in luck, my dear. I think I have some apple tea in here somewhere."

Gaynor made her way slowly over to a high shelf stacked with jam jars, full of leaves and dried herbs. She reached up and began roaming them with her hands. She was too small to see what she was grabbing at, yet it seemed she knew exactly where everything was.

Once located, she brought the correct jar down onto the counter.

"You know, unlike Arrowood that cleanses the stomach, they say apple cleanses everything else. It's a very misunderstood fruit," she hummed to herself whilst she started the tea making process.

Becky sat, staring at a brown stain on Gaynor's wall. It reminded her of her own wall, the one she shared with that lying, cheating bastard.

"Of course," Gaynor said, delivering the steaming-hot mug to the table after a lot of clattering about, "I've always had to seek alternative medicinal arrangements. I'm not one for apples."

Becky reached over to the mug, only half-listening. The fragrance of the sweet apple brought her back to earth.

"Oh gosh, Gaynor," she said, taking in the scent. It reminded her of her mother's cooking. "That smells lush"

"Oh, it's not that I don't like apples as such," Gaynor chuckled. "It's the pips, dear."

Becky took a quick sip—it burnt the tip of her tongue. She now yearned for her mother. She wanted to be comforted by a familiar hand.

"The pips?" Becky asked, absentmindedly. "What, choking on them, you mean?"

She looked at Gaynor as though she was mad. How could they be having this innocuous conversation when Becky's marriage was falling apart?

"Not choking, no. It's just that in ancient potion-making, apple pips were seen as somewhat of a poisonous ingredient. Sure, one or two won't harm anyone. But in vast quantities, they can kill."

Becky frowned.

"Apple pips? That's crazy."

"Oh, I might be old, dear, but I've not gone mad yet. A lot of people don't know this about Granny Smith, but her pips are riddled with amygdalin," Gaynor said, making her way back over to the sink. "Sod's law, isn't it? Such a lovely fruit, harbouring such murderous capabilities."

Becky brought the cup away from her lips and sat perfectly still as the word dropped onto her. *Amygdalin.* She had heard it before. No, not heard—*seen*. She had seen that word written somewhere.

"Amygdalin?" she said aloud.

"Oh, yes" Gaynor nodded, her back to Becky. "It's calamitous, that stuff. It's like cyanide."

Becky rolled the word silently around her mouth, before putting her cup down and sitting bolt upright.

She suddenly remembered exactly where she'd seen it.

■■

At first, Abbie thought the site was a scam because her laptop screen went completely blank for a few seconds. She tapped it lightly, cursing Charlotte for coercing her into opening up a virus on her computer.

"No, no, no," she kept saying, wondering if she could really live her life as it was meant to be lived if she was suddenly without access to social media.

Before she could spring to any more conclusions, however, her screen illuminated, displaying a simple typed line, white on black.

"Join our revolution."

Abbie pouted her lips as she read. She had no idea what to expect from here on in, but she knew there was no going back.

The typed line then disappeared. Out of the blackness, the screen began to fill with lines, moving from the outside in and vanishing, spinning about like some vintage animation. Finally, the lines settled themselves into place, underneath various text headings, which had appeared from different sides of the screen. *"Beginnings, Developments, Infrastructure, Threats."*

It was a fairly rudimentary design. There were no fancy shapes or dazzling imagery. It was just white on black—effective and succinct.

With trepidation, she clicked on "threats" as she had been instructed, and a similar dashboard appeared.

There were further subheadings, too many for her to explore now.

"Who They Are."

"What We Know."

"What We Do Next."

"Guidance and Conduct."

She thought she had better choose "Who They Are" to start—it was best to begin with the ground-level information.

The page opened up with a page of text.

"Witch Hunters—Are they a real threat? By Scillica."

Scillica. Was that another of Charlotte's aliases? Who knew?

Abbie continued on.

"Under the rule of The Oracle, we are led to believe that the real monsters out there are those that call themselves the Witch Hunter General, a society that has existed in the US since the early

settlers arrived, paranoid of the natives who already inhabited the land and their lack of westernised, orthodox belief systems. The punishment these hunters bestow on those who still promote such beliefs echoes the barbaric nature of their ancestors. Never has the phrase "burn the witch" been so prophetic.

However, in reality, the threat is much, much worse. Regan Fasmir of the Wiccan Order of Boscastle noted in her writings:

'We benefitted not by feayring those who crispened our flesh or who cut the tongues from our open mouths for little more reason than because we did not denounce our fayth and follow theirs. We feayred more our sisters who, at his instruction, handed us over to the bad man to repent for themselves. Our own kin did sit amongst us and yet they had already killed us. And as Christians bear hatred in the devil, he is nothing but one of them who had but fallen. The witch who eats with us yet poisons our bread is the much grayter foe.'

What we might take from this is that elder Wiccans were more concerned with corruption within the circle than they were of being hunted by their enemies.

We have since gained information that it is actually the work a little-known, but much older, UK-based society called The Gorgons. They have been infiltrating circles for centuries but have never been a large enough group to ever take *down The Order itself. Like assassins, they have managed to ingratiate themselves into covens as a spy might pervade a community. But it is only recently that The Gorgons have joined forces with the Witch Hunter General and, knowing that they have the right people in the right places, it is likely that the WHG is set to light the wick and bring down the entire Wiccan community.*

Not only this, but they operate in specific locations throughout the world. Places that are synonymous with Wiccan pilgrimage. They trade under the bogus name of Med Users Ltd.—the HQ of which is located in Salt Lake City in the US. They use separate business locations as laboratories for engineering 'magic-bending', the reversing of a dark spell to bend it back onto the caster, with destructive and debilitating consequences. Often, the victims of magic-bending fail to recover from their affliction.

Abbie frowned as she read. There it was again: magic-bending. But why were the WHG analysing it? Surely using magic was against their principles.

We have reason to believe that the WHG are now using magic-bending to entrap witches. It is a bold move that has not been used before, but in this uncertain political age, the WHG has appointed new, more radical members who will try any method necessary to inflict pain on the magickal community. We have managed to locate a file that holds the whereabouts of these locations in the UK, namely Boscastle and Pendle. However, the biggest threat comes from a relatively unknown village in Gloucestershire, the site of the meeting place of the original Scandinavian magic-benders. Underneath is a picture that we have managed to glean from a classified WHG newsletter. While we are too small an army to fight this scourge alone, we are appealing to those of you out there to raise the alarm in your covens. If you know any of these women, who are known to us to be part of this secret order, we urge you to identify them on this page.

Underneath this text was a black and white, grainy photograph of a group of people standing outside of what looked like an old, abandoned warehouse.

Abbie's eyes searched the picture. Staring back at her were three women, standing in the middle of a larger crowd. The three women were smiling, evidently proud of themselves. It was a relatively old picture, possibly from the eighties. The three women looked young. One of them had the instantly recognisable half-grin that Abbie knew as Miss Eames, headmistress of Winchcombe School, and another younger woman with a curly crop—she didn't look familiar. But the face of the final woman hit her like a bolt of lightning. The hair was longer, but the face—it was undeniable.

Underneath was written, *Med Users Ltd. — Oxeten.*

Abbie closed the laptop and caught her breath a moment as her heart pounded in her ears.

Oxeten? This was right on their doorstep.

She brought her hand to her mouth as she pondered the severity of the situation. All along, the WHG had been operating right under their noses. No wonder Odette had been brought in.

This was fucking serious.

She looked around her. She no longer felt safe. She had to tell Gaynor.

■■■■■■■■■■■■■■■■■■■■■■■■■■■■■■■■■■■■■■

"So, there *is* a pattern?" Gaynor asked, her thumb wedged against her top teeth.

"There has to be," Becky said. "There is some significance with Miss Ware being poisoned with Amygdalin."

Becky's mind flashed back to that momentary glimpse of Brenda Ware's toxicology report.

"Apple pips..." she pondered. "I think it's a message. Whoever is doing this wants us to find clues."

"So you think the enemy is leaving us some kind of code?"

"There was something Abbie said about Miss Wicks. Something about a nail?"

Gaynor stuck a finger in the air.

"Yes, it was driven through her finger, or thumb or something wasn't it? That was a bit random, I grant you. I would never have thought of it."

"But that's just the thing," Becky said, "you have never had to. Winchcombe has been plodding along like Wonderland for so many years. Why would you ever have to think outside the box? Gaynor, we are dealing with someone whose magic is advanced, whose calling card is to be cryptic, incisive and cruel. It's the work of a bloody psychopath!"

The word made the old woman bring a hand to her chest.

"This is the way the world works now," Becky continued, getting up and pacing the floor. "It's full of cyber-attacks, scams, online thievery. It appears that magic is evolving with technology. We have to think one step ahead if we're going to solve this case."

Becky let out an exasperated sigh—she was beginning to think they were the worst crime-fighting duo in history. It was all questions and nothing in the way of a solution.

"Rachel Power?" she asked Gaynor, who was still stood pensively.

"Savaged," Gaynor sighed. "By some ... hideous, bloody beast."

"Beast," Becky repeated to herself. "Beast, beast, beast."

"I think..." she started, a smile breaking across her face. "I think I might have cracked it."

As the hospital staff rushed around seeing to the wounded of yet another Saturday night in Cheltenham, something in the very bowels of the hospital stirred.

On a cold slab, surrounded by blue walls, a pair of bloodshot eyes sprang open. The hands, previously limp and lifeless, suddenly balled into clenched fists. The neck twisted, and the body, a woman, tried to sit up, but something was impeding her. Thick ribbons of material were holding her in place. She squirmed but could move very little. She pushed but made no progress. She fought but it was a battle that could not be won.

With anger and frustration, she writhed and thrashed, banging the sides of the slab as she did, in an attempt to loosen the strip. With her hair wild about her face, she contorted her neck so that she could just about grip the restraint with her teeth and, like a rabid animal, began to gnaw away at the fabric.

It wasn't long before the ribbon snapped. Blood dripped from her mouth and down the front of her naked breasts. A tooth dislodged itself and she spat it across the floor.

Once sat up, one cold, white foot smacked to the floor, followed by a second.

With her mouth hanging open, she sniffed the air.

And with that, Miss Wicks stood up.

"What do you mean, children?" Gaynor was perplexed.

"Don't you see, these killings, these possessions. They're all following stories from fairy tales."

Becky was making frantic hand gestures to illustrate her point.

"Brenda Ware: poisoned by an apple, just like Snow White. Anne Wicks: seemingly dead, but really asleep with a nail driven through her finger. Sleeping Beauty pricked her finger on a spinning wheel, remember? And Rachel Power: a beauty, savaged by a hideous beast. Fairytales are stories for children. It all ties up somehow, I'm sure of it."

Becky looked down at her own protruding belly

She was shocked at how much of a maniac she sounded, yet overjoyed that she, the little sparrow that everyone thought would amount to so little, the plain Jane with no qualifications or ambitions—*she* had cracked the code.

"Fuck," she said, momentarily forgetting the company she was in.

"Sorry."

"Don't apologise, dear—my thoughts exactly," Gaynor gasped.

Suddenly a sharp bang on the door broke out, making both women jump.

"It was silly really," Catherine said, "I can't believe I ever listened to them."

"Who?" Robina asked, filling up Catherine's wine glass for the second time and handing it over. She was still nursing her first.

"Those women at the school. They were always going to do whatever Rachel told them to," Catherine sniffed, taking hold of the glass and pressing it to her lips.

Robina nodded in recognition.

After a hefty swig, Catherine carried on.

"I mean, if they had told me that Rachel was going to jump off a cliff, I would have done it." She suddenly brought a hand to her mouth in shock. "I very nearly did."

"What?" Robina said incredulously. "You were suicidal?"

"No," Catherine said, "I mean I booked a bungee jumping lesson after she did it in Mexico."

Both women laughed at the ridiculousness of it all.

"And now," Catherine said soberly, "look at what's happened now. Mauled to bloody death at her own party. I mean, what the actual fuck?"

Robina bit her lip. She didn't want to have to discuss this any further with a non-magickal person. But she had to admit that she was enjoying Catherine's company, even though the last time she had been there, Robina had been dying for her to leave. This time around, however, it wasn't the same. She was vulnerable. It was like the crown had well and truly slipped and underneath, she was the haphazard and clumsy woman that Robina could so relate to. She made bad choices, she liked a drink. And yet she had not realised that it was her imperfections that were what made her perfect.

She watched Catherine, staring into the bottom of her wine glass, her makeup slightly smudged, her hair a little wonky, dressed in less-than-flattering clothes. As an ordinary woman, she only looked more beautiful.

Catherine awoke from her trance and smiled a lopsided smile to no one in particular.

"Saul never liked going down on me," she said soberly, "and his cock is minuscule."

Robina had no idea what to do with this information and looked around awkwardly.

"My mother always used to say, a man should be styled in the office and wild in the bedroom." Catherine laughed at this. "Silly old cow, what would she know?"

She looked at Robina with watery eyes.

"Your mother died fairly young, didn't she?" Catherine said, rather tactlessly. "What was that like?"

Robina sighed.

"My mother was a wonderful woman," she said. The words sounded rehearsed.

Catherine scoffed.

"Yeah, right," she laughed. "I mean, we love them to bits, but they're always making us pay for not being them when they secretly resent us for it not being the other way around."

Robina scrunched up her face as she tried to dissect the thought.

Luckily, Catherine's phone burst into life, playing the opening strains of Eva Cassidy's *Songbird*. She put her glass down as she fumbled around in her pocket for the thing. Once found, she stared at it in a moment of drunken confusion before pressing the answer button.

"Helloooo?" she spoke into the receiver, her lazy eyes rolling around in her head.

Something suddenly made her sit forward.

"What is it?" she said firmly. "Sophia, calm down. Speak slowly, I can't—"

Robina watched, wide-eyed with concern as Catherine's brow furrowed.

As if on cue, her own phone buzzed in her cardigan pocket. She pulled it out and looked at the illuminated screen. It was a message.

"Are you in? Need to talk. Laura."

It was nearly ten. What on earth could she want at this hour? Ten was the time to be cuddled up with the cat, getting tips off re-runs of *The Great British Bake-Off*, not consoling the town's entire population of troubled women.

She slid her phone back into her pocket and looked up at Catherine, who had risen unsteadily to her feet.

"I've got to get home," she said, stumbling about in a nervous frenzy, trying to locate things around her. "It's an emergency."

Robina stood up as well, thinking she could assist just by being upright.

"Gosh, what's wrong?" she asked with concern.

"It's the babysitter. The kids..." Catherine was breathing heavily as she brought her wrist to her temple. "They're not in their beds. They've—"

A panicked look crossed her face as she struggled to comprehend what she was about to say.

"She thinks someone might have taken them."

■■

Wing ascended the stairs. Her head was hanging low.

She had been honest with Joanna, despite her protestations—she just couldn't give any more. She had lost faith in her ability to do the right thing with her magick. She was no match for life's cycle, and when illness or trouble came knocking at the door, there was nothing any sort of spell could do. It was the Deity's will.

She had released Jacqueline of some of her pain, carrying it around with her, to the detriment of her own health, but that was the absolute limit of her powers. She couldn't erase the damn illness and banish it forever. She had prayed endlessly to the Deity for forgiveness, mercy, redemption, and yet there was nothing that even he could do. All this blind faith, this devotion to a higher power—it was all for nothing. Nothing could stop death taking it all away.

She knew she had to go back to her homeland, just for a while. She needed to return and reconnect with her faith. To live in servitude to the Deity. There were retreats up in the mountains, run by devotees who would put her back on the right path. Thirty solid days of quiet contemplation and prayer, cut off from the outside world, in order to realign herself with the teachings of her ancient ancestors. She needed to stop posing with these western witches and their wishy-washy ideologies. She had to get back her faith. Without it she would feel empty, unable to provide for her family, unable to be herself. She had been losing herself for a while now. She had been allowing Joanna to get to her. She was a doormat. Her faith was the one thing that had been stable through all this and she simply could not let it slip away from her.

She couldn't bear to tell the children that she was going. She couldn't cope with seeing the hurt in their eyes, believing that it was something they had done that had pushed her away. She would have to explain that it was just a necessary thing for her to do if she were to love herself a little better. Surely, they would understand that? Richard would support her. He trusted her, respected her. He was a good man—he deserved a good wife.

As she reached the top of the stairs, she heard a clatter from outside. It was unusual on her quiet little cul-de-sac and startled her a little. Probably the neighbour's cat getting at the bins again. She would have to check that it had not tipped rubbish out into the street like it had a few weeks ago.

She stepped onto the landing and trod the few steps it took to reach Dara's room. She put her hand on the wood and pushed the door open.

Something wasn't right. She felt a surge of searing adrenaline shoot up from the pit of her stomach.

There, against the far wall, Dara's bed lay empty.

That couldn't be possible. It was way past ten—Wing had put the child to bed herself.

No, no, no, no.

She rushed across the hallway to Kit's room and pushed the door open.

Again, an empty bed. His curtains were open, and the moonlight illuminated the vacant frame.

She took a few deep, stabilising breaths before quickly stepping out of the room and crossing the landing to the bathroom. The door was open, but she switched the light on anyway. The room was deserted.

How long had she been downstairs, staring into nothing? Had the front door been opened without her knowing?

She looked at her watch. Half-past-ten. Richard was away this evening in Birmingham. It would take him an hour to get back—that was far too long. She had to speak to Odette. Something was seriously wrong.

She descended the stairs two steps at a time and went to grab her coat from the hook by the front door.

Just as she went to pull the door open, she heard the clatter outside again. But this time, it didn't sound like something as small as the Willis' cat. It was something bigger.

∎∎∎

Laura was pacing the kitchen.

"I don't know what to do," she kept saying.

"Laura, you really are going to have to tell me what's going on." Robina hoped she was sounding assertive rather than whiny. "Otherwise I can't help you."

Laura seemed completely wired. On the brink of tears yet composed enough to keep herself from crying. Robina wished that she could control her own emotions like that. More often than not, Robina would find herself climbing into the nearest cupboard when she felt unbridled tears were about to flow. Then she would have a Bakewell tart and try and forget about it.

"I don't know if I can," Laura said, sniffing and wringing her hands. She looked as though she was trying to work something out in her head and yet meeting a heap of dead ends. "All I know is that I have *fucked* everything up."

"What have you ... messed up?" Robina corrected herself. Laura had been in her house for less than ten minutes and she appeared to have brought an ill wind in with her.

Laura stopped and looked at Robina, her face hard and serious. She looked defeated and yet determined.

"That Becky," Laura said, "you know her, right?"

Robina nodded.

"She's pregnant with her husband's baby," Laura said.

"Well, of course," Robina mocked as if it was a ridiculous statement to make.

"Yeah, well..." Laura said, casting her eyes to the floor. "That makes two of us."

■■■

"You are absolutely sure?" Gaynor said, grabbing Abbie by the shoulders.

"Yes!" Abbie cried. "I know what I saw Gaynor, I am telling you, I am totally, one-hundred-percent sure."

Gaynor's face had become grave. The sparkle in her eyes had been replaced with a touch of menace.

"This is outrageous," Becky put her hand to her mouth. "I mean, this is totally unbelievable."

Gaynor swallowed hard. Abbie's news had sent utter shockwaves through the three of them. It had changed everything. No one and nowhere was safe. If what Abbie had said was true, then the coven was now totally exposed, and they would have to act fast.

Gaynor released Abbie from her grip.

"So, what do we do?" Becky asked. "How can we possibly—"

"We need to get to Joanna. Get the ladies together and take action," Gaynor said firmly.

"But how can we? I mean, for shit's sake, look what has happened so far," Abbie said, her heart pounding. "How the hell can we stop this? We're only a bunch of country bloody bumpkins, what can we do?"

"Abigail," Gaynor said, holding her hand out, "do *not* underestimate the capabilities that the women of this coven possess. Between us, we are an extremely competent circle of immense power. We have managed to free Brenda Ware of her magickal shackles and lay her to rest—we can do the same here."

Gaynor walked slowly around the table.

"Remember how disillusioned you were while you were studying? How much it pained you not

561

to be able to put that into practice? How you slaved away night after night, longing to just get out there and start throwing spells around?" Gaynor said, stopping momentarily.

Abbie rolled her eyes and nodded.

"Well, this is it, my dear. This makes all your whining worth it. Now, put your pedal to the metal and come on." She motioned to Becky to move towards the door. "We need to get to Joanna's. We'll be safe there—her house is sacrosanct."

Just as Becky went to make her way over to the door, she noticed Gaynor move over to the Welsh dresser, open a drawer and slide a small, leather-bound pouch into her pocket.

Gaynor looked ahead as she did this.

"An anthame?" Becky asked, recognising the shape of the pouch as being similar to the one that Gaynor had lent Becky.

"It's for protection," Gaynor said flatly. "Now, let's pray to the goddess that I don't have to use it."

With that, the three ladies made their way out of the room.

■■■

Wing was standing on her doorstep, holding her breath in. Something was out there—she could feel it. There was movement on the little street.

562

She whispered a small incantation under her breath, closing her eyes for a brief moment. Though why the Deity should help her now after she had doubted him so, she could not answer.

Another noise made her eyes open. The air was soft and still. Nothing else seemed to disturb it. Her ears felt as though they could hear for miles through the inky darkness. A few street lights illuminated the pavement, bathing the tarmac in a dusky orange glow. Suddenly, a figure moved to her left and over the road, it was low to the ground, as if crawling. She stepped further out into the night and closed the door quietly behind her.

She stooped slightly to try and get a better look, straining her eyes to see, but she could only make out a protruding limb from where she was standing. She moved enough to see the figure dart out of the shadows and disappear behind a parked car. It was far too large to be a domestic animal—it almost looked like a human who was bent out of shape. It moved like a feline yet had no tail or ears.

Wing took a deep breath and clenched her fists into tight balls.

Swiftly, the figure leapt like a big cat out of the darkness and crouched low onto the pavement, moving away from her house.

Wing was a good few yards behind it, vowing to herself that, if it had her children, she would tear it to pieces.

It began to crawl faster.

Wing was on its tail.

■■■

"So, that's why Eames chose here. It's near to the original site of the magic-benders," Becky whispered, trying to keep up with Gaynor, who had now taken on quite a stride for a woman of advancing years.

"She was obviously hell-bent on finishing what her father started," Gaynor said. Her voice was stern, and her movements were quick. Even Abbie was falling behind.

"Alice Eames taught most of the members of our coven at that school but, not being a witch, she wouldn't ever have been able to target us all at the same time," Gaynor said. "Now come on."

She turned off of the road. The other two stopped a moment to catch their breath as Gaynor hurried down a short slope and through the wrought-iron gates that sealed the park that led to Joanna's cottage.

"But we still don't know why she chose those women—women who are not part of The Order. I tell you, she was trying to send us a message," Becky was still calling after her.

"The best criminals always leave clues," Abbie said, absentmindedly. "There's either a pattern in the killings or a significance in the order of the victims. Sometimes killers take trophies from the bodies."

She gave a noncommittal shrug.

"How do you know all this?" Becky asked, thinking back to how cool Abbie had been in front of the security guard in Cavendish House.

"I mean, have you ever—"

"Fuck, no!" Abbie said incredulously. "But I have a strange fascination with it. Can't say I haven't been tempted a few times."

Becky gave a small snort in appreciation of the quip.

"The fairytale thing is bothering me though," Abbie said. "Back when it was all kicking off, I remember getting this weird text message."

Becky looked at her.

"What did it say?" she asked.

"Something about being the fairest of them all or something," Abbie grimaced.

"Snow White," Becky nodded. It was more evidence to confirm her theory.

Becky and Abbie started walking again, following Gaynor's path through the gate. The old woman had slowed a little as she made her way out of the line of sycamores and onto the edge of the grass. The park was large and surrounded by trees, with a long fence running along the left side, separating the green from the pavement. Joanna's cottage was situated at the far-right of the lawn—they could see the lights from her front room glowing in the distance.

The two women picked up speed to reach Gaynor. Although the night was pressing on,

Becky expected to see people in the park, but nobody was about.

Suddenly Gaynor stopped. The other two nearly crashed into her.

"Something's not right here," Gaynor said. The three women stood, looking around them. It was immediately evident that they were on their own in the middle of an open pen. They were exposed and in a very dangerous position.

Becky could hear her heart thumping in her ears.

"Should we run?" she whispered. Joanna's lights were just a few yards away. If they could just sprint to the edge of the green, then—

As quick as a flash, Gaynor turned to her right and threw her arms out to the line of trees from which they had just emerged.

"*Emergo dexremdi,*" she hissed, stooping low with her arms still outstretched. "Show yourself!"

■■

Wing watched as the thing picked up speed, hunched low to the ground, moving stealthily down the embankment to the park and through the open gates. It began to gallop like a greyhound. She too picked up speed, trying to run and maintain her balance at the same time. It had been so long since she'd done anything that came close to exercise. She cursed every deep-fried treat she had ever consumed.

But she couldn't stop.

The thing had spotted something and was now closing in—it was heading for the open space.

■■■

The ladies held their breath, but the night remained still. After a momentary pause, Abbie giggled awkwardly, but Gaynor did not move— she kept her palms out and her eye trained on the opening in the trees.

But then, out of nowhere, a shriek reverberated across the park and like a rabbit from a trap, something pelted out of the bushes.

A prone, half-naked beast came bounding toward them. With the same gait as Brenda Ware, it ran, its teeth bared, and its mouth smeared with an angry red. A tangle of matted, blonde hair fell about its face like a horse's mane. At the sight of it, Becky had the same dreaded feeling that she'd had at Rachel Power's party. This was the same kind of beast that had attacked them that night—a human transmogrified into an enraged animal.

Gaynor gasped, and Abbie shrieked. Becky shielded her belly with both arms as the thing rapidly closed the gap between them. It tore a circle around the three, fencing them in, never taking its bloodshot eyes off its target. Its skin was grey and dirty, its human face twisted into a portrait of inhuman malice and rage. As it neared

Becky, eyeing her with a satisfied leer, the thing lay back on its haunches as if to pounce. It brought its hands up, with fingers hooked over like claws and ran its slimy, pointed tongue across its rotting teeth.

Becky didn't have time to remember the incantation that she had recited the last time this had happened. Her mouth babbled as she struggled to remember the words. All she could think of was protecting her baby. She was about to have her throat torn out by this beast and suffer the same fate as Rachel Power. But she had to live—she could not go down without a fight. She must survive for the sake of her baby. Becky held a painful lungful of breath in and braced herself for impact.

But then, the beast's face changed. Its expression morphed from one of fury into one of surprise. Becky watched in amazement as its neck suddenly snapped to the left as its face continued to contort as if it were trying to fight an invisible noose around its throat. It crashed to the ground, its teeth desperately snapping away, inches from Becky's feet.

In shock, Becky looked over. There was another woman here, one she recognised from the meeting at Joanna's. She was short and squat, holding out her hands in front of her, her palms out flat.

"*Pai, mai, ne!*" the woman said, moving around, still a fair distance from the writhing beast.

The beast went to jump back up, but the woman brought her hand back down.

"*Ne!*" she shouted, and the beast once again came crashing down to the earth. Its tongue flapped out of its mouth as it bit the air. It bore the twisted face of a woman possessed by an inherent evil.

"Say the spell, Becky!" Gaynor's voice broke through Becky's hypnosis and made her turn her head.

Becky looked back at her friend, absolutely dumbfounded and panic-stricken.

"It's okay," Gaynor said, "you just need to remember the spell. Go back to that place, let it consume you. Let it in. You need to try to go back there."

Becky started to breathe heavily. She was worried that she might suffer a panic attack and collapse. She couldn't think under this pressure—it just wasn't coming.

"It's okay, child. Breathe," Gaynor said forcefully. "Let it take you over."

Becky began to slow her breathing down and closed her eyes. Listening only to the flow of air in and out of her mouth, it was as if the noises around her were muffled. She concentrated on her own heartbeat. One … two … three…

With that, her head fell backwards, and her eyes rolled up, just like before. She heard the words come into her mind—they were soft, they were low, but they were clear and comforting. The voice repeated itself—slowly, concisely. This was it. She felt safe.

Becky raised her head up and opened her mouth.

"Palo Mortis Release Embegum," she said slowly and deeply.

"Go in peace."

A huge crackle echoed through the trees, followed by a blinding stream of light that shot up to the sky. It was so instantaneous that it was barely noticeable—it vanished almost as quickly as it had materialised. Becky's vision returned just in time to see the beast's body slump, broken, to the floor.

There was a moment of silence within the group, as the ladies all glanced around at one another. Abbie looked shocked, Gaynor stood firm, and the shorter lady was nodding slowly. The park, once again, fell into silence. A bottle being kicked in the distance broke the tension.

Becky looked down at the pile of crumpled limbs that lay in the grass.

"What was *that?*" she asked breathlessly.

"That," said Gaynor, "was Anne Wicks. Well, her body at least."

Becky looked at the face. The angry expression it had worn before had softened.

Now, she looked almost peaceful. Becky could see the similarity between the woman on the ground and the photograph she had seen on the wall of the school, from underneath the visage of dried blood and dirt that was now smeared all over her.

"Right. We'd better check that nobody witnessed that," Gaynor said sternly, as she went to kneel down and check the woman's pulse. "And then we need to get rid of this body."

■■

Joanna could hear some sort of commotion across the park, but at this moment, she couldn't have cared less. She didn't even bother to go and twitch her curtains. Damn kids and their bloody fireworks—it happened all the time, and usually weeks before the fifth of November. It was hardly worth getting her seeking globe out for.

She carried on stirring a drop of whisky into her tea and turned the radio up. Radio 4, her comforter. Someone had once told her that she should listen to a peapod or something. That they had all sorts of interesting topics from witchcraft to war films. But she couldn't be figged with all this new-fangled technology. She still owned a record player *and* a cassette deck and that was modern enough for her. Nothing that came in an MI5 file, or whatever it was called, could compete with John Humphrys and Engelbert Humperdink.

571

She stared at nothing. This is what she had become, was it? When drinking scotch in the evening was preferable to sorting out vital order paperwork, she knew there must be something wrong. What had happened to her?

Oh, what did she care? The Order was falling down around her ears. Odette had swiped her authority out from under her nose and Bernice was loving every second of it. Bernice indeed. Burns his name was—William *bloody* Burns.

She briefly smirked to herself.

She had severed all ties with Abbie, her wayward protégé. Wing had all but turned her back on her faith. People she knew were getting possessed left and right, while she could only sit there and do nothing.

Never had she seen a shambles like it in all her fifty years at the head of the Winchcombe sect. Wiccans were a dying breed—at this rate, there would soon be none of them left. Social media had all but obliterated anonymity. Now witches were sharing spells and hexing each other via the internet. It was crazy. No sanctity, no consideration or respect for tradition, protection and honour.

She took a small swig from her cup—the liquid burnt its way down into the pit of her belly. She wiped a little from her lips and pulled the throw tighter around herself.

Out of nowhere, a sharp bang on the door caught her attention.

"For goodness' sake," she cursed to herself. "Who can that be at this hour?"

She looked at her watch: 10:45 pm. Couldn't she have a moment's peace? That was the trouble with living on the edge of the park. All sorts of ne'er-do-wells would make themselves at home in her shrubbery once the nights began to draw in.

Well, she wasn't about to move. Let the little, cherry-knocking buggers tire themselves out. But then the knock came again, harder and louder.

She chucked the throw off of herself and tentatively made her way into the hall. Sliding the chain onto the door, she pulled the handle down and opened it towards her.

Gaynor's face appeared in the gap, flanked by that Becky girl—and Abbie.

Joanna paused for a moment, eyeing them with a heedful glare.

"Joanna," Gaynor said impatiently, "will you let us in please?"

Joanna remained silent. She didn't want to speak to this lot tonight. If they were going to come at her with their stories of concern, she didn't want to hear them. She just wanted to finish her bottle of Glenfiddich and drag herself to bed.

Gaynor shook her head in confusion.

"Joanna!" she snapped. "Open the door—we need to talk to you."

"No!" Joanna said, pulling the face of a petulant child.

Gaynor frowned at this response.

"What's going on? Pull yourself together, woman, it's important!" Gaynor said in a terse whisper. "It's about the *circle*."

Wing pushed herself forward, blinking back tears of hysteria.

"My children," she said firmly, a slight quiver in her voice. "My children might be in danger."

Joanna let out a mournful sigh.

"I'm sorry," Joanna began, looking down at the floor so as not to meet the gaze of the women she was about to abandon. "If it's about the circle then I suggest you contact Odette since there is little I can do any more. Now if you'll excuse me—"

She went to close the door on the women, but Gaynor pushed her foot into the gap.

The two witches looked icily at each other for a second before Gaynor spoke.

"You silly woman," Gaynor scolded, her frown deepening as she spoke. "It's her we've come to talk to you about. Now open this *bloody* door!"

■■

"Oh my," Robina said, mopping up the coffee that she had managed to awkwardly spill everywhere in response to Laura's revelation.

"Yep," Laura said, staring into her mug.

She turned to look at Robina.

"Do you think I'm a total bitch?" she asked.

"Well…" Robina muttered, sweeping the kitchen top with her gaze. Jessie-Cat blinked back at her from her seat by the kettle. "I think you've made it extremely hard for yourself."

Laura shook her head.

"I didn't mean for it to get out of hand—I just wanted a baby so much." She put her other hand around the mug.

Robina didn't really know what to say. She had never been faced with this sort of dilemma before. And she didn't really know Laura well enough to offer her anything more than shop-bought advice and half-baked comfort, both of which would sound patronising and make Robina feel uncomfortable.

She just smiled. It was diplomatic—and that suited her fine.

There was an awkward silence between the two of them as Laura sipped her coffee.

"Are you going to keep it?" Robina said, a little more matter-of-factly than she had intended.

Laura took the cup away from her lips and cast her eyes toward the adjacent wall.

"I have to."

■■■

"I don't care," Joanna said, aware that she was causing a scene on her own doorstep. Luckily her garden was surrounded by thick bushes, so her neighbours were unlikely to hear.

She had let the other women in but was now standing with her arm out to block Abbie from following. Consequently, the group were collected around the doorway.

"*She* ... is *not* coming in here," Joanna shrieked. "She is *not* coming into my home after she attacked me!"

"Oh, don't even go there!" Abbie protested. "You had it coming!"

"I was doing," Joanna snarled in Abbie's direction, "what any other seasoned member of The Order would have done when challenged with the insolence of youth."

"Joanna," Gaynor hissed as she stepped towards her, "are you really sure you want to bring such attention to yourself? The way you're carrying on, the neighbours will be coming around with pitchforks to take us to the gallows any minute. Now drop your arm and let the girl in."

"She is not setting foot in my house ever again," Joanna stood firm. "She is a threat to The Order and I am in the process of having her reprimanded."

"Oh, what a load of bullshit," Gaynor said. "You don't have the authority to do that and you know it."

"I *beg* your pardon?" Joanna's eyes were bulging out of her head.

Gaynor leaned over to Joanna and whispered curtly.

"Have you forgotten what you were like as a young witch?" Gaynor eyed her with a warning glare. "Do you think, after what you used to get up to, that anyone at The Oracle would take your allegations seriously? Honestly, woman, I knew you were an old stuffy-knickers, but I had no idea you were such a hypocrite."

Joanna's face dropped—she knew when she'd been had.

"Now, do we want to pull at this thread while we're all stood in your doorway, or shall we go in and sort this mess out?" Gaynor asked defiantly.

With pursed lips and an angry frown, Joanna reluctantly dropped her arm.

"Thank you," Abbie said sternly and made her way into the room.

Joanna closed the door behind her.

Wing and Becky walked into the front room, followed by Gaynor and Abbie.

Joanna was the last in, still smarting from the previous exchange.

"Right," Gaynor said as the ladies gathered around her, "we need to contact the rest of the circle. Bernice, Robina, Laura—"

"I don't want her here," Becky said instantly, looking around at all the others, then back at Gaynor. "I don't ever want to see that woman again."

"Not you as well?" Gaynor said, eyeing Becky with a hard stare. "I'm not having this, ladies. I'm not having our personal issues getting in the way of our responsibility to protect those around us, do you understand? Leave your problems at home and get a bloody grip."

Becky knew better than to argue further. She pulled the same tight-lipped face as Joanna and took a step back.

"Okay," Gaynor said slowly, "I think we need to start at the beginning."

NINETEEN

Joanna looked completely shell-shocked by everything that she had just heard.

"So … where is she now?" she asked the others.

"We had to drag what was left of her into the bush in the hope that she doesn't get discovered. I mean, we couldn't very well carry a body all the way here between us could we?" Gaynor answered. "We were lucky that we weren't spotted. We'll have to go back for her."

Abbie placed Joanna's ornate telephone receiver back in its holder.

"Well," she said, "I got hold of Robina, Laura's there too apparently—but I can't seem to get in touch with Bernice."

Becky grimaced at the thought of that adulteress bitch breaking bread with her friend, telling her all the sordid details of her nights in bed with Becky's husband. It made her sick to her stomach.

"Well, Abbie, I think you need to tell us what you saw on that internet site," Gaynor said, sitting down to rest her wearying legs. Up to this point, she had been running on an adrenaline reserve that she didn't know she had. Now she was stationary, her knees began to feel weak.

Abbie seemed apprehensive at having to address the group. She was normally used to sitting there, chewing her hair, rolling her eyes and staying, for the most part, defiantly quiet.

"Okay," she said, in a small, modest voice, "I have been talking to this witch up North. Scotland, to be exact. We've been chatting over the net for some time and—"

"You've been disclosing your magickal status over the internet?" Joanna said in disbelief. "Are you actually raving mad?"

"Joanna, please," Gaynor pleaded, holding out a hand as an attempt to diffuse Joanna's fury. "Go on, Abbie."

Abbie looked at her feet, unsure of whether to continue. She would have to admit that she had broken the sacred code in order to get this information and she could tell it wasn't going to go down very well.

"So, she told me of this group—The New Realm. It's an alternative order, for those who want to break away from the circle."

Abbie swallowed but her mouth and throat were bone dry. She couldn't bear to look up and register her sisters' reactions.

"So, I checked out their website. I entered a protected area that named and shamed people from WHG. Apparently, they've been setting up businesses throughout the country—the world, even."

"Yes, we know this. Odette told us that Eames was part of this operation," Joanna remarked indignantly.

"Well, yes," Abbie continued, not wanting to look Joanna in the eye, "but there were pictures of these warehouses. They are disguised as places of business, but they're not. They are really terror factories. According to the site, the WHG themselves have been practising magic-bending in these places to use against The Order. But the largest one is on the old pilgrimage site of the original magic-benders, and it's in this county—it's in Oxeten."

Joanna cast her mind back to the story Odette had told them, of Alice Eames' father, supposedly spared by the WHG for practising magic-bending. So that's what the old goat was planning. She was going to carry out her father's dirty work. But if what this girl was saying was true, he had not only given the WHG the names of those who taught him the spell, but he also taught the WHG how to use the spell themselves. Wing slowly lowered herself down onto the nearest chair.

"There was a picture of Miss Eames out of the front of this building," Abbie said. "There were a few other people with her—some I didn't recognise, but one I most certainly did."

Joanna nodded, eager for Abbie to finish her sentence.

"I believe it was the other daughter who Miss Eames' father left behind," Abbie said, a slight tremor in her voice.

"Standing with her arm around her sister, Alice ... it was Odette."

■■

The taxi turned another corner and Bernice was now beginning to feel desperately unsure. This area was quite far out really—she hadn't expected it to be so remote. The car had taken her through one tiny village after another. Each one, she thought, might be where this guy was meant to live, but then they carried on out of the other side. The taxi continued down a long and dark country lane, where the hedges began to narrow, and the lights dimmed.

As the red wine began to wear off, she had started to seriously doubt her decision to come out here at all.

How could she just jump in a taxi and go out into the sticks? Was she really stupid enough to take that risk for a bit of carnal affection? She watched as the illuminated red number on the fare meter crept up and up.

After what seemed like hours, the car pulled up onto the dirt track of a seemingly abandoned site. Over to the left was a large farmhouse and to the right was an abandoned warehouse. Both looked completely deserted and desolate, with no lights on anywhere. The only illumination came from a single lamp post in between the two buildings.

This was such a bad idea.

"This is it, love," the driver said, switching the car's interior light on and looking over his left shoulder. "That'll be £42.50 please."

Bernice reached into her bag for her purse while simultaneously undoing her seatbelt. Her heart was pounding. She was pretty sure that she shouldn't leave the sight of this taxi driver, but part of her wanted to take the risk. She gave another quick glance over towards the farmhouse. What if there really was no one there? What if it was a trap?

She had heard about this. Transphobic people going on Facebook, getting their victims alone just to beat them up—horrible things like that.

She looked down at her feet, feeling totally naive and ashamed. Why was she acting like a lovesick schoolgirl, believing this guy's nonsense and getting swept up in a complete and utter fabrication? Had she learnt nothing about putting her faith in another human being? No one could be trusted.

"Do you know what," she said, suddenly feeling a little panicked, "it looks like my friend is out. I think I should just go back home."

"What, this isn't your place?" the driver asked. "I did wonder—it looks empty. I thought you might be one of those posh birds who has two houses."

She smiled, feeling quite flattered.

"Tell you what," he said, "I'll switch the meter off and you can just run and check to see if anyone's in—you've come all this way."

She looked into his kind eyes. He had a nice face, slightly podgy, with a small moustache.

"Okay," she said, "thank you."

Bernice smiled bashfully as she opened the door and cautiously got out of the car. Looking around her, she pulled her cardigan tight. The air was still, the night calm, but there was still something inherently not right about this set-up.

She walked tentatively across the driveway towards the farmhouse. Acres of land surrounded the two buildings, but it was all void of activity. She stepped cautiously over a small, stone pathway and up to one of the ground-floor windows. It was dark inside, so she cupped her hands to get a better view. The room was completely empty, save for a few dust sheets draped over some furniture.

It had confirmed her suspicions that she had been pranked—she wasn't going to chance it. She would be a fool to stay anywhere that she didn't feel completely safe. She would just return home and chalk it up to a rather silly and expensive mistake, made under the influence of cheap, supermarket Shiraz. She was used to being continually rejected—one more wouldn't hurt. Much.

Turning on her stiletto heel, she made her way back across the forecourt to the taxi. She opened the door and peered in.

"Sorry, but I think I'm going to—"

Her words disintegrated in the air. The front of the cab was completely deserted, and the keys had been taken out of the ignition. Pulling her head out of the car, she looked around but there was no sign of the driver.

Perhaps he had gone for a wee, or a fag—maybe a little stroll? It seemed unusual but possible. He wouldn't just leave his taxi unattended, would he?

She turned around, half-closing the car door.

She gasped as he appeared immediately in front of her.

This time he was not smiling—his face was dark, and his soft eyes were now hard and menacing.

"What the fuck?" she said, but he stopped her before she could continue.

"Sorry about this," he said coldly as his hand shot out towards her neck. He locked his fingers around her throat as she gasped in shock. With his other hand, he struck her forcefully across the face.

She cried out in pain as she brought her own hands up to meet his. She attempted to lurch forward, but he kept pushing her back.

She tried to fight him off, but he was strong—unusually so. She was not a small woman, but he seemed to have an unbreakable grip. She clawed against his leather jacket, looking into his handsome but aged face. His greasy black hair—the snarl on his lips.

"Why?" she managed to gasp as his hand tightened around her throat. Her shoes scrambled on the stone as he forced her down to her knees. She could feel the breath being squeezed out of her as his fingers closed together. Her handbag dropped, sending various items rolling across the ground.

"You really should have stayed at home," he said through clenched teeth.

Her hands felt limp over his, the last of her energy draining as she fought for breath.

The last thing Bernice saw was his smile as she slumped back onto the ground.

■■

At first, Joanna had looked positively stupefied. The very idea that one of the High Priestesses of The Order was moonlighting as a witch-hunter was absolutely preposterous.

"Why?" Joanna said bitingly. "Why on earth would she have something to do with the WHG? I mean, are you completely crazy Abigail?"

"She's not," said Gaynor, "what Abbie is saying is true."

Joanna began to smile.

"And what have we got to base this on?" she said with a mocking laugh. "I mean, has anyone checked out the verification of this *ludicrous* allegation? Has anyone considered the ramifications of what making such a claim could do to a witch? You could be banished from the circle altogether—forever."

"I know," Abbie began to explain through choked tears, "but I know what I saw."

"Oh, I see," Joanna spat, "well if Abbie saw it then it *must* be true!"

"Actually, *Joanna,*" Gaynor said, stepping forward, "that is exactly what happened."

Joanna stared at her, open-mouthed.

"She told us, and we believed her," Gaynor said, raising her chin to face Joanna's cynical glare, "because that is what women do."

A sharp rap on the door broke the silence.

"It's okay," Laura's voice came from behind the glass, "it's only us."

The collective relief was palpable. Everyone but Becky relaxed a little.

Joanna nodded at Wing, who got up and marched over to open the door. The remaining ladies stayed silent. As Wing came back into the room with Laura and Robina in tow, Becky cast her eyes to the floor and moved to the other side of the lounge. Laura, noticing this, also looked downward. There was immediate tension in the room.

Gaynor looked at the two women. She gave an almost imperceptible shake of the head.

"For goodness' sake," Gaynor began, her voice severe and her tone hard. "The goddess makes her message plain and yet we do not heed."

She waited a moment.

Becky was embarrassed but she did not dare to look up. Gaynor waited a moment more before speaking again.

"Look at us," she said, looking around at the women, her adopted sisters. "A room full of interesting, talented, gifted women. We have let everything get in the way of what really matters. Vanity."

She cast a glance at Abbie who instantly looked away.

"Shame."

Wing was the next to glance to the wall.

"Pride."

She turned to Joanna, who took a deep breath in.

"*Men.*"

Laura and Becky were still looking at the floor.

"We should be supporting one another, trusting one another. Standing together."

Gaynor began to walk over to a chair. The other women listened as she spoke, their eyes fixed on anywhere but in her direction. They were almost too embarrassed to admit that she was right.

"Now, I don't know what has been going on between us that we can barely be in the same room as one another," Gaynor said, "but it is to stop now. We are part of the oldest, most well-preserved and protected muliebral societies in the world. An institution that has been unifying women for centuries, long before the suffragettes were throwing themselves in front of horses and millennia before the oldest of us even took our first breath. We are mothers, life-givers, nurturers, spell-casters, fortune-tellers and children of the goddess and yet we let mistakes tear us apart. We should be hanging our heads in shame."

Gaynor sat down slowly in her usual chair. She was tired. Tired of this life, of its loss and its strain upon her heart and her head. Tired of the scourge of womanhood and how long she had been carrying the burden around, with a complete lack of support from her counterparts.

"When I first joined The Order, all those years ago, my mother said to me, 'Gaynor Bess, you must remember that, though a sister might wrong you, and boy they might, she is still a sister. Mother Earth could blow a gale that knocks you off your feet and into a muddy ditch, may damage your underskirts and wet your knees but she is still your mother. The goddess will challenge you every single day, but she is still your protector'." Gaynor looked up, her eyes moist. "One of our sisters has passed over to the dark side and we are going to have to work together in order to bring her back into the light. But not just one of us—all of us."

The room was still silent, but the ladies had now turned to face Gaynor.

"It may take time to forgive one another, to weave the thread together and mend the tapestry, but for tonight, we *must* stand alongside one another if we are going to succeed. Can I trust you all to stand by this pledge?"

The ladies began to look around at one another. Their eyes met—they searched each other's faces for some recognition, a trace of forgiveness, a flush of remorse. Becky captured Laura's eye as Abbie did Joanna's. Each woman looked away in turn, some nodding, some smiling in acknowledgement.

"Good," Gaynor said, rising to her feet. "Now, we must find out where the hell she is hiding. If we make it in time, we can stop her."

∎∎

"I just don't get it," Becky said.

She was sat on the sofa between Abbie and Robina. Laura was standing with her arm around Wing, while the older ladies had moved over to Joanna's dining table.

"There must be some way of leading us to her," Becky said, exhaling deeply.

Laura went to speak but thought better of it—she'd done enough to Becky this evening without stopping her mid-flow.

Gaynor and Joanna had unveiled Joanna's seeking globe and were concentrating as they sat before it on some dining room chairs. They prayed to the goddess to give them a sign that might uncover Odette's whereabouts. However, all they were drawing was blank clouds of grey in the swirling sphere, like a CCTV tape that had been erased. It appeared that Odette had used her advanced magic to block out any possible traceability.

"She'd be doing this for attention," Joanna said spitefully. "A woman like that doesn't just leave a trail. It would be well-planned, methodically undertaken. If this doesn't work, Abbie, you're going to have to try your enlighter."

Abbie nodded reluctantly—as if she hadn't already tried that.

"And we have already figured out that it is in some way connected to children?" Robina asked, "Because, funnily enough, Catherine Clements got a call from the nanny saying that she thought her children had disappeared."

"It true," Wing said, stepping forward, "my kids are out there, and I not leave them. They will be cold, they will be scared."

Becky put her arm around Wing—she was much smaller than she was, so she had to stoop slightly.

"Don't worry," Laura said reassuringly, "we'll find them. This will all be okay."

Wing tightened her lips together and nodded. She didn't want to make a fuss. Even though her heart was breaking, she did not want to appear selfish. What could Odette have done with them? Would they be together or alone? It didn't bear thinking about—they had to do something.

The room went silent for a moment.

"Hold on," Laura said, looking around, "aren't we missing someone?"

Joanna scoffed slightly.

"I couldn't get hold of her," Abbie said desperately, "I did try"

"Are you sure you had the right number?" Robina asked. "She doesn't always answer the first time."

"Yeah, I think so," Abbie said, "I never ever use her number, to be honest, we don't really speak outside of the circle."

"Crazy, isn't it?" Laura said. "I don't either."

There was a brief pause before Abbie tentatively spoke up.

"Did you know her?" she asked. "Like, before?"

Laura shook her head timidly.

"Before what?" Wing asked slightly over loudly.

"Well..." Abbie said, playing with the tips of her hair. "Before she was, you know—*Bernice.*"

"Abbie, that's enough," Gaynor said from her position in front of the globe. "She has always been Bernice."

The ladies became silent again.

"It's funny about names isn't it?" Abbie said, inspecting her nails. "I mean, we all have them, but they are literally only a tracking device. Our first names track our parents' impulses and our surnames track our ancestry. Surely, back in the day, we all would have been called the same—Smith, or Jones, or whatever.

Bernice lived by one tracking device and then decided to choose another all of her very own. One that marked a change in her destiny. She just erased all trace of herself and created something new. And now all memory of ... whoever she was, just remains in the past. Like an old skin. I wonder why she chose that particular name to carry on with."

Joanna huffed as the seeking globe swirled through an image of yet another dark road that, frankly, could have been anywhere.

"Burns," she said exasperatedly.

"Sorry?" Abbie asked, confused.

"Her name was William Burns. That's how she came up with Bernice Williams," Joanna sighed in frustration. "I mean, it's pretty simple when you think about it."

"William Burns," Becky whispered to herself. She rolled the words around her mouth.

A thought suddenly struck her like a lightning bolt and she sat up, her eyes wide.

"William Burns," she said aloud, causing the other ladies to turn and look at her.

"Quick," she said anxiously, "give me a pen!"

Laura walked over to the coffee table and grabbed the biro that was resting there. Abbie leant over and took an empty envelope from the window ledge next to the sofa. They both handed their finds to Becky.

She snatched the pen without looking up or saying thank you. She was still sore and, as motivational as Gaynor's earlier speech was, she still wasn't ready to make nice with the woman who had been sleeping with her husband.

"Who was first?" Becky said, putting the thought to the back of her mind.

"What?" Joanna remarked.

"In the victim line. Who was the first to be possessed?" Becky said,

"Brenda Ware," Gaynor answered, looking over her shoulder.

Becky wrote it down.

"Next?"

"Rachel Power," Laura answered. Becky frowned at the sound of her voice but kept writing.

"And then Anne Wicks?" Becky said.

"Yes," Abbie confirmed, "though, in truth, she was the first to be taken."

"Brenda Ware, Brenda W, Brendaw," Becky muttered. "Is that a word? B, Ware."

She stopped.

"B, Ware... *Beware.*"

Her heart began to race

"Beware, R, Power. *Beware our power.*"

Her mouth went dry.

"A, Wicks. Anne Wicks? Wicks Anne."

She swallowed hard.

"Wiccans."

Gaynor and Joanna halted their work with the seeking globe and turned around in their chairs. Abbie sat up intently and Wing moved closer to absorb what she was hearing.

"Wiccans beware our power," Becky said. "That's the message."

There was a moment of silence as the information sank in.

"That is so fucking cool," Abbie said, momentarily forgetting the gravity of the situation.

Becky shot a look at her.

"What did you say the name of the warehouse was?" Becky asked.

"Oh shit, I don't know," Abbie said, reaching into her pocket for her phone. "I saved it on Google Maps."

The ladies began to move forward as Gaynor and Joanna got to their feet.

Abbie swiped her phone screen a few times before tapping on it with her index finger and reading the name out loud.

"The North Oxeten Wick? Wherever that is."

"North Ox Wick," Becky said, writing it down. "No, Ox, Wick. N, O, W. *Now.*"

Becky stopped talking and looked up, her eyes dark and expression grave.

"What does it mean, Rebecca?" Gaynor said as the ladies all watched in silence.

"The message," Becky said. *"Wiccans beware our power, now…"*

Her breath held in her throat as she tried to force the words out.

"Now…?" Abbie asked.

"…now William burns."

■■

When Bernice awoke, she couldn't see anything. This sent her into a blind panic and her breath came rapidly out of her nose. A hessian bag had been placed over her head which covered her whole face. All she could see was dull shapes through the sack. She could also feel that she was tied to something that ran the length of her spine and that her hands were behind her back and bound.

A piece of cloth had been taped over her mouth. Beads of sweat were forming on her forehead. Where the hell was she? What was happening to her?

She could hear movement, but from far away—it was as though a silent audience was collecting below her. She sensed that she was higher up than these others, but there was flooring beneath her feet, so she wasn't suspended.

She wanted to call out, but the tape was that tight around her face. She was not sure that anybody around could help, even if they did hear her. Wherever she was, whoever had taken her, she knew that she was in trouble, but she had no idea how much. Would anyone find her when this was all over? Without telling anyone where she was going, surely no one would come looking for her. Just another sad, gender-confused statistic who took themselves off to end their miserable existence. Is this what her son would read in the paper when she had been reported missing?

Salty tears stung her eyes and her breath became more panicked and short. Was this how she was going to die?

There was a smell that permeated through the weave of the sacking, it was like soil and hay as if she were in a stable or something. She tried to move her head about, but the sack was tight, and her throat was still sore from where the taxi driver had throttled her half to death.

She sobbed a little, her saliva soaking into the cloth that bound her mouth. It tasted of blood and dirt.

The talking had stopped. The only sound she heard was her breath inside the bag. It seemed to fill the room.

Whatever was going to happen to her, she hoped it was painless—and quick. She couldn't help but think, however, that it would be neither.

■■

Joanna's car was cramped and uncomfortable.

She'd had a little alcohol this evening but still insisted on driving, even though both Abbie and Gaynor had offered. Her little Nissan Micra was rarely on the road, but tonight she would do the honourable thing and drive the rescue vehicle to the scene of the crime. Gaynor rode in the passenger seat, her eyes fixed on the road, while Becky, Wing and Abbie squeezed into the back.

Laura and Robina had opted to go and remove Miss Wicks' body from the park and transport it to Oxeten. Once they had sorted out this mess, they would give her a proper burial. *If* they sorted it out. Odette was not going to be easy to take down if what Abbie had said was true. But how on earth had someone who was so high up in the WHG managed to infiltrate one of the securest institutions in the country? It was totally unfathomable to her.

Unless The Oracle herself was in on it? No, that couldn't be. She had been their matriarch for so many years and was such an inspiration to leagues of generations. She wouldn't just buckle at the eleventh hour and breach the anonymity of the sisterhood.

No, Odette must have been working alone or, as Becky and Gaynor had insisted, with the help of the children of Winchcombe. This was all too bizarre. There must be a damned good explanation as to how and why this had been allowed to happen and Joanna was determined to seek it out.

She pushed the stick and the car ground into fourth gear. Everyone instinctively gripped onto the nearest fixed handle for stability.

"My gosh woman," Gaynor said, "when was the last time you drove this thing?"

"I prefer to walk most places," Joanna responded defensively, "but if you would prefer to get there by broomstick then be my guest."

Gaynor laughed.

"That takes me back," she said.

Joanna stole a quick glance at her.

"Did you ever fly one?" she asked.

"I'm not *that* bloody old."

Joanna waited a moment before laughing.

"We're about thirty minutes away," Abbie said, her phone navigating them through the winding roads.

Wing remained silent, staring out of the window, lost in contemplation and reciting pleas with the Deity in her head. She promised to be more abiding, more pious, more submissive, if only her children could be returned safely home.

She blinked back tears as the car hit another pothole and they all jumped out of their seats. Becky held onto her belly.

"We could be twenty minutes away," Gaynor said, "if you would put your *blasted* foot down, woman!"

"It's a fifty-mile-an-hour zone," Joanna protested.

"Oh, come on," Gaynor said with a wink, "where's the risk-taking, youthful witch I remember from the seventies? The one that would kiss all the boys and smoke cigarettes in the back of her Corvette?"

Joanna shushed her quickly.

"Not in front of the others, thank you," she scolded.

Joanna looked in the rear-view mirror. Abbie beamed back at her, eager to press Gaynor for more.

"You forget how much I know about you, Joanna," Gaynor said, looking at her affectionately. "Actually, you seem to have forgotten a lot of things recently."

Becky hunched forward from the back seat, as much as her bump would allow.

"Have you two known each other long?" she asked.

"Too long," Gaynor said over her shoulder before Joanna could answer. "I mean, I didn't move to the area until '83 but I knew this one knocking around at circle meetings from years before that."

"I don't think anybody wants to know about that," Joanna said.

"What was she like?" Abbie said, sliding further forward in her seat.

Gaynor eyed Joanna with consideration.

"Stunning," she said with a staunch authenticity.

"Oh *stop*," Joanna gushed, "you're going to make me crash this car."

"Honestly," Gaynor continued with a soft laugh, "you were a heartbreaker. Always took herself far too seriously though. She wasn't one to be distracted in study and practice, but outside of tutelage, she was down the bar drinking Coca-Cola and twisting with the best of them."

"As if, Gaynor Richards—you're full of it." Joanna waved a spare hand about. "Now come on, have some respect for those in the car who are worried about their loved ones."

Wing had now closed her eyes and was mouthing words of silent prayer.

"I was a lot older, so my days of jumping and jiving were over, but this one—" Gaynor smirked. "What was that Beatles song that you used to sing? All the time, forever wailing it. What was it? *Love Me Tender*?"

"Give me strength, that was Elvis!" Joanna playfully mocked, keeping her eyes on the road, but with an imperceptible smile on her lips.

There was a short silence as the car trundled along—all of their heads bobbed to the side in unison as they ran over another small pothole.

"It was *Love Me Do*," Joanna said.

Abbie and Becky cooed from the back seat.

"Ace man," Abbie said, "I love the Beatles."

"How does it go?" Gaynor asked Joanna.

"Are you kidding me, woman? I'm not singing now!" Joanna cried incredulously.

"Ah go on!" Gaynor pleaded. "I can't remember how it goes."

'Well," Joanna called, "if Abbie loves it so much then she can help me out."

"Okay," Abbie agreed before she started singing. "*Love, love me do—*"

Joanna joined in.

"You know I love you—"

Joanna caught Abbie's gaze in the rear-view mirror and smiled.

"I'll always be true—"

Joanna's eyes remained locked on Abbie, smiling back at her. She suddenly felt such affection for her, the little girl who she had taken under her wing and nurtured, tutored, guided. She was now a young woman with her own aspirations and dreams. A young witch in a new world. She would have to do more to protect her in a practical way. Not scold her just for wanting to learn and explore her craft.

For so long, Joanna's devotion to The Order had restricted the depths into which she had explored her relationships. It had diluted her personality, turned her into a stuffy, old maid with no real time for anything else. Her piety left no room for mistakes or errors. She had always tried to do right by The Order and yet somehow, she had pulled herself out of a meaningful existence. If they made it through tonight, she would work harder to change this. To understand the women who she held dearer than she had thought.

"So pleeeeeeease—"

Joanna's eyes flicked sharply back onto the road.

Out of nowhere, emerging from the darkness, two small faces appeared in the headlights.

"Look out!" Gaynor shrieked as she noticed the two, horror-stricken children about to go over the bonnet of the car. Their eyes were blackened, and their faces frozen like two white *Scream* masks.

Joanna yelled out and swerved a hard left, sending screams up from the back seat. The car left the road and went plunging bonnet-first into the hedgerow. The air-bag deployed just before Joanna's head hit the wheel, forcing her back against the headrest.

They remained stationary for a moment before she felt the car rock and then fall over onto its left side.

Before she had time to check on the others, she passed out, the nervous cries from her passengers still ringing in her ears.

■■■

Laura huffed as she pulled back the huge blanket of leaves. Robina was keeping watch.

"You know," Laura said, scrambling down into the undergrowth, "that you're now guilty by association. The reason that they've got me to do this and nobody else is because I fucked that woman's husband."

Robina winced at the swearing.

"I'm sure that's not true," she said, wrapping her cardigan around her. It wasn't particularly cold, but the very thought of being out looking for a dead body in the park was sending an unpleasant shiver down her spine. Even more unnerving was the possibility that the thing might come back to life.

"Ha!" Laura mocked, rolling her eyes to herself. "Yeah right. I'm sure I was given this task because of my *marvellous* orienteering skills."

"*Look*," Robina hissed, "is she there?"

"Hold your horses," Laura said, squatting a little further and holding the torch ready. She was also carrying one of Joanna's large suitcases, unzipped and ready to be packed with the broken carcass.

Opening out in front of her, surrounded by trees, was a rather large clearing. Laura moved the torch beam from one side of the space to the other.

"There's nothing here," she said, exasperated.

Robina screwed up her face. Bending in closer, she whispered through the branches.

"Are you sure?" Robina asked.

"Yes," Laura retorted, "there's nobody here."

"They said they dragged it to the middle.

"I know what they *said*," Laura bit impatiently, "but I'm telling you—it's not here!"

Robina shivered again. Suddenly, in the distance, she saw the flicker of a light from the far side of the park.

"Quick," she called to Laura, "we need to get out of here."

Laura let out a defeated sigh as she took one more sweep of the area before scrambling back out from under the fauna.

She stood up next to Robina, brushing herself down.

"Look," Robina said, pointing to the other side of the park. There were more lights approaching through the trees, followed by voices.

"Harry?!"

"Chloe?!"

"Poppy?!"

More names followed. The desperate cries of anxious parents filled the air.

"They're looking for their kids," Laura said, grabbing the suitcase. "We can't hang around. Come on—let's get to my car."

Laura turned around and started to walk back to the road, Robina following in hot pursuit.

"What do you think this is all about?" Robina asked. "I mean, why would Odette want to capture these children?"

"I'm fucked if I know," Laura said, pressing the button on her keys as the lights on her car winked in response. "But I guess no one suspects children, do they? An easy way of getting vast numbers to do your dirty work while going unnoticed—quite clever really."

"Hmm," Robina said pensively.

"Look, get in," Laura said, walking around the car to the driver's side. "We really need to join the others if we're going to stop that crazy bitch. There's not much we can do about the body now. We'll just have to come back some other time."

Robina opened the door and slid uncomfortably into the passenger seat.

Laura opened her door and jumped into the driver's seat, slamming it behind her. As they both buckled up they looked at one another.

"Do you know how to get there?" Robina said.

"I have no idea," Laura remarked, "but I'm hoping that my phone does."

She slid her seatbelt back and reached over to the back seat. As she turned her head to look, she let out a shocked gasp.

"Oh fuck," she whispered.

"What?" Robina said, turning to look in the same direction.

As she did so, she too let out a gasp.

Sat on the back seat were two children, perfectly calm, with their hands in their laps. One was a girl of about seven or eight, the other a much younger boy.

They said nothing, just sat quietly on the seat, totally normal, but for one unusual feature— their eyes were completely black.

Robina began to hyperventilate, but Laura put a comforting hand on her side.

"It's okay," Laura said quietly, as Robina's face twisted into a panicked grimace.

Suddenly the little girl decided to speak.

"What were you doing out there?" she said curiously, directing her head towards Laura, her black eyes reflecting the light from the street-lamp that was shining in through the window.

Laura tilted her head, trying to seem unafraid, even though her heart was racing.

"We were..." she began, "looking for something."

Her words were cool and measured. The little girl looked at Robina, then back at Laura.

"Like what?" the girl said innocently.

Now the boy, too, was looking at Laura.

"Just—" Laura kept her eyes fixed on the girl's dark spheres. "Just something that we'd lost."

The girl blinked, as did the boy. Then she leant forward, her golden locks falling about her shoulders as she reached down into the footwell of the seat. The boy kept his eyes on Laura.

"This thing you lost," the girl said, keeping her head down, "was it this?"

She sat back up straight and held out her right hand.

What she held in her tiny fist was grey and dripping with red ooze. She held it by a scruff of blonde hair as it hung gruesomely from her hand.

Swinging to and fro was the decapitated head of Anne Wicks.

Robina screamed louder than she'd ever screamed before.

∎∎∎

Joanna's eyes sprung open.

She blinked, hoping to block out the pain that was screaming at her from her left temple. Her vision was blurred, and the night was dark. She felt the cold, hard ground on her belly.

Something wet was running down her cheek. She had a sneaking suspicion she knew what it was, but she tried not to think about it.

She thought of moving her arm, but it was heavy, and it ached. She didn't want to make any sudden movements, considering she didn't know where she was or what she might have broken.

All she remembered was hearing the screams from the others and the grind of twisting metal before her sight had clouded over.

Where were the others? Did they make it out alive?

She moved her head to the side, panting quickly.

She was no longer in the car, she knew that much. There was dirt on her lips and the mild night breeze tousled her hair. She was face down in the earth. Someone had obviously dragged her out of the wreckage. But who? Was it one of the others? Were they okay?

"Gaynor," she whispered into the dark, but there was no reply. She felt alone as if there was no other presence around her.

She shut her eyes, trying to listen to her surroundings. All her years of being super-alert had taught her not to give herself away, especially if she thought she was in imminent danger. She would just have to lie here until something presented itself—then she would strike.

She said a silent spell under her breath.

"Mesum mornato protectis."

"Clothe me in protection."

It wasn't much, but it might keep her hidden from any immediate peril.

She was going to have to look around if she was to plan her next move, but her neck was sore, and her temples were throbbing.

Slowly, she moved her head to the other side. Her mouth brushed the soft earth and covered her chin in soil, which she spat out.

She was in a field. High crops obscured her view. She could only see a distant tire protruding through the plants. The car must have turned over. Perhaps her instincts meant that she had managed to unbuckle her seatbelt and throw herself into the brush before the car hit the ground. Did that mean that the others were still in the vehicle? If so, she would have to get them out.

She bent her left elbow—it was stiff, and a searing pain shot up to her shoulder but at least it didn't seem to be broken. She then did the same with the right. Slowly, she put her wrists into the earth and lifted her chest off the ground.

The pain in her head intensified and she screwed up her eyes in response.

She gradually flexed her neck back to try and loosen it up but the impact with the headrest had damaged it and she stifled a scream as the pain coursed through her.

She dreaded to think where the others might be. Hurt? *Dead?*

What had she swerved from? Two children with black, crystalline eyes and slack jaws. This kind of possession broke every rule in the book.

It was the work of someone who had been in prime position to steal ideas of the very worst kind of magic from its pulsating source—Oracle HQ. Not only that but to bewitch *children?* Just what were they dealing with here? She needed to find out, and she needed to move quickly. She put all of her weight on her right arm, lifting herself on to her side and landing flat on her back.

She looked up at the stars for a moment or two before something moved into her view, something that made her breath catch in her throat. A black shadow was standing over her— she couldn't make out a face, but it was dark, and she screwed up her eyes in an attempt to see it better.

Before she could cry out, something was put over her head and tied at the neck. It smelt of damp and pressed against her face. Firm hands grabbed her legs and pulled her away by the ankles.

■■

"Hello?" Becky called out, not that she was sure that anyone could hear her. The bag over her head was muffling all sounds around her. "Can you hear me? You need to let me go, I'm pregnant. Please, I'm pregnant."

Her head was aching and there was a pain in her ankle. She remembered nothing after the crash—just the ringing in her ears from the shrieks of the other women.

Becky let out an exasperated cry. She couldn't hear any voices, just a shuffle of feet. She could tell that the lights were on and that the sounds were coming from below her.

She could hear other voices crying out, but she couldn't distinguish who it was.

"Gaynor?" she called, turning her head to the right. "Robina?"

There was no audible response from either of them, even though Becky was straining to hear.

She knew that she was tied up. Her hands were bound behind her and a long, thin pole was pressing against her back.

"Please," she pleaded, beginning to hyperventilate, "I can't breathe. I need to save my child."

The tears then came thick and fast. She was terrified, not just for herself but because she may be starving her daughter of vital oxygen. Her cries came out as muffled sobs. Gooey saliva bubbled out from her lips as the tears ran down her face.

"Is anybody there?" she called out again in desperation. "I need to get some air."

It was sweltering under the bag. The heat had hit her when she had eventually come to. She found herself slumped against the pole, tethered and tied to the spot, struggling to breathe and sweating in the intense warmth.

She suddenly heard footsteps come towards her. They sounded like heels on wooden slats. She had no idea if she was standing on the same floor as the footsteps approaching her until they came closer and she felt the boards underneath her feet vibrate. She felt a hand tug at her hair and the bag was lifted off.

At first, the light stung her eyes. She squinted, shaking her head and gasping for air. But as her vision adjusted, the true horror of where she was began to register. She looked around as she took the whole scene in.

She was standing on a thin ledge, around five metres off the ground in what looked like a large barn, with breezeblock walls and a high ceiling. It was a huge space, with hay and straw littering the ground below. There were tall spotlights shining directly on the ledge, but the second half of the room was in complete darkness. It was impossible to gauge how far it went back and whether, indeed, there were more horrors lying in wait. Two long ladders led up to the ledge, which was wide enough to fit two people and looked as though it had been purpose-built for whatever was going on here. She glanced downwards. Below her, a hundred-or-so children stood, looking up at her. They shared the same emotionless expressions and had completely black, shark-like eyes. Every one of them stared up at her, not speaking or moving.

Worse still, she recognised almost all of them—from assembly at St Patrick's.

She cast a glance over her left shoulder and noticed that she was not alone on the ledge. Other bodies were similarly bound and tethered to separate poles some two metres apart from each other. She watched in stupefied silence as a tall, brutish-looking boy with curly hair and the same dead eyes as the children below was slowly walking along the ledge, pulling the bags off of the heads of the other captives one by one.

Abbie was first, Wing was second, Gaynor was third and Joanna was last. Each of the women looked bewildered as they were introduced to the scene below them. Their faces were speckled with dirt and dried blood. As they noticed each other, they gave startled, little cries of acknowledgement.

Abbie was closest to Becky—she caught her eye.

"Abbie!" Becky cried frantically. "What's going on?"

But Abbie's eyes were glacial. She was staring down at the children, a look of indescribable terror written across her face. Gaynor was trying not to be affected by the sight of the kids, but her head was retracting as if she wanted to move herself away. Wing was closing her eyes and whispering to herself. Joanna had locked her lips and was looking surprisingly defiant.

Becky looked back down at the sea of small faces, blank yet eerily menacing. The children's eyes followed the boy on the ledge as he took his place by the second ladder, inches away from where Joanna was stood.

'Hey!" Becky called, noticing a couple of the boys in the crowd. "Harry, Archie! Up here!"

Every child turned their head to face Becky, but their expressions remained frozen.

"Help us!" she cried again.

"It's no use," a voice shouted up from below— it was familiarly depthless. "They won't help you. They can't."

The women looked down, following the direction of the voice below.

A man stepped out from beneath the ledge. He wore a leather jacket and had a slight belly. He had a messy side parting of black hair and dark, South Asian-looking skin. He stood in front of the children and put his hands on his hips, staring up at the women with gloating, threatening eyes.

"And it's no use screaming because no one will hear you," he said. His voice did not seem to fit his demeanour. It was low and clipped, but ultimately feminine.

He brought his hands up in front of him with his palms to the ceiling.

"So glad you could make it, ladies. And it's amazing that you're relatively unscathed after such a ... dramatic crash," he said, his tone dripping with sarcasm. "But we are happy to see

615

you. We've been waiting a long time for you to arrive."

TWENTY

The guy in the leather jacket smiled up at them. A gold crown flashed at the back of his mouth.

Becky frowned.

"Please, I need you to let me down," she pleaded. "My baby ... I need to sit down, or else my baby—"

The man sniggered.

"Stop whining," he said, a look of anger crossing his face, "I've heard enough of your damned whining to last me a lifetime."

Becky closed her lips and sniffed.

"Hey!" Abbie was the next to shout, the man turned to look at her. "Who the fuck are you exactly?"

He sneered at her.

"You," he said, pointing an accusatory finger up at the young girl.

"You have a filthy mouth," he laughed, "and look where that mouth has got you—in a whole heap of trouble."

Becky looked over at Gaynor. She looked white, she wasn't saying anything, and her mouth hung open as if she was paralysed.

"Please," Becky begged, "please don't hurt us. Just let us go and we'll walk away. We won't breathe a word of this to anyone—will we, girls?"

She looked at the other ladies, who didn't respond—they just kept their eyes fixed on the man.

"It's too late for that," he said, turning to two of the black-eyed children. One looked familiar. A tallish girl with beautiful blonde locks. It was Sienna Clements.

The man took Sienna's chin in his palm.

"Go and get the canister," he said to her. Sienna nodded slowly and turned to walk out of the barn.

Becky began to panic as her eyes followed Sienna, who was not walking in her trademark slow, elegant strides, but in a more regimented fashion.

"What are you going to do to us?" Becky shouted, turning her focus back to her tormentor.

He waited a moment, holding his gaze upon her.

"In 1642," he began, directing his attention to each of the women in turn, "accusations of witchcraft peppered the Gloucestershire villages. Women who nursed and cared for infants were accused of being responsible for the children's seemingly spontaneous and erratic behaviour. They were also thought to be imposing scratches upon their wards' arms and inflicting aggressive welts on their skin."

The women stayed silent as he continued.

"Stories of the conjuring up of blacks dogs and insidious spirits arose. Of women cutting themselves and letting blood into the fire, mauling animals and shapeshifting into unimaginable horrors. They were said to have used the black magic of the underworld to wreak the devil's work on the defenceless little humans under their care.

The only way to purify the unclean soul of someone so immersed in such darkness was to bathe it in the eternal light of the flame. To scorch the soul so badly that the evil within it went up with the smoke. The only way to emancipate the heart within her breast was to burn the body of the witch."

Becky's eyes filled with horror. She looked over again at the other ladies who had similar looks on their faces. Joanna was the only one who held her fixed stare.

"Of course, that is what history tells us," the man carried on, his tone softening. "In truth, the burning was only half of the story. Before the flame could lick the skin, the genitals were invariably mutilated, the teeth and the fingernails removed. Their tongues were cut out so that they could not communicate with the devil in death, their breasts were hacked off and feet thrashed so as not to be able to seduce him through dance in the afterlife. They were forced to drink liquified base metals and their hair was plucked from the roots. By the time they reached the stake, they were begging their tormentors for the comparatively painless death by burning."

He looked up once more.

"Let's just say that tonight ... I will be merciful."

With that, Sienna emerged from under the ledge, holding a large, red petrol canister. It was almost as big as she was and yet she was not buckling under its weight. Becky flinched.

"You can't do this," she shouted, "you can't! I'll do anything, please. Just save my baby!"

At this, the man smirked and let out a guttural laugh.

He advanced towards the base of the ladder and began to climb up.

"You know," he said as he slowly ascended, rung by rung, "the only way to properly anoint the ground that has been desecrated by the sin of witchcraft is to make a sacrifice."

Becky watched, terrified as the crown of his head appeared up the ladder, half a metre away from where she stood on the ledge.

She tried to step back but her movement was restricted.

"But not just any sacrifice—it would have to be a blood sacrifice," he continued as he came into view.

"And we're not talking goats or lambs here."

As he clambered up onto the ledge and made his way over to Becky, his hand travelled to the seat pocket of his black jeans. He looked even smaller up close. A squat, ageing man with full lips and angry eyes. A lascivious grin spread across his face.

Becky's eyes widened as he brought out a pouch from his back pocket. She recognised it as the one Gaynor had hidden on her person before they left the house.

"And what better human sacrifice than a witch's unborn baby, with the very blade that is blessed for her protection?" His teeth were bared now as he brought the blade out of the pouch. It was small and dull, but sharp.

Becky started to squirm as involuntary tears fell from her eyes.

"Please, no..." she said. "I beg of you ... please. Please don't hurt my baby."

He moved closer to her. He smelt of expensive perfume, not how she expected him to smell. He brought the blade to her belly, never dropping his gaze. She felt the hard edge of it press against her. Becky's breath became short. She closed her eyes, waiting for the searing pain, the flow of blood. She hoped that in cutting her open, he would kill her too. She did not think she could cope with the loss of her daughter—she'd be better off dead.

"Why don't you ask your grandmother to save you?" he said, through clenched teeth—a little of his saliva landed on Becky's cheek.

"*Stop!*"

It was Gaynor's voice.

"You've had your fun. Why don't you stop tormenting us, you coward?" she said.

Becky opened her eyes. The man's gaze had shifted over to Gaynor. She remained pale but had maintained a sense of composure.

He held the blade forward as he strode purposefully over to the old woman.

"Something to say, hag?" he said as he thrust the blade forcefully towards her.

She pursed her lips together, looking at him with steely blue eyes.

"Just one thing," she said in response, keeping her eyes fixed upon him.

"*Esperius bectum.*"

"*Vala,*" came his reply. A blue light encircled the knife but immediately vanished.

"Come now," he said, "do you think I don't know how to block your washerwoman magic? My dear, it's all I've been studying for the last two years. You're lucky I didn't bend it back to strike you in the face."

"Why?" came another voice—this time it was Joanna's. "Why are you doing this?"

"Oh," the man said, "I wondered when you might pipe up. Almighty Joanna, she who must be obeyed. She who when push comes to shove can't even hold her own clan together. I mean, incompetence isn't the word, is it?"

Wing continued to mutter under her breath. Becky didn't know whether she was biding her time or trying to summon something. Either way, she was not connected with the rest of them. Abbie remained silent.

"I should have known," Joanna said. "People like you don't just turn up, out of the blue and start throwing their weight around. That is not how The Order has ever operated."

"Oh," the man laughed, "those troglodytes? Call themselves a tight-lipped, secure institution. They're not even able to keep the WHG out."

"What do you mean?" Joanna asked accusingly.

"The WHG have had plants working there for years," the man grinned, "Gradually chipping away, indoctrinating followers and keeping mum until the right time came. And here it is—the beginning of a revolution."

He held his arms out.

The women looked at each other. All of them, except Wing, were wide-eyed with confusion.

"Aren't you honoured that you are the gateway into the new dawn?" he said, turning to the rest of the ladies. "The moronic inhabitants of a sleepy Cotswold town. You'd never have a clue how to manage yourselves when the revolution came—you're all so backward. Even your police force believe anything we tell them. And now the time has come. We've set it all up right under your noses. I mean, how stupid can you be?"

Abbie shook her head.

"What revolution?" Joanna asked incredulously. "How have you done this? What are you hoping to achieve? *What* is going on?"

The man turned to her, pointing the blade in her direction.

"The eradication of witches—*for good*," he said, a delight in his voice. "Finally, the WHG are going to obliterate the practice of witchcraft. We're going to do to this place what we should have done years ago—burn it to the ground."

He shifted his focus back to Becky.

"We are going to sterilise this little disease once and for all and *you*—" He gestured to the entire group, the blade still in his grasp. "...are going to be the poster-girls for the whole event. We are going to show the rest of your little cult what happens if you don't obey our rules. Soon, they'll be begging us to spare their lives as well."

Gaynor gritted her teeth.

"Burning witches is nothing new," she said. "You've not stopped us in the past and you won't stop us today, even if you kill us all right now. The WHG are just barbaric radicals. You always have been. You're never going to stop an ancient institution by sacrificing a few harmless women!"

"Don't patronise me, *witch!*" he spat, turning back towards her. "Your sort have been bewitching innocents, terrorising communities and hexing my ancestors for years. And for what? Power!"

"A good witch only uses her magic for good," Joanna cried as if reciting it from one of her study books.

He turned to her again.

"Oh, is that right?" he said mockingly. "You're pure as the driven snow are you, Joanna?"

He came closer to her, leaning forward as she brought her chin up to face him.

"Why don't you tell your *sisters* what you did to Floella Michaels?" He ran his tongue over his teeth.

Joanna flinched at the utterance of the name.

"That was a long time ago," Joanna said, the tremor in her voice giving away her anxiety.

"Yes, of course," he said, turning to the others, "but then, considering it was *such* a long time ago, they still haven't allowed you to become a High Priestess, have they? Even though your years of painful dedication to the cause would ordinarily make you a shoe-in. Ruling the coven with an iron fist, never letting anyone step out of line, governing by unnecessary fear—all so you could convince the powers that be that you were worthy of redemption."

Abbie looked sullen.

"What is he talking about?" she said to Joanna, who had cast her eyes to the floor.

Abbie looked from Joanna to the man and back to Joanna.

"What does he mean?" Abbie said, urging Joanna to respond.

Joanna chewed her lip as she slowly looked up and swallowed hard.

"It happened years ago," Joanna said, stopping to take a heavy breath. "When I was at college. There was this student. We studied together but she was also in the circle."

"She knew something about you, didn't she?" the man said, a smile spreading across his lips. "Something you were keeping from mother, the renowned Oracle Archivist."

Joanna looked at him with disgust and swallowed again.

"We had been to my mother's archivist library, a whole group of us—the younger members of The Order, that is. We were messing about, trying to find out unusual spells and such, but that stuff was all highly classified. You couldn't just thumb through it without proper authorisation. Anyway, we found a key in my mother's desk that opened a locked filing cabinet and there we stumbled upon a poorly-archived prophecy," Joanna said shamefully. "Even now, I can't remember what it said—it was something banal, innocuous. And we swore that the information would never get out, or else my mother would lose her job. But Floella was racked with guilt. She couldn't sleep for worry. She would come to class looking distraught and ill. Not eating, not resting."

"So ... what did you do?" Abbie asked through clenched teeth.

"We were certain she would tell. She was on the edge. She wanted to rid herself of this awful feeling, but we couldn't afford for her to blurt out that we had done it. We were young—we didn't understand the severity of the situation." Joanna looked at them with fear in her eyes. "So ... we hexed her with a silence spell."

Not totally sure of what this meant, Becky looked around the ladies for a reaction, but there was none.

"It was a simple spell to put a stop on her saying certain words. They just weren't able to come out of her mouth. She would go to speak the word *prophecy* and she would simply be unable to say it. It's simple, juvenile magic, but we were amateurs—we didn't know what we were doing!"

Joanna was pleading.

"It's okay," Gaynor said comfortingly.

Joanna sniffed.

"It went wrong. She ended up brain-damaged. It was irreversible," Joanna looked again at her feet. "She ended up bed-ridden, unable to feed herself or go to the toilet alone."

The tears fell from Joanna's face.

"Her parents couldn't cope in the end. She needed round-the-clock care," she continued. "They tried to get the papers involved to warn others of the danger of practising witchcraft, but no one would listen to them. People thought they were crazy—selling stories about spells like radical, religious folk. So, out of desperation, they smothered Floella in her sleep."

Abbie and Becky both audibly gasped. There were a few moments of silence as the man chuckled softly.

"How the hell did you get away with it?" Abbie asked through choked tears.

"It was a different world," Joanna whispered, "it wasn't the same as it is now, we didn't have rules and regulations—you just kept quiet. I have been living with it all my life."

Abbie shook her head.

"All the times you have shouted at me for trying spells outside of a regulated safe-house," she said, the volume of her voice building with her rage, "and all the while you've been responsible for *this!?*"

Joanna looked up.

"It was for your own good," Joanna begged, "I didn't want you to have to go through the same torment."

"Bollocks!" Abbie screamed at her. "You're a fucking hypocrite!"

"Yes, she is," the man said as he approached Joanna. "A total and utter hypocrite. And a murderer."

"But ... what do you want?" Becky said. "Why are you here? How are you connected to Odette?"

The man laughed.

"Oh, you are stupid," he said, turning to face her, a mocking leer on his lips. "Stupid, little, entitled witch girl. I can't wait to see The Oracle's face when she finds out what happened to you."

"Why?" Becky cried incredulously.

Joanna looked at Becky—she was ashamed and defeated. Tears left inky tracks down her cheeks.

"That..." Joanna said, nodding towards the man. "That *is* Odette."

TWENTY-ONE

"So, you're here to finish what your father started," Gaynor asked in a broken voice as the man slowly began to descend the ladder. "But why now?"

He reached the bottom of the ladder and walked up to a vacant Sienna who held out the petrol canister.

He took it from her and began to pull off the lid.

"I'm not at liberty to answer your questions," he called up to them. "You're my captors—I'm the one who asks the questions."

"Why all this? Why the warehouse, why the children? Why didn't you just kill us when you had the chance?" Gaynor asked. "We've been alone with you plenty of times."

The man turned.

"How would me disposing of you in Joanna's little hovel benchmark the beginning of a global campaign?" he asked. "We want to show The Oracle and her heretic followers that we mean business, but also that, with the right skills, WHG constituencies across the globe can stage their own large-scale cleansing rituals. Think how stupid The Oracle will look when she realises that all this has happened from inside her offices. That we have managed to learn, from her, all the magick that was necessary to overthrow her. She's even led members of her family to the slaughter."

"And the children?" Gaynor asked. "Your sick little idea, was it?"

He unscrewed the canister lid, throwing it on the floor, and began to pour the liquid liberally across the straw-littered ground.

"Well," he said, "I guess I can't take all the credit. You see, unbeknownst to your archaic, little society, the WHG have been rolling with the times, researching the pace of new technologies."

He stopped.

"Did you know that with just the right amount of spell magick combined with the relevant technological know-how, you can create an app that hypnotises people, merely with science and robust coding?"

He smiled into thin air.

"Fascinating. All we needed was someone to bring the software into the area in a small suitcase and set up shop. Simple really. Not as cumbersome as it used to be—all that bewitching from door to door wouldn't have been the most economical way to start a revolution. No ... en masse was far more effective."

He was still distributing the petrol.

"But, children?" Gaynor asked in disbelief.

"How were we to know that the app would catch on with the kids and their smartphones? They came to us, not the other way around. Don't be blaming us for them wanting to sign up for something exciting and rule-breaking. They even came up with the innovative calling card method. Ingenious really."

He scattered the liquid around as the children moved out of the way, their eyes still looking skyward.

"Who'd have thought that leaving secret messages on the bodies to correspond with fairy tales would be so effective? Better than I could do. It even led you right to us. Recruiting bewitched children is really beginning to reap its rewards. They are the future, after all."

He let out a malevolent giggle.

"Ironic too," he continued. "It's as though the kids are getting their own back for what those old bitches did to them all those years ago."

"It was proven that the children who testified in the witchcraft trials were lying!" Joanna shouted.

The man shrugged.

"Then it's just a happy coincidence," he said.

"Happy? You really are sick," Abbie spat.

"Well," the man said, looking up at her, "with the so-called New Realm planning their own uprising and stumbling upon our capabilities via their spy website, we had to act fast. Couldn't be rumbled now, could we?"

Abbie bit her lip and looked away.

"And, even though they were amateurish, being of that age, I suppose no one would ever suspect sweet, little children of being involved in a major genocide operation. So, we've been virtually untraceable," he said. "One thing I am intrigued by though is how you—"

He pointed towards Becky with the canister.

"How *you* ... managed to bring a spell back to life that has been dead for hundreds of years—you will have to teach me that one."

She sneered at him.

"Oh, you won't be able to," he said with a mirthful snort. "You'll be dead."

He walked around the length of the ledge, scattering the liquid around like water.

"Interesting concept, magic-bending. Once you manage to infiltrate the spell with a cell..."

He paused for a moment.

"...you can manipulate a bent spell to do just about anything. Bewitch innocent people, keep them alive. The bending options are infinite. But there will always be sacrifices."

"Your sister?" Gaynor asked.

"Alice?" the man scoffed. "She was just the scapegoat. She was lying to us. She wanted to

633

denounce our father—she didn't want any part of the operation. She said that she had no money to invest in our revolution when all the while she was stashing Brenda Ware's life savings away at the school. Devious bitch. She had to go."

Becky whimpered as she remembered Alice Eames' warning to her on the grounds of the school the day she was escorted away.

"So, she was innocent?" she asked.

The man shrugged.

"You could say that."

"And you killed those innocent women just to lead us here?" Becky cried.

"You killed them," he smiled up at her. "We just set them up."

"And you learned this ... this *illegal* magick ... from your father, I suppose?" Gaynor asked defiantly.

The man's face grew ashen.

"You leave my father out of this," he said flatly.

"Your father was a turncoat. He betrayed the sect that he was once part of to spare his own life," Gaynor responded.

"My father," he shouted at her, his eyes ablaze with resentment, "was a pioneer. He invented magic-bending after years of study. He invited those Swedes over here to teach him more, only for them to hand him over to the WHG. He saw an opportunity and he took it. He shared his magic with the opposition to exact his revenge on The Order. It made him a legend. Who knows—if they hadn't turned him in, you and I could be in the same boat."

"But it was *illegal.* That's why he was exiled, leaving you two girls on your own. Separated and alone," Gaynor said. "A real legend of the faith."

The man stared at her malevolently and then spat on the floor.

Suddenly, as if from nowhere, Wing opened her eyes and began to speak. After all this time, the sound of her voice startled the man momentarily.

"What..." she said, slowly and confidently. "What have you done with Bernice?"

The man's eyes flickered with a dark malice.

"Oh, thank you for reminding me," he said. "I nearly forgot that little freak of nature. It truly has been the triumph of the whole operation. Luckily *it* will get the recognition it has always wanted."

He motioned to two of the older children.

"Wheel it in," he said. The two boys walked slowly and silently to the back of the warehouse. This half of the room had, thus far, been bathed in almost complete darkness.

"Your wonderful Bernice," he said, with a charmless grin, "will be the ultimate belle of the ball."

A sudden grind of metal made each of the women look towards the back of the warehouse.

The squeak of wheels filled the space. The sound rang in Becky's ears.

Out of the shadows came a structure, tall and ominous. It was a large tower of scaffolding, several metres high. Bound to the bars was a large, wooden trellis that stretched ten metres across and spanned the entire vertical length of the structure. As the two children brought it forward, the others parted to let the structure through.

Becky's eyes pricked with tears as the horror of what was on that structure dawned upon her.

It was a body, strapped to the trellis with rope and cable-tied at the wrists and ankles. The arms were outstretched in a Christ-like fashion, and yet the torso hung forward. The head was covered in a hessian bag that was tied at the neck. The body was motionless.

The cable ties were cutting into the flesh, leaving angry wounds that gaped and bled. The bag was also bloody, covering the head as it hung, lifeless over the chest.

The body was dressed in a torn, white dress, stained red and brown with blood and dirt.

"My *God*!" Joanna screamed. "What have you done?"

Tears streamed down her face as the rest of the women gasped in shock.

The man laughed—it was satanic, inhuman.

"Well, it did fight a little," he began.

"Stop saying '*it*'," Joanna screamed. "Bernice is a human being!"

"Oh, come now." The man's face changed. "You were the one who threw Bernice out. You couldn't give a toss then, so why are you so bothered now?"

"I was wrong," Joanna cried. "Let her down. She doesn't deserve this!"

"Hey," the man stopped her, angrily. "We need a blood sacrifice. I saved this silly bitch's baby—what more do you want?"

Becky started to sob loudly. She saw no way out of this. She was going to die here. Her daughter would never get to take her first steps or speak her first words. She would never hear her laugh or cry. She would be silenced before she even had a chance to draw breath.

The man poured the last of the canister onto the straw and tossed it aside.

"Stand back, children," he said as he brought a box of matches out of his breast pocket. "It's time to burn the witch."

The children began to back away from him and into the darkness of the warehouse, their eyes still fixed forwards.

"*Wait!*" Gaynor cried.

The man looked up.

"Let us see your face, Odette," she said, slowly. "Show yourself! I want to see you, woman to woman, before you sentence me to my death."

The man held her gaze for a moment. She eyed him with a stony glare.

"Why?" he asked in a curious manner.

"You may be able to hide behind your mask and your adolescent army, but it doesn't disguise what you truly are," Gaynor said. Her words weighed heavy in the air.

The man put one hand on his hip.

"Oh, really?" he said, mockingly. "And, pray tell, what am I?"

"A rank amateur," Gaynor said. Her face changed expression from one of despair to one of confidence and defiance.

"Oh?" he said again, in a more sceptical tone this time. "An old, has-been witch, tied up, ready to be *chargrilled* at my instruction, is telling me how amateurish I am. Well, do tell me, *madam*, how you are more experienced than me. I mean, with your age, presumably, comes a bit of wisdom, so how is it that you haven't yet managed to save yourself? And you call me an amateur!"

"Well," Gaynor said, "if you were any kind of professional then you would have tied these ropes yourself."

The man's face dropped as the realisation hit him.

"These kids may have bought into your computer games, but knot-tying isn't their strong suit, is it?" Gaynor said smugly as she brought her hands out from behind her back and raised her arms up above her head.

"*Sapranza!*" she shouted, as the rope flew from her wrist and shot towards the man's hand, whistling through the air and wrapping itself around the matches, crushing two of his fingers in the process. Not having time to respond, he yelped in pain.

"*Velamosa!*" Gaynor shouted again. The rope that bound the other ladies' feet and wrists unravelled and dropped to the floor.

Becky collapsed to her knees, her arms wrapped around her belly.

"Come on!" Abbie exclaimed, grabbing her by the shoulders.

"*Hara!*" the man shouted, sweeping his hand through the air.

They lurched forward as the ledge came free from the wall and began to descend.

"Look out!" Abbie yelled, throwing herself over Becky. "*Barand!*"

A sudden, white flash of light produced a protective bubble around the two of them. The light cushioned the impact as the ledge crashed down into the straw. Dust rained down on them from above.

"Are you okay?" Abbie asked.

"Yes, I'm fine," Becky said. "I'll see to Bernice—just get that *bitch*."

Abbie nodded as she looked about her. The man was attempting to plough through the sea of children, who had now collected at the back of the room. The infant bodies began to crowd around him, providing him with a human barricade that made him all but disappear behind them. Their eyes were fixed forwards as they shuffled into place, protecting the man from the five ladies, three of whom were picking themselves up off the floor. It was only Gaynor who remained unresponsive. Joanna rushed over to her

"Go!" Becky called over to her. "I'll look after Gaynor. Just get Odette—stop her!"

Joanna looked apprehensive but nodded as she went to follow Abbie.

It was Wing, however, who was leading the pack. She raised her hands up, her fingers trembling in the air.

"Pai, tao, mai!" she shrieked, her voice high and strong. *"Poa, pow, pow!"*

The crowd of children began to part as Wing touched the back of her hands together and separated her palms in a sweeping motion. They moved slowly at first, but then more and more began to fall to their knees as the force from Wing's fingertips prized them away from each other. The children began to fall forward into the straw.

"Tse man kaysoh mi!" Wing bellowed, striding further into the sea of falling children. They continued to scatter until the enemy was visible again, only now, the visage had been cast off,

having served its purpose. Odette turned from facing the back wall and looked Wing dead in the eye. She was stood in front of two huge double-doors that led out of the warehouse, presumably intending to make her exit. The light from an outside lamppost streamed in through an adjacent window, illuminating her face. Her complexion was white and her features hard. Without glasses and makeup, she was unrecognisable. She looked serious and cold, far from her usual, preened self. A truly hard-faced woman, as the goddess had intended her to be, her dead heart written in lines across her face.

Her eyes were uncharacteristically wild with mania and her arms stretched out in front of her, her fingers wiggling with purpose.

But Wing's were faster.

"Kaysoh mi dow!" Wing called out, clenching her fingers together and swooping her palms up. Suddenly, Odette's torso twisted around, her back arched up and her face contorted in pain. She began to cry in agony as Wing opened her palms with one quick movement. With that, Odette was flung backwards, smashing into the doors. She crumpled to the floor, face down.

Wing brought her hands back down to her sides as Joanna and Abbie joined her.

"Good job," Joanna said as she put a hand affirmatively on Wing's shoulder. Wing gave a pinched smile.

Odette brought her elbows up and clambered into a crawling position. Her shoulders shook as she pushed herself back. She was laughing, a terrifying, raspy cackle.

"Is that all you've got?" she said, her voice cracking but still intimidating.

She fumbled around in her jacket pocket as Wing brought her hand back up.

"Stop!" Odette said, bringing out a small, black box. "Any more, and I kill the lot of them."

She held the box aloft.

"One press of this button ... and every single child in this building dies," she said as if she were holding a bomb.

Wing put her arms down and outwards, to block the other two from moving forward.

"You see, it's not all magic," Odette continued, getting up from her knees into a standing position. "Sometimes it's just good, old-fashioned computer networking. Every single child has been groomed by our app long enough for it to impregnate a little something into their psyche. And luckily, that network is remote. If I log off, so do they. Even your children, Wing. Call it ... insurance."

Odette nodded towards Wing and positioned her tongue between her teeth.

"You thought I'd make it that simple? That you could just overpower me with your novice hocus-pocus and that would be the end of it?"

Odette laughed. "You witches are so behind the frigging times."

The three women stood firm, their breathing heavy but their eyes focused. They were at a stalemate, and their options were zero.

"Now," Odette said, flicking her hair out of her eyes, "you're going to get back over there, and I am going to finish this—"

But she didn't finish.

For at that moment, the double doors burst from their hinges as a car came crashing through them, sending shards of wood catapulting through the air. All three women dropped to the ground as nails and dust flew towards them. Odette turned in shock as Laura's BMW ploughed straight into her. Her chest bounced off the front bumper with an almighty thud, as her whole body fell back and disappeared underneath the chassis. The box she was holding sailed into the air and landed softly among the supine children.

The car came screeching to a halt, inches away from where the three ladies were crouched. In a swirl of dust, they could just make out a figure getting out of the passenger door. As the smoky cloud cleared, they saw Robina standing over them.

"Fuck..." Abbie exclaimed. "I mean, what the actual *fuck?*"

The door opened from the other side of the car and Laura stepped out.

"Did we get her?" she asked, with an excited mirth.

"I think so," Joanna answered. "Back up, Laura. We need to check."

"Okay." Laura got back in the car and started the ignition.

Abbie, Wing and Joanna got to their feet and watched as the black car reversed back through the doorway that it had blasted through moments ago. The room suddenly filled with exhaust smoke and shreds of straw, so much so that they could barely see the ground they were stood upon. Laura cut the ignition and quickly exited the car, running over to where the other ladies stood. As the dust settled, they looked to the floor, where Odette's body should have been.

Fully expecting to see her bloodied, motionless corpse, instead, there was the taxi driver's battered leather jacket.

"She's gone," Joanna cried, turning and holding a hand to her temple. "She's bloody *gone!*"

A crash made them all look back.

"Wrong again," Odette said. This time she was stood on top of the car, her arms outstretched. "You really don't learn, do you?"

With that, she brought her arms down.

"*Wesmavo!*"

Suddenly, Laura was catapulted backwards towards the ledge, where she was slammed against the wall and thrown to the ground. It all happened so fast that she didn't have time to scream, let alone protect her pregnant tummy from the blow.

She landed next to Becky, who cried out in shock. She had been trying to revive an unresponsive Gaynor for some time and was now cradling her head in her lap, brushing the straw from her face and pleading with her over and over to wake up.

Odette moved her hand over to Joanna.

"*Ves—*"

But Joanna's bark was even louder.

"*Balumo!*"

A lightning bolt shot from Odette's hand but an even brighter one from Joanna's batted it away.

"You can't save yourself, old woman!" Odette shouted. "Give up and surrender."

Joanna kept a stern eye on her enemy as she called over her shoulder.

"Abbie, you need to do something for me," Joanna hissed. "You need to open up The Chasm!"

Abbie looked stunned.

'What?"

"The Chasm, you know how to do it, I taught you."

"But I—"

"I'm giving you permission to do it—so *bloody* do it! *Vestaa!*"

Another bolt was deflected by Joanna's quick hand.

This time Odette brought both hands out.

"*Vizomora,*" she began, circling her hands around, "*cambara!*"

"*Gleftand sello!*" Joanna brought her hand up as two lightning forks crept through the air from Odette's fingertips. A brighter fork intercepted them from Joanna's own hand, just in time. The two forks met in the middle, emitting a giant spark of electricity that fizzed and popped. Both women kept their hands out in front of them, as the forks bent and crackled against one another.

Abbie looked around her, not knowing what to do with herself.

"Um..." She closed her eyes, trying desperately to recall the spell from all those years ago. She remembered the book—it had been bound in black leather and smelled of mould. She remembered the words, scribed in calligraphy. She remembered Joanna's stony face.

"Never—" Joanna had said. "*Never* speak these words out loud. Ever. To *anyone.* You can never undo this spell. Do you understand me, Abigail?"

In her memory, Abbie had looked down. As the recollection came back to her, Abbie began to sway forward and back.

The words bubbled on her lips as she traced them on the paper with her mind's eye.

"*Cactum imperis avalganha parisum. Cactum imperis avalganha parisum*"

She had mouthed the words as she had read them. She had been very young, still oblivious as to what they meant or how serious they were. It was the last time she had ever let the incantation pass her lips—until now.

As she stood there in the straw, Abbie found that she was saying the spell out loud. Robina was also reciting the words, closely followed by Wing. The chant continued as the women looked up, their eyes rolling back in their sockets.

From where Becky was sat, unable to tend to an unresponsive Laura without leaving Gaynor, she could see that, behind Odette, the gap where the doors were hanging off their hinges was beginning to stir. It was as if the whole of the back wall had been painted onto a layer of canvas that was stretching and rippling. Dark shapes started to form as its surface began to retract and warp. Hand-like figures were now pushing against it as if something behind it was trying to reach towards Odette through the fabric of the blackness. Was this The Chasm opening? If it was, she could understand why the witches were so afraid of it. Though it was frightening, she was totally mesmerised by it.

Suddenly, Laura made a sound.

"It's okay," Becky called out to her. "Laura, I'm here, just stay still if you can. You took quite a fall."

But as Becky looked beside her, she saw that Laura hadn't yet moved.

It was then that Becky realised that the sound was coming from the scaffolding.

Odette looked behind her as she stumbled forward off of the roof of the car and onto the bonnet. She was now scrambling to get away from the black mass over her shoulder, as well as attempting to keep Joanna's lightning at bay with her own. But the thick darkness behind her was threatening to grab her with its inky, clawing fingers. She had never seen this kind of thing before. She had no idea what it was, and she had no intention of finding out.

Wing, Robina and Abbie moved forward, their arms rose up to the sky and their eyes glazed over as if made of marble. Their words became louder and heavier.

"Cactum imperis avalganha parisum. Cactum imperis avalganha parisum"

Odette began to let out little squeaks of desperation as her lightning sparked and fizzed. She looked back at Joanna, who remained calm, a smile spreading across her lips. As the swirling space behind Odette grew bigger, the car that she was on top of began to creak and moan as it jolted and slid backwards, becoming enveloped by the encroaching darkness that was swimming and pulsing, moving forward towards Odette.

Odette jumped off the bonnet, bringing her hand down and breaking the lightning fork. Joanna too brought her hand down.

Joanna looked at the frightened woman before her.

"It doesn't have to be like this," Joanna said, reaching out her hand to Odette, "It doesn't matter how hard you try, you can never underestimate the power of the sisterhood. You can only give in to it."

■■■

"Child?" Agatha's voice echoed in her ear. "Are you there? Are you ready?"

Bernice began to stir. She wanted to speak but she couldn't. She had little energy and the back of her head was throbbing with a searing pain.

She wanted to cry out to Agatha for help, but it was impossible. Her mouth was bound up and she knew she was nearing her end. How could this ghost or apparition help her now? She must be hallucinating, delirious with the pain.

"Oh well, that's where you are wrong," Agatha said softly as if answering her thoughts. "I can help you if you are sure you are ready."

Bernice didn't know where she was or what was happening. All she knew was that she was restrained and there seemed to be no way out. Her head hung forward in defeat.

"Well?" Agatha asked again. "Are you ready?"

Bernice had no sense of what she was agreeing to—what Agatha was asking. Instinctively, she believed that she had to say yes.

"Okay," said Agatha.

"Follow me."

●●●

Joanna's hand remained in the air, reaching towards Odette. Just as she was about to take it, Odette paused and raised her arms back up.

"Children!" Odette shouted, her voice raspy and hoarse. As quick as lightning, the stunned children, who were all face-down on the floor of the warehouse, their mouths still hanging open, began crawling stealthily towards Joanna. They were on her in seconds, clawing at her ankles, fighting over each other to grab her skirt and arms with their tiny, pinching fingers.

Joanna faltered, unable to free herself from the clasping hands of the dozens of glassy-eyed children who were now attempting to pull her away from Odette. Wing and Abbie, still in their trance, were all but useless, connected too intensely to the open Chasm. If they now broke that connection, it might close, and they would fail. As the car's bonnet began to disappear into the huge black mass, Odette laughed. It was malicious and cold. The triumphant cackle of a truly insane woman.

But Joanna fought.

She let out an enraged growl as she ripped her arm from the clutch of one of the little girls— then a leg. With all her might, she wrenched herself forward, using what little strength she

650

had left to twist her way out of the many-handed grasp. She allowed her skirt to rip and her cardigan to slide off her shoulders. She kicked off her shoes and finally managed to escape the throng of hands.

"*Barand,*" she muttered. A white light enveloped itself around her as the bodies began to fall back, leaving her momentarily free, facing her enemy.

Joanna knew that this was her moment. She was going to have to make the biggest sacrifice of all to take this woman down—to protect The Order. It had to be her, and it had to be now. She needed to allow a break in magic between her and Odette, seize the moment and run. To use her energy to sprint forward and surprise her enemy, throwing her into The Chasm. If Joanna was to fall too, then so be it. For what she had done, for the life she had taken, it would be the only recompense. She could either live as an outcast for the rest of her life, or her legacy could live on in her wake. A fallen hero who sacrificed herself at the last to save the generations that would come after her. It was the least she could do for Floella.

She took a deep breath as the white light pulsated around her. She started to bring her hands down.

Gaynor sensed what Joanna was about to do and her eyes snapped open, making Becky jump.

"Joanna, no," Gaynor whispered to herself. "You can't do this—you won't make it!"

"Gaynor?" Becky asked. "Don't move, okay? We're going to get help. Just stay where you are."

It was then that she heard the structure in front of her begin to move.

Joanna knew that she was facing very real danger, but she was adamant that, in order to preserve this world that she had given her entire life to, this ancient sect that owed so much of itself to the bravery and integrity of its gifted sisters, she would have to become a martyr. She brought one hand across herself and the white protecting light went with it, exposing her.

Odette stopped laughing and stood to face Joanna. Her hair fell about her face and her lips curled into a grotesque grin. Joanna braced herself. She was ready to do this, ready to propel herself into her adversary. She brought her fists up and her right elbow back. Stepping forward on her left foot, she prepared to launch forward onto her right.

But she didn't get the chance—a force to her right suddenly threw Joanna from where she was poised and sent her careening into the straw. Someone had pushed her aside. She looked up just in time to see a white robe fly past her, a tangle of blonde hair and flailing limbs. The ear-splitting sound of an animalistic scream. She saw a body launch itself at Odette, smacking her full-pelt in the sternum and sending her flying backwards.

The whole thing happened in seconds, yet it seemed as though time had slowed down. Joanna watched in amazement.

The figure wrapped its arms around Odette, hugging her tightly as it forced her into the abject blackness.

"No!" Odette shrieked in terror, her head thrashing about as she tried to fight the figure off—but it wasn't budging.

"Get off me, let go of me—*no!"*

Both bodies fell into The Chasm. Odette fought an arm free as she scratched at the air, trying to find something to clutch onto, but there was nothing. She let out a nerve-shredding howl as the two figures disappeared into the vortex. The black mass swirled around them before the clawing hands closed around their bodies. The last image was of Odette's face, suspended in the air, twisted in anguish and despair. A frozen death mask of horror stared back at Joanna as The Chasm swallowed her whole.

The scream continued on in Joanna's ears, long after the mass had vanished. It inverted upon itself, over and over.

"Break the chain!" Joanna screamed.

Abbie, Robina and Wing dropped their heads and fell backwards into the straw. With that, Joanna watched, open-mouthed, as the canvas faded into nothing but a pinprick in the distance.

She rested her weary head on to the ground. Suddenly, she felt a hand around her shoulders. Then another, and another.

One by one, the children began to regain their composure and move towards her. They silently formed a group around Joanna, embracing her and holding onto each other.

Abbie, Robina and Wing moved into the crowd, Wing searching for her own children amongst the hordes of others who were now huddled together.

They were a human wall of bodies, clinging tightly to the person next to them, without saying a word.

At the back of the room, Gaynor started to sit up, but she winced in pain.

"Careful," Becky said.

"I'm fine—the goddess looks after me," Gaynor said, her voice soft and weak. "She's done a bloody good job tonight, anyway."

Becky laughed as she wiped tears from her cheeks.

Abbie, Robina and Joanna stepped through the throng of children. Abbie had her arm around Joanna, who looked exhausted and upset.

Robina immediately ran to Laura, who was stirring in the straw, sitting her up and brushing the strands from her face and hair.

Becky looked up at the women and smiled a lopsided smile.

"Was that—" Joanna started.

"Yes," Becky said, unable to control the tears in her voice.

"She broke free," she sobbed. "She saved you. She saved *us.*"

The six women turned and looked at the scaffolding structure. The ropes were untied, the cable ties had been cut in two and dangled limply from the trellis.

Joanna began to weep, letting her head drop to her chest. Abbie put a comforting arm around her shoulders.

"I'm sorry," Joanna said through a flood of tears. "I'm so very, very sorry."

"In the end, Bernice..." Becky continued, a tremble in her voice. "Out of all of us ... she was the strongest woman."

Joanna nodded and wiped her nose with the back of her hand.

After a few moments of contemplative silence, Gaynor was the first to speak.

"Bernice may well have been the strongest individual," she said, looking around at the faces of her friends, her adopted sisters.

This small group of women who had doubted themselves and each other, they had united against adversity to bring down one of the greatest foes that The Order had ever seen in Gaynor's lifetime—and that had been a long lifetime.

"But in the end, we were stronger together," Gaynor said with a heartfelt smile.

EPILOGUE

Catherine sat on the edge of the bed, staring at the tiny bundle that stirred as it slept.

"She's perfect," Catherine said. She was not as imposing as usual. She spoke quietly and without the tinge of judgement in her voice that Becky was so used to.

"Thanks," Becky said, keeping one arm under her daughter's head and straightening her top with the other. "I know."

"And have you thought of a name yet?" Catherine asked.

"I was thinking of Bea," she said, looking down at her daughter.

"Bea," Catherine repeated the name, as she mulled it over.

"Well, my mum was Beatrice, and I'm Becky. And, of course, Bernice. Three incredibly strong women. I'm sure she will live up to the legacy."

Catherine nodded and smiled.

"And has Dom been in?"

"Yes, he's been in a few times. Brings me little treats and things. He's being very sweet," Becky rocked her baby in her arms.

"Are you two going to work things out?" Catherine said.

"I don't know," Becky answered truthfully. "I think us two girls are going to see how we get on alone first."

There was a moment of silence. Catherine put her hands on her lap. Today, she was dressed in a simple t-shirt and jeans—no makeup and her hair was down. Becky had hardly recognised her when she walked in. She looked fresh, young and approachable.

"I'm selling the house," she said. "It's too big, too grand. The children and I are going to downsize and see how we get on as well."

"I'm happy for you," Becky said with a smile and looked back down at her sleeping daughter. She really was the most beautiful thing Becky had ever seen.

"Becky," Catherine leaned in and put a hand on her arm, "I just wanted you to know that what you did for our children, what you all did, what you're doing now, being so brave and doing this all on your own—"

Her eyes pricked with tears.

"I..." Catherine said. "I am so grateful. You saved us, saved our little town. You're an inspiration."

Becky looked into her eyes. They were sad and tired but full of sincerity. It was the one time she hadn't had to brace herself for the backhanded aside.

"Thank you," Becky answered.

She held the moment before she spoke again.

"Catherine," Becky said, "I would be really honoured if you would be Bea's godmother. You're a good friend and yet another strong woman for my daughter to look up to."

Catherine suddenly looked flushed. She blinked back tears as she let out a little whimper of appreciation.

Catherine nodded and squeezed Becky's arm.

"I'm so pleased," Becky said.

And she meant it.

∎∎∎

Joanna and Abbie sat in the corridor. Joanna in her best two-piece suit and Abbie in a beautiful, gold dress. Abbie's hair tumbled over her shoulders and her eyes sparkled with excitement.

"So," Abbie said, popping her lip-gloss back into her bag. "What happens next then?"

"Well," Joanna said, glancing down at the pamphlet in her hand. "We sit in the hall, and when our names are called, we go up and receive our award."

"I'm so bloody nervous," Abbie said, rubbing her palms together.

"Language!" Joanna scolded before softening and nodding. "Sorry—I've done it again, haven't I?"

Abbie rolled her eyes and nodded. She looked around at the posh hallway. It was the first time Abbie had ever been to London, let alone the halls of the infamous Oracle HQ.

"So, will we get to see her then? The Oracle?"

"Of course," Joanna said. As she leant in, Abbie could detect a hint of musky perfume. "The coven is being decorated for bravery and courage. It's a highly sought-after accolade and will set you up for life in the sisterhood."

Abbie raised her eyebrows.

"If that is the direction you want to take, of course," Joanna corrected herself, remembering her promise to her fellow witches after the events at the warehouse. She made a pact with them that she was to be more inclusive and open-minded towards her sisters if they allowed her the time to adapt. She didn't want Bernice's sacrifice to have ever been in vain.

"But why did you choose me, out of all of the others, to come here with you?" Abbie asked.

"Because without your tenacity and bloody-mindedness, we never would have taken down that bitch," Joanna said in a hushed whisper.

"Language..." Abbie smiled.

Suddenly the tannoy system crackled into life.

"The Winchcombe Order to The Great Hall."

"That's us," said Joanna, rising out of her seat.

"Joanna," Abbie said, as she also stood up.

"Abigail?"

"You did it," Abbie said. "You don't have to repent anymore."

Tears began to well up in Joanna's eyes, and so Abbie pulled her in.

There they were, two sparring partners locked in a loving embrace in the hallway of Oracle HQ, while the staff continued going about their days around them.

Something caught Abbie's eye as she pulled away.

"Hmm," she said.

"What?"

"I thought you said that The Oracle's real name was a big secret. You've always said that," Abbie said.

"It is," Joanna agreed, "but probably not here. I mean, she does have to work here after all."

"I was going to say because it's written up on that wall," she nodded towards a plaque hanging in front of her.

Joanna turned to look.

"So it is," she remarked. "Right, come on, we mustn't keep them waiting."

The two collected their respective bags and began to walk down the hallway.

"Madam Holmberg," Abbie whispered as they stepped up to the big doors that led into the hall. "I thought her name might be a bit more exciting than that."

661

Gaynor was outside on her little garden bench, waiting for Robina to bring her tea. The sun was breaking through the willow branches and casting little triangles of light onto the grass.

"It's beautiful out here," Robina said, as she stepped out of the back door with two mugs. "I'm glad to see you're feeling better."

"Ah, well," Gaynor said, putting a hand on her sore knee, "these old legs aren't what they used to be. But there's still life in them yet. Of course, it has helped you coming over every day to look after me."

Robina smiled as she sat down and passed one of the mugs over.

"It's the least I can do," she said.

The two women sipped their tea, enjoying the silence around them, save for a bird tweeting in the distance.

"You know, your mother was a very good witch," Gaynor said, looking forward.

Robina nodded as she cast her eyes solemnly to the ground.

"But she was not a natural caregiver," Gaynor said, moving her eyes over to Becky's root, which was now cascading over its terracotta pot. It was just starting to bud.

"You can be the best witch in the world," Gaynor said pensively, "but it's much more of a triumph to be a good person."

Robina thought for a moment and smiled to herself.

■■■

Wing descended her hall stairs, running her hand along the bannister.

The children were in the front room, watching television. Richard was in his study. The house hummed with activity. It was just how she liked it.

She walked into the lounge and sat on the sofa. Dara and Kit lay on their tummies on the carpet staring at the images on the screen.

Kit turned to his mother, little specs of biscuit dappling his mouth and chin.

"Mai," he said, looking at her with those brown eyes of his. The ones that melted her heart.

"Yes, Dek Dek?"

"Are you still going to go back to Thailand like you said?" he asked.

She sighed and smiled. She thought of Jacqueline and all the friends she had in the circle. How life goes on, things change. How it is possible to break years of entrenched self-consciousness just by uniting power with other women.

"Sometime…" Wing said to her son. "Sometime you gain strength from staying right where you are."

He wrinkled his nose up as if he didn't understand, which made her giggle.

Because she understood.

■■■

Laura took a few steps up to the door. She was sure that this was the right house. Her head ached—it was a dull thud that she couldn't shake off.

Ever since she had returned home, bruised and a mess, she had suspected that things were not right inside of her. Crashing to the floor of the warehouse was certain to have upset things, but she didn't want it confirmed.

She'd had to go to the doctors anyway to check for any broken bones that she may have incurred when Odette threw her against the warehouse wall.

He had been very sorry, she could tell. But there was nothing he could do.

She had walked out of the surgery in a haze, not knowing what to do with herself. She couldn't face going back to the coven. It had ruined her life. These women and their "gifts"— they were nothing more than ticking time-bombs, pissing about with magic like they were playing a board game.

She had carried on walking until she had somehow found herself on this street. The name was embedded in her head, almost as if a force had led her here.

She took a few more steps up the pathway towards a white painted door. She knocked three times.

She didn't feel anything anymore. No intense happiness, no crushing defeat. Just a numbness that had dulled her mind and her emotions. She didn't want to think, or laugh, or cry—she barely wanted to exist.

After a few minutes, she heard footsteps echoing down an empty hallway behind the door.

The sound of a latch being slid across proceeded the twist of a door handle. The painted face of an attractive, young woman appeared from the inside of the room. She had a white complexion, with perfect, cherry-red lips.

"Hello," Laura said, suddenly feeling under-dressed and ugly in front of this immaculately made-up woman.

The woman said nothing but continued to look at her with sparkling blue eyes.

"I'm sorry to bother you," Laura said, "but I'm here to collect a suitcase."

The woman looked at her with concern for a moment or two. She opened the door further, just as two smaller faces appeared at her side—a girl and a boy. Their eyes were black, and their mouths hung open. Laura gasped as she saw the children.

"Hello, you two," she said. "Fancy seeing you here. I thought I left you in the park."

Laura looked back at the woman who glanced down at the two children. The little girl nodded slowly and looked back at Laura.

Then the woman smiled.

"We've been expecting you," she said and opened up the door.

THE END

Special thanks to my Editor
Andrew Fenn

and Thomas Cambridge, as ever

28589934R00367

Made in the USA
Columbia, SC
14 October 2018